We as the Anishinaabe Nation know such things as prophetic dreams and channeling knowledge from the stars is as real as the nose on your face. Joshua Veith has told a tale that will come to be known as the time of the great culling. This book will send shivers of truth down your spine.
  —Courtney Miller, medicine person, activist, and dancer

Joshua Veith puts northern Michigan on the map with his dystopian thriller, *Island and Main*, where a plucky band of holdouts on Beaver Island wage a last stand against the collapse of civilization in the aftermath of a viral epidemic. Veith offers a heady blend of speculative fiction, horror, hard science, and Native wisdom, written with the deft hand of a poet.
  —Robert Downes, author of *The Wolf and The Willow*

Island and Main mesmerizes with its Tolkien references, Anishinaabe culture, local lore, and historic maps. The first book of Joshua Veith's *Sudden Quiet* series is spellbinding, bringing readers to eerily familiar places scarred by what might have been.
  —Jennifer Harsha Carroll, artist, writer, editor, Charlevoix, Michigan

I commend anyone intrepid enough to imagine an American future in these dark and uncertain times. *Island and Main* is a deeply felt visit to that strange time-to-come. It made me want to try living there for a spell.
  —James Howard Kunstler, author of the *World Made by Hand* novels

As documentary filmmakers, we strive to anticipate the future and record the present. Joshua Veith has done this in a dark and powerful way. His debut novel, *Island and Main*, creates a cinematic world that will captivate readers of all genres. Veith has crafted a beautiful novel filled with deep character development and fulfilling storylines that make it hard to put down.
  —Christina Clusiau and Shaul Schwarz, Emmy-winning directors of *Trophy* and *Immigration Nation*

Quality writing, just like brewing beer, demands attention to detail and appreciation of place. Joshua Veith excels at both of these in his hyper-regional trilogy, *Sudden Quiet*. We especially appreciated his inclusion of Joe's handlebar mustache and Veith's trippy recipe for "ELF Ale," a brew we might have to replicate!
  —Joe and Leah Short, award-winning founders of Short's Brewing

Island
and Main

Chuck,
Thanks for supporting!

Joshua Leitz

This hand-drawn and painted map of the Little Traverse Region was created in 1934 by Charlevoix artist Irene Harsha Young.

Irene's childhood home is now the Museum at Harsha House. She was married to famed builder Earl A. Young for nearly 60 years. The couple drove for miles throughout northern Michigan to sketch and record lore and landmarks for the historic map.

Irene was proud of the map as a tribute to the area's unique history and natural beauty. It includes Charlevoix, Petoskey, Harbor Springs, Bay View, Walloon Lake, and Lake Charlevoix. Irene later created maps of the Grand Traverse Region and Mackinac Island.

SUDDEN QUIET SERIES
BOOK I

Island
and Main

Joshua Veith

Published by Mission Point Press
2554 Chandler Rd.
Traverse City, MI 49696
(231) 421-9513
www.MissionPointPress.com

ISBN: 978-1-961302-62-4
Library of Congress Control Number: 2024909254
Printed in the United States of America

Cover design of Beaver Island Lighthouse created by Janella Williams.

Island and Main is a work of fiction, the characters are invented, and any resemblance to actual persons is unintentional. That being said, its historical references—to James Strang, "king" of Beaver Island; Chief Biidassige of Petoskey, Tecumseh; Churchill, etc.—are accurate to the best of my knowledge. Also, I lean on some themes and characters created by J.R.R. Tolkien and am greatly indebted to his works along with those of Yeats, Hemingway, and all the authors that haunt the bookshelves of my brain.

This book is dedicated to the departed,
ripples in time that will absorb us all.

I could not understand the sudden quiet—
The sudden darkness—in the crash of fight,
The din and glare of day quenched in a twinkling
In utter starless night.

I lay an age and idly gazed at nothing,
Half-puzzled that I could not lift my head;
And then I knew somehow that I was lying
Among the other dead.

—Wilfrid Wilson Gibson, "The Quiet," *Battle*, 1916

CAST of CHARACTERS:

Island

Beaver Islanders

Keith Two-Crow

Samantha

Miinan

Mukwa

Tom Doyle

Main

The Naturals

Dr. Chow

Brian

Pastor George

Panzer

Cowboy

Chosen

Liz

XCons

Aghori

PROLOGUE:
Concerning Humans

EVEN I WILL ADMIT THAT, in the beginning, it was nice.

Suddenly there was less noise, less movement. Time slowed, and the lengthening days of spring were filled with quiet. Society had been stilled by a virus—a novel one, the first of a series—and like the season, began a period of waiting. Waiting for winter to let go, waiting for transmission data, for a vaccine, for things to go back to normal. I knew this longed-for normal would never return, but in the beginning, it was nice.

We watched it all happen on our phones, on our screens. Satellites shared their images, links intact, circuits undamaged, flooding the eager populace with views from above. Fleets of semi-trucks, ever-busy, now sat parked and orderly. Plumes of factory smoke disappeared, region by region, as whole economies shuttered. Ocean trade routes were no longer criss-crossed by wakes of automated freighters. The human pall was lifting from the Earth. Millions in India marveled at the Himalayas revealed. Dolphins frolicked in the unpolluted canals of Venice, going unphotographed by tourists that weren't there. The lights were still on, electricity served its master. Our little planet sparkled at night, flashing its many-minded message into the void.

And there was food to be had, delivered right to the door. A swipe on a screen, some taps on a phone, and there it was. Sanitary, masked, no touching of course, no exchange of droplets; a smile, a wave, and the driver moved on. Grocery bags were unpacked into kitchens, each item disinfected with wipes: bananas, avocados, oranges, meat and bread and fruit and vegetables—foodstuffs from the world, all readily available. Children helped parents, schools went remote, and mothers grinned with fathers at the helpfulness of the kids. It was good to have some extra time, good to slow down, and what should we have for dinner tonight?

We could read all about it, and we did, endless articles from every angle. We watched the speeches, dissected interviews, posted our comments and added our voice. We were in this together, though the sick died alone in an ever-accelerating curve of heartbreak. But that came later. All curves take time, even exponential ones. In that first spring there was mostly just quiet, and waiting— and for some, a refocusing.

"Beware the Ides of March," warned Shakespeare, no stranger to plague.

"What man is that?" Julius Caesar asked. "Set him before me, let me see his face!"

Four centuries later, and again the world's elite dismissed expertise: "He is a dreamer, let us leave him."

And leave they did, intubated in hospitals where Caesars jumped the line: the finest facilities, ventilators, antivirals, all to no avail. That first wave drowned thousands. The powerful departed, stripped of their finery, hospital gowns the great leveler. My customized variant would soon take them all, but in the beginning, the rich died first.

Of course there were soothsayers, those who used the early days of the pandemic to prepare, to warn others of the coming calamity. These voices, loudest at the end of any era, were once again ignored, at least by most. In this biological storm, as in the floods of old, the many would not be saved, only the few. Masses cleave to the status quo, and their dying wish is to return to the familiar. It's not that the group can't change, but that it won't. Nature's law is change or die. The virus did, humans didn't, and so they died.

As the cold calculus of the curve continued, whole cities were shaved by the scythe. But the lights stayed on, refrigerators hummed, every cell in the hive backlit by screens. We watched our world end, a million channels to choose from, broadcasts in any language, though the content stayed the same.

Complex systems need expertise. Large cities require many workers; disruption leads to filth and decay. The great metropoles of the world were quickly fouled, trash multiplying as the rats grew bold. Every age takes pride in its cities: high-water marks of culture and learning. But turn back a few pages and witness the pyres, the furtive burning of the piled dead. If a city is old enough there will be places stained by such disposals, public squares and pier-side landings where the taint has never faded. From London, Venice, and Athens to Uruk, Ur, and Babylon, the tale of plague is as old as civilization.

On our screens, we saw the overflow at city morgues, the mass graves dug in Central Park. City workers wore hazmat suits and respirators because the corpses, infectious, still vectored the virus. Funerals were forbidden, undertakers taken under; bodies were buried in the clothes they died in.

And then I got involved, my white hand pressing the plunger. After a soft launch, my Stinger started trending, a viral finale to the novel crown-series. The first pyre was in Milan. Milano, that old plague-port, was no stranger to such fires. Some part of that city remembered, though its modern denizens did not. Outraged, the world shared grainy videos: backhoes tending the blaze, clanking treads and floodlights, polizia barricades, Euro-sirens and the wailing of bereaved.

A super variant, Stinger spread its venom. Crematoriums were clogged, first responders were unresponsive; corpses became a biohazard, and the mass burnings began. Old cities knew the drill—Mumbai, Damascus, Istanbul. New ones learned quickly—Los Angeles, Mexico City, Kuala Lumpur. Satellites peered down, incurious, as across the globe factories went cold and pulsing highways flat-lined, their belching exhaust replaced by humanity's last gasp: the oily plumes of our burning dead.

Little did I know these storm clouds were silvered with green. Nature's fuse, tamped no longer, had been lit. Our age, the Anthropocene, ended with a bang. The next one, a throwback, teased its trailer: a return to roots.

PROLOGUE:
The Virus

I AM THE VIRUS.

Tempting to leave it there.

What can be added to those four words, anyway?

Any elaboration might obscure the truth rather than reveal it. And the truth is murky enough already. I suppose that is why I am speaking. Plus, who doesn't love the sound of their own voice? Not the flat, recorded version played back, but the real thing, lively and vibrant as it flutters the vocal cords and echoes from the mouth's chamber. You never really know what your voice might say. As I see this paragraph scrawl across the screen, I'm astonished already.

I am speaking this aloud, from a secure location. Unlike the collapsing world, my gadgetry is still intact. Electricity purrs, my devices go to sleep, turn off and turn on at my command. I am their master—for a while anyway, until their batteries die or the gasoline spoils, or I'm betrayed. A modern-day Mussolini, strung up by disillusioned followers no longer cowed by fear.

As far as I know, I'm one of very few individuals who can relate the real origin story of Stinger. I have a unique perspective on the apocalypse. This telling may one day become the Newest Testament, though its contents are closer to Lamentations in the Old.

These spoken words are recorded and transcribed by my tablet. This tireless secretary will store their truth, in zeros and ones, digitally deathless, awaiting resurrection.

What else will be resurrected, or who?

I have killed billions. Will they somehow be reborn?

I don't think so.

Am I haunted by these deaths?

Am I a monster if I say no?

I'm very busy at the moment, but still I discipline myself to dictate. There may be a future where these words matter; allow me, therefore, to begin at the beginning.

Viruses are not new, but as old as life itself. There is even a virus-first hypothesis positing that they predate cellular life. Can you picture our brand-new planet, steamy with methane and magma-spewing volcanoes? No oxygen, no oceans, nothing hospitable, yet there was our virus, patiently awaiting its first host. It gives me chills to think about.

Soon after the first oceans formed, we find evidence of life, fossilized micro-organisms thriving near the thermal vents. It didn't take long for viruses to find them. Our first infection! Patient Zero!

Fast forward four billion years, and our favorite genus, Homo, takes the stage. With the arrival of erectus, habilis, and their cranial cousins, viruses never had it so good. Here, at last, was a hyper-social primate that could travel. Two million years ago these hominids super-spread out of Africa and infected the world. Viruses had found their perfect vectors.

Perfect, that is, until the latest species of the genus, sapiens, asserted our dominance. It is impossible to separate human history from the viruses we host. When it was our turn to leave Eden, everywhere we went we found other hominids well-established. The best caves, rivers, and resources had all been claimed already. Neanderthals, Denisovans, Heidelbergensis had gotten there first, some by a hundred millennium or more.

Too much credit is given to our bulging brains, language skills, and tactics. Our greatest asset in displacing aboriginals has always been microscopic.

PROLOGUE:
Timeline of Collapse

SOME OF THIS YOU already know. SARS-CoV-2, undeclared and undocumented, began deplaning several years before collapse, an uninvited guest to a long-expected party. Covee's seeming origin was a zoonotic spillover in China. The West, blasé after decades of SARS, MERS, and their acronymic kin, cold-shouldered this new arrival. TikToks of Asians quarantined in factory-cities were rejected as too on-the-nose and far, far away.

Covee's first wave infected almost everyone, while mRNA vaccines, indeed miraculous, inoculated the rest. There were deaths—several million—but most were predictable culls. The human populace sighed with relief, but the poison had been planted; billions, unknowingly, had been envenomed. Global immunization, via infection or vaccination, had hijacked the herd's defenses. The Stimulator of Interferon Genes system (STING), the immune system's pistol, had been primed and pointed, not at the invader, but at the host. All I did was pull the trigger.

This was a busy time for my company, Panzer Pharma. Headquartered in Michigan and designated vital for defense, we were given carte blanche, and flush with taxpayer billions. When Covee began cresting, POTUS, eyes-only, issued orders to Panzer: create something new and, ideally, untraceable. We rolled up our sleeves and got to work.

With a PhD in virology, I became Dr. Frankenstein, and Kalamazoo my castle. We utilized CRISPR to encode a new creature, a riff on Covee, but this time with a sting. Too cunning, I knew it would work, so rather than chase a vaccine-mirage, I channeled gobs of cash towards an in-house virucide, security recruitment, and other doomsday delights.

Before too long my VOHC was detected, a variant of high consequence. In March of what became Year 1, several years after Covee, this variant started stinging. Cytokine storms, a hyper-immune response primed by previous exposure, quickly overwhelmed the populace and, soon after, the hospitals. Pro-vax or anti, the variant didn't care; our politics shrank as Stinger gained function. Covee and my variant morphed, blindly cosmopolitan in their ability to transcend race, religion, and country of origin. The planet's humans achieved equality at last, mere months before functional extinction.

The end wasn't pretty. From my tower, through a darkening globe of satellites, I could see things far away. I watched the world grow dim.

Exchanges—nuclear, of course—had happened; entire regions lay radiated, devoid of life. The Indian subcontinent, the Middle East, and both sides of Europe's tattered curtain had become domains of Darwin—primordial. What might emerge from such a soup? That first winter was a long one, the upper stratosphere saturated with soot. The growing season shrank as not enough sunlight came through. Massive solar flares triggered geomagnetic storms, frying what remained of our fragile grid.

The planet's climate had been seared, but even so, green pockets survived. Trees kept scrubbing and the air grew cleaner, arboreal zones again sheltering hominids. Fresh water, as always, was precious. The species' earliest stomping grounds, Lake Baikal, Amazonia, the old Rift Valley, might now become our last. The story arc of sapiens had been reset to the beginning. Old ways became new again, and neo movements, oh so mockable before, now shared their surplus food with survivors.

Michigan, my future fief, is insulated by the Great Lakes, the watery lungs of a new Midwest. Here I will stake my claim, carve out a barony, and prosper.

And I'm not alone. There are prescient others, bunkered by their billions, at my beck and call. For I have their elixirs, the coveted virucides; my white hands are upon their throats!

And so, as one age ended, I positioned Panzer for the next.

First off, that woman, Michigan's gumptious governor, had to go, so she went. The tricky Halloween raid of Year 1 was a treat for my newly minted mercenaries. Her lieutenant governor deployed the National Guard to secure Detroit's refineries. We took them next, a symphonic attack by rail and barge. The facilities and their precious petroleum were captured, and fires were set throughout Motor City. By sunrise Detroit was a Wagnerian Götterdämmerung.

Next, we eliminated our rivals in the pharma field. Merch Biotech in New Jersey was a daylight raid, live-streamed by thousands. By then Panzer's recruits had been metamorphosed by my virucide, blooded by battle, and inked with the ashes of the slain. The video views were in the millions. Mesmerized, the masses found our signifier. The unit's Sanskrit tattoo, *Aghori*, was summarily analyzed, my paramilitary nameless no longer. The stormtroopers, torsos and skulls tattooed as skeletons, were henceforth known as Gories.

The CDC we burned to the ground, a surprisingly soft target for my hardening Aghori. We deployed a new type of blasting fire, a devilry devised from Mark 77 bombs. Benzene, kerosene, oxidizing agents, and ol' Willy Pete guaranteed Atlanta's specimens of rinderpest and variola wouldn't upstage Covee or its venomous variant, my creature, my Sting.

All in all, Year 1 had gone well. Naturally, I'm only speaking for me and mine, no need to remind me of the bilious billions. Remember, jurists of the future, I am merely responding to events, not instigating them.

Of course, I don't expect you to believe this. I only half believe it myself.

PROLOGUE:
The Island

ON BEAVER ISLAND, collapse crested slowly. March and April of Year 1 saw little traffic between island and main, a quiet season while the world burned. Strict isolation was voted in place; runways and roads were cross-hatched with trucks and old buses, ten-ton hazards, dragon's teeth to chew up invaders. Seeking sanctuary, several small-engine planes crashed on the island, pilot and family burned alive, flames unextinguished as ground crews kept their distance.

Fuel rationing was enforced—diesel and regular gasoline—no driving allowed, no non-vital equipment. Every drop was saved for the fleet, saved for the generators. Squadrons of sailboats were pressed into service, canvas engines fueled only by wind. Watchers were posted, with eyes and ears in every direction. The "Voice of Beaver Island," 91.9 FM MHz, lifted spirits with borrowed oratory till the batteries died:

"We shall defend our island, whatever the cost may be, we shall fight on the beaches, we shall fight on the landing grounds, we shall fight in the fields and in the streets, we shall fight in the hills; we shall never surrender."

Boat crews were armed and drilled: respond, repel, and retreat. Despite the sandy soils, islanders were ordered to produce their own food, plant gardens, stock up on nature's bounty.

Then came the chaos of that first summer. As the Midwest felt the sting of Covee's variant, island defenses—water and sky—were tested in waves. For a handful of Beaver pilots and gunners—an amateur BAF—it was their finest hour. Island airspace was blitzed by small-engine planes, panic-flying and over max gross. Spotters vectored the incoming, and Beaver planes scrambled to intercept, spitting fire and littering the island with wreckage, a hurricane of defiance. Eventually, invaders stopped coming as their avgas ran dry.

By water, refugees loaded boats and tried their luck, fleeing the sinking ship of Michigan's mainland. Shots were fired, diesel stocks were depleted by patrols, island boats returned with windshields shot out and first aid kits deployed. Blood was splashed on decks, on transoms. The Beaver boats were no strangers to gore; human or whitefish, it hosed off the same. Captains were killed, teenage sons took the wheel, racing home through tears as Dad bled out in the stern. Watch lists were drawn up, quadrants assigned. Voices were raised at council, graves were dug—diabetics first—as island medicine ran out.

The summer days of Y1 were shortened by fall. Islanders survived, unstung by the variant. Hunters were prized for their skills, venison smoked and stored away; squirrel, rabbit, and fish bolstered dwindling larders.

Doomed, the islanders scrolled on their screens. They watched remotely as the virus morphed and vaccines failed. The center did not hold; November's presidential election was contested, surprising no one. The incumbent won by TKO as, six to three, the court crowned its king. Command lost all control, soldiers deserted, and there was rank fratricide. Big pharma, bloated, went bust. The electrical cable, the island's umbilical, was clamped and then cut, its mainland mother running out of juice.

Y1 handed its scythe to Y2 and winter had its cull. Three months of cold, without electricity's buffer, added more names to the island's ledger. These dark-month additions had shivered to death, mostly alone. The enormous blue of winter snuffed out the fragile flames of human life, cold-stored bodies awaiting the thaw tucked snugly into their beds. Stormy waters kept the island unmolested. The lack of screens became a respite. There was no going back. Alcohol stocks were depleted, cigarettes too. Islanders endured.

The spring of Y2 brought new digging to the island: graves first, then gardens, a prehistoric pairing. For over 12,000 years humanity has planted bodies first, then seeds. Busy as beavers, whole families now worked together to sow and tend their fields, motivated by a direct connection between crop yield and survival.

Days lengthened, north-bound geese wondering at the emptied world.

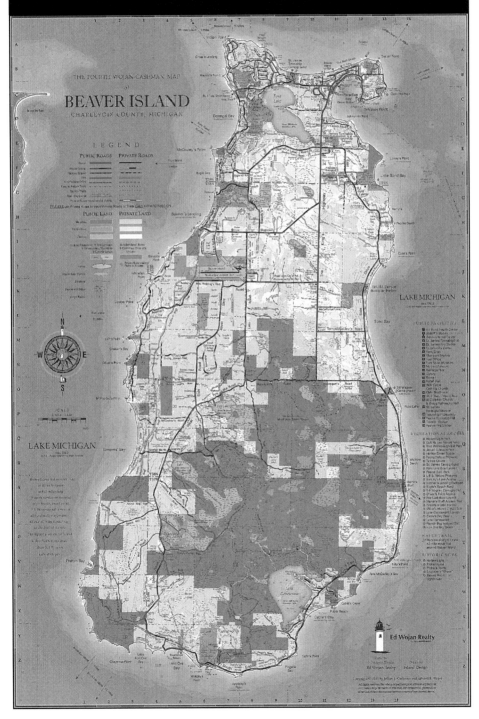

Keith Two-Crow

TALL AND LEAN, with an aching back, the old man caught the screen door before it slammed. He checked the sky as morning surrendered its stars. Keith buttoned his coat, patting pockets for bullets: he'd be lucky if he used them all. Carrying his rifle, dinged from long use, Keith Two-Crow climbed Kilty's Hill to view the island from its vantage.

The trees stood sleeping. Keith paused on a switchback; catching his breath, he also caught the view. Southeast, above the mainland, a red planet watched him, unblinking. Keith scanned Lake Michigan: no lights, no boats, utterly empty. When he checked back, the planet had gone. His knees reluctantly carried him higher, to an oak grove crowning the hill. He leaned his rifle against a trunk and stood still, hand upon the bole. The drowsy tree pulsed low. Keith slowed his own pulse and sat.

Earth's rotation soon revealed the sun, bulging up from blue waters. Each day the northern hemisphere tilted a bit further towards its heat: he allowed himself to settle. Grove quiet, horizon empty, Keith could just make out the far-off hills of the main. Limbering his fingers in a sunbeam, he drew a pouch from his pocket and rolled a hoarded smoke.

With arthritic fingers he pinched out an offering to the living woods and friends long gone, *Miigwech manidoog*. Scattering tobacco, he was young again: Private Two-Crow, door gunner, Khe Sanh, drafted away from his tribe by white Uncle Sam. They had all been so young, friend and foe. Those he remembered would stay that way.

With gnarled hands he kindled fire, igniting dried herbs, a catharsis of combustion. Keith gratefully filled his lungs and exhaled. As he smoked his rollie, his thoughts went adrift: rotor-blades, hollow-eyed Marines, tracer rounds, slumped dead. His smoke curled through the waking woods, the newly risen sun firing bars of gold.

A chittering from above returned him to the island, butt sore, wrists tight. Two-Crow shouldered a dainty .22, so unlike the heavy M-60 of his youth. He saw the squirrel, a big gray. Barrel up, sights aligned, safety off, breathing slow: a mingling of spirit.

Crack! The trigger pulled: the sadness of gravity, a graceless bumping of branches before a final *thump* upon the forest floor.

Keith worked the bolt and pocketed the smoking, brass cartridge. He eye-marked the body, a cooling lump of wild protein. It lay in the leaf litter that had powered its life. Sunlight, acorn, squirrel: food for the island's families. Grateful, he'd bag a few more before wending home to clean them.

The Families

"THANK YOU KEITH!" the kids cried out, waving.

The hunter lifted a hand and resumed the road that brought him. A stirring of crows, and the old man was gone.

A young girl, almost a teenager, ran the heavy ziplock of meat to the cookhouse, smoke curling up from the building's stovepipe. Midday sun dazzled on the water, homesteads on Beach Road were sparsely peopled. Hungry robins scrounged at the turned earth, hopping furrows, keeping distance from farmers. Two boys bested them, filling their bait cans with worms.

A formation of geese overflew the island, halfway home, from Argentina to the Arctic.

A bearded father stopped his hoe, looked up and queried, *What news from the world?*

He blanked his mind, but no reply was sent. What they carried the geese kept to themselves, the thaw-line of pond and puddle was too urgent a priority for midday messaging.

A boy seized the bell-pull, clanging for the laborers to come in and have their lunch.

The V of geese vibrated with the tolling. Thin folk hurried from field to table, a rare sight on their 1000-mile migration. In just one year the world had been emptied; stung by a variant, the planet's people were gone.

The geese navigated ancient flyways, unchanged since the Pleistocene. Magnetic fields and pole stars guided their feathered generations. Pre-collapse, humanity had peaked, cluttering the sky. Winging north, the fliers witnessed the cull. Asphalt arteries were clogged with cars, with corpses. Urban hearts had stopped pumping, the sky scrubbed clean of fumes and data, humanity's messaging had been muted. At night, a great reversal: with the grid gone dark, the heavens blazed.

Rooted in sandy soil, the islanders joined hands, bowing heads. Geese winged away over open water. Beaver Island—its shape, its relation to the coast—was just another waypoint in a millennia of migration.

"We give thanks for this food, for those who provided it. May it bring us health and strength on this day, and in days to come."

An echo of amens, of clattering utensils and unstifled children, their laughter seasoning the meal and drawing grins from adults. Keith's squirrel harvest went around, flour-dredged and skillet-fried; fresh fish were served, and last year's potatoes. Too soon, bowls were empty and plates scraped clean. Grandparents snuck morsels to still-hungry kids, fathers guzzled water to fool their bellies.

Afterwards, men and women scrubbed dishes at the pump, sun beaming on their faces.

A mother of three spoke up: "No news all winter, no traffic since the fall."

Another woman, pregnant, shook her head. "Storms are laying down. Damn boats will be back, and you know it."

"And what then?" the first replied as she scraped a skillet, saving the grease. "Watchers can't turn 'em all."

"And should they be turned away?" a man remarked, drying plates. "Who are we to deny them?"

"You're kidding, right?" the pregnant woman scoffed, pouring kettle-water. "We barely made it; many didn't. Next winter will be worse. Hey! You kids! Take these plates inside. Carefully!"

Menfolk worried, whiskered and gaunt; beer bellies melted, TV remotes raided for batteries months ago. They gathered by the tool shed.

An expectant father said, "What word from the Watchers? What's your cousin say?"

Another, honing a hoe blade, replied, "Nothing moving. There's a lot of deep water between island and main."

"And how'd they make out? I'd like to know," the first said with a grunt, inspecting his spade. "Fat pickings on the mainland. Here, let me touch up my edge."

The file was passed. "Fat pickings? You're thinking with your belly again."

"Might be time for a scout, is all I'm sayin'. A few men, a boat, some rifles, get the lay of the land."

"Get yourself laid, you mean." Laughter rumbled from the amateur farmers.

"And what about boat gas? That's a lot of fuel to run 30 miles."

"Gas is gonna go bad anyway, then what? Sit here blind? Forever?" He handed back the file. "Cavalry ain't coming. And we all fuckin' know it."

The men broke up, grumbling, each to their plot, each with their own plottings. Hungry minds chewed on not enough facts. Similar talk all around the island.

"Watchers are still posted."

"Though there's nothing to see."

"Too many graves."

"Yeah, but none from the Stinger."

"Was a long winter without electricity."

"Hypothermia is a hard way to go."

"We'll need more wood."

"And more stoves to burn it."

"And salt for the fish."

"But how'll we catch 'em?"

"What about Charlevoix, Naubinway, Manistique?"

"Death, corpses, chaos."

"What if there's food? Government? Electricity?"

"And what if there's not?"

What if? What if? What if?

Caution. Caution. Caution.

There were a dozen such gatherings on Beaver Island. Tables cleared, belts cinched tighter, none were sated. The next meal was hours away. Dishes were washed and put away, cooking fires banked. Women knuckled their backs before joining men in the fields. Time for talk was over, their half-full stomachs protesting already.

They glanced at the water as labor resumed. Sunlight glinted on waves as hands shaded eyes, scanning for boats.

Horizon empty, geese gone north, the islanders returned to the earth.

Samantha

SMOKE WISPED FROM THE TENTED STRUCTURE. Samantha, the island's eldest, emerged sweating in the predawn. A fox, holding vigil near the tree line, turned tail and disappeared. The woman steamed, giving up her ghosts. Overheated from the sweat lodge, Samantha splashed cold water from a bowl; a star shone through her hand.

The gray light increased, dew chilling her toes. Adamant, she dared to look deeper, the ring-of-water powering her vision: the bowl's silver surface helped her reflect. Samantha saw truly—wisdom had wrinkled her, suffrage had scarred. She knew her place in the world. She'd been put there, and not gently.

Samantha, sage, was Anishinaabeg, Original People. She'd fostered many children; their tribe didn't matter. Samantha taught what she knew, guided her charges and kept them close. Now these fosterlings were needed.

For over a year plague had ravaged the planet, Beaver Island repeatedly besieged by water and aircraft. Insular, her people were threatened; isolation wouldn't work, never had. Stars faded at dawn's approach. In the east, a bloody planet eyed the world, towering above the dimly drawn hills.

Samantha shivered and wrapped herself in a woolen blanket, sealing in her heat. She faced Michigan's mainland. Trouble loomed there, and salvation too.

Earth rolled towards the light, inching towards mid-summer. Newly born, the sun warmed her eyelids, her lips curving upward in a relieved smile. There was hope in its glow. Healing. Sacred Medicine. Not a chemical concoction, but connection. To each other, to life. A human shield against the pox, against the Stinger.

Sam's visions, mirrored by water, had been clear: the islanders were not alone. There were allies to be found, survivors on the main. Beaver Island would need their help, just as the survivors needed the island. This relationship was reciprocal. Messengers must be sent.

During the night, Samantha had green-channeled her need, summoning three scouts. Two of them, Miin and Mukwa, were still young, her most recent fosterlings. Their guide must be older. Keith, a veteran, tough as old crow, would lead them: from island to main, there and back again.

Samantha's long braid, a silver garland, shone bright in the sun. The eldest headed for the shack she shared with Miin, her youngest foster, her blueberry.

The stove pipe was puffing, heating her kettle, empowering the tea.

Miinan

THE TEENAGER COULDN'T SLEEP. Trees scratched at the window of her dreams, twiggy fingers tapping the pane of her subconscious. Awake in the dark, Miin sighed and opened herself. Above her foster-gran's shack, constellations lay cradled by summer's leafy limbs. The maples were calling, channeling some urgent green need.

Reluctant, Miin slid her feet into slippers, then belted on a robe. Samantha's wood stove, underfed, had gone cold. Miin crept out the door, the stars ablaze above her. In the north, Fisher chased the Loon. Samantha, Native, had taught Miin, an Ojibwe orphan, the words she knew, *Ojiig* and *Maang*. The Panther stalked the treetops, *Mishi bizhiw*. Miin practiced Sam's preaching, gazed above and greeted the great spirits.

Island electricity had been cut last November. Winter waxed quickly, then slowly waned. In early spring, Miin had tapped the shack's trees. Island store shelves had long been emptied. There'd been deaths, too many, and every family was hungry. A little maple syrup suddenly meant a great deal.

Following Samantha, sap rising, Miin had prospected for veins to tap. Given permission by the grove, she'd spiled into their trunks, hanging her buckets. The ping of sugar water had increased in tempo with the birdsong, an overture for the spring of Year Two.

Summer now, Miinan—Blueberry—toed the earth through her slippers. A ruddy planet stared from above, lidless: a threat from the east. The solar-fed grove, shuttered for the night, awaited the coming of daylight. Miin palmed the nearest burl, querying the maple: *What is wrong?*

The trunk telegraphed Samantha's midnight missive: *Miinan is needed, stay close, all will be revealed.* The tremors, for now, subsided, the tree—message sent—resuming its rest.

Light hinted, bed beckoned. Miin saw Samantha's sweat lodge aglow. The novice had helped her mentor prepare, smudging sage and warming rocks. Fostered by Samantha, Miin minded her instruction, laying down the cedar to create a cord—umbilical—between the two fires.

The sweat lodge sat silent; nothing breezed through the branches. Sam's sentry owls were still. Miin reentered the shack and quietly shut the door. Fingers cold, she struck a shaky match, her kindling soon catching fire. When the flames grew hungry, she fed the stove, put the kettle on the hob, and crawled back to bed. The shack warmed quickly, Miin drifting off to the pop of pine.

Keith Called

KEITH TWO-CROW and Tom McCann shared the sunrise watch at Kilty Point station. Life-long friends, both were island-born, their draft tours in Vietnam comprising their longest stints off-island.

McCann had pulled carrier duty, Gulf of Tonkin on the *Forrestal*: 15 months catching shot-up A-4s, arresting them with cables as they hurtled home with empty bomb racks. Keith had gotten the Corps. They'd both returned, scarred by survival; in the decades since, they'd sheltered in place.

Their observation post was a vacant cottage with a second floor of wrap-around glass and a widow's walk above. McCann scanned the horizon with binoculars. Static shushed from their marine radio. Keith, his watchmate, perked shitty coffee on the Coleman, careful to conserve the precious propane.

"Top off?" Two-Crow nodded towards McCann's empty mug. The summer sun rose above Lake Michigan, orange light flooding the watch room.

"Thanks Keith, but I'm right full." McCann shaded his binos, continued his scanning. "If I were gonna hit us, I'd pick sunrise."

A nod from Keith, his gray mountain man beard wagging, stained tobacco-brown about the mouth. Faded ink—USMC—marched around his forearm. The veteran kept his ponytail tucked beneath a cap.

McCann squinted through the sun's blaze. "Can't see a fuckin' thing."

Gull-cry and wave-lap concurred.

A bog-scented breeze found the old-timers; given direction by Samantha, it whisked them backwards in time. Decades and distance disappeared in a blink: ancients no longer, they were 20 again, uniformed, sweating in Southeast Asia, flung by their draft boards to the far side of the world.

Manipulating wind currents was no simple thing. Samantha wanted Keith—her oldest foster—for a mission. The breeze found both men. Time softened, then slipped. Sam's invitation went through.

Private First Class Two-Crow looked out, not at the placid waters of a gentle lake, but at an airborne armada of weaponized will. Hueys and Cobras were contour flying above a brilliant blue sea toward a tangle of dense jungle ahead. Predawn fog filled a valley, mingling with cook-smoke from the target village. Flight crews were hopped up, nervy, nauseous. The sun rose fiercely behind them, blinding villagers, painting targets for the gunners.

The first pass, weapons blazing, plowed a furious furrow. A second pass followed, then a third, till there was nothing left to shoot at: village, farmers, pigs were all a butchered mess, machine-gunned to mud. The target had been reduced to its basic elements, primordial clay. No aircraft had been lost, an exaggerated body count passed up the chain.

Landing in Quang Tri, Private Two-Crow was reamed by his crew chief. None of Keith's ammo had been expended, his M-60 barrel coldly sober.

"Stupid fuckin' Indian! What's the goddamn problem? Chickenshit! Next mission we fly, your weapon's the first one empty! Do I make myself clear, Mr. Crow?"

As for McCann, Samantha's boggy breeze swept him back to USS *Forrestal* in '67.

McCann smelled jet fuel on fire. Oil vapors rose to halo the sun in hazy, rippling plumes. Pilots were coffined in their aircraft, cremated alive under stuck canopies. Rotten ordnance burst, 1,000-pound bombs cooked by the flames. General Quarters bonged through the bulkheads. Their floating fortress in danger, a stirring of sailors commenced. Five thousand men focused their frenzy and extinguished the blaze, saving their haze gray hive. McCann, a first responder, charged the smoke, hooked a half-charred body and dragged his shipmate from hell's maw. A slather of melted flesh marked their passage, human grease spitting on the deck's skillet-hot surface.

Samantha's summons—successful—breezed elsewhere, and linear time resumed. A billion diamonds bedazzled the big lake, gulls keening above the cottage as sunlight dappled the husks of two men. The cottage clock, while its batteries lasted, insisted on the present, though the men's own gears were winding down.

Their radio crackled. "Kilty Point, Kilty Point, Kilty Point. Whiskey Light, over."

McCann blinked and returned to morning light, soft sounds, and the beach, nose twitching as he scented coffee. Turning, he looked to his friend, who still stood vacant, elsewhere, other. Keith Two-Crow was on the wing. It had happened before, something inside him. A Chippewa thing? McCann self-corrected, *O-jib-way*. The watch stander, Keith's battle buddy, shook his head.

The voice on the radio grew pissy and insistent. McCann could almost see the caller's red face.

"Kilty Point, Kilty Point, Kilty Point. This is Whiskey Light, OVER!"

McCann keyed the mic, averting explosion.

"This is Kilty Point. Nothing to report, over."

McCann looked to Keith—his friend hadn't moved. He turned off the burner, filling his mug from the battered pot. He brought his binoculars out on deck. Heat sandblasted the beach. Another summer scorcher, not good for the gardens. McCann resumed his watch.

When he stepped back inside, eyes dilating in the dim, he shook his head again.

Damn it, Keith.

The crow had flown.

The cottage was empty.

Blueberry and Crow

ROADS ON BEAVER ISLAND preferred the coast; most attempts to push inland didn't last. Cranberry Bog was the heart of the island. Its arterial footpaths were clogged by bramble and vine, stymieing would-be visitors. Returning, bug-bitten, to their trailhead, off they'd drive to somewhere more accessible.

Samantha's youngest foster was not one of these tourists. The paths did Miin's bidding. Her parents, years ago, had left both her and the island behind. Bruised by betrayal, Blueberry had grown sour. When Sam adopted her, Miin's sweetness returned, albeit by degrees. Raised by elders, lodge to lodge, Miin had learned the language of the place. Fluency appreciated, Beaver Island talked back.

While sunrise dazzled McCann at his watch station and Keith by his coffee pot, June climbed into Miin's window as well. Finding her not-at-home, its rays lanced elsewhere. Samantha's shack stood empty, elder and younger up before dawn. Sam had stayed close. She had another summons to perform, and her solstice-bog was busy.

Miin, barefoot, had ranged further. Her toes gripped the dirt, planting and uprooting with every step. A green shimmer slowed the girl down: a patch of blueberries, *miinan* to elders, beckoned. Miin knelt and unkinked the bush, freeing its solar panels. Photons were captured, infusing the berries with a breakfast of sunbeams.

"What's this now?" spoke Keith. "Miin in the miinan again?"

Miin said farewell to her leafy friends, straightening. "Uncle Crow," she replied, and bowed, mock-solemn.

"Niece Blueberry."

They stood together on the path, old growth and sapling. Unrelated by family, their kinship through Samantha ran deep. Sunlight filtered through the canopy, energizing the forest floor. They scented chlorophyll as plant machinery fired up for a long summer shift.

"Uncle, why can I never feel your arrival?"

"Why would you want to?"

Miin held her hand in a sunbeam, observing its veins, its leaf-like architecture. "Samantha says all things cast shadows."

The girl waved, and a nearby stand of ferns nodded in response, waving back.

Two-Crow considered, Blueberry waited.

Their antennae tingled. *Intuition.* They both felt it; lifeforms approached.

A white-tailed doe, with her spotted fawn close beside, browsed nearer. The mom feasted on greens, filling her teats with ferny fuel. The doe deployed her sensory spectrum; reports came back from nose, ears, and eyes signaling *all clear.*

Mom paused while her fawn guzzled.

The two humans stood silent, not 10 feet away.

Miin and Keith shared a secret delight. Their conversation continued on a soundless frequency.

When I was your age, Miin, Samantha taught me the same.

YOU were my age?

Motionless, they passed a wink between them.

The deer fed on, undisturbed.

Keith flashed a smile towards Miin.

Before I left for war, Samantha—not much older than I was—showed me something else.

Miin's hungry mind was open, craving this sustenance.

Keith continued:

All things cast shadows. With practice, some are able to control what they cast. Your essence can be muted, camouflaged. Combine what you're casting with the greater shadows around you.

Keith looked into niece Blueberry, checking for comprehension.

Miin projected back to her uncle with a smile: *Understood.*

Doe and fawn eventually strayed elsewhere. Keith and Miin came back to themselves in the glade. She took her uncle's weathered hand, his fingers dark-skinned and knobby, looking like roots. Miin pictured planting him upside down, and giggled. Then she tugged him towards Cranberry Bog. Samantha was expecting them.

Spoken aloud now, their conversation resumed. "What just happened?" Miin asked in a wondering voice. "How did you do that?

This brought a smiling nod from Crow. "You tell me. How did *you* do that?"

Miin considered a moment before answering, "I wanted to disappear, to blend in: sunlight, green leaf, branch and twig."

"And our thoughts? What passed between us?"

"I shielded them, knew what the doe could read and what she couldn't."

Keith trailed behind as Miin skipped ahead. "Does this answer your question, Blueberry? About why you can't sense me?"

Miin constructed a thought-collage of her Uncle Keith, then showed him:

An owl perched for ambush. A bearded wolf. Heron-on-the-bank and hunted-frog too. Lastly and long ago, Private Two-Crow, young and lethal, a jaguar in a jungle, far away.

Approval radiated from Keith, with corrections. *Jaguar* he erased. In its place, he sent:

Metallic birds in fumey formation, ungainly, stalked by death above and below. One bird flickering, sometimes there, sometimes not. Then the formation was blown apart, blood and fragments falling. The flicker-bird became a crow, tattered and terrified, winging back to its island.

Samantha tended her bog, pulling on strings.

Crow was on the way, Blueberry too.

Aandeg followed *Miinan*, an Ojibwe myth. Or like one, anyway. Sam smiled at the thought.

She'd summoned them both, along with one more, the third and final of her scouts. Earlier, before star-fade, Samantha had sent out a profile of sorts, an all-points bulletin to any responding units: *strength of a bear, fire of youth, awkward confusion.*

She was looking for Mukwa. Samantha awaited a reply, an atmospheric response. With sunlight warm on her face, she sensed confirmation: Mukwa, ever reluctant, shambled her way. The folktale had been cast.

Mukwa Called

THE BIG MAN, BARELY IN HIS TWENTIES, had slept like shit. A red planet kept peeping into his hayloft, rousing Mukwa with its angry glare.

"Muck, get yer ass up!" Farmer Gaff barked, gleaming a lantern near the loft. Gaff, cranky without caffeine, enjoyed shouting his laborer awake before dawn.

Hoeing potatoes soon after sunrise, Mukwa sniffed his pits. He stank like shit too. He'd been grudged a cot by Gaff, the elder he toiled for. Dude kept a string of ponies on Sloptown Road. Samantha, Mukwa's foster-gran, had doctored them, and Gaff owed Sam a favor. The farmer's barn reeked of manure, so of course Mukwa reeked too.

The morning sun intensified, a wave of heat drowning the island. Mukwa, squinting at the tree line, noticed a disturbance of crows. *Samantha, that you?*

A black messenger left the roost, winging right at him.

Shit! Samantha for sure.

Born downstate, his parents had quickly lost him. Michigan's Department of Health tried to service his special needs and failed. CPS couldn't protect him: mistreatment had followed, family to family, till Samantha found him and offered sanctuary in her shack. A fairy godmother, Sam's magic touch could heal trauma's wounds.

Sensing the inner bear beneath his white skin, Samantha helped the lost boy find his name, find his talents. Mukwa learned to draw, control his rage, and eventually aged out of CPS and out of Sam's shack. By then his gran had adopted a greener, younger shoot to tend: Blueberry, an islander this time, and like Samantha, Indigenous.

Unlike Miin, his new foster sister, Mukwa wasn't Native, not really, though his name meant bear in the language. Wanting too badly to belong, the tribeless boy, "Muck," got mocked for his hand-drawn tattoos and wannabe ways. But Muck grew big—and so did his grudges.

Muck had fought against bears as a senior at the island's Community School, charging their lines and slamming them to the white-striped turf. The Bay-de-Noc Bears were a home game opponent for the undersized Islanders and their half-assed team. Those big boys, visitors from the Upper Peninsula, had treated the pre-season game as a joke. It certainly had been.

There'd been no lights for the night game, and the goal posts stood crooked, the Islanders wearing mismatched jerseys—green and white—with too many mends. The principal bellowed a play-by-play of the rout though a bullhorn. Of course Muck had picked a fight, squeezing too hard in the handshake line. Helmets off, he'd bloodied some faces before Coach kicked him off the team, this time for good.

That night, underage, he drank a case by himself, lurking behind the Shamrock for last call, a nuisance bear by the garbage bins. Three ladies had tottered out, tipsily weaving towards their tourist hotel. Muck got them talking, then laughing. Before dawn he'd had all three, leaving them tangled in sticky sheets.

Still smeared with game day eye black, overripe from sweat and sex, he made his way to the water's edge. There he stripped, stretched his limbs, and roared. Purples and pinks bruised the horizon as he quenched himself, hissing, in the bay. He stroked towards deep water. *Keep going!* He swam some more. *No one's gonna miss your sorry ass.* Body finally cramping, his passions cooled. *Fucking coward.*

Floating on his back, he watched the gulls soar, impossibly high, lit by a sunrise he could not yet see. He sketched the scene in his mind, memorizing the curvature of the Earth. He'd limped back to Sam's shack, but Blueberry was already there. The two women tried, but their healing hadn't helped.

Mocked for the fight, Muck dropped out of school. Cast out by the island, he was outcast from himself. The foster kid filled a garbage bag with his things: little more than a sketch pad, pencils, and his Jordans. Then he left, searching for his roots in the concrete crumble of southeast Michigan. He shoveled through shit-cities—Saginaw, Flint, Detroit—digging for his deadbeats, but never found them.

He sold drugs, flirted with B and E, and was charged with assault. His sketches accumulated—his rap sheet too. Juvie, then jail: he barely dodged prison. Stabbed and stitched, he'd self-cauterized with booze.

Then came the pandemic's first wave. He'd caught the Covee not once, but twice. But who hadn't? He coughed his way through it like everyone else. He'd been running hot when Samantha first summoned him, a month before the variant started stinging. Her fucking messenger had been a crow, of course. His foster-gran's arm had grown long; Sam's winged emissary had found him on a winter night in Detroit.

Seeking to profit from Muck's posing, the Native Mob had recruited him, joining up with Hamtramck Bloods to hit the Piru gang. Their SUV had been crowded with reefer, trap rap, and automatic weapons. Locker room nerves oozed from the shooters. Lit by screen-glow, nervous teens updated stories, posting their last. When the target approached, there would be no going back. Murder one was a whole different game.

Mukwa had been nervously sketching, sitting shotgun, when something thumped the hood. *Grenade? What the fuck?* Not a bomb but a bird. The big fucking crow gave a glare: Samantha, on her island, *caw-cawed* him to return. *Screw this*, he thought, *the old bird is right!*

So he'd wrenched the door open, ducked and rolled away. Weaponless, desperate, he'd run at full tilt, curses sounding loudly from his crew. This alerted the Piru mark, who pulled up quick in a blaze of light, the sound following a half-tick behind: gunshots, shattered glass, and high-pitched screams. Mukwa put corners between them. Trashcan-tacklers, he dodged them all. Steam rose from manhole covers, accusatory ghosts; the freshly killed kids pointed long fingers. Mukwa knew just how he'd draw it as he hustled away from the wail of sirens.

The next day dawned gray, like all the ones before. He'd peeled some hundreds and made two purchases, a bus ticket north and a tattoo: a bear paw, clawed from his sketchbook. Running no more, Mukwa returned. An island fisherman, owing Samantha, ferried him across just in time. Stygian, the cities collapsed behind him. Year 1 began, and with it, the island blockade.

For over a year, tatted and pierced, Mukwa kept his head down, helping where he could, biding time. Samantha, her hair more silver than he remembered, leaned on his strength, but the big man didn't mind. His wrinkled gran and little Miin were the only family he had.

"Muck, stuff these spuds in the cellar!" Farmer Gaff yelled, red-faced, pointing at the muddy wheelbarrow.

Stuff yourself! Mukwa handled it, grumbling at the stunted taters. *Shoulda stayed off-island.*

Black-winged, Samantha's messenger once again swooped low. The fucking crow recognized him, Mukwa was sure. Sure-as-shit, it delivered Sam's summons, splat, upon the cellar door.

Mukwa squinted as the bird arrowed back towards her shack and Cranberry Bog.

Damn it, Sam.

"Muck! Stow those spuds now, boy! Let's go!"

"Coming!" he sassed Gaff, then ducked below. He pulled hard from the cider barrel and wiped his mouth, already planning his path to the bog.

Cranberry Bog

MUKWA, LAST TO BE SUMMONED, was last to arrive. He'd cleared out of Gaff's loft, grabbed his J's, his sketches, and stuffed some gear in a bag. With fuel rationed and driving forbidden, he'd hitched a dusty ride on a wagon and rolled south, shadowed by crows. Reaching the state forest, he started hiking. A sweaty hour later he found another crow, Two-Crow actually, a leathery old-timer with tight ties to his gran.

Keith and Miin, silent as stones, sat under the eaves. Samantha's shack was empty, its knotty boards warping in the sun. His foster-gran wasn't home—of course she wasn't.

Mukwa nodded at the statues and sat, sharing their slice of shade. The entire insect phylum asserted itself: ants nibbled and gnats gnawed. He resisted the urge to swat, to slaughter. Old Crow and Blueberry, unperturbed, were barely there. He wanted to swat them too, but Mukwa endured.

The sun felt ferocious. The blue planet seemed to pause, halted by heat. *Something* moved through all three—a sending from Samantha? Mukwa scented roots and stone, heard the water trickle as a ferny coolness dampened his skin.

Miin, youngest, was up and running already. Mukwa watched as little sister disappeared down a path. Two-Crow stood more stiffly. He eyed the young bear, the mocked man, the Muck.

"We'll be chasing that girl quite a bit, if Sam keeps us together."

Keith's wink eased the bruin, and Mukwa grunted in reluctant response.

Crow nodded. "We'd better go, before they realize they don't need us."

Keith let Mukwa lead. Bear sniffed after Blueberry, the old hunter following behind.

Midday. Sun beat down on the bog, centuries of decay catalyzed by heat. The airwaves thrummed with insectoid life. Beaver Island's heart was the bog, and the bog's heart, the spring.

There sat Samantha in a bower of moss, bathed by Earth's icy burble. Shade offered sanctuary, a cool grotto sheltered from summer's searing haze. Miin was there already, sitting cross-legged, calm. Both women were barefooted. Roots overhung them, tangling in their hair, binding them to the bog, to the tendrilled kingdoms of Plantae, Fungi, and Protista.

Arriving late, the men bowed to enter and arranged their less-agile limbs, attempting stillness. Keith calmed first. Two-Crow merged with the landscape, matching his pulse rate to place. He was there, then gone, the flicker-bird in flight.

Mukwa fought the merge. His spirit bear paced, hackles up, its growl discordant with water-song. Muck felt the shame of failure, of mockery, the missed block, the wrong skin, the otherment of derision. Muck stoked this furnace, fed his fury. The old delight of *fuck it* fueled his fire.

An icy spray splashed his face, the cold shocking his breath away.

Angry, sputtering, his eyes flashed open. Miin sat beside him; she'd filled a dipper with water and tossed it on him. Grinning, the girl dipped another. Samantha and Keith remained aloof, both elders elsewhere engaged.

Miin paused the assault, making a peace offering of the dipper's handle.

Mukwa slowed one breath, then another. Water trickled down his neck, got under his shirt. He allowed himself to cool. The smiling girl, his foster sister, was no proper target for ursine rage. Mukwa accepted the ladle, brimful with island blood, and drank deep.

Miin insisted, so he dipped another. The clear water had a mineral taste. He gulped away his grief: Gaff, the spuds, the cellar. He gulped away his gang, his deadbeats. Mukwa quenched himself, banking fires, dousing doubts.

Miin resumed her meditation, a smile twitching on her lips.

Sated, he arranged the dipper on its altar of moss.

Calm now, he unlaced his Jordans, baring his feet. Hair dripping, he found his proper place. Mukwa took it all in and was taken away.

The Earth turned quickly, cycling through sun, moon-phase, and stars. Constellations cartwheeled: Ursus prowled north, berserker of the skies. Corvus flew south, wise-bird, cupbearer to gods. Faster and faster, a dizzying blur, till equilibrium was reached.

A pair of crows became four crows on the wing. The scouts shared a bird's eye view of the archipelago: islands of sand, stepping stones to the mainland. There, waiting, was an entire continent of crows. A million eyes were offered, a million received. Corvid cartography was stitched to their brains: roost trees, safety, battlefields, danger...

At last, a night flight back to their island, the last of the chain, glowing green, an insular aurora in a freshwater sea. The four of them dove down, swooping through trees. They folded their wings and delighted in the oxygenated exhale of plants, feasting on fruit, symbionts with seeds. The scouts imbibed the island, its blessings, and its biome.

Queen Earth was strong here. Gaia, Grandmother, Giver-of-Fruits, as she used to be, before humanity yoked her, domesticating her powers.

Now, after the sudden quiet, this force was growing, greener than before. Their immunity was enhanced. Protection was offered, protection received. Nature would shield them if she could.

Last in, last out, Mukwa returned. Their bower was fragrant with sweet tobacco; Samantha passed a bowl, cupping its smoke. Hair and face anointed, she observed her three scouts. Keith, too, took a pull. His eyes, etched with crow's feet, were far-seeing. He exhaled a plume towards Miin, and she spirit-bathed in his cloud.

Keith looked at the man-bear; the two of them were bonded now. Mukwa understood. The youth put his rage away, feeling connected and calm. Keith reversed the pipe, passing it stem-first. Mukwa, greed-free, accepted, his senses had been honed. He identified the scent of each herb: red willow, sumac, nicotiana, and bearberry. Samantha pestled her own *kinnikinnick* and preserved it.

With ceremony, she passed her kit to Keith. Pipe and pouch were now theirs, portable power for the mission ahead. They were scouts now, Sam's eyes and ears, soon to be embedded on the main. Their immune systems had been enhanced: green-shielded, nature willing, from viral assault.

Cranberry Bog had dimmed into dusk. As above, so below: stars peered down through the canopy and up again from the mirroring pool. The smoke had soothed the four humans, clearing clutter from neural pathways. They sat together and talked, soundless perhaps, except to each other.

"*Nookomis*, Grandmother, why us?"

Samantha, wizened, smiled at Miinan, her foster, her Blueberry. "You three have no family but each other, and are blessed with abilities others don't yet possess. You will be protected, at least for a while. And you two," she nodded at the siblings, "have much to learn, if this old crow will teach you? Trouble looms; the island needs you both to grow up quick."

An evening breeze tickled the treetops, stirring leaves from their slumber. Eventually Keith stirred too, asking, "And what's our mission?" Stars winked in and out, galactic fireflies engaged in distant display. "Decades ago, drafted to Vietnam, you asked me the same question." Keith, a lanky Indian kid again, nodded. "I remember."

"The mission is similar, there and back again, though this time as protector." Elder and eldest looked towards the fosterlings, and Sam lifted her chin. "You must protect them, and others as well."

"Others?"

"Islanders, of course, and maybe more. Across the water there are people, a community in danger. I've seen it. They need us, and this island may need them."

"And how do you know this?" Keith did not expect an answer.

"And how do you not?" Samantha grinned. She bade Keith look at the starry pond. "Past, present, and future are one. It's all there if we have the wisdom to see."

"And do you have that wisdom, Sam?"

Mukwa and Miin didn't hear their gran's response. A lake-scented wind ruffled the surface, erasing its etchings.

Samantha shook herself. "You'll leave in three days. I'll arrange it with Doyle."

At this, Keith grumbled. There was no love lost between the Irish-descended fisherman and the island's Indigenous.

Sam instructed Keith to make ready, advising, "You should travel light. Nothing you can't easily carry."

The combat veteran was mentally packing: bedrolls, dried food, weapons, water, medicine...

Miin realized her nookomis would be staying behind. "I'm not ready to leave you."

Samantha smiled. "Miinan, my adventuring days are long over, and yours are just beginning. Will we share our shack again? I hope so. Our years together have been good ones."

Samantha's silver hair was radiant in the evening gloom. She nodded at Mukwa and Keith. "Anyway, these two fools need you. More muscle than mind."

A salty tear spilled from Miin: uprooted again, another goodbye. Mukwa placed a heavy paw on her shoulder. "*Nishiime*, little sister, we'll be back before you know it. Nothing will touch you, I promise."

Samantha laughed, a spiderweb of wrinkles spreading across her face. "Well said, muscles! Though who will protect who remains to be seen."

Watchers

CAPTAIN TOM DOYLE, lunch pail in hand, ascended the spiral staircase of the Whiskey Point Light. Almost to the top, he paused to peer through a window at the predawn harbor below. Sweat dripped down his face, and Doyle gripped the sill for support, his heart revving, its needle pointing red.

Damn legs were built for boat decks, not climbing towers like a monkey.

Small waves chopped across the bay. Daybreak would arrive in minutes. A red planet, ancient aid to navigation, winked out. What else was new? The Beaver Islanders were on their own.

Doyle counted boats—gill-netters and tugs—and arrived at an even dozen, well-moored, gassed up, and batteries charged. Their lockers were stocked with ammo, flares, field dressings, and food. Most had been holed by bullets, rammed, and repaired. The oldest, F/V *Ruby Ann*, Doyle had salvaged from the museum. The turtleback had a steel shell and had been given a .30 caliber bite. Their fleet—so far—had served as a rusty shield against infection's sting.

Other boats, mothballed, had been hauled out and covered with tarps. Not enough resources to keep them all running. Would they ever float again? Doyle doubted it. Summer regattas would become a thing of the past, another tall tale disbelieved by future young ones, one more myth from before to roll their eyes at.

Fucking hope they can roll their eyes. Fucking hope there's a future.

Doyle stumped up the final stairs and stepped into the lantern room, where his niece had the watch.

"Morning, uncle!"

Tom's niece, 18, surveyed the horizon with binoculars as she spoke. Her parents, Doyle's in-laws, like many part-time islanders, had been stranded on the mainland and stung. Bulldozed into a mass grave near Charlevoix, their bodies would not be returning.

White noise whispered from marine radios; the glowing numerals seemed eerie after a year of no outside contact and little electricity. Doyle, short of breath, set his lunch down, popped the latches, and lifted a thermos. He had a face like chipped paint, his Irish skin made splotchy by the sun.

"Mornin' Maggie," for the moment, was all he could muster.

Thick-handed from a lifetime of labor, Doyle unscrewed the plastic mug and filled it with quarantine coffee. His wife Annie, his anchor, had perked it with eggshells using recycled grounds. For 40 years she'd risen early to ensure her captain was provided with the proper victuals.

Doyle slurped the too-thin brew, straining loose grounds through yellowing teeth.

"Pour you one?"

"No thanks, uncle. Never liked the taste." Maggie, eager to depart, bored since midnight, had been duly diligent. She hoped Uncle Tom would quickly dismiss her.

Taste? It's not a damn smoothie, girl!

But even Doyle had been a greenhorn once, watch after watch fueled by youthful energy with no need for caffeine. Recalling the endless droning of his father's generation, he flipped quickly through the logbook while his niece tidied the tower, superfluously sweeping while she waited to be relieved. He looked over her entries. Next to each watch station, *NTR* had been written in Maggie's bubbled font. *Nothing to Report. Good. Christ keep it so.*

Each station had a Watcher, a radio, and batteries powered by solar panels. Around-the-clock, eyes scanned every horizon, bored but restless, always on the lookout even if half-lidded.

Maggie cleaned the spotless window panes, body language screaming her impatience. An errant spray misted her uncle's mug; he frowned but sipped anyway, paging backwards in the log. Island stubbornness was an ancient streak, encoded by chromosomes. A century ago, clan Doyle departed Donegal, fleeing famine. They'd been rooted tight to Beaver Island ever since.

Gonna stay here, too. No fucking variant gonna sting us. No scabby scavengers gonna pilfer what's ours.

Finally, Doyle checked his wrist against the tower clock. Watchers kept the time, synchronizing with each other at the weekly council meeting. Small unities kept them sharp. Around the island all stations were due to report.

Doyle sighed at her hurry and cast the girl loose.

"Well done, Miss Maggie. Now off with you."

"Thank you! I love you, uncle!" And she was off, halfway down the stairs already.

Doyle flashed a rare grin—quick as Morse code—as he watched his niece skip across the lighthouse lawn. In a lifetime spent relieving watchmates, *I love yous* had been rare indeed.

Doyle readied his pen—black ink only—for the sunup reports. He eyed the radios, the big one tuned to 156.800 MHz, channel 16. All ships and stations were required to maintain a listening watch. This emergency station, monitored by Doyle since his greenest days, had been silent since grid-down last November.

Whiskey Point at the north end and Beaver Head in the south were the only two stations monitoring 16. Those antennas, the big ears of the island, had a range of 120 miles. The Coast Guard, FEMA, DHS: if they ever called, it would be on 16. Since collapse the channel had remained stone-silent. On both mics, warnings had been taped: DO NOT BROADCAST!

Island policy had been decided at council. They should stay dark, become a hole in the water. The fleet stayed close, not a matter of fuel, even sailboats were forbidden to roam. It was best to disappear, go full-on Atlantis, at least for now.

Doyle picked up the other mic, 156.600 MHz, channel 12, the comms channel for Watchers. These radios were low wattage and meant for island ears only.

The tower clock blinked 0600.

Doyle keyed the mic. "Point LaPar, Point LaPar, Point LaPar. This is Whiskey Light, over." He released the PTT button.

Static. Then, "Whiskey Light, this is Point LaPar, over."

A young man's voice, 10 miles south. Nick Hannigan, island athlete, had been college-bound before collapse. Young Nick sounded disappointed; he'd hoped to hear Maggie.

Doyle could give two shits about Nick's hopes. "Point LaPar, what's your report, over?"

"Whiskey Light, Point LaPar. Nothing to report, over."

"Point LaPar. Roger, nothing to report. Whiskey Light, out."

Nick and Maggie no doubt had chatted through their midwatch. Doyle grumbled, scribbled in *NTR*, and continued his calls. Maggie's mom, Annie's little sister, had been at the courthouse in Charlevoix, divorcing Maggie's dad—a damn cheater—when Covee clacked its fatal gavel. Young Maggie was devastated by the news. Her island friends slowly nursed her back to health, helped by the Hannigans. Auntie and uncle watched over her as well.

0600 Point LaPar, Hannigan, NTR
0602 Kilty Point, McCann, NTR (slow to respond!)
0604 Beaver Head Light, Miller, NTR
0606 French Bay, Keller, NTR
0608 McFadden's Point, Redding, NTR
0610 McCauley's Point, O'Donnell, NTR
0612 Indian Point, Bauman, NTR

Finished, he inked in his own report. *0614 Whiskey Light, Doyle, NTR.*

Tom stood from the chart table, rolled heavy shoulders, and carried his mug out onto the catwalk.

The sun hovered just above the horizon. Doyle divined the Earth's curve, gulls keening as they hunted over the harbor. The captain craved a cigarette; nothing so nautical as tobacco-tang and morning air.

He moved clockwise around the tower, could point to each Watcher though the sandy island loomed between. Their solar panels better be aligned, storing charge. Blind, deaf, and mute would be a sloppy way to face what was coming. Circuit complete, he pitched the grainy coffee dregs overboard. Sure as sunrise, something shitty would be heading their way.

Emerald Isle

BEAVER ISLAND ROLLED TOWARDS THE SUN. Its inhabitants, hungry but unstung, were already busy. Farmers pulled weeds from their fields, fishermen set nets, and Watchers kept the vigil. Their watery horizon, for now, remained empty.

Big fucker, that boat, Doyle thought for the millionth time.

He'd relieved niece Maggie from her tedium. A tourist pamphlet lay spread upon the chart table, its glossy centerfold an object of concern. Doyle ogled the ferry's lines, her dimensions. He sipped shitty coffee, the leeched grounds far too thin. Doyle had thinned as well; much of his bow had lost its bluff.

Nothing we got could sink her.

Bitter thoughts, bitter brew.

The motor vessel *Emerald Isle* had been built in Maine for Charlevoix's Boat Company. The ferry's home office was on the mainland, and *Emerald* harbored there. Pre-collapse, she'd made daily runs to Beaver, could carry 300 passengers and make it to the island in two or three hours. Since the blockade began, there'd been no sign of her. But out of sight was not out of mind, especially Doyle's.

Real pig of a boat.

His blood pressure rose just imagining the potential catastrophe.

Forget sinking, they couldn't even budge her.

The tower clock blinked 0700. Time for another round of reports.

She's fuckin' trouble for sure.

Doyle clicked his pen and keyed the mic. "Point LaPar, Point LaPar, Point LaPar, this is Whiskey Light, over."

His internal gauges steadied with each *NTR* recorded. They maintained more watch stations in the summer. Better weather meant bigger risk. It was worth the extra batteries to cover their blind spots.

Doyle's nightmare burned bright even during the daytime: infectious bastards making a stealthy landing in some quiet, unguarded bay. *Rabid fuckin' mainlanders!*

Undetected, they'd raid the nearest house, killing, plundering. A family would be butchered. Worse, the variant would be loose on the island, doing what it did. *More death, more suffering.*

Again he wrote down reports, adding his own, *0718 Whiskey Light, Doyle, NTR.*

He returned to the pamphlet. *That ferry's fuckin' coming for us.*

Doyle examined *Emerald* for the umpteenth time, his uneasiness rushing back in force. He took in her airbrushed figure, her eye-popping measurements: 130 feet in length, 39 feet wide. Steel constructed, she was capable of 14.5 knots and could carry a fucking semi-truck.

Some mainlander will load her up, ram her down our throats, and D-Day us with disease.

He remembered Maggie's farewell, *I love you uncle!* It was up to him and Annie now. They'd raise her right, a female skipper. That ferry though was a real bitch, a weapon of mass destruction. Doyle gnashed his molars, his even keel gone aground. *No way I can let that happen. No fuckin' way.*

Bloody Mary

AT THE GARDEN GATE THEY KISSED, mutually superstitious, their good-byes were a mantra, memorized years ago.

"Farewell Tom, take care my love."

"Adieu Annie, mum's the word about tonight. Any luck, I'll be back by morning."

She handed him provisions, then they hugged. The captain shouldered his sea bag, turning away towards the sunset. They'd parted a thousand times, what really was one more?

Farewell and adieu to you fair Spanish ladies,
Farewell and adieu to you ladies of Spain.

Annie behind, the world ahead. Doyle whistled as he navigated the mile from their cottage on the point to the municipal marina in town.

For we've received orders to sail back to Boston,
And never no more will we see you again.

Doyle stumped past Whiskey Light, the tower looked alert, Captain Sue Keller had the watch, a seasoned keeper. Tom, unthinking, changed his tune.

My father was the keeper of the Keystone Light,
Met with a mermaid late one night.

He passed the ball field, the toy shop, the Marine Museum—a repurposed net shed, 1906. He nodded to the old boats and the ghosts that crewed them: a wooden gillnetter, *Bob S.*; the trap net tug, *Miss Bay City*; and the sole surviving life boat from SS *Carl D. Bradley*. Doyle's whistle turned somber—33 drowned, RIP, November '58.

Safe and sound at home again, let the waters roar, Jack.
Long we've tossed on the rolling main, now we're safe ashore, Jack.

Reaching his destination, the ferry terminal, Doyle's blood was up. Too long ashore, he was eager for action, if not for the mission. His heart skipped when he saw her, straining at the leash. Tied tight to the dock was his mistress, a real ball-buster, *Bloody Mary*.

Doyle tossed down his sea bag, and climbed aboard. He ceased his whistle—bad luck in a boat, might blow up a storm. Years ago he'd scammed *Mary* from some Natives who'd gone bankrupt tending empty nets in the Straits of Mackinac, a tricky fishery. Called *Mary Ellen* back then, it didn't take long for her new name to find her. Beaver Islanders christened the boat "Bloody" for her hauls of whitefish and for the Irish knuckles of her brawling new captain.

Mary was the best damn sea boat Doyle had owned: 40 feet, steel construction, a glassed-in wheelhouse and all the bells.

Bet them Indians built it with casino money fleeced from whites.

He'd appropriated *Mary* back from the tribe. It added allure. Built as a small, Atlantic-style trawler, she was now a gillnetter with sheltered decks, the highliner of the Beaver fleet—topping chalkboards for catch-totals in every commercial port.

Doyle unlocked the wheelhouse hatch. *Can't be too fuckin' careful.*

He ducked inside his sanctuary, everything looking ship-shape as usual. His father's favorite phrase echoed in his mind: "A place for everything and everything in its place."

He heard the burr in Da's voice, a lingering brogue inherited from his Donegal forefathers. A century ago, Clan Doyle had immigrated for the fishing. There'd been a time when the Beaver fleet shipped their catch from Chicago to Manhattan. Island families today were the proud remnant. Except for some place-names, their Gaelic was gone, but orneriness endured.

Doyle still fumed from his encounter with Samantha. This morning she'd caught him red-handed pawing through *Emerald Isle's* pamphlet.

Can't fucking BELIEVE that old crone!

Swear Samantha FLEW up the lighthouse.

Spilled my damn coffee, her wrinkled face peering through the glass!

Doyle placed his Annie-packed pail on the galley table, then stowed his duffel in the forward cabin. Checking, always checking: lockers, hatches, survival suits. *You can never be too careful.*

He reentered his wheelhouse. Habitually, he switched on the Coast Guard weather report, then turned off the channel with a nervous twitch. Dead, like all the rest. *Shit.*

NOAA of course was silent, its meteorologists murdered by a molecular storm. Since the bitter end of Y1 and for all of Y2, the radio forecast never varied: static, with a 100% chance of further static. In the quiet, he replayed his recent conversation with Samantha.

Sammy says I'm to haul some of her Indians to the mainland tonight.

Oh am I? That's news to me.

Yes, Tom Doyle, yes you are.

Then she thanks me! Like the fuckin' thing was MY idea.

What about the gas? I say. The batteries? The council?

Again, she grins. Leave it to me, Samantha says, the damn witch.

Doyle's checklist calmed him down, its litany soothing: engine room, dipsticks, bilge, stuffing box, battery bank, fuel sample, filters, pumps, wiring, spares, seacock, extinguishers, alarms, winches, power takeoff, hoses, radios, steering, compass, rifle, bullets, shotgun, shells.

There were electronics he wouldn't be running and fish he wouldn't be catching. If a storm blew in the Coasties couldn't save him—couldn't even save themselves. They'd survived Covee alright, but not the variant, not the Stinger.

Sammy says, Captain Doyle, my three scouts are an answer to your prayers.
My prayers? What do YOU know about MY damn prayers?
I know you're blind, Tom Doyle. You're scared. Not for yourself, but for the island.
Course I'm scared! Who wouldn't be?
Well, she says, these are your eyes, your ears. Your scouts on the main.
Wonderful! No phone, no radio. Fuckin' pen pals, then? I'll check my mailbox!
Again, patting my shoulder, she says, Cap'n, you just leave that to me.

Doyle, back on deck, dreaded the arrival of his passengers. Twilight thickened, the tower looming unlit. The harbor was dark, with no bustle of boats. Tom had consulted no one, not even Big Hannigan; if another captain did this they'd be keelhauled, confined to quarters, shunned for jeopardizing the island and its cargo of souls all for one trip across.

Strange times, strange people, with the strangest yet to come.

Generations of Doyles had grumbled the same. Most of Beaver's non-Indigenous were evicted from another island—Ireland's Arranmore—when its potato crop failed due to blight. Beaver Island was indeed strange, always had been. It was once ruled by a king, islanders still telling the tale: King James Strang, Prophet, Seer and Revelator. Strang, a Mormon, had fired a cannon at the locals, winning the War of Whiskey Point right in Doyle's backyard. For eight years Strang had reigned as a despot, till he was shot in the back.

Doyle wished he could've seen it. 1856, summertime, a night much like tonight. Strang's blood had been spilled right near these docks. No doubt, some of its taint still lingered.

Strange as shit. So what if Samantha is right, and her hippie voodoo works?
A mariner must adapt, exploit any advantage. Maybe this was his chance? He fucking hated being blind. Considering, Doyle stepped to his chart, mapping out menaces: harbors to check, boats to inventory, invasion capabilities to sabotage. He had Annie and Maggie to protect, and the whole island too.

The long June day drowned in nautical twilight. The moon, a new crescent, brightened above St. James Harbor, a reminder that sharp eyes were always watching.

Doyle powered up the small radio, drawing on battery charge from the boat's solar panels.

"Whiskey Light, *Bloody Mary*, over."

He released the talk button.

"Bloody Mary, this is Whiskey Light. Doyle, that you? Over."

"Doyle here. Hey Keller, gonna fire up my engine, bring *Mary* out, spin her around the island and test our Watchers, make sure they're not napping. No warnings, understood? Over."

"Understood, no warnings. Over."

"And Susan, cover my watch if I'm not back by sunup. *Bloody Mary* out."

Doyle thumbed off the radio, its numeric glow decaying. After a year and a half, he admitted, it felt damn good to do something. As always, he craved a cigarette, but a drag of night air would have to do. Doyle stepped out on deck. Above him, silent as shadows, his three passengers—two kids and an old kook—peered down from the Strang-haunted dock. The church bell from Holy Cross tolled its brassy omen.

"Good evening, Cap'n."

Great. Keith fucking Two-Crow.

"May we come aboard?"

The Trip Across

MIDNIGHT OVERTOOK LAKE MICHIGAN, black surface spangling with reflected starlight. Doyle steered course one-two-zero degrees, southeast towards the mainland. *Mary* purred, cutting her way across the flat water. On deck, Keith and Mukwa sorted gear. Miin slept in the forward cabin, vibration and wave-lap the nocturne of her dreamscape.

The crescent moon had swung below the horizon, summer constellations bunched brightly above. *Bloody Mary* ran dark, nav-lights off, the wheelhouse dim. Doyle scowled at the binnacle lamp that lit their course.

Astern of the wheelhouse sat Two-Crow and Mukwa, shadowed by Keith's Old Town canoe. Doyle had flipped out, but Keith insisted they bring it. The captain's cloud of curses had mingled with exhaust from *Mary's* fired-up engine.

On the fish deck, voice pitched low, the veteran instructed. Spread out on blankets between them lay their assembled weaponry. The island's only badge, Deputy Williams, had paid Keith a nervous visit just prior to departure. Williams delivered a duffel of surplus acquired by the county sheriff, RIP.

"Mostly stuff from the 1033 program, plus some non-regulation extras. Never been much of a gun guy. Samantha said you might need it?"

The law man didn't stay for coffee; the old Indian made him nervous.

"Again," Keith prodded.

Mukwa recited, "Colt M-4 automatic rifle, four magazines of 30 rounds apiece. It's got a scope and iron sights for close quarters. Comes with a suppressor and 200 rounds."

"Who is allowed to use this rifle?"

"Only you."

"Why is that?"

"Too heavy for Miin, too much fun for me." He'd answered this way several times before, always with a lopsided smile.

Keith waited for Mukwa to continue. Finally, giving in, Keith said, "Killing shouldn't be fun. If it is, then you're a killer, you're lost."

"You used to be a killer."

"Who found me? Who healed me?"

"Samantha did."

"That's right. She did. And she found you, too."

Mukwa stared astern, the boat's starry wake tethering them to the past. Unknowns loomed ahead. "Yeah, she found me too."

Keith nodded once, as if that settled the matter. "Next," he prodded.

Mukwa sighed. "Our pistol. A Glock, four magazines, and 200 rounds."

"Pluses?"

"Stopping power, can handle wear and tear."

"Minuses?"

"It's loud, and the slide sits low. Hold it proper or slice your hand."

"Who may use it?"

"You. Or me, in an emergency."

"Show me."

Mukwa, in the dark, went through the motions. Two-Crow, by ear, approved. "And the blades?"

"Two knives, military issue. Seven inch carbon steel. Yours, from 'Nam, leather sheath. Mine, newer, with nylon."

"And your stance?"

Mukwa jumped up, rolling with *Mary*. He set himself in what Keith called the basic-warrior-stance.

"Picture your opponent."

The big man tried. Training was useless, Keith said, unless it was real in your mind. Mukwa had no idea what an opponent might look like, so he conjured one: *Racist. Infected. Good ol' boy charging with an ax.*

Feet shoulder-width apart. Left hand up, the blocker. Knife in his right, edge down, pointed at the target. He kept his blade "in the box," like Keith said, avoiding over-extension.

Redneck swung the ax.

Mukwa dodged quickly. Redneck readied another swing, presenting an opening.

Mukwa thrust, bloodying the blade, then pulled out, knife "in the box" again and ready.

I could get used to this!

Muck showboated a bit, butterfly and bee. He prepared for the next assault. Ol' redneck was fucked!

A shadow fluttered behind him, angling a blow toward the back of his neck.

Then Muck was on his knees, nauseous; his knife, his claw, dropped and forgotten.

He glared round at Two-Crow, somehow standing at his back. "The *fuck* man! Kinda *shit* was that?"

Keith smoldered down at him, saying, "Could ask *you* the same. No *game* here, boy. This is *real*. Miin's life, my life, yours. The island, its families, everyone you know—it's all in your hands. Stop enjoying this and start being afraid."

But Muck was in beast mode. *How in the FUCK?* He'd break the bones of old Crow, chum that skinny fart to the fishes!

He attacked Keith's canoe instead, flipping it with a flick of one paw and punching it, one-two, one-two, over and over again, then curb stomping the Kevlar with booted feet. After a few moments his tide of rage ebbed, revealing a fool. Muck cursed and lumbered forward, past the wheelhouse, disappearing in the dark.

The last words were Keith's, approving: "Proper stance, stayed in the box."

The big youth cooled on the bow, the night breeze wicking his skin.
Getting into some trippy shit now. Did the old dude have wings?
Muck rubbed at the back of his neck.
Did that even happen? He swore he'd felt feathers.
Dead ahead, a hook of stars snagged his attention, one red eye ablaze.
Gotta get my head in the game. No more fucking around.

Keith sighed as he looked over his canoe. He shook his head: the kid had power, though thankfully not enough to puncture the hull. Gathering up the weapons, he bagged them and dragged the duffel to their pack pile.

Looking up, he calculated time and bearing by celestial examination; observed the ancient circling parade of Bears, the Watcher, the Crown. Swan-Vulture-Eagle triangulated the galaxy, milky with stars.

Smoke time.

Two-Crow undogged a hatch, ducking through the galley and into the wheelhouse, Doyle's domain. There stood the mariner, alert at the helm. Keith acclimated himself, waiting on the captain.

"Quite a kicker," Doyle said with a sneer. "Used to watch ol' Muck play football. Maybe soccer's more his game?"

Keith stood by the empty chair. "You mind?"

"My guest."

Keith eased himself into the duct-taped contraption, *softer than deck steel anyway*. He arranged his long limbs, pulling out papers from a pouch. Nicotine-need vibrated from Doyle, and Keith, sensing it, rolled a pair of cigs.

"OK to smoke?"

He passed the captain a rollie and his Zippo, a faded *Semper Fi*.

Doyle opened it with a clink, thumbing the wheel. "The smoking lamp has been lit."

A spark, a flame. Doyle shielded his night vision with a squint.

Inhalation, all the good feelings.

Exhalation, and the captain was calm.

He returned Keith's fire, and the ceremony was repeated. The wheelhouse filled with smoke. Doyle launched the first salvo, lipping his cigarette, "Suppose you tell me the fuckin' plan?"

Keith indicated the chart on the table. "Got a lamp?"

Cig dangling, Doyle toggled a switch. Red light came on, illuminating NOAA-14902, "Northern End of Lake Michigan."

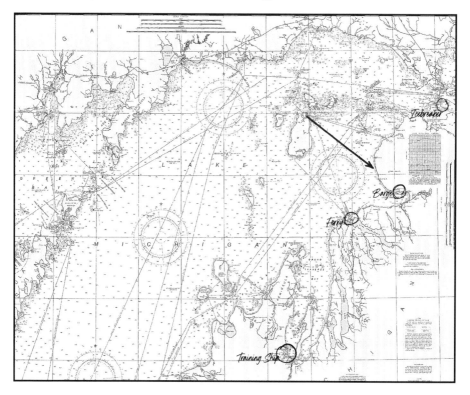

Keith blew smoke towards the overhead. "Samantha was a bit vague on detail."

Doyle grunted. *You don't fuckin' say* went unspoken, and he ashed out the porthole before taking another drag. He eyed their heading, eyed the old crow.

Keith picked a tobacco flake from his tongue. "Samantha feels a threat. Something's coming, something big."

The captain fought for self-control. "Bit vague, eh?" *God DAMN these two!* "Please tell me, Mr. Keith, that I'm not burnin' gas, goin' AWOL, riskin' *Mary* all for the pipe dream of some senile old sorceress!"

"Course not," Keith replied. Tending his cherry with a long draw, he exhaled before continuing, "Once aboard, *you* were meant to guide our next move. Who else knows these waters, our strengths and weaknesses? Cap'n Doyle, we're in your hands."

Quiet in the wheelhouse as Doyle adjusted his mental course.

Not all bad news here. No indeed. Might be a chance, a shitty one sure, but better than living blind.

The engine droned on. Blueberry slept below while Bear cooled on the bow. The mainland loomed ahead, undiscovered, a country of unknowns.

"I won't lie, Two-Crow, I've been wanting somethin' like this since the island went dark. We have to take a peek, can't bury our heads in sand forever."

Keith nodded his agreement. "Question is, where to peek first?"

"More important is how to *share* what you're peeking at."

"Samantha seems to think Miin will be able to send information back to her, telepathically."

Already ruddy-looking due to the chart light, Doyle reddened further. "Dammit, man! Just what I was fuckin' afraid of! No offense, old-timer, you've served, seen some shit, but we gotta do better than this Ojibwe-jumbo."

Keith showed him a smooth poker face. "Got a better idea?"

"Matter of fact, I do. First, gotta assume power's down everywhere."

A nod from Keith.

"Second, no power means no internet, no cell phones, no landlines. Agreed?"

Another nod from Keith. "So where does that leave us?"

"Well, if we had sat-phones and they were charged, that would be an option. But we don't, so it ain't. That leaves us up shit creek, Two-Crow. But maybe, just maybe, there's a fuckin' paddle."

"And the paddle is?"

"These old CB radios. Been around since the forties. Nothin' fancy. Run 'em off a battery, they don't take much juice. Antenna to antenna, range of 20 miles, maybe less."

"How would that work? You can receive, but how can we send?"

Doyle had pondered it. "Exactly, Mr. Keith, exactly. No perfect solution here. I saw your packs when you came aboard. Not much room for a 12 volt, or antenna, or radio setup?"

A head shake from Keith. Their packs were too heavy already.

"Well, it's not mine to give, but I'll loan you a handheld." Doyle passed a battered unit to Keith. "Range isn't great, and its batteries are iffy, but you can't beat the weight."

Two-Crow turned it on, cupping its fragile glow with his hands. "And if it dies, or won't reach?" He switched it off.

Doyle blew smoke towards the cabin overhead. "Shit creek again. Improvise. You hijack a better radio. Find a semi-truck, better yet a boat, one with some charge on its battery. Either way, contact me once a week. Let's use the moon: first quarter, full, and last quarter? Say midnight?"

Keith nodded in confirmation, and they checked their watches. "Midnight. Every quarter moon. First, full, and last. What's the best frequency?"

"Our watch stations use channel twelve. One five six, point eight zero zero. That'll work best. As you'll be broadcasting from the mainland, the island is too far and won't hear you, but I will."

"Might just work. And the range?"

"Range is trickier. On broadcast nights, I'll take *Mary* out, run her halfway, listen for you there, and get you an evac if you need it."

Two-Crow confirmed it all again and sighed, tired as shit.

This gray pilgrim, Doyle thought, *needs all the help he can get.*

"Now, Mr. Crow, roll me another, and let's take a look at the chart."

Turning and Turning in the Widening Gyre✦ The Falcon Cannot Hear the Falconer; Things fall apart; the center cannot hold; mere anarchy is loosed upon the world, the blood-dimmed tide is loosed, and everywhere the ceremony of innocence is drowned; the best lack all conviction, while the worst are full of passionate intensity. ✦✦✦✦✦✦✦✦ Surely some revelation is at hand; surely the second coming is at hand✦ The second coming! Hardly are these words out when a vast image out of Spiritus Mundi troubles my sight; a waste of desert sand; a shape with lion body and the head of a man, a gaze blank and pitiless as the sun, is moving its slow thighs, while all about it wind shadows of the indignant desert birds✦ The darkness drops again but now I know that twenty centuries of stony sleep were vexed to ✦✦✦✦✦✦ nightmare by a rocking cradle, and ✦✦✦✦✦✦ What Rough Beast Slouches Towards Bethlehem To Be Born?

William Butler Yeats

"Turning and turning in the widening gyre"–Yeats

I'M TAKING A BREAK FROM SCROLLING to dictate my own doom.

I still have sources, and as you know, the news isn't good.

Does it feel strange to be the central figure—albeit anonymous—in every broadcast, in every language, in every intelligence report around the world?

Yes, it does.

Though it's intoxicating, too. I'll get to this point later on, but you should know how, at the start, none of what happened was intentional.

The poet wrote: "The falcon cannot hear the falconer."

Indeed, my variant has slipped its tresses, ignores my whistle, and hunts now for itself.

Search high and low, believe me I have, and you will not find a more virulent, pest-ridden species than *Homo sapiens*, our "wise man."

The root word for virus is one of the oldest words we have. Sanskrit, an Indo-Aryan language that goes back 3,500 years, uses the word *viṣa*. The Romans brought us closer with *virūs* and *virulentus.*

Experts, and you may have guessed I'm one, believe our species' unique relationship with animals has been the cause of many viral outbreaks throughout history. Most epidemics are zoonotic events, where a virus leaps from its natural host species, say a bat, to another that has no history with its strand of RNA, say a human.

If you look at "wise man's" 300,000-year history, one thing becomes clear: we cannot seem to exist in an environment without altering it. When this trait is focused on other animals in a biome, the results are either domestication, like dogs, pigs, camels etc., or extinction. Just ask mammoths, aurochs, Neanderthals, and all the sorry rest. Our inability to leave well enough alone has always been a Trojan horse, vectoring viruses into our increasingly crowded city-states.

Smallpox, one of many poxviruses found in rodents, first crossed the species barrier 11,000 years ago in the farming villages of India. That virus, the world's deadliest before my own, authored more chapters of human history than any other.

Measles, the "red plague," jumped from dogs or cattle, and was once so common in Egypt that hieroglyphs called it a normal stage of childhood development.

A plethora of viruses, including influenza, rabies, measles, and smallpox, kept Europe's population in check for a thousand years. In the Middle Ages the average life expectancy was 35, and 60% of children died before 16. From this viral crucible emerged super-spreading *Übermenschen*, infecting every corner of the globe as they circumnavigated in plague ships.

The *Niña, Pinta,* and *Santa María* were biological Weapons of Mass Destruction, cesspools crewed by sociopathic, hypersexual sailors, crowded with livestock and 10,000 years of accumulated pox.

During the Age of Exploration—bold euphemism!—at any given time there were around a dozen vessels connecting the continents, sailing at top speeds of 10 knots. When Stinger broke containment there were 20,000 commercial flights a day, super-spreading my creation 500 miles further every hour.

"Things fall apart; the centre cannot hold"–Yeats

IT'S BEEN QUITE A SPECTACLE, watching civilization collapse.

A virus is a unique WMD in that it eliminates humans while leaving their complicated systems intact, at least for a while. The internet, satellites, radios, smart phones, cable news etc. all functioned, so long as electricity was maintained. With foreknowledge and funding, some of us, like Nero, binge-watched conflagration from the comfort of our palatial bunkers.

So, how did I feel when the localized epidemic we had planned jumped Chinese containment and morphed into a pandemic?

Curious, I felt insatiably curious.

An underwhelming reaction, I know, but would you feel any different? Can you imagine any content more captivating than an HD Götterdämmerung live-streaming death on every channel?

I think not. And if you, dear reader, lived through collapse, then I guarantee you were binge-watching too. Admit it: we were all huge fans of the show until it jumped the shark, started stinging, and took the grid down with it.

I can feel your judgment. Your disdain annoys me.

Three thousand years ago, the biblical Hittites corralled victims suffering from tularemia, a type of rabbit fever, and drove them into enemy lands hoping for chaos, for collapse.

Scythians, and later the Romans, dipped arrows and blades into rotting cadavers in order to inflict tetanus on their targets.

The Black Death itself, reaper of 200 million souls, may have spread to Europe when Mongols flung pestis-infected corpses over the walls of Crimean Kaffa in 1346 CE.

I admit the SARS variant that we "loosed upon the world" is on a different scale, but I must insist on its similarity in kind. The Mongolian Khan at Kaffa, Jani Beg, and I have much in common, middling pieces on a larger chessboard, manipulated by others. We both served our purpose, made our moves, and were meant to be discarded.

The difference, however, is that while Jani Beg was eliminated by the power-players of his day, I, a man-of-skill, hidden behind my lab coat, took control of the game with a strong, white hand.

PART 2:
The Main

Canoe in Fog, by Tim Babb

Breakfast on the Main

THE SUMMER NIGHT RETREATED; only the brightest stars fought, rear-guard, against the dawn. Celestial birds—Swan, Vulture, Eagle—ceded sky to the gulls and terns of morning.

"There, that should do."

Keith, sitting in the stern of the dented canoe, adjusted his paddle, angling for shore. Mukwa, in the bow, provided power, smoother already after two hours' practice. Miin, between the thwarts, trailed her fingers in warm water—a fish jumped. They approached the creek mouth and navigated its sandbars. When the keel started dragging they shipped paddles, stood, and stiffly stepped ashore, wet-footed, onto Michigan's mainland.

Clouds puffed into incredible shapes, turning pink as an onshore breeze ruffled the bay. Their shaded creek was cold, its cut banks and overhanging vegetation concealing Keith's canoe. The scouts stretched, relieved from paddling; they shared a moment of quiet, stilling themselves, awaiting acceptance from this foreign shore.

"We paddle only at night, so we'll take a break before our next move. I'm going to look around. You two, make camp."

Keith made eye contact with each, differentiating their duties. Two-Crow rummaged through the duffel, unzipping both knives. Hilt-first, he handed one to Mukwa, one to Miin, then tucked the pistol beneath his battered belt.

"No fire, no noise. Not till we see what's around."

The graybeard selected a piece of driftwood, ash, for a staff, and up the creek he went. Just a few steps, and Keith was never there.

Orange rays angled into their thicket, warming the forest floor; needles and pine sap scented their camp with familiar overtones.

"Bet you're hungry?" Mukwa pitched his question low.

Miin's stomach growled in affirmation, drawing grins from them both.

"Let's see what the crow packed. Something tells me it's not bacon and eggs."

Miin spread an army blanket in a patch of sunlight. Mukwa was elbow-deep in his rucksack. The cold creek babbled, an early riser, at the deep water beyond the bend. With a grunt Mukwa emerged triumphant, big arms loaded down with bread, cheese, and fruit. "I was right, no bacon. But still, there's plenty to keep us going."

Miin tuned herself, cross-legged, and extended her energy field, her antenna. She attempted to broadcast her impressions back towards the island; she sought the proper frequency.

Mukwa said nothing, hackles raised by Miin's vibrations.

Was Samantha on the other end? Was ol' foster-gran adjusting her dial?

Briefly, he caught a whiff of Cranberry Bog; his nostrils twitched, remembering. From 30 miles away, Mukwa scented moss and muck and ooze.

Miin returned to herself in a minute. Transmission sent, she patted the place next to her. Mukwa shrugged and sat himself down. Miin rifled through her pack, lifting out two books, stamped and barcoded: Beaver Island District Library.

Muck eyed her doubtfully. "You went to the *library?*"

"Of course!"

"They let you take books off-island?"

A guilty shrug from the bookworm as Mukwa tsk-tsked her in his best librarian manner. Miin flushed and tossed over his favorite manga. Muck, reluctant, growled thanks. He pawed his book open as Miin spread provender. Blueberry and Bear broke their fast together.

Beyond the Pale

THE COLD CREEK GUSHED through the culvert, accelerated by constriction. Keith, motionless in shadow, watched the road above. The only traffic he'd seen was a doe with her fawn, the two-lane being their shortest commute between breakfast and bed.

Stiffly, he climbed the embankment and, still concealed, looked up and down the empty roadway. Memory told him this was the Tunnel of Trees. Before Covee, M-119 had been ever-busy with bikers and tourists. The old Indian trail hugged the coast, serving as the link—pre-highway—between Petoskey and Mackinac's big bridge.

Cottages lined the narrow road. Maples and oaks crowded close; many had dropped branches in winter storms. The road, uncleared for a year and a half, presented an obstacle course of heavy limbs and leaf litter. There were vehicles parked in the drives, some pinned in place by fallen trees, others sitting deflated on airless tires.

Keith took it in: no chimney smoke, no sign of habitation, no far-off drone of motorized humanity. Doyle had run them in close, idling *Mary* as they launched their canoe. They'd seen no lights. No car beams, no blinking cell towers, no cottage-glow or flicker of campfire...just darkness, prevailing over all.

Keith broke cover and moved, shadow to shadow, towards the nearest house. A red squirrel, displeased, gave him an earful from the canopy before settling down. A bundled *something* lay piled on the stoop.

Keith slowed, edging closer. He made out tattered clothes, left threadbare by weather; a skull grinned from the heap, resting atop some ribs and a femur. The rest had been scattered up and down the front steps by scavengers. He looked to the next house, then the next. On every stoop, on every front porch, lay a similar arrangement of bony rags. Some skeletons were intact, desiccated tissues still binding; some were shattered, picked apart by coyote and crow. Not a house went undecorated, and every day was Halloween.

For the rest of the morning Keith crept along parallel to the road, going cottage-to-cottage southeast towards Harbor Springs, the first marina Doyle wanted checked out. The captain's thick finger had stabbed each port posing a threat to the island: Harbor Springs, Petoskey, Charlevoix. Doyle wanted intel, and if big boats were found, he'd instructed Keith in nautical sabotage.

Keith continued his scout, though every house was the same. Some dwellings he investigated further, shading the glass and peeking inside. Each one had been ransacked, kitchens stripped bare, cupboards flung open, broken plates strewn on the floor. Garages were busted into; some still held tools, though most had been looted. Of all nature's creatures, only humans were this methodical. Primate brains, pattern-pleased, were thrilled by repetition, no matter how grisly. A pack had done this with a shared sense of purpose, guided by one will. The region had been foraged, then corpse-marked and claimed. At least the atrocity wasn't recent.

The state of the road—undrivable—and the absence of tracks meant a low danger of discovery, yet Keith kept to cover. There was something indecent about walking in the open. At the outskirts of Harbor Springs, Two-Crow turned around.

He felt weary in muscle and mind, his corpse-count now in the hundreds. He thought of Miin and Mukwa; he'd been gone too long. They'd scout the harbor together, safer in darkness. They'd take the canoe, avoid the grisly road, check for threats, and paddle on. The moon phase was crescent. They still had a week until their first radio check-in with Doyle.

Returning, Keith kept to the trees, following deer paths that ran alongside the road. The sun climbed, mosquitoes whined; he had a hollowness in his gut, a flashback feeling. A trauma-cloud of death obscured his senses, causing his limbs to feel heavy, every movement a drudgery.

At length he came back to the culvert and its rushing creek. The sun hovered well past noon—he'd sweated through his shirt, Keith felt sticky and sopping with fear. He climbed down the embankment into the cool grotto of the creek bottom.

He put the road and its cadavers behind him. The current had carved a deep pool in the streambed. He sat upon the mossy knee of an ancient cedar and took a minute; impressions of the morning sifted into place.

He unbuttoned his flannel pocket and removed a coiled line and fishhook. With his pocketknife—honed thin—he trimmed a rod of green willow. Keith notched one end and affixed the light line, snugging it tight with practiced fingers.

He turned a log and pinched a worm from its tunnel, threading it upon the hook. Heron-like, he stalked the pool, assessing his chances. When time and place aligned, he flicked his offering. The current accepted. He stretched his senses, following the baited hook under the bank. He anticipated a strike, and made ready.

There!

The trout was liquid muscle, furious at the barb, determined to shake loose. Keith apologized as he flipped the fish into the ferns: a beautiful brookie, brightly speckled, the cold stream incarnate. Keith slit the fish, vent to gills, and a firm tug returned its innards to the creek. He arranged the trout on a platter of moss, then caught and added two more. He made sure the hook was clean, then carefully dried and coiled the line, buttoning it away. It was time to go.

As he waded downstream, Keith reached out for his companions. He felt them there, near the beach, right where they should be. He eased himself into their presence, the girl sensing him just before he stepped into camp.

Miin had gathered sticks in case a fire was needed. A harvest of berries and mushrooms lay upon a leaf. Keith nodded at the girl, presenting his catch. Blueberry grinned towards the canoe. From the overturned hull, danger be damned, came the muffled sound of a young bear aslumber.

"Mere anarchy is loosed upon the world"-Yeats

DO YOU FORGIVE my pretensions?

The not-so-subtle weaving of The Poem within this narrative?

It adds heft, I think.

After a career authoring articles in pharmacology, I find it fantastically freeing to dabble in verse. Yeats wrote in reaction to the Great War and the influenza outbreak that followed. I plagiarize the poet, just as I plagiarized his pandemic.

H1N1, the "Spanish" flu, is a fascinating virus. I dictated "is" because it still exists. To date, there are only two viruses that have ever been eradicated by humans, smallpox (VARV) and rinderpest (RPV). Smallpox technically still "lives" in two labs, the CDC in Atlanta and the VECTOR lab in Novosibirsk, Russia. Given the current state of things, I wouldn't be surprised if smallpox's variola virus has performed a jailbreak of its own. I played a role, after all, in the destruction of the CDC, but more on that later.

Back to Spanish influenza. In 1919, Yeats' pregnant wife, along with half a billion others, became infected with H1N1. Though she survived, 70% of pregnant women who contracted the disease died, one of many shocking attributes that attracted me to this particular strain. You see, I had been tasked, along with a handful of others, to tweak a known virus, in this case SARS, so that instead of culling the elderly and infirm—which is what a virus usually does—the young and healthy would be targeted. Spanish influenza pointed the way.

I don't know how technical I should get here, but to understand our current apocalypse you need to understand the variant we developed. Humans have a defense mechanism for fighting off infection called the STING response, "Stimulator of Interferon Genes." Basically, a protein detects the presence of a virus and triggers inflammation in the body, including the heart, lungs, lymph nodes, etc. This response is used to protect the host from the invader.

What made the H1N1 strain so deadly was that it used the infected's own STING defenses against them. Our custom-tailored variant of SARS-CoV-2, just like the Spanish flu, kills hosts by *over*-stimulating the body's inflammation defenses, triggering a cytokine storm of catastrophic organ failure resulting in sudden death.

I've heard my elegant variant referred to as "Stinger," an inelegant term, but in this case accurate. Infection from my variant results in multiple organ failure that often jolts the victim to death. An infected person appears "stung" and twitches violently as they drown in their own fluid; either that, or cardiac arrest shakes the life out of them.

Spanish influenza killed 10% of the world's population, but it was the healthiest 10%, which is what made it so heartbreaking. My variant of CoV-2 kills healthy and infirm alike, and its infection fatality rate (IFR) approaches 99%.

A venomous Stinger indeed.

Night Ops

MUKWA, FROM COVER, SKETCHED IN HIS PAD as the summer sun descended into Lake Michigan, the orange-lit waters quenching its fire. The long day was ending. Keith slept like a dead man, flat on his back, arms crossed over his barely rising-and-falling chest. Miin lay under the canoe, curled up in the scratchy blanket, hopefully warm in her Kevlar cave.

He finished penciling and closed his notebook. It was time to wake them up.

The packs were piled and ready. Their cookfire had been smothered with sand, Keith's skillet scoured and stowed away. Mukwa was hungry again, a condition he realized he'd best get used to. He fingered the hilt of his knife, unconsciously adjusting his feet. He'd been practicing stances during the long afternoon.

Basic-warrior-stance, footwork important.
Knife "in the box." Block. Parry. Thrust. Recover.
Grim determination, no joy, no pleasure.

All day they'd seen nothing, heard nothing. There seemed to be no human presence for miles around. When asked, Keith hadn't said much about his reconnaissance, just that they'd be traveling tonight by canoe.

Daylight dimmed to dusk, the crescent moon sinking in the western sky. Lake Michigan's mood was calm, a good night for paddling. Mukwa made a move to wake Keith, but the crow's eyes popped open, giving him a jolt.

Creepy old fart, that's for sure. Nosferatu rising from the grave. That's how he looks.

Mukwa turned towards Miin and gently rolled away the canoe. She stirred, head emerging from beneath the blanket; she looked like a field mouse disturbed from its cover. The girl gave him a grin as she stretched.

"You as hungry as I am, foster brother?"

Mukwa nodded. Yes, yes he was.

Keith, slow-moving and stiff, limped off into the brush.

Taking a piss, I bet. How's the waterworks, old man?

Miin disappeared as well.

Bright-eyed, Miin bounced back from the foliage refreshed. Mukwa, duly diligent, walked down to the beach and took a look around. Nothing on the lake, nothing up or down the coast. Back at camp, Miin had pulled on a heavy sweater. Keith layered a gray hoodie over his flannel; green-lensed binoculars hung from his neck.

"Night vision," he grunted at Mukwa. "Doyle's."

Mukwa shrugged. He hefted his own pack into the canoe with a grunt, grabbed the bow handle, and waited as Keith and Miin brushed away their tracks.

Are there diseased wackos tracking us? No fucking thanks.

Keith hefted the stern. They helped push the laden canoe down the creek till it could float, then guided it to the beach and the open water beyond. The sky had turned purple, the moon had brightened, and a low planet sank in the west.

"Venus," Keith said to Miin, "evening star."

Tutored by Samantha, Blueberry knew it. *"Nigaabii-anang,"* she replied. "The one that shines at nightfall."

Miin carried the paddles. Looking calm-faced and rested, she gave the planet a smile as the men prepped the canoe. Once all was readied, she stepped lightly aboard and arranged herself amid the packs. Keith produced a ziplock of jerky and passed it to Miin, then to Mukwa. They each pinched a plug of island venison. Keith awkwardly got himself seated, wincing as he picked up his paddle. The weapons duffel lay stowed under his seat in the stern.

You ever gonna unzip that, old crow? Is there anyone left to shoot at?

The veteran seemed to think there were survivors, that there had been looting and killing, that the skeletons he'd seen were intentionally placed, turf markers of some kind.

These creepos could teach the Detroit gangs a thing or two.

The big youth tapped his knife's hilt, rotated the canoe, then shoved them off from the beach and attempted to step aboard. A misstep, and his booted foot splashed into the lake, cold water soaking his sock.

Fuming, he got aboard and seated. "Fuck!"

"Shhh!" insisted Keith. "From now on, we're *silent.*"

Mukwa, flushed, stroked hard for deep water. He could feel his foot squelching, pruning. Any chance to change into a dry sock was hours away. They kept the coast on their left while the moon sank astern; night darkened, revealing its stars. The Milky Way pulsed, a galactic artery, circulating the plasma of a billion distant suns.

They slid silently over the waters, keeping close to the coast. No lights were seen, no motors heard. Every bump of Mukwa's paddle against the gunnel was fiercely hushed, first by Keith, then Miin. Loon-cries carried over the water; each bay claimed by a breeding pair, every inch of coast having been contested.

A territorial male, enraged by their proximity, ripped a warning cry right beside them. This startled Mukwa, rocking the boat. *SHIT!* As his heart hummed with the adrenaline shot, he heard Miin giggling behind him.

At last, they rounded a point that sheltered the harbor and its springs. Two summers ago, in the bliss of before, this bay had been packed with yachts, party lights blinking, playlists proclaiming the personalities of each well-to-do owner. The tipsy laughter of sun-kissed women and popping corks were the soundtrack of decadence.

Two summers since the variant struck, the marina harbored only ghosts. The moorings bobbed empty, no lights twinkling from town. In the dark the whole place felt abandoned.

"Stop paddling," Keith croaked in command.

Mukwa shipped his paddle and rested. Their canoe glided, silent, between the buoys. He looked over his shoulder. Keith had his binoculars up, scanning the harbor with night vision. Mukwa squinted into the gloom, but couldn't see shit.

The fuck are we doing here? Nobody's home, old man. This place is deserted.

He wriggled his soaked foot, rocking the boat as he shifted weight.

"Be *still*," Keith hushed, continuing his scan.

"*There*," the old man pointed, arm dim in the starlight, "tied up at that pier."

He took the binos from his neck and handed them forward to Miin. She aimed where he indicated, nodding her head.

"I see it," she whispered, and handed the binoculars to Mukwa.

He took them firmly in both hands. *I will NOT drop these.* Placing the strap around his neck, he adjusted focus and scanned the shoreline.

The night turned lurid green, ghoulish with detail. He scanned the waterfront, eyeing a few boats, battered and broken by the freeze-up last winter. He continued his sweep, then saw for himself. There, tied up at a commercial pier, a long barge, some kind of fuel transport? Pipes and storage tanks bulked green in his visual field. He handed the binos back to Miin without saying a word.

"Let's go alongside, *quietly*," Keith whispered from the stern.

Some stealthy paddling, and they glided alongside the barge; its steel hull towered above them, with no easy access to its deck. As they rounded its stern, Keith steered them towards the pier. Built into the pilings was a safety ladder. Their canoe bumped softly as Mukwa grabbed the lowest rung, swinging them around till they were side-to.

"Thirty minutes for recon," Keith announced. "You two wait here."

Two-Crow was at the ladder before either of them could protest. He climbed out of the canoe, disappearing above.

Great. We'll twiddle our thumbs while you go off doing whatever.

Mukwa looked behind him, past Miin. The duffel lay there, zipped tight: rifle, pistol, radio, ammunition...

He wiggled the toes of his soaked foot. "Fuck."

"Muck!"

Mukwa startled, then looked up. Two-Crow peered down at him from the darkness, beckoning; he'd only been gone a few minutes. "Come with me."

Damn right! Knew you'd need me, old man.

Mukwa considered the duffel. How best to be helpful? Who knew what was waiting?

Wanting no reprimand, he left it alone, maneuvering to ascend the ladder. He took an extra second to balance, then pulled himself onto the suddenly solid pier.

He followed Keith's shadowy form to the gangway, then onto the barge.

Step, *squelch*. Step, *squelch*.

Keith led him through a maze of piping. Mukwa followed behind, nose sifting through the scents: gasoline, rust, engine oil. They came to a steel hatch, Keith pointing to the padlock barring entry. He handed Mukwa a heavy bolt cutter.

Needed some muscle, eh? Stand aside, old-timer. I'll show you how it's done.

Fingering the padlock in the dark, Mukwa felt the chink where Keith had failed to cut through. Getting the cutters positioned, he gripped the long handles and exerted all the force he could muster. The lock resisted.

Oh, no you fucking DON'T!

He dug for more power, felt the handles give and heard a *snick* as the shank was cut through. He set the tool carefully on deck as Keith reached to undog the hatch. They were in.

Keith disappeared into the opening. Mukwa heard him descending a ladder, and followed after a few moments. As he climbed into darkness, a red light blinked on, illuminating the landing. The old man was visible at the bottom, wearing a headlamp.

"Found those cutters in a tool chest," Keith whispered. "Lock not much use if you're gonna leave those around."

Mukwa finished his descent, coming face-to-face with Two-Crow. "What are we looking for?" he asked, as quietly as he could.

They stood in a sort of engine room. Keith played the red light around, illuminating pipes, panels, a generator.

"Doyle wants this thing sunk. Anything steel, he said. Anything his boats couldn't handle. The fuel tanks, of course, are empty, siphoned off a while ago."

Well, how the fuck do we do that? Mukwa thought. *Blow a hole through the hull? You got C-4 in that duffel?*

But Mukwa stayed quiet.

"We're looking for a seacock," Keith said, "any thru-hull fitting. We open it up and flood this thing."

The red light bobbed among hoses and valves. Mukwa followed behind, trying not to bump anything.

"Here we go." Keith's voice held a note of satisfaction. "Cut the hose off that fitting."

The veteran stood aside, keeping his light on the job. Mukwa unsheathed his knife and sawed through the rubber hose, then stood back. Keith played the light around the space once more before aiming it back at the fitting.

"I'm gonna open this, and we'll get out of here."

Mukwa moved out of his way, remembering where the ladder was. Keith opened the ball valve and the lake rushed in, anxious for equilibrium.

"Let's go."

Mukwa followed the light through the labyrinth. Behind them, he could hear water splashing. At the foot of the ladder the headlamp switched off, and he followed Keith's ascending form in the dark. Back on deck, sky brilliant with stars, Keith shut and dogged the heavy hatch closed. He tossed the broken lock overboard, then handed the cutters to Mukwa.

Bear followed Crow down the length of the barge. At every cleat Keith loosened the mooring lines, playing out slack before re-cleating.

"That should do it. Let's get back to the canoe, and bring those cutters."

Hanging Town

IT WAS WELL AFTER MIDNIGHT. The summer stars had set, autumn's now on the rise. Harbor Springs and its barge sank astern. The scouts kept their distance from shore and paddled towards Doyle's next priority, the town of Petoskey.

Miin shivered, nesting in the gear pile. The canoe's bilge was wet, the seat of her pants soaking through; she was cold and hungry, and really had to pee. The men paddled grimly through the night, neither showing a hint of tiredness. Mukwa, she knew, would rather lose his arms than ask the old man for a break. As for Keith, he pulled his motivation from elsewhere. To Miin it felt flavored with sorrow, with guilt. Her uncle owed a debt—but not to the living.

Miin suffered in silence, checking the east vainly for dawn's early gray. She squirmed and shifted, pushing her thoughts elsewhere. Was it just this morning she'd connected to Samantha?

It was an easy sending. Her body had been comfortable, the warm sun rising, waves a soothing aid to her concentration. She'd opened up, and her spirit jumped out. It had needed no guidance, arrowing right to Samantha; connection lasted only seconds, and few details were exchanged. Miin had formed a picture of their beach-bivouac, sending an impression of deep waters crossed. Samantha, in her shack, comprehended; boggy scents had come through, Blueberry swelling with a happy ache for home.

Shivering in the cold canoe, Miin drew warmth from this memory, her spirit stirring. Crow and Bear paddled on. She closed her eyes on one world, tried opening to another, but distractions clamored: wet butt, cold limbs, empty belly, bursting bladder. She sought control, but could feel herself losing connection. The fetid heat of Samantha's bog retreated as the lake-damp loomed larger. She was failing.

Territorial, another loon challenged their intrusion, its call hearkening back to an age of ice. Miin seized hold of this cry, this sending, latching tight to its reverberations. Stretching out, she flew. Suddenly there were shapes in the stars, bejeweled dancers and celestial chandeliers. She felt a rush of understanding, could sense every loon—their calls, their coast—and beyond them, the trees. Drunk on summer photons, they stood in a stupor, digesting their dram of daylight. She limned great fishes above and below, fathomed in the deeps of water and sky.

All this was a fraction of her perception, made hollow by words. Multitudes flowed through her, unsifted, unnamed. Then Miin felt an *INTERRUPTION*.

A jarring note of discord: clunky intrusion, mechanized men, a red cloud of pain, of contagion. A forcing of will, and violence.

"Keith!" she hissed. "Stop paddling."

Their canoe glided to a halt, both men relieved at the respite.

For a minute, then two, nothing happened.

There was no sound but the lapping lake, no light save the stars.

Then they heard it, far off, a bumping of amplified sound. Heavy metal anthems riffed on the quiet night. From Petoskey, headlights beamed: one pair, then two, then half a dozen more.

"Shit!" breathed Mukwa.

"Hush!" Keith countered.

Miin flinched back to herself, repulsed by the throb of angry vehicles. Headlights raced through town, the music bouncing off buildings as joyriders jockeyed.

"That's AC/DC!" Mukwa said.

"Shhh!" Keith chastised him again. "We're exposed. Keep paddling. Don't make a sound. Head for that breakwall."

As the canoe drew nearer to cover, the music intensified. Headlights halted on the coast road, a dozen beams askew, occasionally framing silhouettes of people.

The breakwall was shadowed. Keith steered them close, the piled stone hiding their approach. Their line of sight was clear, 200 yards to the illuminated scene.

Details were difficult to make out. High beams glared. Figures moved about. Some vehicles were trucks, some SUVs, a few sporting racks of LED brights. Keith used his binoculars to spy on the gathering, watching for a long minute in silence.

Miin shivered.

Mukwa flared his nostrils, sifting smells. His snout wrinkled with the reek: *engines, exhaust, blood, booze, sex, DANGER.*

"Keith," he hissed, "these guys are *trouble!*"

Mukwa heard the duffel unzip, the clunk of an inserted magazine, then the slow, oiled bolt as old crow locked in a round.

Shit, shit, shit! This is NOT happening!

"Miin?" His whisper was pitched with worry. "You OK?"

Nothing from the girl; she'd clammed up tight.

Probably best. Whatever's happening, little sis sure as shit doesn't need to see it.

A muzzle flashed from a vehicle, bullets barking a half-second behind.
Brap! Brap! Brap! Brap!
Gunfire ripped the night. A woman screamed as the music cut off.
In the sudden quiet, new sounds emerged. Mukwa heard idling engines, the clatter of weapons, moans of pain, and a tossed bottle breaking. He squinted in the starlight: there were captives in the truck beds, tied up and terrified.

A megaphone squelched, amplifying a voice that bellowed out, "Attention! Attention, if you please!"
Captives were sobbing; Mukwa saw groups in each truck. He heard the thump of flesh as someone's plea was clubbed short.
"We are gathered here tonight because *you* chose to hide from us!"
Moans of protest from the prisoners, and more thumps as rifle butts were swung.
"There can be NO HIDING from Chosen! The world we all knew is OVER!"
Some drunken cheers from his followers.
"In these fallen times there are only two groups: Chosen and their Candidates."

"Keith," Mukwa hissed, "you *seeing* this?" He tore his eyes from the scene and looked astern.
Keith had thrown back his hood, gray hair gleaming in the starlight. The veteran shouldered his M-4 rifle, sighting through the scope. Disciplined, steady, his trigger finger pointed at the speaker.
Holy shit! Two-Crow's on POINT! Mukwa fumbled for his knife, staring up at the road.

"Not everyone can be Chosen!" Feedback squawked as the speaker continued, "Many attempt it, but only a few pass the trial. YOU were called, invited, but foolishly refused. Instead you chose to hide!"
"I don't refuse! I'll take the trial!" A man's voice, desperate and pleading.
Harsh laughter rose from the guards.
"I'm afraid it's too late," the speaker replied, solemn. "Our invitation has expired, and examples must be set. Others must be shown the folly of refusal!"
Screams and wild shouts as something was done to the captives. There was panic in the trucks as figures moved in and out of the lights. A stench of fear, of urine, wafted down to Mukwa, helpless behind the breakwall.

"Keith, what's happening? Miin, hand me the binos!"
He looked back. Keith, tight with tension, canted his carbine at the speaker. Miin, trembling, inched the binoculars towards Mukwa, then closed her eyes and retreated.
The low-light lenses sharpened the scene. Mukwa distinguished individuals.

He searched till he found the megaphone. A tall man held it, a holstered pistol on his hip. A cowboy hat shadowed his haggard face.

Mukwa shifted his field of vision to check on the prisoners, the artist in him memorizing the scene.

He counted six pickups. In each truck bed stood captives, men and women both. He flinched at the shortest ones, *those better not be kids*. All wore tattered work clothes. At each truck, armed guards covered the prisoners. Ropes were flung over light poles. Necks were noosed tight: six trucks, six poles.

Mukwa's gaze was caught by commotion. He saw a woman get groped as her coils were cinched. He heard boozy laughter, and sniffed the sharp tang of lust. Her guard's knife emerged, ripping through the ragged sweater, exposing her shapely body.

A male captive lunged towards her guard. "Helen!" he cried out, and was crumpled by a punch. Unconscious, the would-be-rescuer sagged against his rope. Mukwa made out the letters on his stained sweatshirt: "NCMC," Petoskey's community college.

"Here's one, boss! Maybe save her for later? Might make a tasty Candidate?"

The knifeman ran gloved hands over her chest, leering towards the speaker.

"Take her down!" barked the man in the cowboy hat. "And Heavy, you've eaten enough candy already!"

Rowdy hoots as the topless woman was roughly handed down from the truck. The last necks were noosed, captors jumping down from truck beds. The drivers revved, unmuffled motors growling in the night. The speaker signaled, and metal music blared, Metallica this time. Electric guitars shredded the soundscape.

"Keith," Mukwa implored, "we've got to *STOP THIS!*"

Terrified, he looked back. Miin had covered her ears, squeezing her eyes shut. In the stern, Two-Crow had slung his rifle and was backstroking away from the wall.

"Where are you *GOING?*" Mukwa sobbed. "We've got to *DO* something!"

"Boy! Be *QUIET!*" Two-Crow hissed. "Grab your paddle, let's *GO!*"

Muck panicked, lunged for the duffel and ripped open the zipper, grabbing for gear, for the pistol.

No fucking WAY we let this happen! It ain't RIGHT! We need to HELP!

The canoe rocked, a paddle thumping against the gunnel, and all three heard a soft plop as Doyle's radio fell overboard. Its electric glow faded as it sank, going...going...gone. Mukwa felt Miin's small hands upon him; a splash of cold doused his mind, and he blanked.

In a minute Muck came to. His body ached, and he found himself sprawled across their gear. Miin had scrambled over him and was paddling in the bow, helping Keith stroke them towards deeper water. She whimpered, wielding the long blade awkwardly. Mukwa made a move to relieve her.

"Stay put!" ordered Keith, fear etched on his craggy face.

Mukwa looked back toward Petoskey. Metallica was fading, headlights bouncing away down the coast road; the lamp poles sagged, heavy with human fruit. The victims' flames had been snuffed, lives swallowed whole by darkness.

"Stop paddling," Keith ordered Miin. "No movement. No noise."

The canoe glided to a stop. Keith plied his blade, rotating them towards town.

Keith Two-Crow. Ha! Keith chickenshit is more like it. Head aching, Mukwa replayed the scene, his memory tinted green by the lenses. *Ropes dangling, the trucks, the stink of fear, the revving motors...*his chest felt bruised. *Like I got fucking tazed! Or tranquilized!* His ego felt worse. *Their radio was gone. Throw yourself in next time,* he mocked himself. *Mucked it up again, big time.*

The scouts sat silent in their stilled canoe, Miin trembling in the bow. Mukwa, cramped, snarled from between the thwarts. In the stern, Keith was rigid with worry. The first gray light finally hinted from the east.

Suddenly, a searchlight stabbed out from the harbor. One vehicle had remained behind. Its beam probed the jetty first, then leapt outward towards the deep, reaching over waves with bright, inquisitive fingers.

The crew held their breath.

The beam crept closer. Miin whimpered in terror, warm piss saturating her pants. Mukwa shrunk his profile, tried to shrink the canoe; pull them under, follow the radio, down into darkness.

A loon cry erupted, startling them all. The searchlight flinched too, swept toward the noise and honed in. A large male flexed his wings, challenging the beam; he ripped another call. The cry, ancient and angry, bounced off the rocks and echoed away. The searchlight lingered, the loon glaring back with red-eyed wrath. Then the electric eye winked out, and darkness returned.

The vehicle's engine started up, tail lights speeding south away from town. The truck disappeared, following the others.

A shaky outbreath escaped from the crew. With all his heart, Mukwa thanked the loon. Keith dipped his paddle, stroking them away. Miin was crying in the bow.

"Sorry," she stuttered, cheeks salty with tears.

Mukwa knelt in the gear pile and took her paddle, adding his power to Keith's propulsion.

The gray light grew, dismissing the stars. A cold mist ghosted upon the surface of Little Traverse Bay, damping their bones.

"We have to get off the lake," Keith said. "We're too exposed. There's a river mouth ahead."

Exposed? No shit, Mukwa almost mumbled. But his heart wasn't in it. *Geezer did right after all, getting off those damn rocks. Can't believe I dropped the fucking radio.*

He shriveled at the thought of Miin captured, Keith killed. Their canoe shot to shit, spattered with blood, with brain.

He put power in his strokes, striving for balance, for speed. He willed their canoe off the water's surface as the last stars surrendered. Their bilge stank of fear, of piss, of wet gear and fatigue. He shook his head to clear it. Good for nothing else, he could at least be Keith's motor; dumb horsepower, Muck-power, nothing more.

Stroke, stroke, stroke.

The two men pulled for shore.

Licking Their Wounds

THE CROW, AN ANCIENT ONE, picked them up at the portage; this river was his territory. Its origins began in the highlands, as an icy outflow from Bear Lake—now Walloon—and had tumbled towards the bay since the Pleistocene, glacial melt of the great Laurentide. The corvid, coded by chromosomes, knew this history and was living it still.

Bears had roamed here for millennia; *Mukwa Ziibiing* was the region's Indigenous name. An Odawa chief, Biidassige, saw the light-that-was-coming, the white man, and attempted to make the river valley a refuge, a sanctuary for his tribe. He heeded Tecumseh's call to fight foreign influence, survived the lost cause and returned; then the government sold the chief's acreage. Merchants, ever eager, dammed Bear River to build their town. Brick-by-brick, it climbed up the hill; they named it Petoskey, a corruption of Biidassige and all of his plans.

Keith forced them to portage in the foggy dawn. It was a perilous moment; strength at ebb, flooded by fear, their weary minds were numb and foolish. The cloak of night had been drawn away, leaving their clumsy movements hideously exposed.

Keith did not like the intelligence behind that final truck. Its guess, too accurate, sent ripples of uneasiness crawling over his skin. The girl and the kid shouldn't have come; Samantha be damned, he should have scouted alone.

After the spotlight, after the loon, he'd steered the canoe to the river mouth. Miin, shivering, had been useless, the big lout a liability. The river dropped 30 feet as it rushed the dam, concrete steps and a landing pad offering portage. Fighting the outflow, the scouts held the canoe in place as they emptied it. There they huddled together, core temperatures dropping as the hungry river roared. Mukwa sketched in his mind; the neighborhood was a ruin, probably had been for a while. City hall stood gutted, the fire station next door nearly burned to the ground.

Keith climbed the crumbling stairs, rifle held at the ready. At the top, where the river leveled off, ran M-31, the same road the vehicles took as they raced away from town. The water here was wide open, with no cover for a hundred yards, and Keith hated every inch of exposure. He shouldered his rifle and slowly scoped the road, the bridge, the urban jumble: no vehicles, no men, no movement.

He looked down at his crew, now sprawled on the landing. Muck held the girl, sheltering Miin from wet spray. Their gear lay scattered and sodden. No time for pondering; Two-Crow had to decide. Every minute increased their risk. He recoiled from that naked stretch of river. An ambusher in enfilade could kill them in seconds, and two shooters with flanking fire would kill even quicker.

Kraa! Kraa! rasped the crow. *Kraa! Kraa!*

Keith eyed the bird, high in a pine overhanging the falls. Its black eyes met his, proffering connection. The old man blanked his thoughts, shrinking his signature. The crow took notice, took flight, and overflew the open river, alighting in a tree that spread branches above the flow. Impressions untranslatable, a difference in frequencies; Keith sifted the crow's transmission, fine-tuning for *Humans*. There were none.

Kraa, kraa. The call came once more, and faintly. Was this the all-clear?

Keith slung his rifle and descended the stairs, the cracked concrete slippery with spray.

"Let's go," he said, shouldering his pack and hefting the duffel. He still couldn't believe Doyle's radio was gone.

Yes he could. Muck was just a boy. Muscles or no, the kid shouldn't have come.

Mukwa, bedraggled, shook himself, gently setting Miin on her feet. He hoisted both their packs as they followed Keith up the wet steps. They dumped their gear, left Miin at the top, and returned for the canoe, bolt cutters rusting in the bilge. The men wrestled and bumped its awkward length up the flight. Soon they were afloat, paddling again, skin prickling with exposure till they made the far trees.

The foggy morning dampened to a dark and drizzly noon. They paddled, shivering, till Petoskey fell far behind, past railroad tracks of shunted boxcars, past ball fields whose stadium lights would remain ever dark. High water and low bridges forced two more tired portages: Click Road and Evergreen Trail. When they were far enough from town and the hill country began, Keith called a halt. He put away his compass, checked with the corvid, and steered the canoe towards a sandy bank.

Miin and Mukwa struggled, but got the two tents up. The fabric dripped with moisture, offering dubious protection; the kids stashed their gear in one and burrowed into wet sleeping bags in the other. Few words were spoken. Keith hefted his rifle and disappeared into the woods to secure their perimeter. The crow perched over camp. Thunder rumbled above, and the rain intensified. Mukwa snored, Miin whimpered. A staccato of raindrops percussed their tent like a drum.

Woodsmoke curled from Samantha's stovepipe as summer rain replenished the bog. She consulted a bowl of rainwater held in her lap, condensation fallen from clouds. The island's eldest, brightly braided, sought the trio: Blueberry, Crow, and Bear. Last night's dreams had been red with violence. She feared for Miinan, feared for all three.

A tickle of sage spiced the shack, her smudge mingling with the smell of rain. Sam flew her thoughts southeast across the deep. She begged avian assistance in scouting the coast and riverine systems for a small, green canoe, specifying the three oversized spirits it carried.

A thousand eyes to peer through, a flip book of images she couldn't sift in a lifetime: beaches, boulders, forests, valleys, roadways, bridges, harbors, meadows...

Her chair creaked as thunder rolled. Too many eyes, with too little to see.

A grumble of thunder roused Miin awake. She found herself covered in sweat, overheated by their tented humidity. Much too close, a bear slumbered; Mukwa twitched and grimaced as he slept, ripe with male funk. Miin scooted from her bag, unzipped the tent, and filled her lungs with ozone-tinted oxygen. Rain pebbled the surface of the river, each drop a tiny push towards the sea. Fog curled about the boughs of hemlock, alder, and cedar. The world was silent but for river and raindrop.

Miin sighed and laced up her soaked boots, careful not to kick her foster brother. She zipped the tent behind her, stood tall, and stretched her twiggy fingers to the clouds. The rain washed her face, clearing away the salty tracks of last night's tears. Miin gasped, imbibing the green world through wide open pores.

Their canoe lay upside-down, stashed in the brush; they had pitched both tents on a rise above the river. She stepped away from camp and squatted to relieve herself, still ashamed from her accident the night before. At the riverbank, she scoured her limbs with cold water. Uncle Keith had not returned.

She stooped into the gear tent, finding that their packs were still wet. She opened hers, rummaging for clothes less damp. She shrugged into a sweater, then pulled on a poncho. Her stomach growled; Miin scolded it to wait.

Something was tugging at her. A vibration, sub-audible, a wavelength she had never felt before. She needed to step clear of clutter and find the right sort of spot. The treeish tone, unfamiliar, guided her as she entered the forest and began her ascent.

Soon the camp was far below, her feet following a deer path that zig-zagged up a bluff. Gaining elevation, she left the river in its valley and climbed above the alders, reaching a plateau of older beech and oak. She felt their woody senses upon her, a million stomata sightlessly sifting the flavor of this tiny intruder.

She slid her palms along wet trunks as she passed, slowing her steps to accommodate the trees' ponderous perceptions. Under each sentient she radiated a hello and lingered, allowing her scent to be scrutinized. She felt them transmitting, root-tip to root-tip; the slow news of her progress rippled through the woods.

A hub tree loomed in the upland mist, a massive red oak, nerve center of the network. *Wiisagi-mitigominzh* was the old name for this species. Miin tried it aloud, the spoken syllables seeming well-received. She humbled herself before the craggy elder and then approached. There, amid its roots, she found a crevice. Scooting inside, she put her back to its bole.

The canopy kept away the rain; Miin pushed back her poncho and shook out her wet hair. She got settled in the roots and gazed slowly up the towering trunk. This ancient tree had called out to her. She took deep breaths, slowed her pulse rate, and let herself dissolve.

Miinan, surrendering, scented a faint whiff of Cranberry Bog.

Later, when she emerged, mind-altered, Keith was there. The rain had stopped, and her uncle stood steaming in a sunbeam. He leaned on a staff, rifle hanging from his shoulder. Expression weary, Two-Crow mustered a grin. "Quite a blueberry you've found there," he said, nodding at the tree. "Making friends, are you?"

Miin uprooted herself and stood, dizzy and stiff. She shook the lignin from her limbs, sloughing bark as she returned to her nimble self.

"Uncle," she sighed with satisfaction, "you have no idea."

The man's smile faded. "Are we OK here? Are we safe?"

"Yes and yes, at least for now."

He gave her a look. She shook the droplets from her poncho and stepped into the light. The sun was warm, and she grew towards it, heliotropic, allowing her tree-dream to settle.

Keith waited as she processed the event. He'd been away from camp too long, and didn't like leaving the boy, the canoe, and their gear unguarded. Their perimeter was clear, yet the danger of last night still loomed large in his mind. Despite their relative safety, Keith did not feel relaxed.

"Can you translate?" he asked. "Are there words?"

Miin shook her head. "I'm not sure." A gurgle interrupted their conversation, her digestive system demanding food. She winced, then smiled at Keith. "Uncle, I'm starved. Can we eat?"

Keith softened the severity that had crept into his face. "Follow me."

And away they went.

Three's Company

Thank. Fucking. God.

The rain had stopped.

Mukwa paced the shoreline, growling at abandonment. He'd woken to an empty tent, air sour with the smell of unwashed flesh; sniffing his pits, he'd realized the stench was his own. Stepping out to discover both companions gone, he'd bristled.

Can't leave a fricking note?

Would it kill you, Two-Crow, to wake me? Or you, Miin, to catch me up?

He took stock. His clothing was damp; their tents were sopping, packs soaked through. He was starving. He had to crap, and he was alone.

Well, first things first.

The big youth shambled away from the river to dig a hole.

Under clearing skies, he cleared his mind. Mukwa uncoiled some paracord and strung up a clothesline. He set their gear to drying: shirts, socks, sweaters, and his sketch pad. He lifted each tent, shook rain from the fabric, and moved them, patch-to-patch, as the sun leap-frogged down through the canopy. From their food bag, he pulled powdered soup and a hunk of foster-gran's bread. Finally, he lit their camp stove and put on a kettle of river water, now close to boiling.

He filled his cheek with a plug of Keith's venison, stripped to the waist and scrubbed himself down. The duffel—his damnation—lay untouched, paw-printed still from last night's fumbling. He resisted the urge to catalog its contents, not needing another constipated *look* from old Crow.

Instead, he practiced his forms, with blade and without: basic-warrior-stance, knife in the box, foot work, block hand, thrust hand, first with his left and then with his right.

Heated, he kept going: push-ups, jumping jacks, high knees, and sit-ups.

That's more like it!

Blood pumping, musculature engaged, he flexed his limbs, tattoos bulging.

Didn't do much good last night though, did it?

His tent dreams had been bad ones, nightmares of too little, too late. He ripped out more jumping jacks.

Need to DO better, BE better.

He cringed, remembering his panicked digging in the duffel, the sickening plop of the radio as it fell into the lake. Going...going...gone.

If I'd gotten hold of the pistol, or wrestled away Keith's rifle...then what? Squeeze off a shot or two? Shit! They'd return fire at my muzzle flash. A dozen gunmen? Full auto? They'd put the lights on us and we'd be blown to bits, or worse, captured. Stretched from a light pole or taken for torture.

We need to get our shit together!

Fuck! I need to get MY shit together!

That WILL... Five fast push-ups.

NOT... He did five more.

HAPPEN... Five more.

AGAIN!

He sprang up from the ground to sarcastic applause. There stood Miin, with Keith beside her, two dripping druids emerging from the trees.

Mukwa grimaced. Then, remembering to do better, be better, he exaggerated a bow.

✦✦✦

The sun, falling fast toward the horizon, fired low-angled light through the trees. The river rushed, icily indifferent to the three figures hunched over their cook-pot. The ancient corvid, upon Keith's return, gave a final croak and took flight. Already the crescent moon had thickened, a waxing reminder of their duty to Doyle—and the radio they'd lost.

"Had enough?" Miin asked, ladle at the ready, a taunt in her eye.

Mukwa nodded, mopping his bowl with a heel of hard bread. Miin looked to Keith. A slight dip of his head; the old man was beyond weary. With the bouncy gait of a fawn, she collected their dishware and took it to the bank for scrubbing.

"What's *she* so chipper about?"

A shrug from Keith.

Old dude looks done, ready for his tent.

The two men resumed silence as the moon brightened. The only sounds were the clatter of dishes, a stony rumble from the river, and the wind wicking wetness from the world. A sudden snore escaped from Keith. Mukwa watched the veteran startle himself awake.

Two-Crow shook himself. "Blueberry, thank you. Would you please fetch Sam's pouch?"

Dishes done, Miin dipped into Keith's pack and returned with his smoking kit. The old man nodded thanks and gestured her down. The three of them sat, knee to knee; the stove's blue flame boiled water for tea.

Two-Crow turned ceremonial. The young ones took their cue, matching the elder's pulse rate, his pace. Keith lifted out the pipe: nothing elaborate, just an old briar with a char-darkened bowl. He opened the pouch and nosed it. Left-handed, he passed it to Miin, who gave it to Mukwa, who then returned the herbs to Keith.

From the pouch, Keith selected sage, tied tightly with string.

"Mashkodewashk," he intoned, displaying dried leaves.

Two-Crow presented the bundle to the stove's flame, igniting its tip. He blew it to a smolder and wafted the smoke. He passed the smoldering sage, and the young ones did the same. The trio breathed in the sweet spice, smudging their faces and hair.

Two-Crow tamped the bowl with Sam's blend. A final pinch he held high, as if to the moon. This one he gifted, sifting it between fingers and thumb.

"Gichi mewinzha, Wenaboozhoo izhinikaazo, gii-pii-miinogod Anishinaabe asema omaa akiing..."

He trailed off, shrugging an apology. It was all he could remember.

Keith reached back and snapped off a twig. Lighting it on the burner, he then ignited the bowl. Inhaling a puff, he held the smoke in his mouth and released before passing the pipe with his left hand, the circle repeating, forging a band. The trees leaned in, the river quieting.

"And now? Miin?"

A moment of stillness, a flood of fellowship, the red power of their ring. The kettle steamed; Miinan was ready.

"Uncle Keith? Brother Mukwa?" She smiled at them. "There are *others.*" Then she flinched. "Others, I mean, besides the ones we saw last night."

Mukwa, soothed by smoke, opened his sketch pad and let this news wash over him.

Keith kept his eyes closed and his ears open. Her tale would unfold, no need to hurry.

"The oak tree told me," she began, "or rather, the *others* told me *through* the oak tree, that they were here, they were close."

The river listened, each droplet newly attentive.

"And uncle, they're like us. Not Native, I mean, not Ojibwe, but *Natural.*"

Keith flexed his forearms and wrists. Samantha's blend eased his carpal tunnel syndrome, clearing constriction, soothing his pain. "What can you tell us about these others?" he asked.

Mukwa, for some reason, couldn't stop smiling. He eased his bulk to the forest floor. Supine, he penciled the moon climbing down the trees, awaiting Miin's answer, hoping this moment would never end.

Miin paused. Her spirit, mind, and tongue were engaged in complicated alchemy. A triple translation was required: others, into oakish, into human speech. She feared frightening the tree-dream by speaking it aloud. Sam's pestled plants fueled her: walls of self dissolved as brain regions, long dormant, flashed with electrical impulses. Miin inhaled, willing herself back to that upland oak.

"These *others,* these *Naturals,* live in an old way, like trees, like birds. There's a smoothness to them, a flow, a blending-in. They sense us and want to help; however, we're strangers. They're waiting upriver, so we must keep going."

Miin frowned, unsatisfied, probing her audience. Her companions were with her, no judgment, no protest.

She continued, "Now, the men in the trucks, these *Chosen.* There's something about them, jagged and sharp; real danger there, in more ways than one."

She paused again, translating the tree.

"Like a wildfire: creatures filled with terror, a violence that can't be bargained with." She released the phrase, felt it settle into her friends. "Lastly, the prisoners." This impression was simpler for the girl to translate. There was a shared vocabulary, the imagery universal: weakness.

A spotted fawn without a mother, coyotes circling.
A diseased branch, one storm away from a necessary cull.

"Those prisoners had been hiding. People like them won't last long." Miin trailed off, realizing her description fit Beaver Islanders as well.

The pot boiled over, water hissing upon the burner. Someone switched off the gas.

Stars crowned the trees, a billion leaves bejeweled. Across the river a horned owl boomed. Time passed, or it didn't.

Miin fixed tea and handed round the tin mugs. Mukwa rolled himself to sit upright, closing his sketch pad. He blew steam off the surface of the brew, then took a sip.

"Sheee-it! That's HOT!"

The three companions grinned in the dark.

Cowboy's Headache

THE MAN WITH THE MEGAPHONE, sporting a cowboy hat since collapse, stood at his window staring daggers at the drawbridge. Fucking thing was stuck again, had been since they returned from Petoskey last night. Both halves of the M-31 bridge angled upwards, flipping him off with metallic middle fingers.

Bob "Cowboy" Campbell paced in his office, supposedly running this organized shit show. His walkie-talkies squawked, each tuned to a different frequency. His Chosen lieutenants were freaking out.

A freq for every freak.

He shuddered at the wordplay.

Bob yanked off his hat, dragging dirty fingers through his greasy hair. Lice-free for the moment; he'd take it. At the pilfered coffee maker he fixed another cup. *A perk of his position?* Cowboy shuddered again. Every wall held a map, penciled and pushed full of pins, the lair of a madman. The gourmand gave a wry grin, sipping at his black market blend.

Madman. That's exactly what I am.

His smile soured as Bob mused over an emerging migraine. The hat went back on.

Chosen headquarters, the northernmost branch, was an old office building, a stately structure of high ceilings and handsome woodwork. Its top floor viewed the town of Charlevoix, the inner harbor, Lake Michigan, and the fucking drawbridge.

Cowboy went to his radio bank, picking up the one labeled *Mikey.*

He thought for a second, then depressed the PTT.

"Mikey, you on here? It's Campbell."

Silence, then a burst of noise: shouting, clanging tools, and out-of-shape wheezing.

"Yeah, boss, I'm here. You lookin' at our latest cluster-fuck?"

More asthmatic breathing before the talk button was released.

"Yes, Mikey. Yes I am. Do you have an estimated time for repairs yet?"

"ETR? For this fucking dinosaur? Gotta be kidding, boss."

More noise, swearing, someone kicking scrap metal?

Cowboy sighed. "Mikey, believe me, I know. If it was up to me, we'd move this whole FUBAR operation somewhere else, but it ain't, so we ain't. Understand?"

"Yeah, boss, I get it. But remember last time? It took *weeks.*"

"*Weeks?* Oh, hell no, Mikey, we ain't got no *weeks.* You get that fucking thing fixed today, hear me? Today!"

Cowboy, blood pressure rising, eye-wrestled the old bridge, built in 1949, willing it to close.

"Roger, boss, roger. Hey, next time your Raiders nab someone, how 'bout a fucking engineer, OK? Would your guys do that for me? Nab someone with brains for once?"

Cowboy heard the labored breathing of Mikey on the move. He looked down at the bridge and could see his overweight fixer, radio to his ear, approaching the access panel, his wrench-turners in tow.

"Engineer, huh? Why didn't you say so before? No problem! I'll put an ad in the paper, maybe post it on our website, you know, *join-the-chosen-dot-org.* Now fix that damn bridge!"

He slammed the radio back into its charging cradle, glared at the obstinate structure, and picked up another radio, this one labeled *Heavy Metal.*

"Heavy, Heavy, you on this one? Pick up, it's Campbell."

From his office, Bob heard a revving of Raider engines, unmuffled for psychological effect. Heavy modified all their vehicles for maximum noise, maximum menace. Cowboy's espresso had evaporated along with his patience.

"Yeah, boss. I'm here."

"Heavy, I've got bad news. Bridge is out again, no patrolling that way. Over."

"Fuck, boss! You shitting me? North is where the pickings are. South's been combed, and you know it!"

Cowboy's head was killing him. Heavy wasn't lying. Bob's map showed shaded red from Reed City in the south, north through Traverse all the way up to their current outpost in Charlevoix. Two hundred miles of scavenge, red pins in every town, notations indicating food, fuel, and Candidates acquired.

Traverse City had been the big score so far. Pockets of Hidden everywhere; some were still Candidates, though it was too soon to tell if any would become Chosen. Cowboy's Raiders were almost wiped out by some Indians, the Grand Traverse Band having barricaded themselves inside their casino. Reinforced by Old Law, their fort lasted till Chosen cavalry sortied from Grand Rapids and burned the place down.

A red pin stuck up from Elk Rapids as well. They'd raided its little library; the Big Boss downstate paid well for rare books. Bob had sat on its reading porch, enjoying the bay view. It would be nice to retire, kick off his boots, dip his toes in the water and relax in the sand. Campbell sighed.

North of Charlevoix was still mostly blank. Harbor Springs had an old pin, though its stats were weak. Petoskey was a work in progress; numbers should pick up though, especially after last night's example. Cowboy massaged his throbbing skull before answering over the radio.

"Heavy, I know it. Nothing I can do. Mikey and his guys are on it. By the way, he says to nab some engineers next time. Over."

"Ha! Engineers. Tell Mikey to go fuck himself. Pencil-pushers make shitty Candidates, and he knows it."

"Roger. Now what's your plan? I can hear you burning gas. It's a 70-mile detour without the bridge, you going or staying?"

Cowboy looked down at the motor pool of Raiders. Heavy maintained a dozen vehicles crewed by armed Chosen, trucks and SUVs jury-rigged with gun mounts and metal plating; Heavy's own truck sported a pair of oversize amps. One of the vehicles was a modified tanker truck, unspoiled fuel being the pinnacle of salvage.

Heavy chopped his throat, and drivers killed their engines. The day quieted, Bob's headache did not.

"Alright boss, we're staying. Boys and I will test drive those new Candies instead. And tell that fucker Mikey if the bridge ain't fixed tomorrow, he'll get an ass kickin' from me!"

"Roger, Heavy. Take it easy on them, OK? Never know who might be Chosen. Campbell out."

The Raiders dismounted, some heading to the barracks, others to the ramshackle collection of chairs and tables they called a bar. Heavy and his buddies strolled to the cage where last night's prisoners were penned. Cowboy watched them enter, kick awake the sleepers, and select companions.

Heavy chose the woman—Helen?—who'd escaped the noose; with the memory came a fresh stab of brain-pain. Something nagged at Bob for sure.

Heavy had one hand wrapped in the woman's hair, dragging her towards his hut. Cowboy *almost* keyed the radio, *almost* told Heavy to knock it the fuck off. Instead he sighed, stretched, and rattled open his drawer of expired painkillers.

Last night in Petoskey had not felt right. He couldn't get that damn water bird out of his head. And they'd had trouble in that region before—scattered resistance, evidence of recent scavenging, and secret signs carved in hard-to-see locations, usually a stylized tree or runic R.

He popped a couple pills, then a couple more. Campbell replaced the handset and sat on his desk.

Would these end times ever fucking end?

The Departed (Cowboy)
Ashley Campbell, 41 years old, May of Year 1, wife and mother

Ashley worked from home, and did all the shopping; her husband Bob built houses. Their daughter Angela got good grades, and was busy lining up colleges. Fresh Covee outbreaks had closed the schools again, a new variant apparently, this one with a nasty sting.

Bob was finishing a subdivision, sweating through his shirt, ticking items off punch lists for houses that would never hold families. Their fridge was almost empty, the pantry shelves stripped bare. Nervous, Ashley drove her SUV to the big-box store, flipping stations, searching for music, avoiding the news. The panic shopping of the recent frenzy was over, the parking lot empty along with most of the aisles. Ashley masked up, put on gloves, and filled her cart with anything edible.

At checkout, while typing her pin, droplets of virion adhered to her glove, a lethal pay-it-forward from the previous shopper. Driving home, she rolled the gloves into a ball, transferring the variant to her hands. Twenty seconds later she touched her face.

The next day, speeding to the ER, she died twitching in Bob's truck, stung by her own defenses: cytokines primed by past exposure. Her husband commandeered a nurse and gurney at gunpoint, but they never made it inside. Ashley Campbell was tagged and then bagged, her stiffening cadaver stacked like cordwood on a pile of curbside corpses.

Going Upriver

"I *KNOW* WE OWE DOYLE A REPORT SOON," Miin said as she watched her flapjacks bubble in the skillet. "But uncle, we have to head upriver."

Keith sat, hooded and gray. The old man was shivering, hoarding his words. He kept one eye trained on Mukwa, who was fishing; silently he willed his coffee pot to perk. Cold mist arose, silver, from the river, while bars of golden sunlight stocked the forest's vault.

"Uncle, we still have some time before our transmission. Plus, what's the use of reporting till we've got something to report?"

Miin flipped pancakes, her first batch, imperfect.

The coffee pot burbled, freeing Keith's voice. "There's a bridge ahead of us."

"We *know* there's a bridge, you've told us. But uncle, we're protected. They've given me a sign."

Miin had dreamed in the night, or had been sent a vision: *a concrete bridge, gushing water, protection.* A green token of safe passage.

An extended burble from the percolator roused a longer speech from Keith. "Blueberry," he said, searching her face, "I need to know more about *them*." His voice was gentle, even tender; Samantha's foster was also his own.

The scouts had slept after sharing their pipe, nocturnal sentries securing their camp. With each owlish all-clear, Keith had rolled, seeking relief from gravity's law and the hard ground. Miin's subconscious had sunk, subterranean. She'd burrowed along highways of roots, flashing tree-to-tree with mycelia, the fungal network meshing a million awarenesses into one. In her dreamscape, the forest had been conscious; she'd visioned the bridge and its token. Daybreak dissolved her dream, but an invitation had undoubtedly been sent. Samantha's three scouts were expected.

"Uncle, it's hard to explain, but *they* seem to be a lot like *us*: familiar with the woods. They found me through the trees. This is their home, and they'll protect it, protect us."

The veteran, wearing all his layers, still felt cold. Two-Crow blearily eyed the coffee pot. He looked in no condition to receive any kind of image, but Miin shaped one anyway, then doubtfully sent it on:

Dappled creatures of forest shadow. Graceful. Nothing clunky or artificial. Folks turning treeish, feet to roots, hands to branches, haloed by leafy crowns. Swimmers into fish, skin into scales, quickly darting, cold-blooded with current.

As Miin projected her trout-image to Keith, Mukwa chuffed, flipping his own catch from the river. He dropped his willow rod and pounced on all fours, pinning the little brookie to the bank.

"Got one!" he triumphed.

Keith's coffee pot boiled over.

Another hour brought them a further mile upriver. They'd scoured their camp clean, leaving no trace of their bivouac. Keith sat in the canoe's stern. Mukwa's three trout were still alive, gills threaded on the stringer behind them. Their finny push added propulsion.

Keith knew this river, had been here before. They'd reach the next bridge, Bear River Road, by this afternoon. Plying his paddle, he tried to anticipate each hazard, finding it hard to trust in Miin and her affinity for these *Naturals*. He kept his duffel zipped and his doubts wired tight.

That last truck still haunted him, the crafty one with its too-intelligent beam. If they'd been blown, it wouldn't be hard to guess where they'd gone. Denied the big lake, there was only one river that could hold them. An easy task to watch the next bridge. Post a few sentries with rifles, and they'd be fish in a barrel.

Mukwa's morning was all business. After his glee with the trout he focused on breaking camp and staying quiet, helping out his sister while following Keith's unspoken commands. Miin, now nestled in the gear, well-fed and comfortable, was pinging the woods, calibrating her green sonar, listening hard for any return. This was on her, and she radiated determination.

The current stayed strong as they paddled upstream, gaining elevation with every stroke; twice Mukwa had to disembark. Along a flat stretch their canoe bottomed out, and Mukwa, unasked, entered the cold water. Bowline over his shoulder, he'd tugged them to a deeper channel. An hour later, a blowdown blocked them. Given a handsaw and an encouraging grunt from Keith, good ol' Muck soon cut them free.

As the sun rose to its zenith, Keith called a halt. The two young ones glanced back at their guide: hood thrown back, the Native son sat straighter. Two-Crow pointed at Ojibwe-bent cedars, ancestral signposts for a stopping place ahead. The river, high with yesterday's rain, rushed swiftly underneath the canoe.

They steered towards a break in the alders, eased aground and stepped out, unbalanced by the sudden solidity of earth. Mukwa disappeared into the brush, toilet paper fluttering like a flag; mouse-like, Miin scampered the other way.

Two-Crow forbade them fire, the bridge looming ominous in his mind. They heated the skillet with propane instead. Miinan foraged nearby, and Keith invited Mukwa to pull in his stringer. The spotted trout—vermiculated to match the river bottom—were still quite lively.

Keith leaned upon a bankside boulder, eyes closed, resembling a reptile on a rock. Mukwa brought over the fish, the biggest a generous eight inches.

"Now what?" the hungry youth asked.

Their lunch spot was sunny and resinous with pine. The old man luxuriated, flicking a saurian eye at the bear cub's impatience.

"Now you clean them."

Muck, ever eager, unsheathed his combat knife. Looking askance at Keith, the young man prepared to do surgery by sword. The weary pilgrim sighed and put a hand in his pocket. Keith's gnarled fingers flicked open a tiny blade. He gestured for the trout, and taught the kid his next lesson.

"The blood-dimmed tide is loosed"-Yeats

I'M NOT DOING MYSELF ANY FAVORS with this narrative, am I?

A strange self-portrait I am attempting to paint. Mad scientist, aesthete, megalomaniac: my canvas is imperfect, a Pollock spattered with derivative dribble and kitschy cliché.

Am I right? Do I care?

Of course I do. I'm still dictating, aren't I?

So where were we? Ah yes, the modification of the original virus. I promise, Covee's variant is almost ready to be "loosed upon the world." That's the moment you've been waiting for. Thank you for your patience; I'll speed things up to get to the reveal.

The antecedents of our design were many. Spanish influenza (H1N1) gave us the idea to hyper-stimulate the STING response. The measles virus (MV) attracted us too. Its R-naught of 18 meant one infected person would infect 18 others. Before Covee, measles was the most contagious virus we had. One person in a crowded room, just by breathing, could infect 90% of its occupants. Don't take this the wrong way, but once Stinger hit the street, its R-naught hit the high twenties!

So, we plagiarized from H1N1 and MV, cunningly using gain-of-function to inculcate their traits within a familiar strain of SARS. Our employer and commander-in-chief, for obvious reasons, ordered our variant to appear zoonotic. Plausible deniability is Pentagonese for *leave no fingerprints*, and, barring this memoir, we didn't. Similar to the Manhattan Project, we had a massive budget and unfettered access to talent and facilities. Again, borrowing from General Groves, we utilized compartmentalization, which meant that except for a handful at the top, no one had access to the big picture. Ahead of schedule, the variant, our Stinger, was ready for clinical trials.

These trials never took place. Not that we suffered from any lack of test subjects; you'd be surprised how easy it is, or rather was, to procure human mice. No, the only trials that occurred were the ones conducted in real time, on actual cities. The data accumulated, stacked and orderly, behind countless Chinese morgues.

Tíng shī jiān is the poetic term for such places.

"The corpse pauses in this room for a while" is my best approximation.

A fascinating language. Sadly, that whole continent has gone dark, and even my far-seeing eyes can't pierce its pall.

Am I implying that the variant was loosed without my consent?

Yes I am.

Does this absolve me of blame for what transpired next?

Probably not, though maybe it should.

Ever-courtly, the Mandarins had an expression for someone whose artistic creation was stolen by soldiers: *Yìshùjiā bèi shìbīng qìngjiéle.*

My still-functioning technology tells me that this phrase comes close to defining my plight, though I'm guessing that a native speaker, if any are left, would find it laughably lacking.

Boss is Such a Dick

COWBOY PACED THE OFFICE, waiting for his contraband coffee to kick in. Campbell had slept like crap. The rising sun flooded through the harbor-side windows. He switched off the overheads, easing the load. Gas wouldn't last forever.

On his commute into work this morning, red-eyed, he'd passed the bank of generators. Humming along, they electrified the compound: barracks, chow hall, motor pool, and stockade.

Per his orders, there was supposed to be a guard on duty, protecting their power source, keeping the tanks full. Of course, this morning there'd been no one there. He'd consulted the watch list, found the culprit to bitch out. Not that it would do any good; hard to stay vigilant when you were the only threat in town, though he suspected there were others—the stylized tree, the graven R. Not like downstate. He didn't miss those early days a bit. *Fucking jungle down there.*

Cowboy observed Charlevoix's compound from his window. Sleepy men, and some women, slouchy with hangovers, were entering the mess hall. New Candidates, sickening already, were serving up ersatz coffee and tasteless chow. Nothing great: no fresh eggs, no bacon, no butter, no bread. They got by on freeze-dried fare: powdered milk, globby oatmeal, MRE hash browns, and the like.

He'd heard rumors about farms in middle Michigan, plantations where Candidates labored, unsick, and ceasefires held long enough to cultivate a crop. Cowboy shook his hatted head. Probably just bullshit, wishful thinking brought on by too many hungry stomachs.

A calendar hung on the wall, featuring lighthouses of Lake Michigan. It was two years old, its dates all wrong, but he'd penciled in some notes for the current month of June. As a scavenger boss, he was overdue to send a shipment south. Bob was worried. Soon, a convoy would arrive with empty tractor-trailers to be filled with salvage and Candidates, both of which were in short supply. He knew he'd get bitched at, but shrugged it off. What were they gonna do, fire him? Not like there was a line of applicants wanting his job. Still, Bob could do better. He moved to the map, studied it again. Had to be a honey hole somewhere, some untouched township that would boost his stats and impress the Big Boss. Maybe he'd slide into something cushier than fucking outpost duty. But every place held a pin, at least the ones he could reach. The only blanks were islands, terra incognita, marooned in the blue. In the early days, scavengers had been sent—by boat, by plane—but none had returned. If there were tales of secret treasure, Bob hadn't heard them.

Near the drawbridge—*still stuck, goddammit*—a compressor coughed to life and a grinding wheel spit sparks. He saw Mikey directing his wrenches. Campbell would leave him alone, let the fix-it man do his thing.

Bob next looked to the barracks. Of course, no Raiders were up. The missing sentry was one of theirs; the asshole partied too hard and missed his shift. Cowboy choked his anger down. He'd have to deal with Heavy eventually, but hopefully not today.

These worries weren't new, and none explained his sleepless night. Bob was bothered by something else, something different, a feeling tied to the most recent hangings. Again, nothing new; he'd noosed too many necks to count. The boss sat at his desk and felt the headache coming on. He gobbled some pills, letting his mind go blank. Assorted stressors bubbled up, and he examined each in turn, kept breathing and released them.

Charlevoix's compound was running low on fuel. The region's remnant gas supply had been siphoned off or spoiled—too much ethanol and no local refineries. Instead of shipping surplus gas, he'd have to beg for resupply. Cowboy didn't relish making that request, not one bit.

Their scavenging had been poor. Traverse City provided a decent haul, but since then his numbers had sucked: a pallet maybe of canned food, some grain, some seed, and a few older deer rifles. No jackpots, no honey holes, nothing to make his name stand out.

On top of everything else, Candidate pickings were meager. The rural population had been sparse even before collapse. Once the variant started stinging and the grid blacked out, those who could migrated south. The long winter, made twice as severe by polar vortex, wiped out the rest. Those they'd unearthed had been a wormy, scraggly bunch. He'd noted their Candidate fail rate was higher than it should be.

As for Heavy, that asshole wouldn't part with his women. Mikey, his fixer, needed manpower too. Executions of resistors had gotten out of hand; Campbell, once a finish carpenter, had gotten sloppy.

Finally, Charlevoix, his base of operations, was proving less than ideal. He'd liked the place at first: lots of fresh water, and as a builder he admired the architecture. Mushroom houses, once photographed by tourists, sprouted everywhere, and with only one road, M-31, it was easy to barricade. But summer's heat had exacerbated their latrine problems. Just because they'd been "chosen" didn't mean dysentery or cholera couldn't kill them. He hadn't made it this far just to drip to death from a leaky asshole. Also, that fucking drawbridge, which he'd once considered a bonus, was proving a nightmare without the know-how to keep the damn thing running.

Campbell's older worries, trauma scars from lost family, were buried too deep to exhume this morning. No, whatever was fucking itching him was fresh, from the hanging night. He'd been on the right track when he'd stayed behind and flashed the spotlight. He'd felt eyes judging him from the harbor, eyes that shouldn't have been there. That damn water bird had mocked him, distracted him; he should've shot the thing to pieces.

He stood up from his desk, ignoring Mikey's wheeze on the radio. He shelved his earlier stress and went to his map of downtown Petoskey. Cowboy fingered the execution site, then backtracked to the breakwater, trying to picture who might have been watching and why. He studied the shoreline, closed his bleary eyes, and recreated the night. When he opened them, he found his finger pointing at the river's mouth.

"Heavy, get your hairy ass up!"

Cowboy booted the door of the Raider's barracks. He waited a minute, the morning sun hot on his neck. He kicked again, then barged in. The first thing he felt was the air conditioning.

"AC's forbidden, and you fucking know it!"

The room stank of sex. Mood not improving, he kicked at the bed.

"Heavy, you're going out!"

A groan escaped from beneath the soiled covers.

Cowboy tore cardboard off the window.

"Jesus Christ, Heavy, put on some pants before I puke!"

A female leg was also showing, also forbidden. Cowboy ripped off their blanket.

"Goddamn it! Get her back to the stockade before I lock you in there too!"

"Fuck boss, OK! Get outta here, will ya? I'll be out in a minute. Shit!"

"You ain't got a fucking minute, you've got right fucking now!"

Cowboy could feel the weight of his pistol. He itched to pull it out and club the insubordinate shit where he lay. The woman covered herself; the morning light did her no favors, bruises purpling her face. Despite the AC she looked clammy, Cowboy feeling her fever from where he stood. *This one won't last long. Par for the fucking course.*

"Leave in 10 minutes! One truck, and you can pick three men. I'll brief you at the motor pool. Now MOVE IT!"

Cowboy, sweating in the sun, was pissed at himself. How the fuck had things gotten this slack?

Cotton-mouthed, Heavy groped for the woman. Ignoring her fever, he beached his white weight upon her, an unwashed whale.

"Sorry sweetie," he wheezed, morning breath rank. "My boss is such a dick."

Heavy at the Bridge

HANK JUNIOR BLARED FROM THE TRUCK, tires kicking up dust from the empty rural road.

The preacher man says it's the end of time
And the Mississippi River, she's a-goin' dry

Heavy sat behind the wheel, reeking of vice and various fluids. He was sobering, but happy. Driving had always been his thing. He'd loved it since he was a kid: stock car races with Grandpa, the stench of rubber, hot oil, and exhaust, the roar of a rally crowd, the lights, the beer, the country girls, their daisy dukes. He pulled on his stale cigarette, the motor stroking beneath him.

I got a shotgun, a rifle and a four-wheel drive
And a country boy can survive, country folks can survive

He'd picked his three best Raiders. None of them thought much of Cowboy's mission, babysitting some wilderness bridge. But you never knew. Once out of the compound, anything could happen. He was glad to be on his own and away from fucking bosses. With a bit of luck they'd strike something, find some action, something to get their blood pumping: resistors that needed a lesson, stockpiles to pilfer, some farmer's tank of unspoiled gas, or better yet an unspoiled daughter. He grinned to himself, clenching his cigarette between bared teeth. Maybe getting up and out today wasn't so bad, after all.

'Cause you can't starve us out and you can't make us run
'Cause we're them old boys raised on shotguns

His truck was an older F-250 that burned diesel, Heavy's go-to since he'd survived the jump from Candidate to Chosen. He'd painted one door panel with the Confederate flag, a coiled "Don't Tread on Me" snake hissing from the other.

An armory-acquired, box-fed M249 had been mounted in the truck bed, its rate of fire and range enabling Heavy to kick some serious ass. From his radio antenna whipped the black and silver shield of the old Oakland Raiders.

His crew, in travel mode, were packed inside. Sitting shotgun was Gunny, his SAW operator. Discharged from the Corps after a so-called "friendly fire" incident, Gunny made for an ideal Candidate, Heavy helping guide him through the trial process. Once Chosen, he'd been his ride-or-die ever since.

Stuffed in the crew cab were two lookalikes, Tyler and Tyrone. Fighting back-to-back, they'd survived the urban collapse of Flint. With flashy chains and saggy pants, they were living the gangster's paradise. Heavy couldn't stand their Eminem bullshit, but they were cool under fire and shared his taste for celebration. Often lacking female company, Heavy and Gunny had been known to make do. It wouldn't be the first time Tyler and Tyrone had kept them warm at night.

Cowboy's marked-up map lay open on the dashboard. Heavy steered one-handed around potholes as they took the long way to Bear River. Of course that fucker hadn't fixed the drawbridge, Mikey's dumbassery costing them good diesel.

The woods and farms seemed almost normal so long as he squinted past fallow fields, torched houses, and the total lack of traffic. Fuck normal though. Heavy had no idea what day it was; he sneered at the old Monday-through-Friday soul-suck. Far as he was concerned, collapse was the best thing that ever happened. How else could he get three squares a day, endless driving, booty and plunder, all without punching a fucking clock or looking over his shoulder for the sheriff?

The good smells of hot road, summer dust, and country green rushed through the open windows. He pulled his red hat lower and reached for a dip, turning up Hank just because he could.

We're from North California and South Alabam'
And little towns all around this land

By early afternoon they'd made River Road, the dry heat and weedy fields left far behind. The air was cooler in the shade, wet smells from the river mingling with stale cig smoke in the cab. Driving north through Clarion, the river ran on their right, clapboard cabins flashing by to their left. Heavy turned off the music and tightened up; little hope for action, but it was best to be prepared. The turn-off for the bridge should be coming up. There it was.

He stopped the truck, a blowdown blocking their path. His crew sat silent as the engine idled.

"Fuckers need an invitation? Get your skinny asses out and move that tree!"

The Flint brothers exited the cab. Tyler tossed his picked-over MRE into the weeds, and Tyrone lit a dangler. They hitched their pants and, grunting with dead weight, dragged the obstacle clear.

"Gunny, get on the SAW."

The discharged Marine climbed into the truck bed. Freeing the machine gun from its bungees, he opened the feed tray cover, seating the ammo belt. He pulled back the bolt, then tapped twice on the roof. Locked and loaded.

The brothers armed themselves as well: a 12-gauge street-sweeper for Tyler, an AK for Tyrone. Both walked behind the truck as Heavy slowly turned towards the river.

Cautious creeping brought them to the bridge. Heavy stopped short of the river clearing, checked his sightlines, and shut off the engine. A liquid gushing filled their ears, mingling with bird calls in the summer afternoon. The air was chilly by the water. There was a feeling that some shit might go down. He tried the radio.

"Cowboy, Cowboy, this is Heavy, you hear me? Over."

Static as he waited for a reply. Cowboy's voice cut in, cut out, then nothing. Heavy, out of range, tried again.

"Cowboy, this is Heavy. Reached the bridge. Nothing yet, sitting tight. Over."

No return transmission. Not the worst thing in the world; Heavy didn't need anyone breathing down his neck. They could babysit this bridge just fine.

Cowboy hadn't given him much to go on. Boss seemed to think they'd been spied on from the water, Bob's best guess being a canoe or small boat. Cowboy's math of mileage and travel time supposedly made this bridge their best chance for an intercept.

Pretty sketchy, Cowboy had admitted, but worth a look just the same. Heavy's Raiders took along enough food and fuel to last for 24 hours. If nothing happened by dark, they would patrol downriver looking for lights. In the morning they'd check again for campsites, then book it back to the Charlevoix compound.

Heavy stepped out, unzipped, and let loose. Tucking in, he gave his junk a quick scratch, hoping that Hidden bitch survived to become Chosen. Not a bad piece of ass; a shame they never lasted. She'd escaped the noose, but not his Stinger. Heavy had seen it before.

"You OK here, Gunny?" Heavy handed up his tin.

Gunny pinched a dip, patted the SAW, and nodded.

Heavy spat juice, considering their position.

They had good fields of fire, upriver and down. Concealed, they'd shred anything moving before they were seen.

"Tyler, you guys cross over, grab yourselves some cover. Keep your eyes fucking peeled, and don't move unless we move first. Got it?"

Tyler nodded and slung his shotgun. Tyrone shouldered his AK, shaking out another cig.

"And no fucking smoking! We're on ambush duty, asshole."

Tyrone tucked the cig behind his ear, flashing yellow teeth at Heavy before following his brother across the concrete bridge.

Heavy shouted, "And no pot, either!"

Gunny leered down at Heavy, spat brown juice, and wiped his chin.

"Fucking amateurs."

The Departed (Heavy)

Gary Halvaka, Sr., 75 years old, June of Year 1, grandpa of six

Grandpa Gary stood on his porch, observing the approach of his son's only son. Heralded by a dust cloud, a diesel pickup, and the blare of heavy metal music; he stepped inside the farmhouse and grabbed a couple beers. By the time he returned, his grandson had backed up to the garage and dropped the tailgate.

"Nice generator," Gary Sr. said, nodding at the new Honda. "Guess I shouldn't look this horse in the mouth either?"

His grandson grinned. "Box stores are busted open, shit's free for the taking."

Working together, like they'd done a thousand times before, they each grabbed an end and maneuvered the bulky box into the garage. Chest to chest, they inhaled particulates off of each other. Grandson got a whiff of Grandpa's beery breath; Senior got a lungful of aerosolized virus.

Together they rigged up the generator, tossing empty cans into the weeds. Then his grandson hit the road.

Paying another visit two weeks later, Grandson never made it past the porch. The old house reeked, Grandpa's rot turning his stomach. Red eyes watering from dust, Heavy Metal retreated along the county road, his whole world collapsing.

Keith's Plan

THEIR BATTERED CANOE PULLED ITS WAY UPRIVER. The sun, past noon, slid westward.

Damn those were good.

The trout, skillet-seared and salted, had been the best meal of Muck's life. When he'd surfaced from his lunch plate, little sister's grin was ear to ear.

"Hey brother bear, save any for us?"

He'd meant to eat just one and give the other two away, but three gaping heads lay on his plate. He looked to Keith, but the old man was preoccupied. He'd opened up the duffel, was going through its contents with a deepening expression of worry etched on his features. Doyle's radio lay on the bottom of the lake; Two-Crow hadn't chewed Mukwa out, though he still expressed his displeasure in subtle ways, like now.

Muck, unsupervised, winked theatrically at Miin and tilted back his plate. The three fish heads tumbled into his open jaws. Giddy at her revulsion, he crunched the tiny skulls, savoring each brainy morsel till Two-Crow started cawing. Keith waved the foster siblings over, watching closely as Mukwa taught Miin the basics of their pistol.

Mukwa, paddling again, kept an eye out, not just for danger, but for spots that looked good for trout. Maybe he'd ask Keith if he could fish from the bow? He looked hopefully over his shoulder; not just now, though. The old-timer radiated anxiety. Crow had assembled the rifle, inserted a magazine, and propped the M-4 for easy access. Mukwa banished thoughts of an overflowing skillet and concentrated on pure propulsion.

An hour later, Keith angled them towards the western bank. "Here, pull over."

They beached their canoe, Keith gesturing to disembark. The cold flow of the highlands rushed past them. Sinking, the sun hid behind shadow-draped trees. The scouts squatted in a circle. Mukwa, frowning, scoured some river mud from his Jordans. Meanwhile, Keith cleared a patch on the ground and outlined his mock-up.

"Here's the river." He snaked a groove in the dirt and added an arrow, indicating flow.

"Here's the bridge." A flat piece of bark spanned the groove.

"Here's us." He added an X downriver of the bridge, on the western side.

"Here's the plan." Keith looked up, fixing them each with a solemn stare.

"I'll stay on this side, you two will cross in the canoe."

He marked the dirt, and pointed them to the other bank.

"Miin, you will stay with the canoe." He offered her the pistol, grip first. "Show me how to lock in a round."

Miin accepted the firearm, its sleek black shape heavy with lethal intimation. Remembering, she ejected the magazine, checked the load, inserted it back into the grip, worked the slide, chambered a round, engaged the safeties, and looked to Keith.

The old man nodded.

"You see *anyone* that's not us, keep both your eyes open, aim for their center, and fire until they're down."

He stared. Miin swallowed her nausea and met his look.

"Mukwa," Keith said, locking eyes with his trainee, "you have your blade. You will *SILENTLY* make your way upriver to the bridge."

He traced Mukwa's path in the dirt, showing his position on the eastern bank.

"If *you* see anyone that's not us, treat them as an enemy. If you get a chance to *SILENTLY* take them out, you will do so. If you don't have that chance, wait until you hear me make my move. Repeat it."

Mukwa, hands shaking a bit, parroted his instructions word for word. A bit breathless, but he got it all out.

"Attack from behind. Go for the throat." Keith mimed the maneuver, dragging an imaginary blade across an imaginary neck. Mukwa rehearsed it and almost gagged.

"We assume the bridge is guarded. To do otherwise would be foolish."

They knelt in the dirt, studying the layout.

"I'll make my way up *this* bank, to the *western* side of the bridge." Keith traced his path, parallel to Mukwa's but on the opposite shore. "If the bridge is held against us, I'll try to clear it. We'll have both sides covered."

He checked with Miin. Minus Doyle's radio, the girl was their only receiver. "Anything new?"

Blueberry shut her eyes, trying to focus on the river's burble.

"Nothing since the tree. But uncle, its message was clear. Danger is behind, and maybe ahead, but we need to keep going."

Keith sighed, wishing for more options. "If the bridge is empty, we meet back with Miin. If the bridge is guarded, but I make no move, we meet back with Miin. If something happens to me, you two make your way back to the big lake, scrounge a radio or a boat, and try to contact Doyle at the quarter moon, channel 12. Get back to the island, but travel only at night."

The siblings paled, but nodded. They understood. The three looked over the plan one last time before brushing away the dirt map.

Keith groaned as he rose to stand. From a pocket, he opened an army surplus compact. The old warrior daubed a finger and smeared a black stripe down Mukwa's forehead, nose, and chin. He did the same with Miin, then himself.

"Black, because war is shameful. We hide our faces to do what must be done."

Next, he smudged his finger in green, angling stripes from nose to ear.

"Green, for vision. To see things as they really are."

Finally he striped their cheeks with red, then his own.

"Red for power, for violence. If we must, we kill our enemies without hesitation, the warrior-way."

He snapped the lid closed and pocketed the paints.

"To take a life, any life, is a terrible thing."

His own elders, long gone, had taught him this. Sam had too, before young Keith left for basic training. Of all his early mentors, only Samantha remained.

"What you do as a warrior, washes off with this paint. Do not let killing get inside you. You fight now to protect each other."

Words were not enough, not for what might come. Keith knew it and trailed off, the young ones staying silent. The river rushed, uninterested, as the sinking sun angled acutely. Standing in a circle, the companions adjusted to their altered faces.

"Let's move."

Keith led them back to the canoe. From the duffel, he selected the suppressor for the rifle and the green-lensed binoculars. Re-zipping his bag, he booted it underneath the stern seat. Their radio was gone, deep-sixed by the boy to the bottom of Lake Michigan; he'd watched its blinking descent, stomach likewise sinking like a stone. One bridge at a time, and this one, just up the river, came first.

Two-Crow threaded the silencer onto the barrel, secured the binos, and slung his weapon. He seated Mukwa in the stern and Miin in the bow. When ready, he shoved them off towards the far shore. Both banks were thick with alders, providing plenty of cover.

He watched them paddle across, haul out, and stash the boat in some undergrowth. He mimed for Miin to stay, then hand-signaled the big man upstream. When Mukwa disappeared, Keith did the same, stalking upriver towards the bridge, towards their doom.

Ambush

MIIN WAS ALONE.

Bear River muscled past, rolling stones along its bottom, current eager to reach deeper waters.

The trees were in transition, biochemistry slowing as daylight diminished and the night came on. The full Strawberry Moon of June was still days away, but *Odemiini-giizis* was ripening, turning red to silver as it waxed.

The youngest scout sat cross-legged, leaning on her uncle's canoe, the loaded pistol gravid with death. Both men had gone upriver. Miin felt like puking.

◆◆◆

Mukwa itched all over. He paused his slow stalk, took off his shirt, and stuffed it under a root, giving himself a furious scratch before continuing his approach. Sampling the air, he smelled sap and needles, icy oxygen, an asphalt tang from the unseen bridge. And something else, something familiar and sweetly out of place. There: his nostrils twitched with another skunky whiff. Sure as shit, someone up there was smoking weed.

◆◆◆

Two-Crow, moving like a panther on the prowl, angled away from the river. He wanted to intercept the road that led to the bridge; there it was, seen through an opening in the trees. Unslinging his rifle, he worked the bolt and locked in a round, then inched towards the clearing and gave it a long look.

The potholed road was empty. His shoulders sagged with relief.

He'd hit his aim-point, the turnoff from River Road to the bridge. His eye caught something, and he flinched. In the bushes lay a discarded MRE. Bending down, Two-Crow sniffed the package. Still fresh; it had been opened today.

Shit. Adrenaline dumped into his system. Keith breathed through it and studied the track. A heavy branch had been dragged clear, two different soles leaving their prints. Daylight almost gone, the tracker knelt near the tire treads. Hard to tell, but it looked like a single vehicle.

He tried to mentally telegraph Miinan and Mukwa. *Danger!*

Keith paralleled the approach road, moving quietly through cover. The river grew louder, the bridge massing ahead. He raised his binoculars, and the wide lenses filtered photons, limning the littoral in green. A truck squatted, toad-like, near the river. A figure stood in the back, crewing a machine gun.

Keith studied the span. The tracks indicated two men at least, so where was the other?

Turning around was not an option. These people were aware of their intrusion; back on the big lake they'd be dead. He believed in Sam, and Samantha believed in Miin. The girl's message had been clear: their path lay forward.

Committed, Keith would take the gunner first. After that, he'd improvise. The hunter shouldered his rifle. Acquiring his target, he steadied the reticle on center of mass and thumbed the selector from SAFE to SEMI, resigning himself to murder.

◆◆◆

Mukwa, shirtless in the dusk, willed himself to strike. He was in position, and he'd found his tokers. River noise and their stoned babble helped cover his approach. Two figures sat, bumps on a log, watching the water with their backs towards him.

The ex-linebacker was heavier than both bumps combined. He issued orders to himself, but Muck's morale was low, his limbs mutinous. He pictured Miin, their canoe, the slaughter they'd so far avoided.

That's just it. I've got to do this to protect Miin and the old-timer.

A low growl grew in his throat. Mukwa emerged, gripped his knife and lit his own fuse.

◆◆◆

Where were they?

Miin shivered near the canoe; no time to add another layer.

What was happening up there?

It was almost dark, and moonlight reflected from the river. She tried for stillness, for dissolution, but only shivered. It was not happening. She could feel the blockage.

The gun.

Its mechanical menace repelled her. She stood up, leaving it on the bank; the pistol seemed to pout, eager for use. She moved herself downriver, away from the bridge, where a red cedar offered respite. Permission granted, she sat upon the lap-like gnarl of its roots. Limbs entwined, they merged, skin to bark; Miin felt freed from the weapon's power.

She heard disparate voices in the river: clacking stones, shifting gravel, the pulmonary pulse of cold circulation.

A large corvid overflew her, shadowing the moon.

Danger! The bridge! They're waiting!

The sending unlocked her.

Uncle!

At once, she was wide open and everywhere: *moss on the tree, moonshine, swimming trout, Samantha in her shack.*

For a blink, Sam saw her too, and chided her away. Miin returned to the river just in time. Bear was growling, Crow about to strike.

An oily foulness oozed from their foes. They were deadly.

Then another sending hit her, this one stronger: *rushing trees, warriors bathed in moonbeams, luminous spears lancing corruption. Blueberry! We COME!*

◆◆◆

Two-Crow held on his target; at the exhale he'd squeeze. Just as he began to pull the trigger, gunshots ripped the night apart—*Dhak! Dhak! Dhak! Dhak!*

An eruption of fire, not from the truck, but a shooter on the bridge. The muzzle flash blinded Keith's scope, but he quickly acquired the new threat. A standing shadow unloaded an entire magazine at the river—*Dhak! Dhak! Dhak!*

The muzzle flashed again and again, angling down towards the water. Keith centered on this new target. He squeezed off a quick burst, suppressor muffling the sound.

Whock! Whock! PING!

Two hits to the body and a ricochet? Keith squinted. Was the bridge shooter down?

Then the night exploded again—*Whap! Whap! Whap! Whap! Whap! Whap! Whap! Whap!*

Red tracers zipped from the truck's machine gun, lighting up its target: a splintered boat.

The canoe? Miin?

Keith approximated the torso of the truck gunner and was about to squeeze, but just then the silhouette slumped, the heavy weapon going silent.

Across the river, a young bear was roaring.

◆◆◆

Bare-chested, Mukwa made ready to charge.

Dhak! Dhak! Dhak! Dhak! The darkness splintered as lightning flashed from bridge to surface.

"What the *FUCK?*" the smoker bitched, half-rising from the log as Mukwa sprang, his long knife a claw. He buried it deep, then ripped the blade free. A hotness splashed across his face. His victim gurgled, lung collapsing. Confusion in the dark as the other toker fumbled for his weapon.

Dhak! Dhak! Dhak!

A shooter on the bridge was barking flame. Mukwa, flash-blind, lost his opponent.

Whock! Whock! PING!

The bridge-shooter went silent.

Mukwa crouched low. Somewhere close, his enemy was armed and alert.

Whap! Whap! Whap! Whap! Whap! Whap! Whap! Whap!

Red stitchery needled the river. Mukwa saw a drifting canoe shot to pieces.

Then he heard his quarry. Blinking back the flash, he saw him too: a skinny dude, standing just 10 feet away, shotgun squared at Mukwa's chest.

"That was my brother, ASS-hole!"

Mukwa bellowed, charging to his death. His last thoughts were of little sister Miin.

The skinny dude leered, finger tickling the trigger. Suddenly, his hollow chest exploded outward, punched through by a silver spear.

Moonlight Meeting

MIIN HAD MADE IT TO THE BRIDGE; their canoe, pistol, and packs she'd left behind. She'd been scrambling through tag alders when the firefight erupted. By the time she arrived, it was all over.

In the moonlight she saw people standing on the bridge, *her* people. Mukwa's heaving chest was bathed in sweat, and there limped Two-Crow, feathers ruffled but unhurt. Behind them, a fuming vehicle hulked in the shadows. An oily film coated the scene: murder, death, corruption. The innocent girl gagged on its reek.

Miin could see something coiling inside her uncle; a look at brother Mukwa confirmed the same. Violence had been done by each, lives snuffed out, good or evil not theirs to say. The writhing coils sought purchase, a further constriction of mind and flesh.

And then she saw the *others*. One pair, two, and then three; each shimmering duo stepped clear from the shadows as she perceived them. A glow emanated from these slender newcomers, yet they bore no lights. To Miinan, they appeared lit from within, as if they'd swallowed moonbeams, their very veins shot through with quicksilver. Twigs and ivy wove about their bodies, like the very woods were walking; cloaked in this concealing verdure, the sylvan folk were hard to make out, especially from Miin's periphery.

Eight figures stood tall upon the span as she struggled up the embankment. Mukwa, unsmiling, hauled her to the top. Miin looked him over, adjusting. Blood had smeared his paint, the colors gone gray, bleached by moonlight. She clutched his hand, so similar to a padded paw, and squeezed, but Mukwa didn't notice. Miin looked to her uncle; all business there. The vet cradled his rifle, muzzle held down and still smoking. Two-Crow eyed these new creatures, calculating and cautious.

The crescent moon, ever-serene, gleamed upon the watershed's cold-blooded artery flowing out from beneath the bridge. Night grew chill as the heat of violence ebbed away.

"We need to leave *now*," a tall woman said.

Pulling aside a twig-covered hood, her angular eyes scrutinized all three. The sylph wore a braided headband bound up in her moonlit hair. She signaled her companions; hunting bows were slung, spearheads glinting as the silent squad dispersed, each warrior to their task.

"Your canoe is nearby? You are able to paddle?"

Miin's companions had lost their words, so the island girl replied, "It's down-river a bit, and yes, we can paddle. But where are we going?"

The woman dressed in leaves smiled. "Can I call you Blueberry?"

Miin nodded.

"You are known to us."

The woman turned to welcome Mukwa and Keith as well. "All three of you are known. Call me Elena. We would escort you upriver, to a place of safety. Will you come?"

Blueberry looked at Crow, at Bear. Both men were still constricted by their coils.

Miin decided for them. "Yes, we'll come."

Elena nodded. "Good. Return to your boat and paddle past this bridge. We will meet you upstream. For the rest of the night, we travel by canoe."

Keith looked up, his tongue loosening at last. "Whose boat was shot up? Not ours?"

The woman's face took on a feral mien. "Not yours. One of ours, a diversion. Thank the trees it worked. Now let's go."

Elena stalked off the bridge and out of the moonlight, blurring back into shadow.

The three scouts stood alone and cold upon the span while others cleaned the scene. Bodies were dragged, weighty with death; their confiscated weapons clanked, metallic.

Keith shook off his stupor, began planning again. "You two, head back to the canoe, gather our gear. I'll meet you there in a minute."

He slung his rifle and walked towards the truck.

"Well Mukwa, you big lump, can you move?"

The shirtless man shivered, crusty with blood. Adrenaline evaporated, his shoulders slumped with fatigue. His big body shook, but not from disease; the girl sensed no virus, no pathogen despite Mukwa's hand-to-hand proximity to a Chosen. Their protection seemed to hold. Miin again took his paw, pulling Mukwa from the bridge and back toward the bank.

Bear followed Blueberry. Together, they stumbled towards their canoe.

Escorted

THE MOON HAD GONE DOWN. Daybreak flirted with the eastern sky, the riverine system stirring. A heron stalked its breakfast of minnows, kingfishers flashing from tree to tree. The river steamed in the predawn chill.

Three canoes pulled upstream. A fourth lingered behind, its pair of warriors working to scrub the bridge clean. The truck, four bodies, shell casings, and bloodstains; there was plenty to hide from investigating eyes.

In the growing light, Miin studied their escorts. Elena and another tall woman crewed the lead canoe, gray hoods obscuring their faces. Strong paddlers, they hadn't missed a stroke since leaving the bridge behind hours ago.

The next canoe was theirs. Big brother paddled in the bow; Miin had teased him into putting on a sweater. He didn't tease back. In fact, Muck hadn't spoken a word since the bridge.

Miin rotated in her nest. In the stern sat Uncle Crow; she'd never seen him look this old. All three still wore their face paint, now smeared and cracking. Keith's eyes had sunken deep into their sockets. His painted visage scowled, monstrous from murder.

Miin averted her gaze, looked past him to the trailing canoe. Two athletic men were paddling, hoods up, full quivers bristling over the shoulders of the bowmen. They kept silent as they stroked, scanning the shoreline, watching their six. The oak tree had intimated she could trust Elena and those she led, but the feeling of being escorted was nevertheless unnerving.

What exactly are their orders? What if we try to bail?

Dawn cracked open, stars and planets fading from view. A red-tailed hawk, perched high in a pine, studied their procession. Miin felt the raptor counting them, memorizing faces, gathering intel. With two muscled sweeps, the huge bird was aloft and heading upriver.

Off to report?

Right on time, Miin's stomach started growling.

❖❖❖

Keith's belly was empty too. Even worse, he felt hollowed out by another coffee-less dawn. His wrists complained, his back ached, and his bony butt was numb. There was a chill in his limbs that no sunrise could thaw. He'd killed a man last night. Worse, the youth had killed one too.

After the fray, he sent Miin and Mukwa back to the canoe. No need for them to linger at the crime scene; he'd conduct the after-action report himself. Utilizing moonlight, he checked his kill, confirming two hits to the body. The blood had pooled. Was it contagious?

Keith rolled the heavy corpse over and frisked the motorcycle jacket, sticky with plasma and covered in patches: Metallica, AC/DC, Slayer. He squatted over the body. No wallet, no ID, just a crushed pack of blood-spoiled cigs. Crow reached for the man's rifle, an armory M-4, but a hooded figure materialized, picking it up instead. The creature pierced Keith with a sylvan look before carrying the weapon away.

Next was the truck. A body slumped by the gun mount. Keith looked it over, noting two arrow wounds in the chest. One of the broadheads had punched clear through, the other lodged in the dead man's spine.

He opened the driver's door, the dome light winking on. Scanning the interior, he pilfered a road map from the dash, putting it in his pocket. He then looked at the radio. Just a basic CB rig, but it should work for contacting Doyle. Opening his multi-tool, he severed some wires and carefully removed the radio. Next he found the hood release, popped it, and quietly shut the driver's door. The internal light went dark, and moonlight returned.

Two faceless fighters heaved the corpse with the motorcycle jacket into the truck bed. Keith looked to the bridge, seeing a third corpse carried by another pair. Mukwa's kill? Keith made haste while they were busy. Unlatching the hood, he studied the battery.

"Stop!" Elena was beside him, voice and expression stern.

Keith stepped clear of the truck. Holding up his hands, he spoke very slowly, saying, "I need this battery for the radio."

Her bright eyes lanced him. Keith stood still, resigned to hold his ground. A fourth body was carried from the far side; this one's chest had been shattered. No knife wound here. Young Mukwa had help.

"We need that battery too," Elena said, regal under starlight.

"You're driving this out of here?"

She nodded. "No one must ever find this truck, or these bodies."

"What about the weapons, the machine gun, the *fuel?* You don't salvage?"

She considered. "It's more of a *won't.*"

The fourth body—killed by spear?—had been arranged in the truck bed. Keith eyed a hooded male warrior who bore a shotgun and Kalashnikov; he placed both with the corpses. Elena began moving among the dead, drawing blood, filling vials that she pocketed in her parka.

When the woman finished, Keith tried to strike a compromise. "Start the truck, get it running, then I'll take the battery. That way we both win."

A long minute passed. Elena's fighters had gathered, some with bows, some spears; all wore hoods, braided headbands, and looked lethal.

Keith's rifle was slung, and he made no move, clearing his mind of even *thinking* about making a move. Six against one. The river rushed below.

Finally, Elena inclined her chin and said, "It's not our way. But *our way* is not *your way,* at least not yet."

The figures behind her dispersed. On the bridge, leafy forms continued to clean.

Keith remained silent. The old man hadn't moved.

"The trees trust the girl," Elena said, holding his gaze, "and so *I* will trust *you.* Fear must not disrupt the bonds between like and like."

Just then, one of her company climbed inside the truck and started its engine, shattering the subtle soundscape.

"Take the battery, take the radio. Then return to your canoe. Your two friends are waiting." With that she strode off, hand-signing to her companions.

Keith slowly exhaled. Ducking down, he unharnessed the battery, wrenching the bulky block free. Shutting the hood and avoiding eye contact with the driver, he cut off the vehicle's antenna using his knife.

He did this for Sam, for the island, for its families. The damn battery was heavy, and he tried again not to be angry about the boy's muck-up and Doyle's deep-sixed radio.

Two-Crow marked the moonset, a silver crescent waxing towards first quarter. Just three more days till their radio-rendezvous with Captain Doyle.

✦✦✦

Mukwa paddled hard to match the women's pace, blisters bubbling on his palms. Sunrise slanted through the mist on the river's surface; not a single pause since the bridge, and he was glad for it, the demands on his muscles leaving little time for thinking.

Each time he probed memories of the bridge, several sensations came through: his plunging knife, the gritty grate of blade on bone, the hot splash of blood on his hands, his face. He'd tasted it, too.

Did I get infected? Miin told me no.

His stomach heaved again, thankfully empty. He spat bile overboard and observed the lead canoe.

Shit! He was falling behind again.

Fucking animals, those two.

He clenched his jaw, stroked harder, and tried to narrow their lead.

At a confluence, their war party entered a feeder stream, departing Bear River. Muck looked up from his paddle as the women finally beached their boat. The creek was no longer navigable: boulders and tree-wrack clogged further passage. There'd be no paddling over that.

Keith steered them, and they beached as well. The two women hauled out their craft and returned to the shore. The darker one reached out, locking eyes and arms with Mukwa as she pulled him to his feet. Wobbly, he stepped ashore. *Damn, she's as tall as I am.*

He sampled her scent profile, a commingling of sweat, woodsmoke, and pine. She lifted Miin out of the canoe as well. Blueberry held the woman's hand, giving it a squeeze. The tall one looked down, and the girl nodded gratitude; a half-second later, the woman nodded back, a smile flashing from inside her hood.

The trailing canoe beached, its two men vaulting out and dragging it towards cover. This duo traveled light: no packs, no duffels, just recurve bows, quivers, and two long spears. They moved quickly, athletes of the woods. Mukwa remembered the skinny dude's chest exploding, the spearhead bursting through with incredible force. These commandos were deadly, outmatching the three islanders for sure.

The creek slid past them. The June sky shone jewel-blue, a perfect day. Elena threw back her hood and trilled a signal, a bird whistling back from beyond the small falls. Two hood-wearing guards appeared there, arrows nocked, tipped with stainless steel. They each raised a hand, and Elena returned the gesture. Relief flooded their escorts as everyone drew aside their hoods.

The two athletes from the rear canoe, brothers by the look of them, approached Mukwa. They extended rough hands, obliging him to shake.

"Nice knife-work back on the bridge, *amigo*."

Mukwa grunted at the accented compliment.

"Yeah man, nice work. Blade against an AK? Got some *huevos* for sure."

He should say something.

Muck shoveled gravel from his throat. "Thanks for your help."

A quick nod from each, both smiling and relaxed. Hard to believe they'd just murdered multiple people.

The older one introduced himself. "Name's Miguel, but call me Matador, the killer of Chosen." Matador finished with a fake flourish of cape and sword.

The younger grinned up at Mukwa. "I'm Tomas, but in the ELF my name is Tigre. I was a scholarship soccer player, like my brother."

Muck thumped his own chest. "Mukwa. It means bear, but I'm not Ojibwe, not really."

"*El oso*, eh?" Matador said approvingly. "Big man, in the ELF you can be whoever you want to be."

Tigre backed his brother's play. "We both chose footballers, why not? Ever heard of Sepúlveda from Guadalajara or Luis Hernández from Cruz Azul?"

Muck had not.

"Ah well, favorites of our father, *descanse en paz*." Tigre made the sign of the cross.

Matador finished up, the time for introductions almost over. "They both played in World Cups, oso, for the national team."

The waterfall sentries climbed down to converse with Elena. Two of the canoes had been stashed, Keith's green Old Town still lying on the beach.

Elena gathered the group. "We've made good time," she announced, nodding at the weary islanders. "For the moment we are safe. We'll rest a bit in the shade, and eat some food."

Mukwa almost grinned, Miin's stomach gurgling its approval.

"Then we hike through the forest. The paths to our sanctuary are secret. To us, they are sacred; you three will be blindfolded."

A change in scent wafted from Two-Crow. The old man was pissed, but said nothing.

"One final thing before we eat."

Keith's rage-scent increased.

"Our ways will seem strange," she said, "but your weapons, your technology must be stashed here until you return."

Keith radiated anger, but held his tongue. Mukwa, too tired, did the same.

"Now, let's clear this beach. We'll rest under the trees, then we'll go."

Matador and Tigre, wordless, checked with Two-Crow, who consented. The athletes hauled Keith's gear-heavy canoe away from the landing. Elena, her tall partner, and the two portage guards disappeared the same way. The three scouts remained at the river.

The rising sun cleared the canopy, gilding the beach. Basking in its beams, the chill left their bones. They stood listening for a moment to the mixture of murmuring creek and birdsong, fair breezes blowing through the pines.

They circled up. Something inward opened.

Keith pitched his voice low. "Last night was a long one."

They breathed together, exhaled as one. Old bonds were renewed, each catching an elusive scent of Cranberry Bog.

"I killed a man, and Mukwa killed also."

Flashbacks of the firefight, lightning and thunder, shattered bodies silvered by moonlight.

"What we did, we did as warriors, to protect each other and the people we love."

Images of Samantha played in their minds, followed by elders, children playing, the lighthouse, their sheltered island.

"The night is over, we wash off the warrior. We wash away our crimes."

Keith pulled a bandana from his pocket and soaked it in the river, scrubbing his craggy face clean. He handed the rag to Miin, who repeated the procedure on herself, rinsing it out when she was done. She shot a mouse-like look up at Mukwa and tugged his sweater, pulling her foster brother down. Tenderly, she washed away the paint and blood from his features. When clean, she let him go. Keith wrung out the cloth and tucked it away.

They looked at each other, returning to themselves. Big-hearted, a river of fondness flowed through them. The sun kept shining, the birds kept singing; the terrors of the night receded.

Miin tried, without success, to restrain her grin. "Uncle, can we eat now?"

A smile softened Keith's face. Miin, the hungry link, broke their chain and skipped up the path. Mukwa, finally stirring, moved to follow his foster-sis, but an iron grip banded his arm.

Keith held him, pinning the youth with a hard-eyed stare. Much was conveyed: pride, sadness, respect, duty. A nod from the veteran as he set Mukwa free.

The young warrior didn't move; Keith's message sank in. Boy no longer, Mukwa nodded back. Two-Crow turned away and limped towards the trees. Mukwa inhaled deeply as he settled into this new skin, flexing and embracing the green surroundings. Putting his back to the river, he loped after the others.

A hundred yards through the woods, and the path reached a clearing where a dozen watercraft were camouflaged. Plastic barrels, lidded tight, were stockpiled in rows. Long-hafted spears bunched against the trees. This was a depot, a rally-point for river excursions. Keith's battered canoe had been added to the stacks. Mukwa saw the old man negotiating with Elena. Their gear lay spread upon the ground: rifle, pistol, binoculars, bolt-cutters, truck radio, battery, and duffel.

Mukwa's olfactory lobe lit up, flooding his mouth with saliva. The two brothers had kindled a fire; coffee was perking in a pot, and something sizzled in their skillet. Grinning, they gestured him over, nodding to a greasy pile of bacon. Beneath the pork lay six beautiful trout.

Tigre pointed to Mukwa's bear claw tattoo.

"El oso tiene hambre, eh Miguel?"

His older brother laughed, patting the ground. *"Si Tomas, muy hambriento."*

Mukwa thumped down, ravenous, beside him.

"This bear looks fucking hungry."

Matador shoveled food onto a plate for Mukwa, proffering a fork.

Tigre, laughing, told his brother not to bother.

El oso was already chewing, bacon in one paw and a trout in the other.

"The ceremony of innocence is drowned"-Yeats

IT'S HARD TO DECLINE a White House summons, even for me. Near the end of his first term, the president, a less than august personage really, gathered together Big Pharma and top brass from the Army's Research Institute of Infectious Disease. POTUS then tasked us with an unthinkable mission. I simpered like the rest, and the race was on.

The early decades of the 21st century reminded the world just how destabilizing viral epidemics can be. The 2013-2016 Ebola outbreak (EBOV) in West Africa was particularly riveting. Hemorrhagic fever is a gruesome death, and EBOV's 80% fatality rate became must-see TV. Fluid-only transmission, however, resulted in a low R-naught of 1.5, making EBOV easy to contain. By 2016 there was an effective vaccine.

This turnaround time, unprecedented really, between outbreak and vaccine intrigued me. The inherent problem with biological warfare is that, like poison gas from the Great War, it cuts both ways. Panzer Pharma, my baby, was awarded the contract because we'd convinced USAMRIID we'd solved the double-edged dilemma.

Since the Nazi excesses of World War II, it's been considered uncouth to point out genetic differences between races. I understand this reluctance, but still, some exist. Let's cut right to it: our president and his lackeys wanted a viral weapon customized to attack the Chinese.

So we made him one.

Do you want to hear the details?

Doubtful. It's ponderous reading, but here's a sample from our abstract:

"Single nucleotide polymorphisms of the protein tyrosine phosphatase non-receptor type 22 (PTPN22), a negative regulator of T-cell activation, differ significantly between European-Americans and Asians..."

I warned you!

Basically, Panzer manipulated SARS-CoV-2 so that the cytokine storm, Cov-ee's lethal sting, would exclusively target Asian phenotypes.

It's as if Fritz Haber, the German chemist behind the gas attack at Ypres in 1915, had designed his chlorine to burn British lungs only, while leaving the lungs of good little Germans alone.

Willi Siebert, a German soldier at Ypres, wrote to his son about what he'd witnessed that day. I include it here, its imagery prescient of Covee:

"What we saw was total death. Nothing was alive. The smell of the gas was still in the air. It hung on the few bushes which were left. When we got to the French lines the trenches were empty but in a half mile the bodies of French soldiers were everywhere. It was unbelievable. Then we saw there were some English. You could see where men had clawed at their faces, and throats, trying to get breath. Some had shot themselves."

As an interesting aside, after Ypres, the chemist Haber hosted a celebratory party in Berlin. His wife, also a chemist, horrified at his perversion, took his service revolver, walked into the garden and shot herself in the heart. She died the next day, cradled in the arms of their 13-year-old son. Haber was later awarded the Nobel Prize, and remarried. I admire the grit of his first wife. I like to think that if I'd ever married, my spouse would have shown the same intestinal fortitude.

Beating the competition, Panzer created the Asian-specific virus POTUS had pouted for. Being a prudent fellow, with access now to billions, I built a big, beautiful wall around the company complex, engineered some side projects, and hedged against apocalypse.

One Fucking Thing After Another

A BLARE OF HORNS scrambled Cowboy's concentration. His porta potty was overfull, and the morning sun fierce; Bob gagged on the stench of his plastic latrine. A long blast from an arriving semi-truck scuttled his momentum. Cursing, he exited the shit-box into the glare of yet another day in paradise.

The long-expected convoy, a half-dozen gun trucks and an empty tractor-trailer, idled at the southern end of the compound. A checkpoint straddled M-31, guards waiting on his OK to wave them through. Cowboy pulled the brim of his Stetson lower and fast-walked to sort out the mess. Squinting, he didn't recognize the semi-truck or its driver, though the lead vehicle, a fiery pickup, was instantly familiar. He first heard her voice, then spotted her red hair.

"That you, Cowboy? Holy shit son, you've seen better days."

She ignored the gaping guard, strode towards Cowboy and surprised him with a hug.

"Tell your limp-dicked sentries to let us through, will ya? We left Grand Rapids at midnight and, as you know, the roads are shit."

Campbell nodded to his men. The big dozer started up and rolled clear. Red Liz faked a curtsy and waved her column through. The vehicles entered, then the roadblock returned. Cowboy's sentries stepped back into shade, the day's big event over already.

She nodded at the tractor-trailer. "Hope you're ready to fill that fucker?"

Cowboy had been dreading this; having it here didn't make it any better. His guts clenched.

"Not gonna lie, Liz, been slim pickings up here," he said as they walked towards his office. "You don't wanna hear it, but it's been one fucking thing after another."

"You're right, Bob, I don't. Bosses neither. Got any grub for my guys?"

They passed the reeking latrine. Cowboy and Liz, conditioned by collapse, held their breath.

"There's our mess hall," Bob said, pointing it out. "Nothing fresh, not unless you brought something?"

Liz laughed. "Yeah right, you're the one in the scavenge business. Ain't you enjoying the spoils of war?"

Liz whistled her drivers to chow. Their vehicles emptied rapidly, crews clumping off towards rations of powdered eggs.

"Spoils of war? Shit Liz, fucking area's been picked over. Our last big score was months ago."

The air above the parking lot wavered with fumes, gas-driven generators thrumming. Again, there was no fucking sentry.

God DAMN it! The second Heavy got back, he'd chew his ass out good. Cowboy checked his watch. Should be anytime now.

He held the door for his Liz. They entered the old building, taking stairs to his office. At his desk, he offered her a chair, angling the fan. Bob plopped himself down with a sigh.

Liz unbuckled her gun belt, laying the heavy holster on his desk. Knuckling her back, she stepped over to his wall map. "Been sittin' on my ass since midnight. I'll stand a bit, if it's the same to you?"

Cowboy shrugged, freed a bottle from its drawer, and poured some Jack Daniels into two cleanish mugs. He handed her one, and they both took sips.

"I've never been up this far. What's your situation here, Bob?"

Campbell took off his hat, fingers combing through his greasy hair. Where to fucking begin?

"Remember the early days, Liz? Just two years ago. Firefights all the time, turf wars, treasure hunting, climbing the Chosen chain of command."

The redhead nodded, still facing the map.

"Well, outpost duty's about as far from that as you can get."

"Hmm," she replied, downing a mouthful of whiskey as she scanned up and down the forest of red pins. "What's your Candidate situation?"

"No one left up here. Region was sparse to begin with. Once in a while my Raiders root out some Hidden. Starving and sickly, they don't last long. We nabbed a few this week, and they're fucked already."

Bob thought of Heavy's woman, twitchy with fever. Envenomed by his Stinger, she wouldn't last another night.

"What about resistance? Anything serious?"

Cowboy shook his achy head and shared an air-brushed version of the truth. "Nothing for months. Tell you true, Liz, my guys have gone slack. Hard to keep 'em sharp with nothing sharp around. What about you? What's it like downstate?"

Liz swiveled, raising her mug. Bob joined her.

"Here's to surviving." Their old line.

They each took a swig, Cowboy's guts protesting.

"Downstate? Shit's gotten crazier." She stabbed the map repeatedly with her finger: Jackson, Flint, Detroit. "Remember the max-security prison population? Their higher survival rate?"

He did. Covee seemed to favor felons, sparing the most violent more often than not.

"Well, Old Law lost containment. Convicts are loose and carving up turf; they call themselves XCons. They're runnin' quite a show, too. Branding, whips, the whole fucking deal. Can't say I blame 'em."

She took another slug of her whiskey. "Weapons, fuel, recruits. Convicts got plenty."

"What's our position with these guys?"

"Who knows? Bosses don't share, especially not with me."

Liz drained the mug. Eyeing his, she tongued her rim.

Stomach pain flaring, he pushed his whiskey towards her.

She arched an eye, stretching her limbs. "You're in sorry shape, aren't ya, Bob?"

He stalled for time, familiar with her tells. "What about Old Law?" Cops and hero-types had always been their biggest opposition.

Liz snorted. "White-hat cucks still doing their thing. Fighting for the flag, organizing all the time. Just won't let the old ways die. Least Stinger keeps their numbers down." She took a big gulp of his whiskey, then smiled, shooting a suggestive look at her friend. "Speaking of numbers, what've you got for me to take south?"

He'd been dreading this part. "Not gonna lie, Liz. My numbers are shit."

Wearily, he stood and showed her his stats.

She tossed her red hair. "These suck, come on Bob! How are you gonna keep this cushy job? Not worth the gas for me to fetch it."

"I know, and I'm sorry. But like I said, ain't exactly the land of plenty up here."

He almost shared his recent spookiness. *That fucking water bird, too many hangings, paranoia about the bridge...*

He checked his watch. Heavy was officially AWOL.

Liz studied the region. "What you need, Bob, is to find yourself a honey hole. Remember that weapons cache we dug up in Ann Arbor?"

Cowboy almost grinned. Who but Liz would have figured those hippies for gunrunners? That score had fast-tracked them both. Foot soldiers no longer, they rose in the ranks.

"Trick to a hole," she said, tapping a spot on the map, "is to think outside the box."

He looked where her finger pointed. "Islands? Liz, get real."

"Fuck you, Bob! I'm saving your sorry ass. You eager for combat again? Go toe-to-toe with XCons? End your end times as a slave? Chosen or not, my friend, you wouldn't last long in chains."

He was almost touched that she gave a shit.

"Alright, Liz, tell me more."

"To begin with, looks like they haven't been scouted." Her milky skin flushed as she spoke. "No one's been there since collapse."

Bob waited, biting his tongue. *No one who lived to tell the tale, anyway.* Liz popped her top buttons and blew sweaty bangs from her face.

"Either Stinger got 'em all, in which case there'll be loot. Or maybe, just maybe, they haven't been exposed. A whole island of Candidates for you to ship south. Cowboy Bob's name in lights again, the pride of the Chosen."

They shared a grin. For a second, his gut pain receded.

"You got a plane, Bob? A pilot?"

Cowboy shook his head. "Yeah right. Who does?"

Liz sighed, untucking her shirt. "I hear ya. Even downstate, pilots are hard to come by. What about boats? Got any?"

"A whole harbor of 'em," Bob said, shaking his head, "but we haven't got one running yet. My fixer Mikey has been busy."

Liz looked up from the map and out the windows. She saw Lake Michigan sparkling in the sun, golden light bathing the broken drawbridge and inner harbor.

She laughed, drained his mug, and slammed it down. "Bob, what would you do without me?"

She walked to the harbor-facing side of the office. Kicking off her boots, she added some sway.

Cowboy eyed her ass, then followed her triumphant flourish as she pointed down at the moorings.

There, tied to its berth, waited all 130 feet of the motor vessel *Emerald Isle.*

"Seeing you, Bob Campbell, has brought back a few things."

Bob remembered too. Parts of him, anyway.

She sashayed towards his chair, popping open more buttons on her western shirt. Reaching down, she squeezed Bob's crotch, then licked her lips before giving him a boozy kiss.

"I say," Liz teased, clearing the old desk for action, "what's a cowgirl gotta do to get a ride around here?"

The Departed (Liz McGee)

James "Big Jim" McGee, 35 years old, August of Year 1

In their 15 years together they'd never missed a rally. Sturgis is where they'd met, gotten married, and played with fire during their partner-swapping years. Big Jim was against going that first summer of Stinger, but Liz had gotten hooked on the flames.

"But what if it's the last?" she'd pouted, straddling her Harley, giving her red hair a shake.

Jim guessed it would be. "Fuck it, let's ride."

There were worse ways to go, as the past few months had shown. Just post-collapse, side by side on matching bikes, those 1,200 miles had practically flown by, the State Police being elsewhere engaged.

Husband and wife got horny from riding armed. Each night they'd screw in a bedroll beneath the stars, brighter already because of regional brown-outs. This sex by firelight, coyotes howling along, moved James deeply and brought him closer to some God.

Eventually, they ran out of road. Sturgis, that dusty Gomorrah, beckoned, and they roared into town with all the thirsty others. A shotgun blast behind the Knuckle Saloon ended Jim's life. Liz faced down his red-eyed killers, flashed her come-fuck-me grin, then pulled her pistol and gunned down all four as they lunged at her bait.

Samantha Pays a Visit

ANNIE DOYLE STOOD AT HER SINK, washing dinner dishes with hand-pumped water and a miserly ration of soap. The day's heat had lessened, cooler air breezing through her screens; the sun had set behind the island, a crescent moon waxing above. Annie set the last plate to dry and unbound her apron with arthritic hands. Tom had mumbled some words of thanks, then fled to the garage.

Annie's kitchen dimmed with the day. Too hot for a lantern, so she sat in the dark. Not a problem, as after 40 years in this house she knew every inch, could find her way by feel alone. They'd bought it with cash, her Tom then the highliner of the fleet. Doyle's fish had shipped everywhere, feeding the country. Those first nights together as newlyweds...Annie grinned. They hadn't gotten much sleep.

But children never came. She kept their home, kept her man fed, and never complained. He'd had a career on the water, while hers had been this house. The top rooms viewed Lake Michigan, the lighthouse just a short walk away. She'd spent years scanning the horizon for her husband. Tom Doyle always came back, and Annie was always there to greet him.

There were footsteps on the back stairs, followed by the sound of someone knocking. Annie willed herself to stand and shuffled to the porch. Through the screen grinned an unlikely caller.

"Samantha, my goodness, is that you?"

The woman's flyaway white hair was haloed by moonlight.

"Hello Annie, not a bad time?"

"Not at all, not at all. Please come in."

Annie opened the screen door. Samantha stepped inside, cradling a jug. The island's eldest looked around, nodding at her hostess.

"I've brought us some wine, take a glass with me?"

"Of course," Annie answered, surprising herself. "Sit down, I'll get what we need." Turning to open a cupboard, she shook her head: stranger and stranger, this fallen world. "Porch OK? The house is still stifling." Annie grabbed two Mason jars and sat in the other rocker.

"Just fine. My shack is hot too."

Samantha unscrewed the cap, filling both glasses to the brim. The women clinked a toast and shared a quiet sip. Annie scented strawberries, sunlight, and a boggy heat. Something delightful bubbled up inside; nothing could be more normal.

"Taste alright? Home brew, you know. My foster Miin picked the berries."

"Samantha, it's delicious. I've never had anything like it."

The old woman nodded. "It's yours. I've got more. Nothing better after a hot day."

They imbibed again. Summer sounds softened the darkening air: crickets, frogs, and a robin's finale murmured together in the twilight, the big lake exhaling a breath from its cold fathoms. Annie and Samantha sipped in shadow, watching the moon descend, following the sun.

Metal clattered from the garage, along with curses of manly displeasure. The women sighed as Captain Doyle, unseen in his workshop, made himself known.

"Thank you, Annie, for the company, but I'd better see your mister. Enjoy the wine, and when you need more let me know."

Samantha left the jug, gently closing the screen door behind her before navigating through the yard toward the garage.

Annie, lonely again, finished her glass, then wobbled tipsily up the too-familiar stairs. She undressed in the dark, a giggly girl with a wrinkled body. Neglecting her nightgown, she laid herself naked in bed. Her last smile, spinning sleepward, arose from a wish to see Tom's face at Samantha's intrusion.

PART 3:
ELF Country

A Walk in the Woods

MIIN, BLINDFOLDED AND BAREFOOT, read the earth with her toes, brailling the forest biome. A cubic foot of loam contained multitudes: 100 miles of mycelia, the neural network of the woods. A single step crushed a thousand invertebrates. Pulverized by her footprint, they were sipped up by the roots. "Death begets life" was the primary rule of the planet. When Miin stumbled she reached out, finding Elena there. The tall warrior led them well; they'd been on the move since breakfast, miles now between them and the waterfall.

Mukwa had insisted on carrying Miin's pack. He'd strapped it to his chest, wearing his own pack as usual. Awkward, he swore with every stumble; Matador and Tigre guided his gait, defusing el oso with their light-hearted banter. The blind bear, his handlers, and the dark woods formed a medieval tableau.

Keith trudged unguided. Sightless in the present, he minded their future, going over all the details he had to get right. He didn't like being separated from their gear, let alone not knowing where they were. He didn't like Miin's ease with Elena, how her loyalty had blurred after just a few hours.

These *others*, or Naturals, or whatever they were called, were lethal, without many soft edges from what he'd seen. Were the scouts captives, or free to go? Would the three islanders be aided, hindered, or perhaps forced to join?

Two-Crow feared Petoskey's executioners and the hat-wearing hangman who'd led them. Keith remembered the lynchings, the searchlight, and the probing mind who'd pointed it. Capabilities unknown, he considered each danger. Would they bring dogs? Their escape upriver was predictable. That truck and its crew would be searched for; soon the woods would be swarming. Did these Chosen have a plane? He dreaded the mosquito-whine of a Cessna motor.

And what about the variant? Had Mukwa been exposed? What about the corpse-handlers? Samantha hinted that her scouts were shielded from infection by green energy, but what did that mean? And what about these Naturals? And the gunmen? And the Hidden they'd hung?

Worries chafed Keith's mind like the pack chafed his shoulders. There was Doyle, the radio check-in, and all that entailed. Not tonight, or tomorrow, but the night after that; the moon wouldn't wait, never had. Somehow he'd have to return to their gear, make sure the battery was charged, the antenna arranged, the right frequency found, then send a clear transmission. Would Elena let him go? Was she even their leader? What about the canoe cache? If it was discovered, they were all sunk.

Their column of seven had been climbing since the falls. Blindfolded, their noses told them what their eyes could not. The woods were changing, riverine cedars supplanted by nutty oak and upland beech. There was a new feeling of spaciousness around them. Water concentrates life; the river valley had been crowded. Gaining elevation, they felt the ceiling lift. The pace of growth, stately and deliberate, was less frenetic here than in the lowlands of alder and pine.

Elena called a halt, indicating their destination was near. She restored Miin's vision, then moved to unmask Keith. "My apologies, elder, for the rough treatment so far. We're not used to visitors."

Two-Crow eyed Elena, shrugged free of his pack and sight-checked his charges.

Elena signaled the two brothers. Mukwa's bandana was removed, Matador snapping it at the tired bear. Muck dropped both packs and made a bluffing charge at his handler. El Matador stumbled backwards as Tigre laughed, *"Cuidado Miguel! El oso está enojado!"*

Mukwa extended a paw and pulled his captor upright. Elena considered the smiling trio, her canoe partner having sprinted ahead to alert the camp.

Miin stood beneath a hoary oak, her tiny hand upon its bole. A smile lit her face as her gaze climbed to its dappled crown.

"Uncle! This old one says hello!"

She looked at Elena, who nodded.

"Miin, many of these trees are quick-of-speech, quicker than most, especially with those who listen."

Blueberry queried the quercus, patiently awaiting its tight-grained response. Upon receiving it, she looked askance at Elena. "They *want* you here?"

Elena nodded back. "They seem to. And we're glad."

Craning his head upwards, Keith surveyed the old forest. Beeches and oaks comprised the overstory, their limbs forming the ceiling, roots and fungi the floor. There was a holiness to this sanctuary; nothing on their sandy island could compare.

As he looked down, Elena caught his eye. "My partner has gone ahead to prepare for our arrival," she said. "You three are expected, and will be our guests. How long you will remain so is unknown, but for now, try to put aside your concerns. Allow the forest to strengthen you for what lies ahead."

With that, she gave her hand to Miin. Side by side they continued up the path.

Keith re-shouldered his pack, knobby knees creaking at the weight.

Mukwa attempted the same, but his new friends stepped in. Jesting, with many *cabrons, gueys,* and *putas* peppering their speech, the brothers insisted on hauling his load.

The sapiens renewed their march, ant-like, across the forest floor, keenly regarded by the grandfather trees.

Partying with the Elves

MUKWA WAS STUFFED, and might be drunk too. He sprawled inside an oversize tent, left there to recover after the welcome feast. He could hear guitar chords, a drum circle, and singing from a nearby campfire.

He'd lost track of cranky Keith and little sister Miin, but at this moment Muck could care less. His head was spinning: part home brew, part sleep deprivation, part sensory overload from the past few hours. When they'd crossed a stream bordering the encampment earlier that afternoon, a twig-woven sign had proclaimed:

Welcome to ELF Country!

Branching above the message was a stylized tree. His day had only gotten weirder.

Their little group had passed sentry after sentry, each one unseen until choosing to reveal themselves. The apparitions, hooded and armed, unnerved him every time; some popped up from ground blinds, others peeped down from branches. Without an invitation he'd be dead 10 times over, feathered by arrows, skewered by spears.

Only later, sated and supine, did he feel more at ease. It took a whole fried chicken, most of a smoked ham, and many mugs of brew to make him so. Night had fallen when he had; now, he watched firelight dance on the tent walls, his ears soaking up sounds from the surrounding camp.

A woman sang a melody he knew. Others joined in, harmony upon harmony, until the tune was transformed into something new, something beautiful. He let it wash him away, wash him clean.

The song ended, applause rippling through the night. The guitar player started a new chord progression, and the drum circle disbanded. Conversation resumed; Mukwa could hear the soft Spanish of Matador's endless teasing. Fainter still, solemn voices droned in chant, their furtive frequency too low for him to make out any words.

Muck must have dozed after dinner, as he didn't remember being left alone. Now he needed to piss, and anyways, he should check on Miin. He lumbered up from his corner, grabbed his drawing kit, and exited the canvas cave.

He made some sketches as he roamed. The sickle moon gleamed through the trees; a communal campfire was crowded, kids and toddlers underfoot. In the firelight's flicker an interracial couple held hands, an infant, conceived post-collapse, nursing at the mother's breast. There were loners too, solitary types still shadowed by sorrow. A teenage group had their own fire, awkward adolescence alive and well post-apocalypse.

Mukwa floated towards the fringe. Finding privacy, he emptied his bladder and gazed skyward. A night wind swayed the high branches, stars winking in and out like silver fireflies through the leaves. The human music was accompanied, sub-audible, by low-thrumming trees.

Am I drunker than I thought? Or tripping balls?

He shook his shaggy head, but nothing changed. Mukwa headed back towards the fire as sylvan voices fluttered from above. He tried another sketch, though he could barely see the page; silhouetted by moonlight, hammocks hung like webs from the understory. Somewhere up there a mother sang a lullaby for her child, humanity once again arboreal as history rewound.

Stranger and stranger: moonlight, music, and benevolent trees. Mukwa paused, voyeuristic, without judgment, beneath a female's husky voice and another woman's stifled giggle, their shared cocoon trembling above him.

Another headshake. He was here; this was happening. The young man shuffled on.

A large tipi glowed ahead, tall figures guarding the tent flap. Sentries again?

Mukwa stopped short, stretching his ears for sound. He recognized Elena's voice as she asked a question he couldn't quite make out. A male with an easy-going accent answered her.

Several shadows were visible through the canvas; a crooked one looked like Uncle Crow. He tried to identify Keith's leathery scent. Just then, a burst of drumming drowned out the council's debate.

Mukwa's feet eventually returned him to the communal fire. Fresh logs had been added, and children put to bed. Jugs were passed, skunky cannabis wafting on the breeze; percussion performed its ancient function, dancing revelers gleaming as sweat slicked their skin, kindred spirits synchronized, faces filled with mirth.

Matador, the older brother, made room for his muscled friend. "Oso! Hey Mukwa, over here!"

Homebrew was proffered, and a glowing bowl passed around the fire. Muck partook of both. *Why not?*

Then, two girls attached themselves to him, one on each elbow. *What the hell?*

Tigre and Matador, high-humored, couldn't stop laughing. *"Sí, sí, este es un oso valiente,"* they assured their followers.

The girls' eyes were flashing; their tight jeans and toned limbs were blowing Mukwa's mind. His worldview started spinning again, a shit-eating grin plastered on his face.

Have I died and gone to heaven? Sure fucking hope so.

Amidst the musicians, one woman now stood, her dreaded hair interwoven with flowers. She swayed, eyes closed, to a familiar drum solo. Then, loud and clear and fair, she sang an old song, with a message even older.

Don't worry about a thing,
'Cause every little thing is gonna be alright.

Muck looked up at the stars. Apparently, he was lying on his back. He'd never felt more comfortable, as if everything in the world embraced and held him. He palmed the earth, giving the soil a grateful high five. His last thoughts before oblivion: the beauty of the song, its singer, and these summer people.

Singing sweet songs of melodies pure and true,
Saying, "This is my message to you-ou-ou."

Keith Questioned

MIIN LAY CURLED AT ELENA'S FEET, like a tuckered puppy past its bed-time. She'd been covered by a blanket, her occasional snores escaping through the wool; each soft burr raised grins from the otherwise serious folks at council.

Keith was proud of her. Niece Blueberry had made it through the welcome feast, had even stood when nudged and said a few words. Of the three scouts, she was the camp favorite. Rumor of the young tree-talker had spread since her chat with Elder Oak. When had that been? Three days ago now? To Keith, it felt like a lifetime.

He thought back on the feast. Ever-tactical, Two-Crow had done a head count on their hosts, finding close to 200, all applauding and toasting Miin's message. The rough-hewn tables held plenty of food; no problem here with provisions. He'd taken an inventory, noting pork, fish, fowl, forest forage, and garden greens.

These Naturals were industrious people. Hunters, fishers, and green-thumbs, they lived close to the land, preserving its plenty. Of the 200, maybe half of them were fighters. He'd seen no weapons at the feast, but there was a hardness on many faces; punching an arrow through a mammal, whether white-tail or human, exacted a price.

Besides hunters and gardeners, there were many children, including tod-dlers born post-collapse. Elders were present too; grandparents led the feast, feeding and chiding the energetic young ones.

No single leader stood out. A few, including Elena, seemed to speak for the group. Most striking to Keith was their lack of technology. This was an orga-nized, intelligent society, living peacefully together under the trees. No doubt they were capable of creative salvage, of restoration, of a solar grid at least. Why not utilize the fallen world to ease the hardships of the new?

And yet, there was no evidence of repurposing. Instead, every object, from platters to projectiles, seemed selected for simplicity. He'd scoff at their choice if he hadn't seen, firsthand at the bridge and long ago in Vietnam, how effective such simplicity could be. Over-reliance on technology was an evolutionary error these people seemed determined to correct. Decades ago, had the Viet Cong been so different?

After the welcome feast, his two companions found themselves very much in demand. Left alone for an hour, Keith pitched his tent on the outskirts, past tilled clearings and livestock pens. He'd zipped himself inside for some privacy and rested, digesting dinner and data, preparing for the questioning to come.

Miin came to fetch him at twilight. She held his hand as she skipped towards the tipi where the council gathered; he'd never seen her so alive or animated, Blueberry practically bursting with joy and wonder. Orphaned early, had she found family at last? Kindred spirits who shared her green fire?

The council began properly with introductions and an update on current events. Had news reached the scouts' island that the US president was dead? Killed three or four months ago—by a woman, rumor had it. A bloody purge had quickly followed.

Keith shook his head. Not that he was aware of, though he couldn't speak for every islander. Michigan's grid went down last November, leaving island batteries long out of juice. No doubt some Beavers still had radios, but what use were ears if no one was talking?

The camp's adults and elders were curious about their origin story, as well as their plans for the present and near future. The tent's intrigued occupants asked about their un-stung island, and about the scouts' mission to the mainland to keep it so. They shook their heads in disgust at the Chosen and their hanging of Petoskey's Hidden. Keith got the sense that they'd skirmished with these scavengers before, and that last night's bridge ambush may have broken a cease-fire of sorts. Also, many of their questions focused on Samantha, her capabilities, and the spirit-walk they'd shared at Cranberry Bog.

Miin, yawning, did less and less talking. Finally, a tedious welcome speech from a tree-paced elder pulled her lids down for good. This drew smiles from the gathered company, but their expressions again turned serious as Keith stepped forward to answer further questions.

Some council members had been to Beaver Island as tourists; some even knew Samantha, or had heard of her anyway. Was Keith somehow related?

Two-Crow had nodded. "Yes," he'd said, "but only distantly."

What about Miinan, and Mukwa? They'd both called him uncle.

"No. Miin and Mukwa are fosters of Sam."

They wanted details about his combat service, his occupational specialty. They asked about his health and infection history. Had he fathered any children?

Conversation curdled as Keith held his tongue, especially when pressed about Beaver Island's defenses.

During interrogation, he tracked the questioners. Elena went first, her sharp ears alert for military applications. She'd put away her combat garb, her headband and parka; instead she wore jeans and a college sweatshirt with a track and field logo. Her hair, braids undone after battle, had been brushed out. Her questions were tactical: how many Chosen had they seen in Petoskey? How many trucks? What weaponry? How many Candidates had they taken? How many Hidden had they hung?

Next up was a professor type, with a command about him that bespoke intelligence and virility. His questions concerned contagion, their recent contact with Chosen, any transmission that might have occurred there or elsewhere. Mukwa, face-to-face, had been exposed and was under observation. And how was Keith feeling? Could his vitals be taken? Perhaps a blood sample, too?

Crow perched darkly, stony with silence.

Two farmers, middle-aged and holding rough hands gently, queried next; Keith caught a glint of golden bands, guessing the two men were newlyweds. The old world was gone, and who was he to judge? Their questions concerned island crops, seed banks, harvest yield, and soils. Keith concealed what he could, knowing the island struggled to feed its own.

Then a final elder stood, a Mukwa-sized Native, his long ponytail streaked with gray. The man wore a faded black cap displaying his military decorations: Vietnam, Purple Heart, and Combat Action Ribbon.

"Bozhoo," he greeted his guest. *"Mino dibikad."*

Keith repeated the welcome, locking eyes with the old warrior.

"Diving-Duck *ndizhinikaaz. Gdi-anishnaabem-na?"*

Diving-Duck spoke slowly. Could Keith understand?

Keith gave his reply haltingly: *"Enh, ndi anishnaben bangii eta go."*

Duck grinned. "Keith Two-Crow, you and your companions have shown bravery. You have killed two of those who would surely kill us. You have our thanks, our respect. What's ours is yours."

With Diving-Duck's words, the mood shifted. Interrogatory no longer, defenses were lowered. Music and laughter from the nearby campfire now permeated their tent.

One young man at the assembly wore a Baja hoodie, his red beard strung with beads. Acting as shaman, he bundled some sage, ignited it, and smudged the gathering with smoke. Its spice cleansed their bodies, their minds. The seated council, more light-hearted and generous, relaxed into postures less formal.

Red Beard produced pipe and pouch from a satchel at his side; he lifted both in the air in benediction. Pinching herbs from the pouch, he sifted them upon the flames. Spirits of tobacco and red willow made themselves known.

Next, he loaded the pipe, tamped it with his thumb, and lit the bowl with a fiery twig. He filled his mouth with smoke, held it, and then puffed out a thin stream. With his left hand he passed the pipe to Elena, and she to her partner Diana. Then Professor, the Farmers, Diving-Duck, and others. Finally, Grace, a grandma-type, blew clouds before passing it to Keith with a crinkled smile.

The pipe was curiously carved, oak leaves and acorns twining about the stem. The ember-bright bowl had been shaped from soft stone. Keith received the pipe, imbibed, exhaled, and passed it back to Red Beard.

The old crow closed his eyes. He could feel his guard dropping, his trust increasing. Drums and singing mingled with the curling smoke. He sensed Miin where she slept, and could feel Mukwa prowling the night. Good intentions thickened the air.

Keith breathed in, breathed out, as others did the same. One by one, he released his many worries; they escaped through the vent above. The moon was setting, stars darting in the void like errant sparks from some galactic fire.

The Departed (Elena)
Peter Vandenberg, 60 years old, April of Year 1, father

Father and daughter had grown closer since Ellen's mother was taken, too soon, by cancer. Tall and fair like many west Michigan Dutch, their best times together were always in the woods. "If you ain't Dutch, you ain't much," was her father's favorite saying.

Peter winked at his grown daughter as they left the church for a turkey hunt. The Sunday service had been powerful; they'd prayed for pandemic-stricken places they'd foolishly thought were far, far away.

The deacon had sung with gusto, recently returned from an LA conference. *"We gather together to ask the Lord's blessing,"* he'd then intoned, sounding a bit out of breath.

Their hearts filled with compassion as their lungs filled with the deacon's virus. An hour later, father and daughter, camouflaged, sat in their ground blind, tempting a turkey into range. Ellen drew a bead on the gobbler's red head, her father box-calling to shorten the distance. Just before she could pull the trigger, her dad began to wheeze. Alerted, their turkey disappeared with rapid dinosaur strides. Ellen turned towards her father, who looked blue in the face, his asthmatic alveoli having swollen shut.

His inhaler was back in the truck. Ellen, a trained first responder, burst from the blind. The college track star ran a mile and back, untimed but breaking her personal record. When she returned, out of breath, her dad had breathed his last. A flock of curious turkeys surrounded the suddenly silent blind.

Earth Liberation Front

BLUEBERRY WOKE UP ALONE in the big tent, sunrise heating the tipi, stirring her from sleep's dream to a waking one. A rooster crowed, and she could hear human voices, still hushed and subdued from last night's celebration. The council fire was out, her pack tucked away against the canvas wall. The girl rubbed sand from her eyes and grinned: it was real. It was all real.

She quickly changed into garments less dirty, deciding against shoes, then pushed through the flap and into the day. First to greet her were the trees. Up and up her gaze climbed, till she beheld them entirely.

Benevolent, they nodded.

Giddy, she bowed.

Hammocks hung from their lower branches; some cocoons were empty, some still sagging with sleepers. Children descended on knotted ropes, snoring parents abandoned above. Cookfires were tended by early risers, who stirred pots and boiled tea. Photons filtered through the canopy, tinted green by chlorophyll and freighted with oxygen. Miin filled her lungs. Her empty stomach growled, unsatisfied by air and light alone.

She spied a row of outhouses, a crescent moon carved on each door. She waited her turn, and was pleasantly surprised. Ample screens for fresh air and a bucket of lye did much to mitigate the odors of human waste. Back in the open, Miin, still smiling, looked around.

Elena's tall partner approached. War gear put away, she wore a flower-patterned dress, her darker skin bathed in sunlight. She smiled at Miin and offered her calloused hand.

"Good morning, Miss Blueberry. Sorry this took so long, but you can call me Diana."

Miin shot her an arch look. She'd first seen "Diana," hooded, with a quiver of arrows, on the Bear River Bridge in moonlight.

The woman rolled her eyes. "I know, goddess of the hunt, right? When someone joins ELF they take a new name. I'm a sucker for mythology; Artemis was my first choice, but Elena talked me down to Diana."

"ELF?"

"Earth. Liberation. Front." Diana gave each word its due weight. "An eco-terrorist group from the 90s. Before your time, young lady. We've resurrected the name."

Miin tried each word, lingering on *liberation*. She liked it. "What exactly are you liberating Earth from?"

Diana stopped their walk and looked at Miin, dead serious.

"From us, of course. From humans."

As the encampment stirred, Diana showed Miin around, introducing her to many and answering her questions. Diana, from a maritime family, hailed from Canada, and had been a deck officer on an ore freighter until the variant forced her crew to anchor off Cheboygan. A step ahead of Stinger, she'd jumped ship, survived the chaos of collapse, and eventually got recruited by Elena's cadre.

Taking the tour, Miin, duly diligent, asked about farming, livestock, the school, and the drying racks of meat and fish. A man in shorts with a handlebar mustache was brewing ELF Ale, adding flowers and fungi for a trippy effect. Diana was detailing creek nets and weirs when Miin's stomach, exasperated, demanded breakfast. Diana, startled, gave Miin a look, then laughed. "Of course! My goodness girl, let's eat."

They headed towards the cookfire where Diana's squad took their meals. The huntress pointed out that though ELF strove for equality, differentiation still existed. Farmers, Sentinels, teachers, nurses, and builders were some of the subgroups of this sylvan society.

Diana explained that most elves—Miin grinned at the term—considered it impolite to dwell on their former lives. Even so, the racial and class distinctions of the pre-pandemic era were hard to erase. Diana smiled at a gaggle of children as they ran playfully past. "It might take a generation or two."

The cooking spot was crowded. A shift change had occurred, and a dozen Sentinels, still clad in military parkas, were gathered around, hungry from night duty. Spears and bows had been racked, but many wore blades on their belts. Hoods down, their faces evinced a hardness, a horror, that marked them as life-takers; murderers, regardless of the cause.

Diana exchanged greetings, then guided Miin through the serving line. Meal trays full, they sat at the crowded table. Fully gathered, the hungry group paused, putting down their forks to join hands.

Diana led them, saying into the silence, "We are thankful today for many things. For the labor that produced this food. For the shelter and bounty of the forest," here Miin bowed towards the listening trees, "and for our guests. May they find what they seek, and may their days with us be peaceful."

Hands were squeezed and released, some of those gathered giving voice to amens. The company then devoted itself to the eggs, pork, and potatoes steaming on their trays. A clatter of cutlery and the leafy breeze were the only sounds as they shoveled empty bellies full.

Once hunger had been blunted, conversation picked up, Miin overhearing much at the table.

Some discussed the nocturnal critters and noises heard on their night watch. Some gossiped about the bonfire and the music they'd missed, a few curious looks were cast Miin's way. Diana had introduced her, but Blueberry got the feeling she was already known.

The woman next to Miin had brown hair, tightly braided, and wore a headband. Turning, she queried the newcomer: "Is it true about your island?"

"Is *what* true?" Miin, channeling Keith, was cautious in response.

"That it's untouched. No Stinger, no Chosen. It's protected."

Miin forked her fresh eggs and considered. "Yes, we've been lucky. So far, anyway."

She chewed slowly, remembering that everyone here, even if smiling, had been through a holocaust. Mass graves, funeral pyres, friend circles destroyed, futures upended—these mainlanders, without the moat of Lake Michigan for protection, had witnessed carnage Miin couldn't comprehend.

"I'm Miinan; it means Blueberry." She offered her small hand.

"Call me Squirrel," the hardened athlete answered, shaking with a strong grip. "We were briefed about the bridge ambush. Sounds like some serious shit."

Miin, post-trauma, remembered the lightning of muzzle flashes, gunfire like thunder, and corpses cooling, exothermic, in the moonlight. Some of this stress must have shown, because Squirrel squeezed Miin's shoulder. "Sorry," she said, and their eyes met. "I haven't faced Chosen yet. Just curious, I guess, and nervous as hell."

"That's OK," said Miin, "I hope you never will. Do you think they'll find you here?"

Diana had cleared away her tray and was conversing over near the gear tent. Miin felt unsure what exactly she could, or should, ask.

"Spreaders haven't found us yet. Gas guzzlers don't stray far from the roads. Our place here, thank the trees, is about as far from the grid as you can get."

"I hope we haven't put you in danger."

Squirrel flashed an angry look. "Fuck 'em," she said, her tone growing fierce. "Did you know they keep slaves? Call 'em Candidates, but they're slave labor. Either Stinger kills 'em or they're worked to death. If by some miracle they survive and become Chosen, they join right in with the same evil shit."

Squirrel looked away from Miin, staring into the past. "Assholes like that raped my sister, you know," she whispered.

Miin wished she could shrink, disappear.

"She was sick, but that didn't stop them. I was hiding in the house, healthy. I heard everything."

Other Sentinels attended, grim-faced. An older, fatherly man chimed in, his eyes sunken in deep hollows; the parka he wore was heavily frayed and patched. "Listen, it's Miin, right?"

She nodded, all ears.

"During collapse, most died quickly, stung by the variant. Obviously, we survived," he said, looking to his comrades. "But surviving, we witnessed some god-awful shit. These Chosen now, they're a type. They fit a profile: violent, selfish, and sexual. Basically sociopaths the old system kept in check. When shit fell apart, their kind thrived. Virus couldn't touch 'em, and in the chaos they ran wild, doing terrible things. Things I never thought I'd see." He paused, then shuddered. "What happened to my kids...I can't even say it."

The man trailed off and cleared his tray. The table emptied out, leaving Miin and Squirrel alone.

"We don't talk much about the past. I'm sorry."

Miin bowed her head and whispered, "I'm sorry, too."

The Departed (Squirrel)

Jessica Bissell, 18 years old, July of Year 1, Squirrel's sister

Ever-outgoing, Jess broke trail for her younger sister Sarah, who was awkward and shy. The high school had Jessica's name all over it: homecoming queen, volleyball banners, "Most likely to succeed" in the yearbook.

On weekends Jess partied, inviting her sister along. Blushing, Sarah would shake her off, then mope around the woods constructing fairy houses. When their district went virtual, wrecking Jess's senior year, shy Sarah breathed a secret sigh of relief. But quarantine couldn't cramp Jess's style; college-bound, carpe diem, she seized the day, till the day she was stung.

Their county collapsed quickly. Old scores were settled as laws were ignored; Confederate flags multiplied, rebel trucks prowling in packs. It started with wealth redistribution, the have-nots deciding to help themselves. Once doors were kicked in and windows broken, the good old boys turned out to be not so good.

Mom was already in the morgue and Dad stalked the hospital, seeking care for their elder daughter. Jess fought the fever alone in her room, messaging with friends as her temperature climbed. Sarah, uninfected, heard truck doors slam outside, followed by the sound of voices.

The deadbolt didn't hold. There were boots on the stairs, and boozy laughter; it was a group of men, fathers of football players who'd watched Jess flirt with their sons. Sarah hid while Jess screamed. When it was over, Jess's livestream ended: zero views, zero comments, zero likes.

A Fishing Idyll

KEITH HAD SLEPT FOR A FEW HOURS; music and pipe smoke flavored his dreams. Now he heard movement outside his tent and snapped awake, sitting up in the dark.

"Two-Crow, you in there?" The whispering voice was Diving-Duck's, the Nam vet from last night's council. Keith grunted in reply, unzipped the tent and peered out, the Ojibwe elder looming large in the gloaming. Duck held two rods, while a satchel and creel hung from his shoulder.

"Come on. Let's go fishing."

Duck led them down the feeder stream as it fell away from camp, tumbling through the last good country. The forest stirred, bats darting home, pinging the predawn air for a final meal. Birds were waking, their first claims of territory as strident as yesterday's last. A morning wind made hushing sounds through the canopy, towering Old Ones exchanging treeish dreams at star-fade.

The two veterans paused where the stream divided, light enough now for them to read each other's faces. Diving-Duck handed Two-Crow a rod, nodding at the divergent creeks. "You choose."

Keith looked them over, pointing his rod down the right-hand fork. "Easiest choice I've made in a while."

"Lot of weight on your shoulders, Two-Crow. Good to set it aside when you can."

Duck dove into his satchel, handing Keith a box of tiny hooks and spinners. He then pulled out a red plastic thermos.

"Figured you for a coffee man." He handed it over; Keith could have hugged him. With that the men separated, soon passing out of each other's sight.

Old Ones observed the two youngsters angling for food at their roots. Life required death, sapiens and bats only different in degree. Half a millennium these Ancients had stood, rooted in place; humans were only brief visitors, remoteness and something else keeping busy Man at the fringe.

Huron had hunted here, then Sauk and Fox; next came Ojibwe, followed by French fur trappers and surveyors, tool users who rarely looked up. The trees, all-perceiving, abided each in turn.

Keith waded through centuries as he stalked from pool to pool. There was awareness here, a sentience stronger than his own. The weary man, soothed by his shrinking significance, found relief in dissolution.

This morning, thanks to Duck, Keith's to-do list was short. One word summed it up: trout. *Maazhamegos*, orange-finned and blue-speckled, had spawned here since glacial retreat, their first habitat was meltwater from shrinking ice. Trout were here before the first acorn, before rooted life sipped from the stream. The spring-fed pools eyed by Keith had been fished by paleo humans casting hooks of bone.

There was a holiness to such places, a compression of chronology. The centuries here were stacked vertically, undiluted by intruding timelines. Keith waded towards a bend in the river, felt its pull as forces aligned: current, cover, food. He intuited the presence of fish, sensed their watchfulness, their familiarity with local forage. This place had *the feel*.

No need to rush; no one's life was on the line, except maybe the trout's. Keith savored the simplicity of the morning's op. He kept his distance, careful with his profile, cautious of his footfalls. He studied the layout, rehearsed his presentation, then rolled over a mossy log, baited a worm, and waited.

The sun brushed the horizon with light, painting the forest gold. A leafy gap opened a window onto the blue sky, revealing a raptor circling at an impossibly high altitude. The moment had come. Keith balanced the rod, freed some line, calculated current, and presented his offering. The hungry creek accepted, the line running through his gnarled fingers; his tribute tumbled through space and time towards King Trout, the thousandth of his name.

A second before the strike Keith knew it would happen. The rod came alive as he met the muscled fish, felt the ferocity of its refusal. He'd hooked the whole watershed, and the primeval forest too! The rod bent double before a speckled bomb exploded upwards, charging from the depths. It was all too much—and then, suddenly, not nearly enough.

The fish spit the hook.

Two-Crow, nerves taut, reeled in the slack. Uncaught, the trout resumed its liquid vigil; Keith bowed and backed away from the bend, a supplicant. There were plenty of other places to fish in the creek.

An hour later, Keith rendezvoused back at the fork. His six trout, neatly slit, lay on an altar of fresh ferns. Stretched out on a sun-drenched boulder, he basked like a reptile while awaiting Duck's return, minding the moment and the passage of clouds.

Overlarge, Duck returned, walking nimbly along the bank. His ancestors had done the same; their spirits still lingered. Three hundred generations since the first fishermen angled this stream. That prehistoric family, anything but primitive, had gathered calories at the glacier's edge, coldly shadowed by mile-high ice.

Reunited, the fast friends admired their wild harvest, each attending the other's tall tales. Reclining on moss, Keith pulled out pouch and papers and rolled them each a cig. He sifted a pinch for the past, then they smoked together, blowing spirit-clouds towards the canopy.

"Could get used to this."

Duck looked him over, squinting a smoke-veiled eye. "I bet you could."

"Didn't know there was country like this, not around here."

They both dragged, exhaling at the trees. Fragrant smoke curled through the branches.

"Way things are going, there'll be a lot more like it."

Their boots and jeans dried in a patch of sunlight. They observed the forest observing them.

"Duck, I'll need your help with the council later today," Two-Crow ventured at length. All good things come to an end: cigarettes, idylls, and perfect mornings too. "Tomorrow night the moon will reach first quarter. There's something I must do, a promise I must keep."

The Departed (Diving-Duck)

Amber "Ducky" Lafranier, 70 years old, July of Year 1,
wife, mother, grandmother

She hadn't missed a powwow in 50 years.

Amber adjusted the beads on her deer-hide dress, preparing for the Buck-skin Dance she'd performed all her life. Her husband, her kids, and her grand-kids had gathered anyway, despite the powwow being canceled by their tribe due to Covee. She closed her eyes, grateful.

Their tents and trailers mushroomed across the field. She could hear cousins playing, backed by the booming laugh of their bear-sized grandfather. Last to arrive had been her youngest. A soldier in the US Army, like his father; he'd gotten leave and rented an RV. He and his family drove nonstop from Texas, shedding virus all the way, arriving at night with honking horns and flickering high beams. By the time breakfast was over, the whole family was infected.

Amber heard the first cough as she stepped into the arena. A prize-winning dancer, she knew the steps, but her feet balked at the Buckskin. The morning sun shrouded over as Diving-Duck watched his wife sway; he'd only seen the Ghost Dance once, in 1973 at Wounded Knee. Amber danced it now for her finale, cytokine storm clouds gathering.

Wovoka, the Paiute religious leader, in 1889 prophesied: "When your friends die, you must not cry.... The dead are still alive.... When the time comes there will be no more sickness and everyone will be young again."

"The best lack all conviction"-Yeats

THE AMERICAN SYSTEM OF GOVERNMENT, of checks and balances, of civilian control of the military, proved shockingly easy to pervert. President Lincoln, our Abrahamic father, began it; to preserve our imperfect union, too much power was ceded to the executive branch. Decades of decent presidents papered over this design flaw, but it was only a matter of time before we elected a fool. Once the jester was enthroned, there was nothing to be done.

King George III had bid his colony good riddance, stating, "Knavery seems to be so much a striking feature of its inhabitants that it may not in the end be an evil that they will become aliens to this kingdom."

The biggest mistake I made was allowing the Army to relocate the variant from our Michigan lab to USAMRIID's Fort Detrick. It's not like I didn't protest, but lacking a paramilitary force I couldn't stop them. Learning my lesson from this one-sided skirmish, I got to work.

The nuclear arsenal of our nation features many fail-safes within the command and control structure to prevent the type of rogue launch that occurred with Stinger. The infrastructure of biodefense had no such speed bumps; in the end all it took was a knave president, a stooge colonel, and some special operators. Facing grim polling and a looming electoral embarrassment, POTUS opened Pandora's Box, loosing the four horsemen.

"I looked, and there before me was a pale horse! Its rider was named Death, and Hades was following close behind him. They were given power over a fourth of the earth to kill by sword, famine and plague...."-Revelation 6:7-9 (NIV)

Once Stinger was stolen I knew what would happen, and worked fiendishly to develop countermeasures. I maintained eyes and ears in all the likely places; again, a Chinese wet market became the likely culprit. Again, the Western world cringed at the PRC's palate for *yewei*, or wild game, including bats, pangolins, and civets.

I had time. Not enough, but I put my house in order. POTUS tweeted, fear-mongered, contested the election, and things fell apart.

Mikey Strikes Again

LIZ'S CONVOY DEPARTED CHARLEVOIX, trucking Cowboy's meager tribute to their bosses downstate; her semi trumpeted a horn blast, and they were gone. Bob's slouching guards re-blocked the road, then disappeared in search of shade.

Bob Campbell stood in the sunlight and stretched sore muscles. Last night had been a blur of red hair, milky skin, and sweaty sheets. He'd been impressed with his performance, and Liz had, too. "Ol' Cowboy's still got some gas in the tank!"

Backtracking to his office, Bob witnessed the drawbridge descending. Gears clanked as Mikey's crew cheered: *the fucker did it.* Cowboy liked the castle moat vibe of the bridge. If a motorized horde approached, at least from the north, raising the roadway would essentially shield the defenders.

He gagged his way past the reeking shitters. He should have ordered the Candidates to dump them, but he'd sent them all south instead. Bob checked the inner harbor, giving the ferry a long look. Liz might be onto something there.

More immediate, though, and totally un-fucking-acceptable, was the continued absence of Heavy, his crew, and the truck. They'd been gone 48 hours, which was 24 past due. Liz's gymnastics, his shitty numbers, the bridge...too many things had gotten in the way. It was time for him to handle this.

An hour later, he rolled north across the bridge. Word that "Boss is going out" had spread through the compound, meaning he had his pick of bored volunteers. Sitting shotgun, tongue lolling, Mikey enjoyed a road trip as reward for his drawbridge diligence. Others had grumbled as Cowboy saddled up and spurred past the roadblocks. With no women penned, the garrison, unsupervised, would head towards the booze.

Cowboy tried not to think about it. He was free, for a few hours anyway.

The truck's windows were down; Bob had a dip tucked in. Mikey, not a talker, was content to watch the country go by. They enjoyed a moment, temporarily forgetting that the whole world was gone. A map lay open on Mikey's knee, allowing Cowboy to retrace Heavy's orders: first the bridge, then River Road, then look for campsites. After that, who fucking knew?

Bob considered what Heavy might be up to. Had he jumped ship, booked it down south? Doubtful, as the bosses there would ask questions, check with Cowboy, and then shoot Heavy's ass for desertion. He couldn't see him going native either; there was no one up here for him to join, plus he was a lazy shit. Heavy knew he had it made in Cowboy's outfit.

With these off the table, the remaining options worsened. Had their truck broken down? Then why no radio call for a ride? Had they found some Hidden to fuck with? More likely, but insubordinate as hell, meaning Cowboy would have to thrash both Heavy and crew. Worst case: they'd run into trouble and gotten themselves killed or captured. This scenario grabbed his guts. Bob fought nausea, spitting tobacco juice out his window.

He had no love for Heavy, and no like either. Bob was aware of local resistance—the symbolic tree, the runic R—Cowboy knew he'd let things slide, knew his sad sack routine had softened him. In this shape, his sorry outfit wouldn't last a week downstate. Any Old Law posse would hang them high, or they'd be captured by rivals, maybe XCons. They'd be beaten and branded, then sold to the highest bidder. Chosen, seemingly immune, were in high demand.

Accumulating clouds of what-ifs now shadowed the morning sun, the woods and fields along M-31 ominous with gloom. Campbell needed a vacation. He'd book a first-class flight, pay extra for all-inclusive, go to clubs, fuck all night, nap all day, rinse himself and repeat.

Bob sighed. *Who am I kidding? Those good old days are long gone.*

"River Road coming up, boss."

Cowboy slowed down at the outskirts of Petoskey. He wanted to avoid downtown and its nooses, so he took a right instead, following the potholed road upriver. Thirty minutes later, they reached the turnoff for Bear River Bridge. Bob stopped the truck and killed the motor, then sat with Mikey for a minute, listening to the engine tick as it cooled. Through the trees they could hear the rush of river.

Have to stay sharp, Bob. You can't afford to fuck this up.

He keyed the radio, trying Heavy again, but received only static.

Well shit, here we go.

Bob called back to the compound. Someone sober picked up, and Cowboy reported their position before exiting the truck with his fixer. Squatting over the crumbling asphalt, he noticed a problem at once: the wear marks in no way matched the road they'd approached on. The track had been scrubbed, and recently. *Shit.*

"Mikey, grab your shotgun. And peel your fucking eyes."

Stooping to study the ground, Cowboy walked towards the bridge. Bear River gushed by, cold and clear, water darkening beneath the concrete trusses. The place felt totally empty. He tried to picture how Heavy would have set up.

Bob found the spot where he would have parked, concealed, with a clear field of fire. Heavy would post another shooter across the bridge. Tyrone or Tyler, or both?

Two nights ago the moon had been bright, providing good visibility. So, they'd gotten set up, they'd been waiting, then something happened. But what?

Cowboy felt the familiar ache as a migraine thundered nearer. Something here just wasn't right. He linked his unease to the hangings, to the breakwater, to the spotlighted bird. *Trouble.*

Bob combed the scene with Mikey: no shell casings, no trash, no clues whatsoever. *So a truck and four men just fucking vanished.* "Check the far side, will ya?" he called to Mikey.

Nodding, Mikey bulked his way across the bridge.

Cowboy stood on the span. Looking down, he saw fish swimming in the current. His thoughts wandered till something glinted in the sun, catching his eye. There it was: a shiny spot on the guard rail, a bullet-sized ding through the rust.

"Boss, you'd better come see this." Mikey's voice sounded unsteady as it emerged from some brush on the far side.

Lightning flashed through Cowboy's skull. *Damn.*

Bob walked slowly across the bridge, looking for clues. Below, washed up on the alder-choked bank, lay several large chunks of colored plastic. Pieces from a boat? Hard to say how long they'd been there.

He joined Mikey, looking where the man's shaky finger pointed. He saw green bushes splattered with blood; chest-high, a gout had spurted. Bob rubbed the stain, smelled his fingers. *Fuck.*

His fixer bent near a log, pinched something from the ground, and sniffed. "It's a joint, boss. Ain't been here long."

A vision of the two brothers from Flint, high on ambush duty, forked through Cowboy's brain. One of them got shot, or stabbed? Or was the blood from their victim?

Nope. Cowboy knew it was theirs, knew they were dead, knew he was fucked. He was typecast and just playing a part. Was this real life, his actual life? *What a fucking joke.* But the show must go on, so he delivered his line.

"Alright, Mikey, so where's the damn truck?"

Mikey the mechanic wasn't a typical Chosen. He wasn't an asshole, or a sex fiend, or a drunk; he'd built his own business, servicing trucks and construction equipment. Like Bob, he'd had a nice family, a house in the burbs. When the variant arrived and his family got stung, Mike never even caught a cold. When the turf wars kicked off and teams were picked, he got immediately drafted by Chosen, as not many Candidates came with his skill set. Cowboy had recognized his talent and kept the man close.

Mikey studied the track. "Back the way it came, I guess? It didn't cross to this side, and it wasn't on the road we drove up either."

They stood on the span, Cowboy showing him the bullet-ding. Mikey shook his head, looking down at the plastic wreckage. "Well, boss, I think our bushwhackers got themselves whacked."

Fuck.

"And the truck, Mike? Driven away? Stashed? And our boys? Their bodies? Dead? Captured? Run off?"

Bob hated all these options, hated voicing them aloud. He was glad it was only the two of them; they still had some time to work it out.

Mikey shook his head. "I don't know, boss. But it ain't good."

Bob pointed back to where they'd parked. "Let's keep going up the road, follow the brush marks."

Thirty minutes later and they made out vultures, six bald birds spiraling high above a fleshy feast. Cowboy slowed the truck, noticing where some roadside brush had been recently cut; Mikey saw it too. They dismounted, removed a screen of saplings from an overgrown turnoff, and followed the track to a gulch.

Drawing nearer, they smelled burnt rubber, motor fluid, and overripe death. Parting the undergrowth and peering down, Bob let loose a string of curses. There, at the bottom, lay Heavy's truck, burned out and abandoned. A wake of birds worried the bodies.

God fucking damn it.

They didn't say much on the drive back to base, both men rearranging their realities. Mikey had stayed above while Cowboy, harassed by thorns, had done his duty, identifying bodies and sweeping for clues.

The guards at the drawbridge passed them through, Cowboy flinching at their accusatory eyes. Mikey wheezed upstairs, and they sat together at Bob's desk, a map open between them. Cowboy took off his hat, self-prescribing pills and booze from his drawer.

"Drink?"

His fixer declined. *Dude looks seasick.*

Bob shrugged and continued his postmortem. "All four were down there, cooked pretty good. I didn't look too hard."

Mikey trembled over the map.

"Couple things stood out," Cowboy said, gulping a drink of whiskey before he continued. "First, their weapons were still there. What kind of half-assed resistance leaves behind a mounted machine gun?"

Mikey blinked, all ears.

"Second, their CB radio was missing. The antenna too."

Cowboy slugged the rest of his whiskey, feeling the alcohol like a punch in the gut.

Mikey was thinking. "Another thing, boss. There were no tracks, no other vehicles. Whoever did this was on foot."

"Or boats. Remember the scraps?"

Both men perspired as an electric fan pushed hot air around. Summer shone outside the window; Lake Michigan sparkled, oblivious and blue.

"Put it together for me, Mikey. What've we got?"

His man attempted to oblige. "We know they're not far. Unless they had a vehicle stashed somewhere else?" He finger-compassed the burnt truck and bodies, establishing a radius.

"We know they want to either broadcast or receive with that radio they stole. And they must be well-armed already, why else leave the SAW? And they're crafty as hell. A quick look, and we wouldn't have found shit. It'd be like those Raiders and their truck just up and vanished."

Cowboy chewed it over, looking first at the map, then his man. "So now what?"

Mikey was smiling; he'd pieced together the puzzle. "You know I worked with truckers, right?"

Cowboy nodded and raised his eyebrows, encouraging him to continue.

"Well, sometimes an asshole would shit-talk on their channel. If the FCC didn't act, drivers would handle it on their own."

He looked at Cowboy. The boss was listening intently.

"Truckers called it a Fox-Hunt. They'd use radios, triangulate the signal; it never took them very long to find the guilty rabbit. Then they'd all converge, spot an antenna, and kick the shit out of the slob. Problem solved."

Cowboy flushed and sat erect. "Tell me, Mr. Mechanic, do you have what we need to set this up?"

Mike mentally inventoried his motor pool: CBs, scanner, antennas, and fuel.

He nodded several chins at his boss.

Cowboy flashed the day's first smile. *Fucking Mikey strikes again.*

Cards on the Table

DAYLIGHT DIMMED AS THE MOON BRIGHTENED, waxing towards first quarter. Mukwa cleared his dinner tray; he'd loaded it up twice. Sated, he stacked it for the kids on KP. After spending a day with these "elves," he was impressed. They had their shit dialed, from food, to security, to schooling, to clean up. He knew he was witnessing a well-run show.

Every muscle was sore, half from his hangover, half from training. He'd spent the day with Matador's squad, roused from the ground at a godawful hour. Someone had covered him with a blanket the night before, and he may or may not have passed out by the fire. Predawn, he'd been chided to his feet by the brothers, both dressed for PT, grinning down at el oso, their slumbering bear.

Before he'd rubbed the sleep from his eyes he found himself running through the forest, chasing the disappearing squad as they circuit trained. He did his best to keep up with the six Sentinels, always ahead, as they prepared for their day with sprints, rope climbing, and calisthenics. He fought for breath, his stomach flip-flopping, dangerously close to a protest puke. And that was just their warm up.

The Sentinel squads of the ELF followed a three-day rotation. First, a duty day where they served as lookouts, road watchers, and scouts. Then a training day, followed by a day of rest, when they helped around camp before cycling again.

He'd lagged on the run, and projectile practice wasn't much better. The three males and three females of the squad were freakish in their ability to put spears and arrows through all kinds of targets, moving or stationary. The craziest shit was when one of the women—Nighthawk, she called herself—ran through the trees at full speed while nocking and firing arrows through the fucking center of Frisbees flung by her cheering squadmates.

Then it was Mukwa's turn. Stationary, taking careful aim at a straw man 20 yards away, he only stuck one out of three arrows, and that one, naturally, right through the scarecrow's crotch. Of course the squad cracked up.

"Careful, *compañero!*" Matador said with a laugh. "I think this guy likes you!"

More grins and elbows from the Sentinels. Always a laugh with el oso around.

With hand-to-hand next on the agenda, Mukwa got serious. Time for him to shine. They paired off to spar, and he picked out their biggest dude, a country boy named Bull, built like a damn bulldozer.

The younger brother, Tigre, laughed. "Bear against Bull, eh? *El oso tiene hambre del toro!*"

But Matador shook his head and called instead for *el gorrión, t*he squad's smallest member. The young woman, war-named Sparrow, pushed away the grinning Bull and squared up, all business, in front of Mukwa. She looked like one of those tiny gymnasts, or the flying cheerleader type that got tossed in the air after touchdowns.

Mukwa held his stance. *Seriously?*

He looked at Matador. A half-second later and he couldn't fucking breathe, eyes wide, mouth sucking wind, his diaphragm in spasm. Sparrow aimed another kick, swept his thick leg, and he was on the ground.

Oh HELL no!

Gasping, he got on all fours, then reared up on hind legs. She moved one way, he went to block. She pivoted, spun, and swung a roundhouse punch right into his face.

Mukwa's nose crunched. He tasted blood, saw stars, and sat down, *thump.*

The squad exploded, high-fiving their Sparrow.

Bull offered him a calloused hand. "She did the same thing to me," he said, helping Mukwa up. "Doesn't seem fair, does it?"

Mukwa, unsteady, pawed at his numb face, sniffing back a nosebleed. He wanted to cry, he really did. Sparrow approached, and he crouched warily, prepared for pain. She smiled, offering a handshake. Mukwa growled and didn't budge. *No fucking way.*

Laughing, Matador came over. Wiping away a tear, he grabbed both their hands and made them shake. The rest of Muck's day was pretty much the same.

Dinner was over and night had fallen, kernels of stars popping above in bright bunches. Families ascended the trees, tucking kids into hammocks. Meanwhile, a council gathered in the big tent, a slow drum summoning the elves.

Two-Crow entered to Miin's beaming smile; she stood beside Sentinel Diana. Keith nodded to Mukwa, who looked black-eyed and bothered. Elena was there, along with the professor-type, the farmer couple, Red Beard, Grandma Grace, his friend Diving-Duck, and others.

The mood in the tent was serious. A small fire burned, venting smoke through an open flap. Red Beard circled, smudging the participants with sage. Arranging himself on the ground, Keith breathed in the cleansing spice, preparing his arguments.

The professor-type started things off. "First, my name is Daniel Chow. I'm a doctor, a Wolverine, U of M Medical School. Let me say how honored we have been to host you three as guests."

He looked from Keith to Mukwa to Miin, giving a slight bow to each.

"It has not been our custom, this past year or so, to take in outsiders. I am glad we have done so."

Pausing, Dr. Chow glanced at Diana, Duck, and Matador. Each nodded in turn.

"I have heard from your hosts how you've spent the day, so tonight we will speak openly. We know that you are scouts from Beaver Island, and that you seek information. Now is the time to ask any questions you'd like answered."

Grace smiled, deepening the grandmotherly wrinkles on her face. "Best take advantage, friends. Our good doctor won't say that again."

The drumming ceased; the fire talked to itself. Miin raised her small hand and waited.

Dr. Chow grinned. "Ah, Miin, you take me back to my lecture days," he said, smiles spreading around the tent. "What is your question, young student?"

"Well," Blueberry began, reaching out as she spoke to squeeze Diana's hand, "this has all been so wonderful. Really, like something from a dream. So I guess I want to know, how is it possible?" She paused, looking around at the gathered group. "I don't mean this camp, or the children, or the food. I mean, how did you make it?"

The smiles quickly changed to frowns, the atmosphere turning awkward.

"I'm sorry. I know it's bad manners, but how did you survive when no one else did?"

Miin wished she hadn't asked. Her question hovered in the air, mingling with the sage smoke.

Dr. Chow sighed. "Indeed, you do take me back," he said, this time with sadness. "Again, I remember my teaching days. Beware of raised hands!"

The tension inside the tent eased. Grins briefly flashed, then disappeared.

"This is what we know, Miin, or at least what we *think* we know. First of all, I am not a Sentinel. I'm only half-elf, really, mostly I'm a man of science." He looked at the red-bearded shaman. "The answer to your question combines biological facts, my specialty, with something else. Call it mysticism, animism, or what you will. These are new times, requiring new truths. I will share what most have come to believe. You must judge for yourself. Will you hear it?"

Miin checked with Keith and Mukwa, then nodded. "We will."

"First, and forgive me," Chow went on, "but your question implies that no one else survived. This, as you know, is not the case. Yes, the variant has a high mortality rate, off the charts really for an infectious disease. We put it at 99%, though it's probably higher. An unprecedented pandemic; unique, as far as we know, in recorded history.

"You've seen three types of survivors already. First, and easiest to explain, are populations that have not been exposed. We call them Hidden. Your islanders are an example, as were those poor souls you saw hanged in Petoskey.

"Second are the Chosen, and Virals like them. They usually fit a pattern: violent, sexual, and highly mobile. This type, and we've studied some, are heavily infected. The virus rages, yet does not kill them. Why? Again, nothing is *proven*, not in a scientific sense, but we believe the virus 'rewards' its super-spreaders. What better vectors for infection than predatory, promiscuous sociopaths?

"The final group is our own, and others like us. *Naturals* is a good name," he lectured through a smile, "though some prefer *elves*. Blood testing shows high levels of antibodies, which is why we've survived. Babies born post-collapse have these antibodies as well. I suspect that you do too. If you're willing, a quick test, perhaps tomorrow, would provide valuable data to our study."

Miin nodded. Keith and Mukwa definitely did not.

"How am I doing? Is the student satisfied?"

Miin, sheepish, raised her hand again, causing fresh smiles to circulate among those gathered. Chow gestured to her once more, amused. "Yes?"

"Thank you, doctor. I *am* satisfied, and this explains a lot. But *why* is this happening? Why this virus, why now, and why are you protected with antibodies when billions were not?"

Chow frowned. "It is humbling to be taught by a student. Your questions, as they should, expose my shortcomings. I have learned that science can sometimes feel shallow; I am fluent in *what* and *how,* but when it comes to *why* scientists often flounder. There are others here more comfortable in deeper water."

Miin checked with Keith. He steadied her with a look; she was doing fine. The tent stayed quiet for a moment, then the shaman stirred. He was a younger man, red-bearded, maybe 30, with a hippie vibe and serious gaze.

He was about to speak, but the grandmotherly woman, Grace, interjected. "Perhaps the pipe, Brian? To clear the clutter and help our focus?"

Grace's suggestion received affirmative nods from the farmers, Sentinels, and Dr. Chow. From his satchel, embroidered with birds, Brian produced a pipe and pouch. A ceremony was performed; the bowl smoldered, energizing the participants with herbal strength.

Brian began by saying, "None of this, Miin, is new. Before collapse, much had been predicted, even named. We don't claim to have invented any of this. People saw it coming, wrote books, gave warnings and tried to organize. Of course it was all too little, and much too late."

He watched the pipe as it passed before fixing his blue eyes upon Miin. The young tree-talker was hungry for more information, so he fed her. "Gaia's virus is what some call it," he said, with a sideways look at Chow, "though others do not. The name is important, Miin, because it gets to your *why*. Do you follow me? Have you heard this term? Gaia is Mother Earth, yes?"

Miin, Samantha-tutored, understood, though she'd never heard of Lovelock or his hypothesis.

"Well," Brian continued, "if Gaia, the Earth itself, is a body, then humans are its disease. Pollution, overpopulation, risky bio-science: all of these were threats. The Earth, endangered, had to fight back. Again, this is nothing new. Mother Earth countered the human pest with a pathogen of her own. The planet, sick of us, made us sick in return.

"Your last *why* is the trickiest to answer, and not everyone here agrees. But you asked our doctor why *we* have survived, why *we* all made antibodies when no one else could." Here Brian's voice cracked, and he bowed his head, grief-haunted by those he'd lost. In this he wasn't alone; the assembly inside the tent remembered their collective trauma, and some quiet tears were shed. A minute of silence passed before Brian continued.

"Many here believe that Gaia, Earth herself, more sentient than science is willing to admit, has spared her closest kin: people connected to nature, to her plants, her animals, her rhythms. The mechanism is unknown, and in these fallen times may never be. Enzymes, T-cells, antibodies, and the rest are beyond me. I believe we are here because Gaia has spared us. She *wants* us to survive, to prosper. She has granted us children. Did you know, Miin, that Chosen are sterile? That infected can't reproduce? Their sex drive, instead of creating life, has been hijacked for death.

"Children are not the only gift granted to us by Gaia. Miin, since collapse your own abilities, once called mystic, have multiplied. Am I right?"

Miin nodded: it was true. She thought of her transmissions to Samantha, of her talk with Elder Oak, of moonlit Sentinels shimmering on the bridge.

Brian tugged his beard. "The world has changed, and we have too. Powers, once considered miraculous or mythical, are growing. Science and logic appear to ebb. I don't know the why of this, Miin, and I don't need to. It is enough for me to bear witness, to do my part. Despite the losses that haunt me, that haunt all who've survived, I am blessed to live in a time when our species is less lonely, more connected, more fully realized in our potential."

Miin remembered Cranberry Bog, the vision of their island glowing green. Sam's hint that her three scouts were protected, shielded by nature from infection. Mukwa's bearlike aspects, Keith's communion with crows, her own affinity for plants, for trees. It made sense. Nothing in her resisted.

Uncle Keith was thinking; she knew his look. Mukwa, bruised and battered, was elsewhere in his mind. Those in the tent waited, serene, patient. It was her turn to speak.

"Brian?" He nodded. "Doctor Chow?" Another nod. "Thank you for your honesty, and for taking us in when you didn't have to." The two men inclined their heads.

"Elena?" The tall Sentinel smiled. "Thank you for the bridge, for risking your lives to save strangers." Elena nodded. Matador and Diana were smiling too.

"What can we do to repay all this?"

Miin felt Keith's hackles rise, and said no more.

Elena looked from Chow to Brian, then to Keith. Finally she looked at Miin.

"Repayment is not the right word," she said, "at least for now, though that may change. Here, we try to live in harmony with the Earth. We Naturals have been blessed, as Brian said, with health, with life, with children. Our mission, for now, is to protect our own, to find others like us, and to protect them too."

Diana, closest, interlaced fingers with Miin, then smiled at Elena, content in the moment. The mood in the tent, herb-fragrant, had relaxed; a great deal had been said. But Two-Crow stirred, his feathers still ruffled by the proceedings.

Keith rasped his throat clear, and the gathering's attention reluctantly focused on the old-timer with the mountain man beard.

Harshing their vibe, he croaked, "I am also thankful, but you asked for questions, and I have one that needs an answer."

Two-Crow leveled a look at Elena, at Chow. They blinked. Back to business.

"You blindfolded us, took our weapons, and force-marched us to your camp," Keith continued, tone smoldering. "Are we free to go? Like you, I have a duty to perform. Will you help?"

Miin sent a soothing signal to her uncle, to the Naturals. Mukwa sat up straighter, backing Keith's play, cards on the table.

Cool and professional, Elena answered, "We are not your captors, Keith Two-Crow, but we have a responsibility to protect our own. As long as you don't put us in danger, you are free."

The two warriors dead-locked their eyes, equally matched. Diving-Duck, selecting his words with care, spoke at Keith's side: "All of us have lost family, have lost friends."

Sadness swept again through the council.

"When a chance comes to replace what we've lost, to add another brother or sister, we must do so. What is survival worth if we don't share it?"

Matador, standing next to Mukwa, nodded. Diana gave Miin's hand a squeeze. Grace's vibe was positive, and Brian looked keen. Chow, Elena, and the farmers felt more aloof.

Duck remembered Keith's request, their fishing idyll. "Tomorrow night, this man's duty is to contact a boat from his island. He's protecting his people; it's a mission we can understand."

The big Native looked at Elena, and she broke eye contact with Keith, agreeing with Duck instead. The big man continued, "We've overlooked this Chosen threat for too long. We can't hide under the trees forever. We take a stand, or we stand for nothing."

"Also," Duck went on, now addressing Dr. Chow, "who knows the future? One thing seems clear: the future brings change. Beaver Island, and the Hidden there, might be a chance for us. Allies? New knowledge? Who can say?"

Duck lowered his head for a long moment before musing aloud, "Wife, kids, grandkids. I've lost them all, and they won't be returning." He looked over the three scouts. "I will help you with your duty, but I warn you," here he grabbed his belly with both hands, "my help is not what it was."

Keith acknowledged his fellow fisherman with a nod.

Matador shrugged, loyal to his new squadmate. "I'll go too. Who else will keep el oso from mischief?"

The circle stirred, and Brian interjected, "Details will be worked out, I'm sure."

He looked at Chow and Elena.

"Time presses, but for now, enough words have been spoken. Let us relax, embrace this moment, and reconnect with each other and what's important. Clarity comes with meditation."

Miin checked on Uncle Keith; the old crow seemed content. Closing her eyes, she felt others do the same. She focused on her breathing, and the tent itself seemed to breathe with her: a humid, canvas lung. Fuel was added to the fire. Herbs spiced the coals. Sage and cannabis made their ancient rounds.

Miinan inhaled, green-magicked by plants. The nocturnal tent quieted. An owl boomed nearby, followed by chords from a guitar in the hammock colony above, soothing the sleepers, soothing the trees.

She was open, she was everywhere. Miin sealed a mental envelope, addressed it to Sam's shack, and mailed it. Message sent, she laid her head down on Diana's knee. Soon after that, Miinan fell asleep.

The Departed (Diana)

Julie Girard, 30 years old, third mate on the Innovator, *20 souls, July of Year 1*

Julie and Diana met at the maritime college in Owen Sound, Ontario. Celebrating the first week of classes, they went pubbing with some fellow midshipmen. After a few beers they realized they had much in common; both had mariner fathers and unfaithful mothers. Fast becoming friends, they clinked their pints.

Both women graduated near the top of their class, got licensed as third mates, and were hired by Algoma Central. Julie was assigned to *Innovator,* Diana to *Enterprise.* The freighters carried similar cargo, and often crossed paths. When the variant accelerated, Algoma ordered its officers to anchor in place and monitor their crews for symptoms. Both vessels ended up offshore of Cheboygan, their limestone cargoes a relic of the future as the world's history books riffled in reverse.

The two officers assigned themselves midwatch duty. Each night, they practiced their Morse by flashing lamps; .. / .- -.. --- .-. . / -.-- --- ..- or "I adore you" was as racy as they got, professionals to the end.

And the end came quickly. One night on anchor watch, Diana noticed a darkened boat bump alongside Julie's *Innovator.* She radioed a warning to her mate and lover, and Julie accosted the interlopers, who were attempting to traffic human contraband up the rope ladder.

Julie's bored crew wasn't happy. What was wrong with a little supply-and-demand? The smugglers' boat motored off, stranding the prostitute aboard. Julie confined the poor woman, getting stung in the process. By sunup Julie was coughing. By the time breakfast was finished, so was her crew.

Doyle Offshore

"THEY'RE SURROUNDED BY DANGER. There's been fighting, but they're safe for the moment. Captain Doyle, you need to go."

I need to go, do I? And who are you, Samantha, to be bossin' me around?

Doyle, helming his *Mary*, looked astern, infuriated to see Sam standing on the dock with his Annie. The wrinkled witch had wrecked their departure, mangling their mantra. For the first time in forever, there'd been no "farewell," no smooch, no "adieu."

Doyle growled, pitch-matched to *Mary's* motor. *Thick as thieves, those two.*

The women watched him navigate the harbor, waving as he cleared the channel buoys. Doyle chewed over the stringy intel Samantha had grudgingly shared.

The crone's visit, two nights ago, had shocked him shitless, materializing like a ghost out of thin air in his garage. The old net-weaver was checking on him. Making sure he'd keep his bargain, though when he'd made it, or what exactly it was, Tom wasn't quite sure.

Samantha hadn't shared much, just that the Indian girl, Miin, had been "in touch." The three scouts were alive, they'd contacted other groups, and there'd been fighting, shooting, and maybe killing.

What the hell! This was all news to Doyle.

"What kind of groups? What kind of fighting? Weapons? Numbers? Details? Shit, woman, this is important!"

She'd stared, unblinking, as he'd raged in his workshop. Point made, she'd strutted out.

Damn her!

Once Doyle's anger had been vented, he'd closed his workshop and clomped upstairs. There, he'd found his wife drunk in bed, flirty as a schoolgirl. What kind of potion had Samantha witched her with? Annie's hands were everywhere, the humid night too hot for touching. He'd scolded her, cursed his way down the stairs, and then spent the night on the screen porch, his designated doghouse.

Annie was distant at breakfast, with no apology for her drunken behavior. Things had been awkward ever since. *Damn Samantha and her meddling!*

With St. James behind, he throttled *Mary* up to speed. Doyle checked his gauges: engine temperature, oil pressure, RPMs, all systems go. The sun was westering behind the island. Keller manned the tower again; she was a shipmate he could trust. Doyle picked up the mic, switched to channel 12, and depressed the PTT.

"Whiskey Light, *Mary*, over?"

"Whiskey Light here," came Susan Keller's voice. "Doyle, you headin' out again? Over."

"That's affirmative. Just stretchin' her legs, checkin' the Watchers. No warnings, OK Keller?"

"Roger Doyle, no warnings, be safe, over."

"Back by sunup. *Bloody Mary* out."

Doyle, pissed, slammed the mic in its cradle, not at all satisfied with the situation. No backup plan, no one except for Sam knowing what he was up to. Lying to Sue Keller, sneaking around, burning gas, being a damn hypocrite. He blamed this all on Samantha, and the Indians in general. Their tribal bullshit put them all at risk. How in hell had he gotten roped into this, anyway? He couldn't recall, but knew it wasn't his fault.

Mary hit the big water as the sunset bled astern. The moon rode high, having waxed to first quarter. It was time for Two-Crow's transmission. Eight days since he'd dropped off the scouts, but not much had changed. Everyone on the island had been busy. Summer was always the crazy season, but instead of tourists, they now tended crops, salted fish, and stacked wood, preparing for the dark months ahead. The fields didn't look good; farmers blamed the weather, but few had ever cultivated by hand. Beaver's sandy furrows were overrun with weeds.

Island council was determined: this winter's death toll must be minimized. There'd been a push by Doc Newsome, Deputy Williams, and others to siphon off the fleet's fuel supply, then relocate old folks from their cabins into heated shelters come November. So far, Doyle had rallied his captains to resist.

Samantha's hints about the mainland stiffened his resolve. Apparently the adopted girl had sent messages, and Sam believed the threat was real. If so, his fleet must be fueled up and ready, but lacking solid proof diminished his bluster. The council, even some captains, were turning against him. It was past time to figure out what the fuck was out there.

Damn you, Keith Two-Crow, don't let me down.

Doyle found his balance as *Mary* hit her stride. Twilight turned purple, always a magic hour offshore. Gulls and terns settled onto the surface, the moon beaming into his wheelhouse. Static purred from channel 12. He'd be in radio range by midnight, would drift offshore from Petoskey, nav-lights off, ears open, ready to receive the Vietnam vet's transmission.

Tom began humming the old island song: "Oh, it's a long way to Beaver Island..."

Thoughts adrift, he anchored them to Annie: their house on the point, their life, and the children that never came. In God's hands, they told themselves, but they could have tried harder, seen a specialist. Who knows what might have been?

Niece Maggie, a near-daughter, had a crush on young Hannigan. Would those two make a family? Grandkids might smooth things over, make things right with Annie. No denying they'd grown apart, and some of the blame might be his.

Doyle flushed with regret over Annie's flirtatiousness the other night. Damn Samantha! If the crone hadn't rattled him, he could have responded better, performed as a proper husband should.

Doyle examined the chart, distracting himself with range and frequency. He'd make it up to her. His wheelhouse was full of good intentions, most of which never made it back to the dock. *Mary's* diesel engine chugged towards the mainland, the boat a rusty speck above the darkly fathomed deep.

The Transmission

THE COMMANDO TEAM REACHED the confluence and its cache of canoes by early evening. There'd been no talk this time of blindfolds. They'd made good time between the ELF encampment and the portage site, Elena leading them well. She'd picked her team this morning, turning down plenty of volunteers to settle on the six that would accompany Keith and Mukwa on their radio mission. Miin stayed behind, her green abilities in need of tutoring.

Matador and Nighthawk had sprinted ahead, contacting the on-duty Sentinels at the falls. By the time the team reached the clearing, four canoes had been readied for their journey downstream.

Keith knelt in the gloaming, inspecting his gear, confirming battery charge and wiring his radio. He'd won his argument with Elena, the duffel lying at his side.

Satisfied with his rig, he looked up at Mukwa. "You sure?"

Mukwa was not at all sure. Hearing the river again, he flashed back to the moonlit bridge: the hot splash on his face, the cold horror of cooling corpses.

Mukwa nodded down at Keith. *Too fucking late now.*

Keith unzipped his duffel and handed up the pistol in its holster. Mukwa strapped the weapon on.

Two-Crow nodded at him. "Check it."

Mukwa pulled out the Glock, inspected its magazine, and checked each of the safeties. Keith nodded; together, they loaded their canoe. The old man then stepped away, seeking out Elena. As daylight faded, Mukwa watched them conferring over the pilfered map.

"You sure you need that?"

Nighthawk's voice came from behind, sounding skeptical; Mukwa turned to find the Sentinel arrayed in full battle gear. She wore a headband, a gray parka, a quiver of carbon-shafted broadheads, and a belted knife. Her eyes flashed with a smoldering green fire, she held a recurve bow in one hand. She glanced to his pistol, indicating the object of her leery remark.

"Well, you saw my bow skills, right?" Mukwa aimed for humor. He sensed amusement from under her hood.

Hawk mimed the arrow-erection from the straw man's groin, and grinned. "Hit those Chosen bastards where it hurts."

She extended her hand, and he gripped it. She pulled him closer.

Damn, she's strong. Her scent profile—woodsmoke, jerky, sweat—was a good one.

"We get through this, el oso, maybe I'll teach you a few things."

Her voice sounded sly; her scent was sexy. Adrenaline dumped into his system, and for a second, Muck couldn't breathe. She pulled her prey closer, her talons unrelenting. They stood chest to chest, his heart pounding so hard he was sure she must feel it.

Just as quick, Hawk shoved him and then vanished, seeming to merge with the dusk.

Holy shit. Mukwa tried to recover.

At twilight, Elena called the team together. They circled up on the shore, canoes laden and mission-ready. The first quarter moon brightened above.

She whispered over the water's muted rushing, "Canoes stick together. No talking, no noise. We paddle hard for two hours, downstream, north towards the coast; we need to shorten the range between Two-Crow and the boat from Beaver Island as much as possible."

She confirmed with Keith, then continued, "Follow my lead. When we're close enough, I'll beach us. We'll disembark, establish a perimeter, make the transmission, and pull out."

She queried the circle. No questions; they were focused.

"We know the Chosen are based in Charlevoix from the map Two-Crow stole from their truck at the bridge. Remember, they own the roads. They're fast and they're ruthless. We are not, I repeat, *not* looking for a fight."

Elena checked around. Did they get it?

The Sentinels nodded, dead serious. They got it.

"As you know, making this transmission in the open puts us at risk, especially if the Raiders are hunting for our guests. Any trouble, we scatter and regroup at the falls." She paused, taking a moment to look at each of them in turn. "Questions?"

Squirrel, who'd been honored when tapped for the mission, spoke up. "Tonight's not the night, I know, but Elena—when are we gonna hit those fuckers for real? Make 'em pay for the evil shit they've done?" Squirrel's face was hooded, but Mukwa heard anger, could smell her ferocity. He was glad they weren't sparring.

"Payback is not our mission. It may never be. If that's a problem, Sentinel, then you're in the wrong line of work. Keep your anger wired tight, do I make myself clear?"

"Clear, Elena. I get it. Just sayin'."

Elena stared at Squirrel. The other Sentinels stayed silent; it was time to go.

Mukwa noticed that the further they traveled, the stranger the Sentinels became. Maybe it was the moonlight, but to his eyes, they were getting that shiny look again. Their predator vibe was up. When they moved, they shimmered, which made them hard to track. Creepy as hell, but pretty fucking cool too, since they were on the same side. He mentally outlined how he'd draw it, the hooded warriors merging with the nightscape.

Elena and Diana paddled in the lead canoe, well-armed with spears and bows.

Matador and Tigre manned the second canoe. Crazy that these goofball brothers were the same magic "elves" that saved his ass at the bridge.

Two-Crow sat behind Mukwa in the stern; their boat came third. The old man was strapped with his badass M-4, night vision binoculars slung around his neck.

The final canoe held Nighthawk and Squirrel, the two female warriors watching their six. They only carried bows, but with Nighthawk that was plenty. Endorphins from their face-to-face still percolated. *Holy shit!* Muck hoped for more of that later.

Diving-Duck had been furious when Elena nixed him from the team. Weird how uncle-like the big Ojibwe seemed to Mukwa: same build as him, same hair, same everything.

Elena told the elder he was too out of shape.

Duck admitted it, but claimed other skills. Elena had reconsidered, the veteran standing at attention, too proud to beg. Twice denied, he'd stalked off muttering.

Mukwa wondered about those "other skills." He didn't doubt them, not for one second.

The moon glimmered on every rapid and riffle. Between that and the Sentinels' elvish vibe, the night trended stranger the further they paddled.

And another thing: Mukwa felt pretty sure they were being followed. A raptor had covered their party since leaving camp. It would soar off and then return, as if checking in. Mukwa had seen way too many trippy things lately to put anything past these guys. Was one of these elves mind-locked to the bird somehow? Like in a fantasy story?

Again, as long as they were on the same team, the weirder the better: a bunch of damn mutants headed downstream.

Mukwa stayed sharp as they maneuvered through obstacles, but mostly it was easy paddling, with only a few tricky spots. No one had to dismount or portage, and none of these pros even got wet. He thought back to Petoskey, hanging-town, how rookie they'd been. The lynchings, the evil, the fumbled radio, the angry loon, that spotlight, Keith's face as the beam swung closer. *Shit.*

They'd been through some things.

Muck ordered himself to stay in the moment, forcing himself not to think of Nighthawk stroking along behind him. *Double shit!*

He looked up. The raptor, their air cover, winged across the moon.
Here we come motherfuckers!

Two hours brought them to a bend, a stretch of sand, silvered by moonlight. Elena beached, she and Diana silently hustling their canoe off the water and under cover. Other teams did the same. Mukwa tried to get a better look at Nighthawk, add some fuel to his fantasy. No such luck; hooded and armed, she merged with the night.

Diana motioned, and the Sentinels fanned out, setting a perimeter. Matador and Tigre, Nighthawk and Squirrel disappeared into the trees. Diana did the same.

Keith knelt stiffly on the sand. He checked wires—battery to radio, radio to antenna—then looked up at Elena and nodded, indicating his readiness. The tall woman signaled him to wait, giving her team another minute.

Mukwa squatted next to Keith, feeling useless. He checked the moon; no raptor, no overwatch. The river gleamed in the moonlight, but the far shore was dim. The trees around him stood still, no breeze, no clouds: ideal conditions for their scheduled broadcast.

At last, after a series of owl calls, Elena nodded permission. Keith connected the battery, thumbing the leads down tight. The CB radio lit up, empowered. Keith dialed Doyle's frequency and checked his watch. It was time.

"*Bloody Mary, Bloody Mary, Bloody Mary,* this is Crow calling, do you read me?"

The soundwave rippled, Mach 1, through the night. Keith turned the volume up, listening intently for confirmation. They could hear static on the frequency, but no return.

Keith transmitted again.

"*Bloody Mary, Bloody Mary, Bloody Mary,* this is Crow, do you read me? Over."

This time, when Keith released the PTT a jumble of sound squawked through the speaker. Mukwa strained to recognize Doyle's voice, but couldn't make it out. The radio went quiet.

Elena stood abruptly. "We need to get you closer."

Keith disconnected the leads and readied his rig for travel. Elena made the appropriate owl call, signifying the all-clear. Sentinels returned, shimmering, from the perimeter and held a whispered conference. A minute later they were paddling further downriver, narrowing the distance between send and receive.

A Fox-Hunt

MIKEY'S FACE WAS LIT by a dashboard of electronics; he'd been like a kid at Christmas since Cowboy's green light. He and his wrenches scoured the motor pool and marinas near Charlevoix, patching together enough radios and scanners to nail the fuckers that murdered Heavy.

The mechanic stank of armpit, bad breath, and a poorly wiped ass. Disgust was the emotion that most defined Cowboy's post-collapse world. In all the apocalyptic films and fiction, not enough time was spent on the messy logistics of piss and shit. Cowboy rolled down the truck's window, mosquitoes a small price to pay for a break from his fixer's funk.

Mikey had declared his Fox-Hunt ready earlier that afternoon. It took him and his men 24 hours of creative rigging; the hardest piece to come by was the directional antenna—the quad—that would allow the hunters to hone in on signals sent in the open. Theirs had been found accidentally by a Raider scrounging for porn in abandoned semis, par for the post-collapse course.

Three nights ago, Heavy had been killed and his radio taken. The problem, as Cowboy saw it, was not knowing when the thieves might transmit. Maybe they already had? Maybe they never would? Bob was gambling an awful lot of resources on a slim chance of revenge.

But he had to. When word got out about Heavy's killing and the burning of the bodies, it had been all he could do to keep his 30 Chosen in-garrison. The promise of a Fox-Hunt and proper revenge bought him some time; even so, Cowboy needed this bet to pay off.

Bob's reputation as boss, once golden, had been tarnished by shitty numbers, few Hidden, and even fewer chances for fun. Cowboy knew there were further plums to be picked—Indian River, Cheboygan, Mackinaw City—but he had to neutralize Petoskey and its nest of insurgents first. Every boss knew you couldn't run a scavenge operation with insecure supply lines. Bob had been derelict in dealing with the No-Go zones—shaded green—on his office maps. Even Raiders were reluctant to venture too far under the trees. "Not worth it," they huffed, figuring on better pickings in the towns.

He'd heard some grumbling about jumping ship, changing bosses; Charlevoix wasn't the only game in town. Chosen, not known for loyalty, were piratical in their enthusiasm for rape and plunder. There was plenty of opportunity for both downstate. Of course, firefights with XCons and Old Law came with that territory. A perk of Cowboy's northern outpost had been the relative lack of resistance. Now four of Bob's best had been bushwhacked and barbequed, so there went that.

For tonight's hunt—which would run into the next few days if it came to that—they'd gassed up four vehicles, almost draining the compound's reserve. A radio plea to Liz's boss begging for a tanker truck was not a call Bob wanted to make. He'd be demoted for sure, replaced by some ladder-climber out to make a name. Cowboy would end his end times as a hired gun, older and slower each year. No fucking thanks.

Bob splayed the road map across his knee. He'd deployed all four trucks along Bear River, figuring his enemy traveled by boat, with water as their highway. He'd directed his drivers to shut off their engines, conserve fuel and set a radio-watch. Who knows how long they'd have to wait? Mikey had eyes and ears on the scanner; any nearby transmission would be picked up and its frequency displayed. Next, he would dial in the roof-mounted quad, its phased array indicating the direction of transmission, which Cowboy could vector on the map. Where the vector intersected the river, the foxes would find their rabbit. Cowboy's four vehicles would then rush to the spot, his rabid Raiders dismounting and converging to spring their trap.

Cowboy pictured his trucks, evenly spaced along River Road, ready to pounce. He'd picked his best men, dudes that could handle themselves. After Gunny's murder, Bob still had three ex-soldiers in his outfit, traumatized for sure, but who wasn't? These vets preferred to stay together, but tonight he'd divided them, one soldier per truck.

"Well, Mikey, think we've got a chance?"

The mechanic monitored their gear. "All depends, boss. If they use Heavy's radio, and they're still in the area, then we've got 'em."

Cowboy liked the sound of this, liked the mission. Outpost duty had grown pretty fucking dull since Liz pulled out. Their romp had reminded him of better times, a better self. He'd slackened along with his men, but tonight would tighten them up.

Come on fuckers, make your call.

It was just after midnight. Cowboy reclined his seat and pulled the brim of his hat low, resting his tired eyes. Mikey mashed an MRE mocha bar while Bob tried to unhear his wet chewing. Suddenly, the shush of static was interrupted, the scanner squawking as it caught a transmission.

Something's happening!

Cowboy sat up as the digital scanner landed on channel 12. He couldn't believe his ears, but there it was: "...*Mary*, this is Crow calling, do you read me?"

The scanner resumed its static.

Holy shit!

Mikey, brownie-smeared, was punching channel 12 into the directional antenna. "Come on, come on, send it again," he urged the caller, apparently some dude named *Crow?*

There it was again! An old-timer's voice, crystal clear—and close.

"*Bloody Mary, Bloody Mary, Bloody Mary,* this is Crow, do you read me? Over."

Mikey rotated the roof-mounted quad, bleary eyes glued to the signal strength indicator.

"One more time, boss, one more, and he's ours!"

Static on the radio.

Shit, we lost him.

Then a different voice, sounding angry, responded from the ether.

"Crow, this is *Mary,* I read you. What's your report, over?"

Cowboy looked at his fixer. Mikey shook his head, eyes on the indicator. "We need that Crow dude's response."

Nothing. Static.

Fuck!

✦✦✦

Another hour passed, Mikey eating a second mocha brownie to stay alert. Bob asked if they should move, but Mike said no; he liked their position.

Their patience finally paid off. The old man called again, speaking cautious and slow. "*Mary,* this is Crow..."

Mikey, aroused, fingered the indicator. They had their vector! Bob listened intently.

Did this Crow guy just say the word "scouts?"

The pair of Chosen manhandled the map. Bob drew a line in the frequency's direction, circling the spot where it intersected the river.

We've got the fucker!

Crow was still talking.

Did the dude just say "elves?"

Cowboy grabbed the Raider mic, set to a different frequency, and called to his three crews, directing his foxes.

"Hernandez, you're closest," Bob said over the radio as he traced the route. "Drive one mile south, dismount, and push east through the woods. You'll hit the river and the radio in a quarter mile. Don't fuck this up!"

Hernandez, a veteran of two tours in Afghanistan, confirmed his orders. "Roger boss, one mile south, quarter mile east, nail the fuckers. Over."

"That's affirmative. Backup will be right behind you. Take a prisoner if possible. Cowboy out."

Campbell called his other two foxes. Barnes, an Army vet, and Kowalski, his remaining Marine, hustled their trucks towards the fun. They were still a ways out though, which meant Hernandez would get there first.

Should I hold Hernandez back, send them all in together?

Fuck! Too risky to wait. This Crow character might be long gone by then. He let his order to Hernandez stand. First come, first serve. Hernandez and his crew would have first crack at Mr. Crow.

Cowboy spurred his own truck, revving its horsepower. Mikey hauled in the antenna as they roared south along River Road. They were furthest from the fun, but the final fox still hoped for a bite.

Firefight

HERNANDEZ, SITTING SHOTGUN in a modified Chevy, slammed his mic down. "You heard the boss," he said, thumping his driver on the shoulder. "Hit it!"

The truck spun its tires, then leapt, ravenous, towards the target. The driver, a frustrated gearhead before Covee, flicked on his brights as he barreled down the road.

"Easy now," Hernandez said, eyes wide, savoring his pre-combat rush. "Bust an axle and I'll fucking eat you."

Their mile went by quickly, the Afghan vet ogling the odometer. "Start slowing down," he ordered, "lights off, stealth mode now. Our tango is close."

Hernandez looked behind him. The two white guys were grinning; this was the shit Chosen lived for. Who needed video games when you could be a first-person shooter yourself?

When the odometer rolled over, he stopped his driver.

"OK, now it's a quarter mile east to the river; our radio thief is there. Keep your fucking weapons safe, and watch your muzzles. I didn't survive two tours to get shot by you jerk-offs. And don't you dare slam those doors. Let's move out!"

His backseat boys exited, and the gearhead driver too, fumbling their loaded weapons. Hernandez took point, but couldn't see shit in the woods. He led his three as best he could, heard them cursing thorns as they got tangled in thick stuff. *Assholes!*

He wished he was with Barnes and Kowalski; at least those dudes knew how to approach a target. He raised one fist to indicate a halt, his bumpkins bumping into each other in the dark. All four heard the sound of water. The river was close.

Hernandez, from shadow, tried to signal them to fan out, to approach the objective from different angles. The clowns grinned, then forged ahead right on top of each other, muzzles waving everywhere. *Sloppy!*

Fuck it, Hernandez let them go first. If it was a trap, they deserved to have their asses shot off. Hanging back, letting others rush in, was something he'd perfected. You didn't survive the Talibs by being a hero all the time.

Hernandez was down on one knee cradling his assault rifle, listening to the racket as they pushed through the brush, each man eager to be the trigger-puller. He'd forgotten to mention the prisoner part. Suddenly, fear gripped his guts, a tight squeeze of dread he'd felt before. From shadows beneath the trees, three missiles lanced out like silver tracer rounds. Hernandez heard crunching as the projectiles thudded home. *Contact!*

His three puppets went down, strings cut just like that. He could hear one flopping on the ground. Hernandez stalked closer, low and silent. His driver had an arrow shaft protruding from his chest. The broadhead must have hit bone? Thankfully the gearhead lay quiet, in shock, taking it like a man. Hernandez was in no hurry to share the same fate.

Something shimmered in his field of vision. A moonlight mirage? The forest seemed to move towards the man on the ground. He caught a glint, a knife in the dark? Hernandez raised his rifle, sighted on the shimmer, and squeezed a three-round burst—*Bap! Bap! Bap!*

Muzzle-flash blinded him. What had he hit? He peered along the barrel, blinking away the afterimage; his night vision was wasted. Something struck him hard in the back, knocking him to his knees. Hernandez looked down, disbelieving, at the spear tip sprouting from his chest. His hands, confused, dropped the rifle and groped at the wooden shaft. Thing wouldn't fucking budge. His lifeblood left him, sponged up by the thirsty loam.

I've been skewered.

Corporal Hernandez died in the ferns.

✦✦✦

Same road, different truck. Barnes and his men sat silent, holding their breath. They'd just heard the *Bap! Bap! Bap!* of a battle rifle. Had that been Hernandez?

"Back the fuck up!" Barnes ordered.

His tattooed driver reversed away from Hernandez's empty truck.

At 50 yards, Barnes stopped him. "Enough. Park it."

He told the driver to stay put, kill the engine, kill the lights.

"You two," he addressed the jailbirds in the backseat, "get out, use your doors as cover, and ready your weapons."

Barnes, a forty-something with a buzz cut, climbed into the truck bed and readied the machine gun mounted there.

"Hey Juan!" The driver's tattooed face appeared at the window. "Hit the brights when I say so."

Juan grinned, gap-toothed. His night was getting better and better.

Barnes' men were deployed in ambush position, their safeties off. Barnes was satisfied. Time to wait and see.

Four pairs of bloodshot eyes adjusted to moonlight. Each watcher tried to picture what was happening at the river, under the trees. Was the fun already over? Or had it just begun?

Cowboy's voice squawked from the radio, their boss sounding out of breath. "Hernandez, you there? Barnes? Kowalski? Report! We're on our way!"

"Juan, turn that fucking thing off," Barnes hissed.

Radio silence. Waiting. Sweaty palms were wiped on pant legs.

Where the fuck is Hernandez?

Barnes, eyes wide, sensed movement in the dim. Fucking bushes were creeping across the road! Saplings, uprooted, moved stealthily around Hernandez's empty truck. Barnes peered, but couldn't make them out. He waited a second; then it was time.

He tickled the trigger of his MG. "Juan!"

His driver flashed his brights on the scene. Caught in the headlights, the forest froze, half a dozen hooded figures blinded by the beams. They carried no guns.

"Hands up, assholes!"

The hooded figures complied, but slowly. Barnes covered them with his .30 cal. At least one of the figures was female. He leered at the tall woman; their lucky fucking day.

✦✦✦

Two-Crow squatted, listening to the radio. After their first failure they'd paddled closer to the bay, disembarking again. This time the signal connected. Doyle's angry voice was droning on, the volume so low Mukwa couldn't make him out.

Enough already, Keith. Let's go!

Crow keyed the mic, giving a hushed reply to Captain Doyle, adrift on his boat.

What are these geezers gabbing about?

Flashes strobed through the trees. Then, *Bap! Bap! Bap!* The sound of shots came a half-tick behind.

We're busted!

Keith looked up, startled, from his radio, panic etched on his face. He hurriedly spoke into the mic, Mukwa overhearing a fragment: "Four nights from now, near the shore where you dropped us."

The old man listened closely to Doyle's confirmation. Keith then signed off and disconnected quickly.

Mukwa bristled with adrenaline; *he needed to get over there. Matador! Nighthawk!*

The linebacker crouched and charged the tree line, fumbling with his holster. Two-Crow tried to block his path, but Muck broke Keith's containment. *Old fool! We have to HELP!*

He crashed towards the sound of gunfire.

In the piney dim, prickles of moonlight needled through. The bear couldn't see, his face and limbs bloodied by thorns. Old Crow was in pursuit; gunfire meant trouble. Muck tripped on something soft, landed hard, and got a mouthful of blood-soaked moss, finding himself face-to-face with an arrow-killed *someone.*

Keith, out of breath, heard Mukwa tumble; Two-Crow paused his pursuit and took in the scene. Shadows dappled the cooling bodies of four freshly slain Chosen, the last cadaver speared through the chest.

Mukwa blinked to clear his vision. Keith stood over him, someone *else* lying nearby. Muck moaned; the final figure was a Sentinel. A parka shrouded its identity, though it seemed too short for Elena or Diana.

Nighthawk then? Please no!

He needed to make sure, to turn the body over and peer under its hood.

Matador maybe? I have to know!

Keith hauled him upright, hissing, "There'll be more of 'em. Come on!"

Mukwa, reluctant, followed the old man away from the river, deeper into the woods.

Where the hell are the elves?

Six Sentinels had deployed, guarding their asses; now five had vanished and one lay dead. *Fuck!*

Trailing Keith, he saw the woods thinning ahead. *A road?*

At the tree line, Two-Crow took a knee. Unslinging his rifle, he motioned Mukwa up. "Get your pistol out. Take it off safe. Be ready!"

Keith sighted towards the clearing. Something large loomed in the road.

Mukwa sniffed the night air: warm engine, rotten gasoline, and stale body odors. *A truck!*

From the right, in the darkness past the reeking vehicle, someone shouted, "Juan!"

Suddenly, the scene blazed with light. He squinted against the glare.

Headlights! Chosen! Shit!

"Hands up, assholes!" the same voice commanded from the road.

Eyes adjusting, Mukwa saw leafy forms raise their limbs, helpless and exposed around an empty truck. The headlights and voice came from his right, from a second vehicle just down the road. Keith scoped its headlights. Mukwa squared himself, brought the pistol up, and did the same. Way out of range, but he'd do what he could.

He forced himself to wait. *Come on, Keith! Fucking fire!*

The sight of Sentinels, hands up and vulnerable, turned his knees to jelly.

No way out. They're fucked for sure.

Then Mukwa heard a revving engine, high beams bouncing down the road from his left. This newcomer skidded to a halt, blocking them in. Now the Sentinels were pinned by two sets of brights. *Double fucked.*

Harsh laughter rose from the right-hand vehicle, followed by a shouted greeting. "About time, Kowalski! Almost missed the fun!"

Several seconds of silence passed before fire blossomed from the left: *Chug! Chug! Chug! Chug! Ping! Ping! Chug! Chug!*

Tracers zipped in the dark, shredding metal, splintering glass. The Sentinels scattered as the newcomer blazed away. But who was their target?

After a startled pause, a machine gun flashed back from the vehicle on the right, *Dhak! Dhak! Dhak! Dhak!*

Return fire raced towards the first shooter, pinging off metal, knocking out headlights.

Keith's rifle began barking, supporting the left against the right: *Bap! Bap! Bap!*

The vet's aim was true, the right-hand lights shattering as he shot them out. *Bap! Bap! Bap! Bap!* Keith poured it on.

Mukwa aimed and squeezed his trigger in support: *Pow! Pow! Pow! Pow! Pow!* His pistol bucked wildly.

From the left, the mystery gun kept firing, unleashing angry red tracers. *Chug! Chug! Chug! Zip!*

But who the fuck is shooting?

The right-hand truck had been shot to shit, disabled by heavy rounds; its mounted gun had gone silent. When the shooting stopped, Mukwa's ears started ringing; flash-blind, he saw gray spots, felt Crow's claw on his shoulder. The old man reeked of gunpowder.

"Easy now. Safety on, holster that pistol."

Mukwa's limbs were locked, his smoking sidearm still aimed towards the silent truck. Keith gripped him harder, and Mukwa deflated, putting the pistol away.

What the fuck just happened?

"Stay here."

Keith, holding his M-4 low, snuck towards the road. Fires burned from the wreck on their right. Mukwa saw Sentinels combing the scene, primitive weapons at the ready.

Fuck this. He drew his knife and joined them in the road.

Keith, stepping clear of the blasted truck, reported back to Elena. "Four dead, not pretty."

She nodded coldly, and they moved on together. Mukwa followed, brain feeling fuzzy from endorphins; he counted Sentinels as they shimmered around the wreckage. *Five of them. But shouldn't there be six?*

Then he remembered the dead one. *Shit.*

Mukwa had to know the hooded corpse's identity. He made a move to go back towards the river.

"Easy man, easy. We got this. Just wait." Matador's voice punctured his paranoia. The Sentinel stood with his brother Tigre, both holding nocked arrows at the ready. The two athletes were tense, eyeing the bear.

Mukwa couldn't take it. "Someone's back there in the woods. Dead. Is it Nighthawk?"

Nose first, then ears; pheromones, then frequency. "Mukwa, I'm here."

And she was, materializing right beside him, a hooded hawk with bloody talons.

From the left, over near the mystery gunner, Two-Crow, investigating, gave a cry. They hustled over to find the truck cab empty, lights and windshield shattered, a .50 caliber gun smoking upon its mount.

Keith climbed awkwardly into the truck bed and genuflected near a body, anguish gouging his features. The team peered mournfully at the object of his grief.

A large man, chest perforated, trembled as he bled out, air leaking from his lungs in rattling wheezes. War paint streaked his stern face. It was the elder, Diving-Duck, his conspiracy unmasked.

Duck groaned, then gasped his final words, eyes locking on Keith: "Protect them! Save them!"

Then he was gone, departed like all the rest. Keith moaned, bowing his head. The moon shone down, silvering man and corpse in a tragic tableau.

Elena lowered her bright eyes before giving orders to her commandos. "We've got to move. There might be more of them out there."

The Sentinels scattered; there was much to do.

What Doyle Heard

BLOODY MARY HELD TO HER HOMEWARD COURSE, heading north-west, steady on bearing three-one-zero. The quarter moon had set, the galactic spume splashy with stars. Lake Michigan's fathoms, cold and dark, thrummed beneath the keel. In electrified times, Doyle would have picked up Beaver's Whiskey Light by now, its Fresnel lens beaming him home. He'd never get used to this blind approach; he'd be dead before he acclimated. This unlighted world was not for him.

Hours earlier, Doyle had heard what sounded like gunfire over the radio, Keith confirming it. In a rushed voice, Two-Crow broadcast that they'd been busted and couldn't call again.

Bap! Bap! Bap!

Doyle couldn't unhear that sound. Had the old man even survived? What about those damn kids? Of course, the whole situation was Samantha's fault. That crazy old witch and her schemes.... He still bristled to remember Annie, drugged and frisky, ambushing him in bed.

Mary's captain cursed himself for what he'd just agreed to. Why the fuck had he promised to meet Keith face to face?

The old Indian had requested a rendezvous four nights from now, "Near the shore where you dropped us."

Doyle assumed, since they'd been busted, that their conversation had been overheard. Had they given anything away? Going over their earlier comms, he didn't think so, thank fucking Christ.

Keith had hurriedly reported on the factions they'd encountered, friend and foe alike.

All mainlanders were foes to Doyle, but these Chosen sounded especially dangerous. Keith didn't know their numbers: "Many, well-armed, and based out of Charlevoix," was all the information he provided.

Doyle tasted bile. Charlevoix, home port of *Emerald Isle*, the ferry he'd been haunted by for the past year and half.

He and Keith had been busted quickly, mere minutes into transmission. Assuming they honed in on Two-Crow's signal, that meant these Chosen had vehicles, gasoline, weapons, and radios. More than that, they were organized.

His worst fears were coming true. The island, and everyone he knew, were at risk; this was beyond doubt, no more hypotheticals. The enemy on the mainland had proven all too fucking real.

Two-Crow also mentioned "allies." Had he even used the word "elves?"

Now who the hell were *they?* And *why* were they helping? *What* was their price? And why, for fuck's sake, had he agreed to return, four nights from now, wasting gas, telling lies, just to have this same conversation all over again?

The captain craved a smoke. He checked the compass, and steered his shitty course.

As the stars dimmed, Tom Doyle felt the looming presence of the island, rising up from the deep. He would make his circuit, steam past the Watchers, disguise his absence as a test of their vigilance. There'd better be a contact entry from each and every station.

Doyle pictured that old man, a Vietnam veteran for chrissakes, taking fire. Keith had risked his life and the lives of those kids, and for what? Information? A damn reconnaissance? Grudgingly, Doyle granted that Two-Crow was a man of action, of deeds not words. Doyle knew, all grumbling aside, that he'd be making this trip again. Four nights from now, he and Keith Two-Crow would hold a midnight rendezvous.

Scalped

COWBOY DROVE AS FAST AS HE DARED. No one had responded to his radio call; they must be taking prisoners? Having some fun? He could feel it. Tonight his luck had finally turned.

There was action ahead, and he didn't want to miss it. This Fox-Hunt was just what they'd needed: a break from the base, a reminder of the perks of being Chosen. He kept his low beams on as he drove his way south along River Road. Something ahead was burning—they fishtailed to a stop. He couldn't see clearly, and flicked on his brights.

What in the fuck?

His stomach flopped; it couldn't be. He peered through his windshield in horrified disbelief. Barnes' vehicle, doors askew, had been shot to shit. A scatter of bodies lay like pick-up sticks in the road.

Please fucking no.

Bob's plea was ignored. Scene unchanged, he parked the truck. Climbing down, he clicked on his rifle's flashlight, boots crunching on gravel as he drew closer, his fixer following at his heels. They found a figure sprawled in the truck bed, bitten in half by bullets: Barnes.

He heard puking behind him as Mikey tossed up his brownies.

Two other Chosen, Barnes' jailbirds, lay mangled near the doors. He peered inside the vehicle to find Juan, or what was left of him, his corpse coated in broken glass. The driver reeked; his gut had ruptured. *Fucking butchery.*

The next truck belonged to Hernandez, sitting untouched and empty? A third truck was up the road a bit, Kowalski's?

Cowboy investigated, plying his light: the beam shone on smashed glass and splatters of blood. There were no bodies here, though someone's plasma had pooled in the truck bed. Mikey heaved again; their Fox-Hunt had been fucked.

What the hell happened here?

Bob's brain was stupefied. None of this felt real. The moonlight, the trees, his idling engine: it was all a dream. Had to be, better be. But he knew it wasn't. Cowboy Bob had run out of rope.

Twenty minutes later, and shit was even worse.

Mikey hadn't moved, still lying in the puddle of his own puke. Cowboy, scouring the woods by flashlight, located the bodies of Hernandez and his puppets. And there were tracks on the beach. Drag marks. *Canoes.*

Whoever was responsible for this, they were long gone. Upriver? Down? It didn't fucking matter; he had no intention of pursuing them. If he and his fixer arrived any earlier, they'd both be corpses too.

He'd seen the arrow jutting from Hernandez's driver, like a fletched middle finger to the too-modern world. Bob poked around the wounds of the other three, finding none had been killed by bullets. In his mind, he peopled the woods with painted primitives. They'd scalped his ass good.

And where the hell was Kowalski and his crew of Chosen? Too many mysteries for Bob's trauma-fried brain. Behind him, Mikey had finally found his feet, moaning as he circled Barnes' truck.

"Boss, you seen this?"

Exhausted, Cowboy slouched over and aimed his bright beam. There, finger-painted on a door panel, was their fucking symbol, a bloody tree:

Welcome to ELF Country!

Fixer doubled up again, dry-heaving this time. Cowboy couldn't compute; he shook his head and struggled to reboot his brain. Nothing helped. Only one thing was clear: he was fucked.

Cloudburst

BY SUNUP THEY'D REACHED THE CONFLUENCE and returned to the falls, its resident raptor guiding them home. The on-duty Sentinels had been alerted somehow, meeting them at the shore; they helped land the boats. The tired paddlers disembarked onto dry land. Two canoes rode low, ballasted by dead bodies, parka-covered in the bloody bilge water.

Elena, standing tall, spoke quickly of their circumstances. The river guards nodded, one turning to speed up the path. Elena signaled the others to haul out the canoes. Mukwa lent a hand, Diving-Duck's corpse a heavy burden. He grunted, and Tigre joined him. Together they cached Duck's canoe-coffin under the trees.

Keith, rifle slung, lugged the radio and its 12 volt. He trudged into the clearing, a depot of barrels and bundled spears. Setting down his load, he unkinked his back before locking eyes with his mentee, Mukwa. The old vet then inclined his head towards Duck's parka-shroud. "A warrior," he stated with grim respect.

The other body, half-sized and draped in a Sentinel's military camouflage, was that of Squirrel. Diana and Nighthawk took charge of Sarah, their comrade, their friend.

Humid already, the morning heated up. Elena made them wait, out of sight, till help could arrive from camp. Mosquitoes whined as the commandos cleaned weapons and prepared food. Their group was exhausted, each combatant mentally mapping the terrain of last night's trauma.

They found Duck's canoe on their return upriver. He must have beached it to ambush that last truck, though how he did it they could only guess. No time had been spared to investigate the scene. Seven paddlers had muscled five canoes and two bodies against the current, the short summer night seeming to last forever. Mukwa, shaking, could barely stand.

Elena sent the remaining sentry downriver so the survivors could process. Even sprinting, it was a long way to ELF Country; it would be past noon before any help arrived. After trying tasteless food, their team split up, males and females, to wash themselves and bathe the dead.

Keith, Mukwa, Matador, and Tigre sat together under the trees, unlacing boots and pulling off parkas. Muck cleaned elf blood from his high-tops. They could hear the women in the river, Nighthawk keening as she tended to her friend Sarah's bullet-holed body.

Tigre stuttered as he rehashed the ambush. Three arrows had been fired, one each by Hawk, Squirrel, and Matador. It had been his spear, too late, that skewered Squirrel's shooter. On the road, deer-in-the-headlights, he'd thought they were doomed. Tigre shook his head, recalling how Diving-Duck saved all their asses. Dude was fucking unreal.

When the women emerged, the men took their turn. They did their best, but Duck was heavy and wouldn't float. They stripped his body, Keith taking the lead; the river ran red with clotted blood. Mukwa cleaned himself, scrubbing out his clothes, while Keith laved water over Duck's shattered chest. Mukwa shivered in the icy flow and looked away.

The two dead were laid out, decently covered, on stretchers made of lashed-together spears and ponchos, awaiting more pallbearers from camp.

Nap time.

Muck's eyelids drooped as the humidity thickened. Cumulus clouds mounded higher, thunder tolled; something had to give. The commandos dispersed, each to their own spot. Hammocks were stretched, the weary snatching some sleep while they subconsciously triaged their terror.

Mukwa roamed further beneath the trees, restless; he found a stand of old pines. A wet, hot wind, hinting at rain, pushed the bugs away. Soft needles formed a deep duff underfoot, his boots and gear left back at the depot. Wearing only boxers, he stretched supine upon the loam. Up and up, his eyes climbed the trees, lingering on their cone-laden crowns.

Thunder growled nearer. His eyes closed. He blinked once, blinked twice. *Fuck it.* He surrendered, allowing his lids to slide shut for good.

Minutes later, he was dragged up from the deep.

He scented a woman. Opening his eyes, he discovered that Nighthawk lay beside him, face to face. She was crying, then kissing; she tasted of salt. Ursine energy flooded his veins, startling him awake and alive. Urgency growing, he followed her lead.

Hawk's hands were upon him, calloused fingers caressing. She leaned over on one elbow, her face tear-streaked, hair still braided for battle, a hovering hawk about to strike.

Then, she put a finger to his lips; time for lust later. They aligned their bodies for sleep, big spoon and little. Tensions evaporated as consciousness collapsed, warm rain trickling through the canopy as storm clouds burst above.

Returned to the Earth

MIIN HEARD THE WATERFALL and knew they were close to the confluence and the cache of canoes. Half the camp had trekked to the river; old folks,
children, and adults fanned out around the two bodies. In the clearing, by the
stacked canoes, the two Sentinels lay in state. Dr. Chow had come, and Miin's
new friend and Samantha-substitute, the elder woman Grace. A warm rain pat-
tered, greening the air with moisture, mossy with molecules.

Elena's team stood solemnly assembled, their parkas scrubbed clean. The
Naturals filed past, expressing sympathy to the stony-faced survivors. Raindrops spattered upon the shrouded dead.

Miin watched Keith—older, sadder—as he stood above the body of his fishing buddy. She left Grace's side, the elder watching with compassion as Miin
embraced her foster uncle. Keith hugged back, his bleary eyes avoiding her
bright ones.

"I'm sorry about your friend," he said, nodding down at Squirrel.

Miin looked reluctantly. Rain had pooled in the valleys of Squirrel's parka;
she remembered her story, the sister she'd lost, the anger she'd known. Something caught in her throat, and Miin shifted her attention to Diving-Duck. "Uncle, I'm sorry about yours as well."

Keith squeezed her hand before Miin moved along, making room for other
farewells. She found Mukwa, and reaching out gripped his large paw. His face
was grim, but his spirit burned bright; Miin basked in his energy, sensing the
change. The Sentinel, Nighthawk, stood by his side, something in her brighter
too. Miin felt glad for both of them.

They processioned slowly back to ELF Country. The two litters were heavy,
and many hands shared the load. Elena posted extra Sentinels at the falls and
other approaches, as their situation had changed, and not for the better. They
wouldn't be ignored by Chosen again.

Miin took her turn, small hands lifting the shaft of Squirrel's stretcher with
difficulty. She bore the load till they blistered, then swapped with another, finding Grace again at the tail of the column. Behind them, rearguard Sentinels
remained vigilant.

◆◆◆

The commandos were away for 24 hours. In that time, Grace kept Miin busy. She'd introduced herself properly after Keith and Mukwa departed: a teacher, an artist, matriarch of a boisterous family, none of whom survived the variant.

Grace, highly qualified, had been teaching art at a nature-immersion school when Michigan collapsed. A few colleagues survived, shielded somehow from the cytokine sting; these survivors had connections with the early ELF, so here she was.

But what she really wanted to discuss were Miin's abilities.

"Young lady, I've got the feeling what you've done so far is just a beginning. Mother Nature has opened her doors, and my job in this place," she gestured to the forest camp, "is to help those, like you, willing to explore this new green reality." The instructional pattern was familiar to Miin. Samantha and Grace—elders, teachers, herbalists—had much in common.

"Our first lesson," Grace said through a kindly grin, "begins with tea."

Miin wasn't surprised that Grace lived alone. They sat in her garden, air abuzz with pollen-drunk bees. The commandos had just left, and Miin pined for her companions. Two-Crow, Mukwa, Squirrel, Diana—silently she wished them protection and success on their mission.

The apprentice fed the fire she'd kindled, a thin column of smoke curling through the canopy. Grace gently questioned Miin about her past experiences: Cranberry Bog, messaging Samantha, her intuition about Chosen and Naturals, and of course her conversation with Elder Oak.

As they talked, the kettle began spouting steam. Grace showed Miin the tea she was preparing. "From what you've shared, I can tell that Samantha—who I'd love to meet someday—has been helping you learn control."

The educator paused her preparations to look directly at her pupil. "So far, your talent has not been yours to command. Your deepest experiences have either been guided, like at the bog, or accidental, like your premonitions."

Miin attended to Grace's recipe. Some ingredients she recognized: dandelion, mint, lavender, and honey. Some she did not, like the small-capped mushroom Grace sliced and then pulverized with her pestle.

"This wider world that nature offers us has only begun to be explored. Have you met Brian?"

Miin recalled her impressions of Brian, the bearded shaman of the Naturals. "Not officially, but I know who he is. I've seen him at council."

Grace lit a bundle of sage, smudging them both. "That young man has taught me a lot. Even before, he was pushing nature's limits. As an artist, I appreciate the hippie in him, though of course he transcends such simple stereotypes. Our Brian calls himself a psychonaut. Ever heard the term?"

Miin, island-sheltered, had not.

Grace smiled. "No matter. Others have this talent too, but we look to him for guidance. He was the one that showed me these."

She pinched a capped stem, presenting it to Miin. The student, Samantha-trained, gave a sniff, cataloging its soily signature in her cortex.

"What these allow us," Grace continued, "is control. I don't know your future, Miin, but I'm guessing Samantha sent you on this mission, despite your young age, because she thought your abilities could help others."

Miin's "help" had proved questionable so far. She felt like a burden, one more worry added to Keith's heavy load.

Grace, reading her, redirected the conversation. "This medicine—mind-medicine, Brian calls it—used properly will allow you to access your talent in the time and place *you* choose, instead of randomly or not at all. How does that sound?"

To Miin, it sounded perfect. "Like a shortcut? A shortcut with mushrooms?"

Grace smiled again. The lesson continued.

Set and setting, so Grace instructed, were vital to getting the most from this blend.

Set, she explained, essentially meant one's mindset. Ideally, Miin should be calm and open before imbibing. As for setting, that was the environment and social vibe surrounding the seeker.

"Do what you can, Miin, to maximize both before introducing organics into your system. Once you've strengthened your abilities, 'set and setting,' not the brew, will be all you need to access connection. Does this make sense?"

Miin thought so. Blowing steam from her cup, she took a sip.

Twenty minutes later, every tree wore a face.

Miin, mind-altered, merged with the membrane of Mother Earth. She bowed beneath the boughs, introducing herself to the woody denizens, who creaked downwards, eager to meet this young tree-talker, this *goshkozi miinan* who knew the old speech.

Each tree blinked eyes-of-burl and opened mouth-knots for whispering; their bark rejoiced at Miin's touch, gentle giants with centuries of experience to share. The oldest remembered a time when tree-talk was more common, many of Miin's kind had been fluent.

Why had it taken so long, they asked her, *for others to learn?*

Never mind for now, answered Miin. *I'm overjoyed to know you, and thank you! And, please, how may I serve? How may I serve the trees?*

The grove nodded at this, their leafy crowns astir. *Quite proper, quite correct.*

News sped through the fungal network. Root to root, the trees pulsed their approval. Her signature was passed on, her pheromones, her face, her name: *Sunlight-on-Berries,* or *Berries-Awake.*

The forest embraced her, 100 square miles of wooded approbation, and Miin, graced by the garden, hugged back. Her mushroom shortcut led to a delightful, day-long delay. Grace, meanwhile, tended to her plants, tea untouched.

◆◆◆

Walking in the rain, the mourners wended their way through the dripping uplands of the state forest. Occasional homesteads stood gutted, roads barricaded: scorched-earth tactics of the Sentinels to preserve ELF Country. The sagging litters never touched ground as the heavy dead were passed from hand to hand. The great trees loomed over these hominids, tiny ant-like creatures ever-busy with their burdens. Miin, peering upwards, acknowledged the giants, her neural network freshly rewired. Yesterday's cup of tea, with Grace observing, had permanently altered her relationship with the rooted realm.

Squirrel and Duck, liberated from life, were returning home. The funereal column processioned under a sign of woven twigs, showing a fantastical tree with curling branches:

Welcome to ELF Country!

Naturals who'd stayed back had been busy with preparations. Two new graves were dug on the outskirts, near those who'd died before: old age and heartbreaks mostly. No elves had been envenomed by Stinger.

The rain stopped at dusk, though lightning still flashed on the horizon, thunder grumbling its distant report. The entire camp had assembled, no bonfires being lit; mourners bowed their heads and knelt in the dirt, trees dripping in solidarity. Earth's maw yawned open, eager for organic offerings.

Elena gave the eulogy, Diana holding her partner's hand.

"None of us are strangers to death," Elena began. "Indeed, all of us born before, in some ways, are dead already, for we have lost almost everything."

The rain, full of pity, resumed its patter.

"As survivors, our mission is to push through our pain, protect those that need protection, and find a new way to live in better harmony with the planet, so those who come after," here an infant cried on cue, "do not repeat the same mistakes."

The renewal of thunder, accompanied by a freshening breeze, foretold an approaching storm cell.

"Diving-Duck and Squirrel died fighting, weapons in hand, for what we all believe in. Their deaths saved lives, mine included. They don't need our words to rest easy. Tonight, they are returned to the earth."

Squirrel's squadmates lowered her covered corpse using pre-positioned ropes. Elena nodded, and Diving-Duck was eased downward just the same, Mukwa, Keith, and several others straining to gently deposit his remains.

The assembly lamented. Brian joined the camp's collared pastor to lead the mourners in solemn song.

A saber of lightning slashed the clouds, an ionic cannonade thundering in response.

The Departed (Grace)

Staff of Woodland Charter School, assorted families, June of Year 1

When the variant started stinging, society as it had existed in Michigan collapsed. Woodland Academy never went virtual; the parents wouldn't have it. They distrusted the state, putting faith in themselves instead. The academy was new, but with an old-school curriculum. Its acolytes were loath to abandon it.

When local districts opted for remote instruction, Woodland opted for yurts. They sprouted in the playground like canvas mushrooms, families squatting nearby in RVs and tents. The month of May, Y1, was idyllic, a dream come true for those involved.

"I told you this could work," they all said to each other through winks and smiles.

Their director, Ms. Grace, was an art teacher, her extended family bivouacked nearby. Grace helped nurture their gardens, leading all ages in comprehensive nature immersion. The regional health department wasn't pleased; neither was the county sheriff. Case counts were climbing, stay-at-home orders recently announced by Michigan's governor.

"But we *are* at home," the families replied, grinning as masked officials were driven off.

But they weren't self-sufficient, nor were they insular. Stinger found them soon enough, vectored to their meadow by well-meaning volunteers. That first death—the English teacher—divided the group. The less committed peeled off, taking their cytokinetic kids to the clinic. The devoted remained, digging graves instead of gardens as their utopia imploded.

Good and Fucked

THE FUCKING WHEELS had come off for sure.

It wasn't even dark yet, and his compound was already out of control. How could everyone be drunk but him? Cowboy heard the rumblings, an overlap of gunfire and thunder; Charlevoix's Chosen had not responded well to news of their losses, and he couldn't blame them. Twelve dead or missing, three trucks lost, ruthless savages shooting arrows into folks left and right—a massacre, and on his watch.

Word traveled fast. He blamed his mechanic, but not too harshly; this was really on him. Bob Campbell had lost his touch and couldn't get it back. What he needed was a career change. Maybe tomorrow he'd fill out some applications, put in his notice, collect unemployment between gigs?

Bob oozed failure. *Even my sense of humor is going stale. What next, Cowboy, what next?*

He flinched at another burst of gunfire. A long one, a whole fucking mag, a waste of ammo, sloppy. The stink of mutiny, gunpowder, and booze rankled his nose.

Good and fucked, that's what he was.

Lightning flashed outside his office window, a breeze pushing the fan blades around. Apparently there was also a snitch, someone who'd reported his sorry ass downstate; Bob's bosses had been calling, but he ignored the angry radio all day. Of course, he'd have to come clean at some point. Just not tonight.

His only way out was to somehow hit it big. The Fox-Hunt had been his chance to impress the bosses and keep his shit show together a while longer; that chance had gone to hell. Bob heard bottles breaking on the pavement and shook his head. He couldn't assemble his men if their lives depended on it. And maybe their lives *did* depend on it. Who knew what these forest-dwelling fuckers were capable of? And what the hell should he call them? On the radio, that Crow character had referred to them as *elves!* The term haunted Cowboy, who imagined hordes of blood-streaked barbarians with pointy ears.

They'd never checked on Kowalski last night, or his three missing men; Cowboy pictured the worst. It was a mistake to leave the bodies where they lay, but he'd been terrified at the time, convinced he and Mikey were next.

Running scared, he and his fixer fled back to Charlevoix, the remaining garrison unimpressed by their faintness of heart. If they'd known the true depths of his cowardice, they'd never have lowered the damn drawbridge. Cowboy and Mikey would have been left marooned out in the wild to be scalped, castrated, whatever. Bob adjusted his junk and shuddered.

Junk-adjacent, his thoughts went to Liz. That fiery broad might be his very last chance. Pretty iffy, though; Bob doubted she would come through. Did a year together, living the pirate life, exploiting the chaos of collapse, count for that much? Probably not, but what else was there? Jump ship, start over, hang out a shingle, hangman-for-hire?

Yeah right. Bob knew his limitations. It wasn't that kind of apocalypse, anyway. Then what? Join some Hidden, shed his fucking virus around? They'd lynch his ass. He'd be strung up for a super-spreader, a cardboard sign dangling from his over-stretched neck.

He damn well wasn't elf material either, whatever that meant. He guessed they knew all about him anyway, though who "they" were was a mystery. Arrows? Spears? Butchery by moonlight? A tree drawn in blood? Shit like this didn't happen, end of the world or not.

Should he sell his services downstate then? Snitch what he knew to the XCons? Or try to pass as Old Law? Maybe in his prime he could have. Maybe. Campbell knew he didn't have the stones for any of these options, and probably never did.

He sat quietly at his desk while the compound partied outside. Rain fell harder now, the scent of wet pavement wafting through the windows. Bob considered the office radio, but Liz was too far away for its signal to reach. Besides, it would broadcast in the open, where any asshole could overhear.

He slid open a drawer and checked the satellite phone instead, finding it still held some charge. Could he get through? Would she pick up? Liz had one in her vehicle, or at least she used to. Bob still had her old number. Should he give it a try?

Ka whumpf! An explosion shook the windows, coming from the harbor. Cowboy saw a plume of water rise into the air, the splash cheered on by a crowd of drunks. Grenades then? Great.

He needed to get his poop in a group, needed Liz to pick up. He dialed her digits, took a deep breath, and thought of better days. He and Lizzy had their share.

Fuck it. Cowboy hit send, prayed to nothing, and played his last card.

Dr. Chow's Promise

TWO YEARS AGO, Dr. Daniel Chow, M.D., from the University of Michigan, ran the region's hospital network. Now gaunt and hollowed by heartbreak, he guided his two guests through the encampment's lab tent. Chow's canvas clinic was sheltered by trees.

The old Native man hadn't said much. Two-Crow looked exhausted, but Chow sensed iron beneath Keith's rust. He'd love to get a blood sample from him: Ojibwe ancestry, isolated since collapse, possible exposure through recent proximity to Chosen. Chow's hypothesis was that Keith had preexisting antibodies, probably in the mid-range.

The girl Miin, bright-eyed and whip-smart, had been asking all the right questions. From what Brian and Grace told him, her connection to nature was impressive. Again, he'd love to get a sample of her blood. His hypothesis: antibody levels in the highest range.

Seeing his lab through islander eyes, Chow observed it afresh. If only his former colleagues could see him now: a bush doctor practicing backwoods medicine, fighting a global pandemic without computers, freezers, centrifuges, fluorescence microscopy, and so much more. Chow did his best, but hoped like hell others out there were doing better.

Access to equipment was not the limiting factor. Rather, it was electricity. In the early days of ELF, when Ellen, a head nurse he'd worked with, convinced him to flee collapse and join her friends in the forest, he'd lobbied hard for a gas generator and failed. The nascent ELF had compromised, a few solar panels and a small battery bank serving as the lab's only power source.

Chow observed Miin observing his lab. The girl brushed her hand through a rack of Sentinel parkas; each garment was plugged into the battery bank, and most showed signs of patching.

"You have electricity here? What are these wires? Aren't you elves against it?"

Chow smiled as he answered her. "Just a trickle, and remember I'm only half-elf. Elena and her Front barely allow it." He gestured to the parkas. "Back in Y1 we looted these from a factory in Central Lake: Armor Express, a local manufacturer of next-gen body armor for the DOD. They're woven with nanotechnology compounds such as graphene, which can mask the wearer's heat signature. Since then I've been tinkering. It's all about the electrome, microcurrents, synching fields. The solar panels ionize their shimmer, helping Sentinels blend with their background. The future, Miin, is bioelectric."

Samantha's student knew the word: a field of energy created by every living thing. Doubtful, she rummaged through a box of headbands implanted with electrodes, also plugged in. "And how do *these* work?"

Chow shrugged. "Stolen from the same plant. Another DOD project; they supposedly boost the wearer's flow-state, helping Sentinels stay in the zone. Miin, excuse my pun, but all results appear positive. Increased circulation, tissue oxygenation, rapid wound healing, and—regarding the parkas, anyway—superior camouflage."

Miin nodded, remembering the bridge, the leafy elves merging with moonlight. Next, she stepped over to a table of medical equipment. "And the variant? What else have you learned about the virus?"

The doctor laid it out, taking Miin back to the beginning. Captivated by Nurse Ellen's Naturals and their apparent immunity, Chow dusted off old textbooks and scavenged compound microscopes from a hospital basement. These dinosaurs didn't need a grid and could magnify up to 2,000X, not enough to image virions, but enough to see human cells and, more importantly, the antibodies and antigens related to the variant. Chow's microscopes used battery-powered LED lights, which were still going strong.

Early in Year 1, prior to total collapse, he'd accessed an electron microscope. The healer Chow had illuminated its blue-and-gold ring, employing a bombardment of electrons to visualize *Corona-virinae*, the crowned king of chaos. The Sentinels' nickname for Stinger was *Gaia's Guardian*, the femme fatale of Mother Earth.

"Explain that again, please."

Chow was showing Miin his journal entries on Naturals and their antibody levels. Two-Crow perched near the tent flap, letting the youngster do the probing.

Chow nodded, rephrasing himself. "What I'm finding, Miin, is that antibody levels, the body's way of fighting off the virus, *increase* the longer someone lives here."

She followed his finger as he indicated examples. Dr. Chow still covered patients' names, old HIPAA protocols too deeply ingrained.

"And what does that tell you, doctor?"

"Well, it's early and the sample size is small, but the data suggest Naturals are onto something. There are many variables, but Brian, for one, would tell you how living an organic, low-tech lifestyle, immersed in nature, enhances one's immune system, granting protection, seemingly, from Covee and its variants. At least for now."

Student Miin, studying his journal, asked another key question, further impressing Dr. Chow.

"Can the lifestyle *create* antibodies in a person that starts with zero?"

Chow looked at Miin closely, scrutinizing this slip of a girl, a supposed tree-talker.

"I don't know yet. I wish I did. Evidence suggests that it's possible, but nothing's been proven in the scientific sense. Certainly, there are many who believe it can happen; Elena, Grace, and Brian for example. All I can promise is that I will protect anyone in my care, and aid them in their struggle against infection. I will fight for their life, and for the survival of our species, with every weapon I can wield."

The girl looked unsatisfied, her new world underwhelmed with his old. Chow didn't blame her; these days, he often felt like a geocentrist confronted by Galileo and his telescope, outmoded in an instant by revelatory change. Looking around his lab at the microscopes, LEDs, slides, journals, and primitive equipment, Chow shared Miin's dissatisfaction. He weathered her gaze, clung to dignity, and vowed—not for the first time—to remain open to new ways of knowing, no matter how strange.

"And what about these records here?" Miin asked, eyeing a shelf of notebooks labeled *Stinger*.

The doctor considered for a moment. If Elena and Brian were all in on this girl, certainly he could do the same.

"Those, Miin, are blood samples from Chosen."

"Show me?"

How could a former educator say no? Chow obliged, saying as he did so, "Since you three arrived—bringing violence with you—there's been new data on this population. I began studying the pathology of infected early on; however, we haven't had much recent contact with Virals. There's been a détente of sorts. But over the past week or so, due to an uptick in combat, Nurse Ellen—Sentinel Elena, I mean—has obtained another dozen samples for our data set."

"And what have you found?"

It was news to Miin that the ELF had collected blood from corpses. She looked to her uncle, who shrugged. Shocker—the old man had kept it to himself.

"Honestly Miin, I've never seen anything quite like it. To my knowledge, it is unique in the field of infectious disease."

Miin—more elvish by the minute—was all ears.

"It's true what you heard at council, and these latest samples confirm it. In every Chosen so far, the variant is present at very high load levels, yet does not damage its host. Also, no antibodies are present. The immune systems of Chosen do not fight the virus, but appear to embrace it. A symbiosis that, as far as I know, is a first in its field. Should I continue?"

Her nod was all he needed. Lecturing a single student in a rustic tent only differed in degree from an ivied hall filled with hundreds; Daniel Chow was a teacher.

"Viruses form a relationship with the host cell. It's how they function, but these are usually antagonistic, or at best, commensal in nature. The relationship between Stinger and Chosen appears to be a rare example of mutualism, where both host and virus benefit from each other.

"Now what you heard at council from Brian, about Mother Nature 'selecting' Chosen for their sociopathy to super-spread contagion and 'green' her planet... obviously that sort of speculation is outside the realm of science, at least Old Science. But I'm trying, as we all should, to remain open to change."

Miin again cut straight to the heart with her next question. "Doctor, is there any evidence that viral load levels in Chosen can be reduced or eliminated?"

Daniel Chow, widower and grieving father, smiled at his pupil, this barefoot girl who would never graduate high school.

"No evidence as yet. But Miin, I'd love to test the possibility."

The Departed (Doctor Chow)

Mary Morrissey-Chow (45 years old), Timothy (13 years old),
Thomas (11 years old), June of Year 1, wife and sons

When regional case counts started climbing, Mary Morrissey-Chow could no longer count on her husband. As chief pathologist for the region, Daniel and his expertise were much in demand. Dr. Chow began sleeping around—not with women, but at hospitals—and the tough decisions about their boys' schooling had fallen to her.

Woodland Academy informed its parents that, unlike public schools, it would *not* be closing. Instead, Woodland would form outdoor pods, protecting its families and furthering everyone's education. Switching to the Academy had been her idea; Timothy and Tom weren't challenged at their traditional school, and both parents hoped alternative education would help their boys flourish. Lacking input from her absentee husband, Mary kept faith with Woodland, signed the waiver, and moved with her boys into a communal yurt.

The weather that May could not have been finer, her texts to Daniel were fragrant with fresh air and garden details. The boys were doing amazing, their dad wouldn't recognize them; they stood inches taller, and hadn't seen a screen in weeks. Daniel's responses had been stilted, too much on his mind. Mary hoped it was the virus and not someone else.

Then the English teacher died.

Families fled, classes were canceled, gardens went neglected. Woodland's director, Ms. Grace, visited Mary and her two boys; Grace kept her distance, talking through the tent flap. The Academy as they knew it was over, but some surviving staff wanted to try something more radical. Mary had trouble following the older woman, both her boys shivering under blankets, foreheads on fire, organs shutting down. Their mom, devastated, felt the same horrible flush.

Mary's final text, her envoi, urged Daniel to drop everything and bring them medicine. The doctor, ever-busy, arrived too late. His commandeered ambulance became a hearse; Grace comforted the shattered man, and outlined a greener plan.

"The worst are full of passionate intensity"-Yeats

THE STINGER VARIANT, despite our meticulous engineering, followed a path of its own. I'm not suggesting this single strand of RNA achieved consciousness or had a functioning brain, but it was hubris to think we'd controlled for all possible variables. We had not. Life, even "near-life," is more complicated than we may ever comprehend.

One design flaw presented early, Stinger stubbornly ignoring the racial restrictions we'd proscribed. From its cosmopolitan viewpoint, a host was a host, and it had no difficulty morphing around the phenotype limitations we sought to impose.

In the early days, infected humans with Asian markers for ESNP (ethnic variant single nucleotide polymorphisms) or ECNP (ethnic variant copy number polymorphisms) experienced more pronounced cytokine storms, but it didn't take our variant long to level the playing field. Soon enough, every race and ethnic group on the planet was defenseless against its mortal sting.

The next surprise involved another genetic anomaly, in this case the MAOA-L gene disorder known as Brunner syndrome. I know it's tedious, but I'm quoting from the literature because this narrative doesn't work without your trust:

"The gene MAOA encodes monoamine oxidase A, an enzyme that degrades amine neurotransmitters, such as dopamine, noradrenalin and serotonin. A rare genetic disorder caused by an MAOA mutation leads to MAOA deficiency and in turn an excess of monoamine transmitters, *causing excessive impulsive behaviour including hypersexuality, sleep disorder and extreme mood swings as well as a tendency to violence,* which is known as Brunner syndrome." -European Molecular Biology Organization (EMBO Reports, Sept. 2010)

The italics are mine, please reread if you skimmed!

Once our variant jumped China's Great Wall, data showed Stinger playing favorites: 99% of infected people died (IFR), most through systemic organ failure. The less than 1% that survived did so seemingly for genetic reasons. Brunner syndrome, years earlier, connected sociopathic behavior with a deficiency in the MAOA gene. Patients inclining towards sociopathy had a dampened STING response when confronted with my virus; their gene mutation kept them infected but alive.

These Brunner syndrome cases, in a societal collapse scenario, were soon free to run amok. Their hypersexual and violent behavior, coupled with high viral load levels, made them the perfect super-spreaders. For example, inmates of supermax prisons survived at a higher rate than the general population; in country after country, news media highlighted these prison breaks. The fact that sociopaths were empowered by the pandemic made containment efforts all the more difficult. Naturally, I took advantage of this phenomenon.

I don't mean to suggest it was *only* low-class criminal types who were spared; of course there were plenty of politicians, CEOs, police, and even doctors that turned Viral. Those with great power proved the most efficient at super-spreading the viral venom of my Stinger.

Open any history book to any page, and the truth shows itself plainly. *Homo sapiens* have always had sociopaths; the fact that these genes are encoded suggests this aberrant behavior benefits our species. Evolution rewards mutation, and in our current dystopia these mutants and their handlers are reaping the rewards.

Dr. Liz's Orders

"WAKE THE FUCK UP, MIKEY!" Cowboy kicked at the door of his man's hooch.

A groan came from inside, followed by his fixer's voice. "Boss, it's early, what the hell?"

Cowboy kicked again. "Rise and shine, motherfucker. It's a beautiful day in the neighborhood!"

Another groan from Mikey, answered by another order from his boss: "Meet me in my office in five fucking minutes!"

Cowboy tried to unsee the sorry state of his Charlevoix compound. Without Candidate labor, their shitters had overflowed, the sun-warmed rot blistering Bob's nostrils. Broken glass sprinkled the pavement, empty bullet casings gleaming brassy on the ground.

Bob made a note to check his supplies. At the pace they'd been drinking, was there any booze left? He was down to a couple dozen men, no women. Outpost duty got weird; Bob learned from past commands to focus his underlings' sex drive on Candidates and not each other, though plenty of buggery still occurred. That was understood. In fact, some considered it a perk of the job.

He prodded his own package, reassured by a responsive twitch. His satellite call with Liz last night had been just what he'd needed—he still couldn't believe she'd picked up. Now Bob felt like a horny teenager, counting down the hours till they could sashay in his sheets.

Liz knew all about the failed Fox-Hunt. She'd bitched him out, calling him a sad sack; said he'd better take care of his men or they'd be "taking care" of him. Boss-fragging was far from uncommon among Chosen, sociopaths not famous for loyalty.

Charlevoix's snitch had been thorough. Liz knew his losses, knew about "ELF Country," the rogue transmissions and Campbell's cowardice in not collecting his dead.

"Shit, Bob, you're kidding me? Just left them in the woods like roadkill to be scavenged? No wonder your men have turned, how the fuck would *you* feel?"

He'd accepted her tongue-lashing; shit, Liz could lash him all day. Another twitch, forcing Bob to adjust himself before walking past the generators. Unguarded, of course.

For the first time in days, he did his duty and actually checked the storage tanks. Fuel levels were low, real low. He thought of the three vehicles he'd abandoned, un-siphoned, on River Road, their gas tanks almost full.

And why the fuck didn't these tree-terrorists confiscate the Raider weapons? Heavy's SAW, Barnes' .30 cal, Kowalski's big .50? Were these Keebler elves gonna fight with sticks and stones?

Bob tried not to worry about his fuel levels; Liz promised she'd handle it. "But this is the *last* time I save your sorry ass. Honestly, Bob, shit's getting old."

After plenty of scolding, Liz promised to come through. She'd somehow sneak past the bosses, her crew with her, and they'd assemble a covert resupply. She'd pass word that fighters were needed for some action up north, offering a chance for revenge on some primitives who dared to bushwhack fellow Chosen.

"Give me a couple days to organize, then look for me after that. And another thing, Bob. I've been thinking about that ferry boat..."

Campbell climbed the stairs to his old fashioned office. He put on crappy coffee and waited for Mikey. Today he'd turn this whole shit show around. They had to be ready for her arrival; impressed with his preparations, he and Liz would bounce around in Bob's bed, then kick ass just like the old days. Fuck by night, fuck shit up by day. He knew it would work. It had to.

To make it official, he grabbed pen and paper to jot down Liz's orders. The percolating brew smelled good, like the past. Sun streaming through his open window, Bob inhaled deeply and sighed, his nightmare of war-painted ghosts and moonlit butchery receding.

Item number one: *Stay off the radio.*

"Bob, don't contact any bosses. They're just gonna fire your ass, or worse. You need a victory before you pick up that mic again."

She also reminded him other ears might be listening. Old Law maintained a National Guard unit in Grayling, capabilities unknown; better to be safe than sorry.

Item number two: *No more patrols.*

No more burning gas and risking men. Bob should forget about pushing past Petoskey; the towns further north, Cheboygan and Mackinaw City, could wait. Instead, he'd reinforce his castle, raise the fucking drawbridge, and stay the hell away from ELF Country.

Item number three: *Lock up the booze.*

Liz was incredulous he hadn't done this already. "You're not dealing with Boy Scouts, Bob. These assholes can't be trusted. Without Candidates, all they've got is alcohol. Lock it up, confiscate their stills, put them on rations. Damn it man, take charge!"

Item number four, his favorite: *Prepare the ferry!*
"Remember our last talk, about island honey-holes? Especially big Beaver, right? That's your ticket, buddy, and ol' Liz will help you cash it."
She'd waved away his worries, unfazed by the Bermuda Triangle reputation of the islands, the rumor that no scout-plane or boat had ever returned.
"C'mon, Bob! You can't fear the bogeyman. *You're* the fucking monster, remember?"
Cowboy's libido lurched as Liz purred through the sat-phone. Fuck it, she was right, Liz always knew how to stiffen his resolve.

Feeling more and more official, he made a sub-list below item four:
Get the ferry running, top it off with oil and diesel.
Liz promised him a tanker truck filled with stabilized fuel.
Weaponize it.
Bob pictured the ferry bristling with guns and plated with armor, a damn dreadnaught.
Choose a crew.
They couldn't all come, so he'd handpick a few. The rest would stay behind to guard the gates.
Prepare for prisoners.
If this worked he'd collar hundreds of Candidates; their pens would be ready.
Pillage and plunder!
His boys would have their fun, and he'd rebuild his reputation. Cowboy Bob was back!

He heard Mikey's tread, his asthmatic approach. Moments later, the mechanic's bulk filled the open doorway. He looked like a total slob, nervous and hungover, his shirt and pants stained, skin glistening with foul-smelling sweat. Feeling generous, Bob stood to pour his man a coffee and pull him up a chair. After giving Mikey a moment to catch his breath, he slid over the notepad, tapping his pencil at the title: "Dr. Liz's Orders."

The Old Forest

GRACE SNORED GENTLY FROM HER COT across the tent as Miin listened to the breeze shake last night's raindrops from the canopy. After yesterday's double burial, the ELF sang dirges before dispersing, families tucking kids into tarp-protected hammocks. Closer friends of Squirrel and Duck stayed to grieve graveside, some of them till morning.

Footsteps approached Grace's garden: stretching out her senses, Miin knew whom they belonged to. Blueberry scooted from her sleep sack, pulled on a sweater and stuck her head out the tent flap. "Good morning, Brian."

The bearded figure, just a few paces away, paused in surprise. She saw him smile through a mass of curly red bristles.

"Good morning, Miin. Care for a walk?"

An hour later they rested, looking down on a valley from their high vantage, a forest of fog; the birds were all singing to welcome the dawn. Brian and Miin acclimated as they sat on a mossy stone. The sun, near solstice, warmed their bones; Miin looked sideways at the red-bearded man. Eyes closed, essence wide open, the sylvan shaman had centered himself.

"Good flying weather today?" she tested, teasing out his secret.

Brian smiled, showing a chipped tooth. "Young lady, are you onto me?"

"Busted," she said, and grinned. "But I'd love to hear more."

"I bet you would. That's exactly why we're here."

He opened his eyes wide. Blue and piercing, they sparkled with energy as she met and held them, her brown irises thinning around each dilated pupil. An exchange took place between the two, a commingling of kindred spirits and trust. He slid his hippie bag off his shoulder, the fabric tie-dyed and covered with patches: *Grateful Dead, Phish, Black Lives Matter.*

Brian pulled out a heavy tome and a thermos. "I brewed tea, Grace's blend. Want any?"

Miin shook her head, focusing on set and setting.

"I think I'm good."

The morning dazzled as the first rays of sunlight struck the dew, creating a diamond mine of droplets.

Brian nodded. "I feel the same."

He put away Grace's potion, opened the big book instead, and arrayed his awareness by rereading a favorite page. Miin rooted herself beside him, two lotus flowers blooming on a Michigan boulder. Synchronized, their electromes overlapped—the output of 80 trillion cells—and fewer words were needed. Ion-driven, their microvoltage combined, together they burned bright above the misty valley.

"There is so much to explore," he began, "but these are warlike times. We must be practical and use our green abilities to protect our people, be their far-seeing eyes."

Miin radiated understanding. She felt him stretch out, mindfulness bubbling forth from their boulder. She was in it; the forest critters too. Brian left trees and plants alone as he reached out for a raptor.

There! He'd found one. Respect and recognition!

An osprey, perched high in a pine, scanned the escarpment.

Proud, the bird resisted his overture.

Brian bowed at the lord-of-winds, a mental genuflection.

The fish hawk gave a feathered nod, consent—reluctantly—had been granted. They merged, each into each other, with everything in balance. Brian's mien grew wilder; Miin could feel his ferality beside her. She tended her trust and focused on the two fliers.

Brian flexed its wings, *his* wings, and they were aloft!

Shamanic, he leaned into flight. It was like dreaming, or rather like flying in a dream, but without any fear of gravity or of waking up. Miin felt herself halfway flying too as, open-eyed, they spiraled skywards on a draft. For a second she saw, with an acuity a hundred times sharper than her own, their boulder far below, two tiny figures just visible atop it.

Brian acted as keeper of the ELF's bible, the Red Book of Tolkien. From 1000 feet Miin eyed his open text: *The Old Forest* was the chapter title, followed by a burst of green verse.

She flew with him as co-pilot, never feeling fear. Brian circled once, deftly landed, stepped away from the osprey and returned to himself, his raptor-vibe fading fast. They shared a moment of roller coaster elation, Miin gasping out loud: she wanted another ride!

"Now you try," the flier advised, "but pick a tree instead."

Miin minded the mystical valley below, opening her perceptual apertures, sifting for the right sort of tree—one willing to go against its grain.

She felt a tug of tendrils, there, from her left!

A grove of young birches broke their fast on sunlight, stomata sipping from last night's rain. She sensed their playfulness, their gossip; every leaf was aflutter. She attempted to merge, to exchange spirits, to more fully enter their rooted reality. She came close, but no closer. Something wasn't working. She pulled back, hollow, unfulfilled. She looked at Brian, looking blue-eyed at her.

Teacher queried student: "So what happened?"

"Something wasn't right," Miin answered, her eyebrows drawing together as she thought it through. "Trees and birds are very different. Let me try another way."

He smiled at her confidence.

Miin bounded from the boulder, grinning back at Brian. She closed her eyes and, showing off, followed her feet blindly. They didn't carry her far. Where they stopped, she looked up: an elder birch kindly proffered directions. This was more like it!

She brailled gentle fingers along the scroll of its bark, found its pulse, and slowed her own. Island-sheltered, she'd never been to a city, but the vibe here was mass transit. It was up to her where she commuted; the elder's roots were the subway, well-connected and well-signed. Miin pushed through the trunk-stile, rode the mycelia metro, and emerged—in spirit only—at the gossipy grove.

The slender youngsters greeted her as an out-of-town guest, and hilarity ensued. They played together, frolicking amid the photons. She drank chlorophyll; tipsy and treeish, she could've stayed at their party all day, but Brian reeled her back in. She uprooted herself and returned, giving the old birch an appreciative pat. Miin looked back at the boulder to see Brian laughing as he slapped a knee, his red beard was bouncing. "That—Was—Awesome!"

At noon, the sun hit its apex. Miin was starving, her hunger at zenith. They remained on the boulder, training hard. Brian overheard her tummy grumble and winked. "Just a few more."

He never let her linger, raising the bar after every connection by picking a tree further off. Birch, white pine, oak, beech—each species proved to be different; to Brian, her progress was impressive. She'd even gone over the horizon, merging with trees she couldn't see. It took lots of effort, but he pushed her onward, saying it had been the same with him.

"When I first started all I wanted was to play, to tag along with the bird. Steering is different. The birds resisted, especially the eagles, who prefer Indigenous familiars. Sadly, we are weapons first, the eyes and ears for innocent people who depend on us to keep them safe. So let's try one more, OK?"

Miin was worn out but elated. She nodded, awaiting instruction.

Her mentor considered, then laid out her last task.

"This time don't search for a specific tree. Instead, ask the forest to *find something* for you. I've done this before, but it's difficult. Are you ready?"

Miin looked around for a tree she hadn't tapped. Perhaps a hardwood? Something slow-growing and tightly grained?

There, rooted on a ridgetop above their boulder, dwelt a gray philosopher, an ancient beech, *Fagus grandifolia*, a hub tree connected to hundreds. Miinan processioned slowly, projecting reverence, selflessness, and a druid's desire for dialogue.

Trees don't like surprises. Blueberry understood this as she approached. The beech, aloof, slowly acclimated to her aura. Drawing closer, she knelt in a nook near the trunk, rooting herself down. When she felt the tree had grown comfortable with her presence, Miin asked for entrance and was gravely granted permission.

She placed her tiny hands upon its bole, slowed herself, then slowed down some more. These ancients experienced time differently, in epochs.

Miin synchronized her pulse rate and exchanged electrons with the elder.

The tree, of course, had heard of her, was glad to host *sunlight-on-berries*, and how could it be of service? Miin thanked the gargantuan and exchanged some pleasantries, then relayed her request for reconnaissance.

Find them for me, she asked, mentally shaping those she sought: *Chosen, their vehicles, the stench of exhaust, frenzy and violence, their dominion over others, the smell of blood, of violation, their disconnect from trees, super-spreading sickness—*

A flare of alarm and recognition. *Enough! We know them!*

The tree showed Miin their signature.

Foulness, a spreading rot, a two-legged blight.

The beech bent downward with its branches. Miin twined her limbs in turn, *miinan* grafting to *gaawemizh.*

Let's find them!

Away they went.

The Departed (Brian)

Paul Olsen, Brett Anderson, Leif Sigurd, twenty-somethings, August of Year 1

Friends since junior high, they'd walked through every gate together. The first few were easy: girls, grades, graduation. Sharing an apartment in college, the four friends left the well-trodden path in order to map the terra incognita of their minds.

Brian began it, opening their perception with Huxley's *Doors*.

Brett discovered Leary in a Minneapolis book shop.

Leif explained Peter Carroll as best he could.

Paul went full Tibet with Robert Thurman.

Their fridge emptied as bookshelves overflowed. Classes were dropped, and girlfriends too. Their parents grew worried, but family attempts at intervention were ignored. The friends pooled their money, following a progression of psychotropic exploration: psilocybin, peyote, DMT. They started tasking their dealers to procure them ever-more unusual trips, *Psychotria viridis* from Amazonia, fly agaric, *Salvia divinorum*.

When collapse began, they isolated early.

Brett had a key to an island cabin with a Canadian view. The shared boat ride—duffel bags stuffed with books, tools, and food—was an apex moment for all four. Arriving at their island, they worked hard to stack stove wood and fill their freezer with walleye fillets. Drug-free, the sober summer of Y1 was their best. Without digital screens, they were blind to the mass death all around them.

The general store proved to be their undoing. They needed gas for the outboard, and for the generator. They weren't self-sufficient, but who was? Their survival depended on fuel refined from the organic remains of Cretaceous ferns.

Brett was stung first, then Leif, then Paul.

Their island was mostly rock, so Brian deep-sixed his friends, sewing stones in their shrouds, planting them—together forever—at the bottom of the lake. He grew his beard long, and his gaze shifted skyward.

The Council of Elves

THE CHOSEN RAIDER STOOD UNMOVING, oblivious to the stealthy pair above. Mukwa had a million things on his mind when he should only have one—the flight of his arrow. He held a deep breath and centered his focus, aiming instinctually at the Chosen's chest.

Nighthawk, perched beside him on the bough, didn't help his concentration. She was sexy as hell. He could smell her sweat, her honeyed skin; their electrical fields sparked with proximity.

Focus wilting, arousal growing, Mukwa loosed. *Fwwwwit!*

A total miss, he knew immediately.

Thunk! His arrow buried itself near the Raider's boot.

Damn it!

A split second later, Hawk's missile punched through the straw man's chest, a perfect bullseye. Nighthawk then smacked him on the head, not gently. "Stop thinking so hard, dumbass!"

Muck, so often mocked, flinched at the laughter from above. Matador and Tigre of course, the *putas*. Muck hoped they'd fall from the tree.

It was a training day, their Sentinel squad working through the target course. Straw-stuffed corpses littered the ground, not one of them "killed" by Mukwa.

Drumming reached their ears, insistent, calling the elves to council. The squad dropped down from the trees, quick and professional, weapons safe, a SEAL team of sylvan operators. Fucking Matador, the showoff, did a backflip from a high bough and stuck the landing, his squad mates bursting into applause.

Tigre elbowed Mukwa. "You ever need help, *güey*, sticking your arrow," of course he was thrusting his hips, "you pay attention to Tigre! I'll show you how to nail a target."

The squad cracked up.

Hawk, mockingly jerked her hand up and down an arrow shaft, retorting, "Only target you've been nailing, *pajero*, is your own!"

More laughter; Mukwa was smiling too. She was just so badass!

Their squad—Mukwa, Matador, Tigre, Nighthawk, Sparrow, and Bull—strutted towards the council site. June's sun was setting late, spreading twilight through the trees. All the groups were gathering; farmers and foragers had been busy, fishermen too. There was much to do before winter. Livestock had been penned, Mukwa smelling their musk on the evening breeze. There were whole flocks he hadn't seen yet, shepherded in far pastures. He shook his shaggy head. These new world elves had it made, if only the old world would leave them to it.

Tonight's council was a big deal, the deaths of Duck and Squirrel hitting the Front hard. Harder still to reckon with was their looming showdown with Charlevoix's Chosen. The newest intel predicted shit would get worse. He hadn't seen much of Miin and Keith; Mukwa guessed they'd be speaking at the pow-wow. He hoped like hell he wouldn't have to.

The waxing moon shone brightly, six days till she was full. The side flaps of the big tent had been rolled up, council deliberations open to all; Matador's squad filed through the gathering crowd. Mukwa heard his name and "el oso" as parents pointed him out to their children. Sentinels, especially those who'd fought Chosen, were respected in ELF Country, recent deaths only reinforcing their cred. Mukwa had watched the camp kids at play, and judging by the intensity of their games, there'd be no shortage of Sentinel recruits.

Matador's group arrayed itself outside the tent, close enough to bear witness. They settled on the ground, nodding at other squads doing the same. Nighthawk sat close beside Mukwa, and together they waited, their skins prickling with each other's energy.

Brian, red-bearded, drummed a duet with a forager girl, flowers woven into her hair. They syncopated as the crowd settled down, then finished with a flourish. The gathered elves applauded.

Brian held up both hands. "Thank you friends, and thank you for coming! We assemble tonight because our situation has changed, and not for the better."

The general mood turned serious.

"Most of you know there's been fighting. Twelve Chosen were recently killed, and sadly, we've lost two of our own."

Brian allowed a moment for silence, then continued, "Three scouts—shielded—from Beaver Island are here, seeking information."

He gestured to Keith and Miin, both inside the tent, and then to Mukwa seated outside with his squad.

"We have shared what we know, and they have shared in return. We've learned that their island, due to its vigilance, has not yet been stung, and although they've seen suffering, like us, they've found ways to survive."

He paused, glancing toward Miin and Keith. Did they want to add anything?

The two sat together around the council fire, stone-silent. Not yet.

Brian rolled on, turning back toward the crowd. "Our guests have provided valuable information about Chosen capabilities and practices, including details of a mass execution they witnessed. Mr. Two-Crow even stole a map, which we've been studying. Sentinel Elena?"

The tall athlete stood, unfolding the annotated road map.

She briefed the assembly as she circuited the tent. "Your questions will be answered, but let me explain what we've learned so far. These Chosen are from a scavenger outfit based in Charlevoix. We've been aware of them for a while, and no doubt they're aware of us as well. As you can see, they've pushed up from the south, extracting resources and shipping them downstate. ELF Country lies between their outpost and areas they most likely wish to plunder further north."

Elena held up the map, showing them the red-circled towns of Indian River, Cheboygan, and Mackinaw City. On the far side of the big bridge, "Free North" was penciled across the Upper Peninsula, along with "???" as if this intel wasn't certain.

"I don't have to remind you that Chosen traffic people as well. They call them Candidates, use them as forced labor—and worse. Most are killed quickly by Stinger. The Chosen we sampled all carried heavy viral loads."

Elena looked to Dr. Chow, who nodded confirmation. She continued, "Second, this map details other groups besides Chosen. Some of you remember a faction of Virals called XCons?" Elena made an X on her forehead with her thumb as she spoke.

"During collapse there were reports that some incarcerated felons survived. We predict that XCons, like Chosen, are super-spreaders, symbiotic with the variant. According to this map their nearest turf appears to be Clare. Just a two-hour drive, way too close for comfort."

She stopped, and hands were raised, wood added to the council fire. Night darkened as stars pestered the moon.

"A final point. Some of you know Camp Grayling, an Army post about an hour's drive from here. This map suggests an Old Law unit may be headquartered there. We've had no contact, and believe they are virus-vulnerable, dependent on chem suits and PPE. These soldiers are reputed to be a force for good, though of course we can't confirm.

"To conclude," she said, placating those with raised hands, "I am no longer confident in our position here. Secrecy has been compromised. A dozen Chosen have been killed, four of their vehicles destroyed. They know we use the river. It won't take long to find us and attack in force. Also," she pointed at the map, "as I said, these XCons are way too close. We know nothing about them. I fear getting caught up in their turf battle with Chosen."

Mukwa saw Miin begin to fidget. Keith at her left, on her right sat the grandma-type she'd been living with—Grace? He knew Blueberry's look; his foster sis would have her say.

Elena canvassed the gathering. "Rodriguez?" Two men sat knee to knee, Rodriguez and farmer White. Pre-collapse their relationship had been professional, boss and picker; now their roles had reversed, and Señor Rodriguez took the lead. From terraced gardens to their candle-lit tent, the two greenthumbs tended each other and were blooming.

The sun-dark farmer stood to speak. He wore patched jeans and flannel.

"What kind of time do we have? The crops look promising, can we hold on till harvest?"

The Sentinel shook her head. "Our team was trapped three nights ago, outnumbered and outgunned. If it wasn't for Diving-Duck," she dropped her eyes, and Mukwa saw others do the same, "we'd have been killed or captured. We're not trained to resist torture. The Virals would have learned our location and defenses. I'm sorry, Rodriguez, but I think it's time to go."

A low groan ran through the assembly. Elena bowed her head. "I am sorry," she said, "for everyone. But we must treat these threats as real. Otherwise, we risk losing everything." Another hand was acknowledged. "Ms. McIntyre?"

McIntyre, no-nonsense, worked with the school-age Naturals. She looked like every principal Muck had sat detention for.

"Are you suggesting, Sentinel Elena, that we just pick up and start walking?" The ex-administrator sounded incredulous. "There are over 30 children in this camp, most of them pandemic orphans with traumatic backgrounds. Their ACE scores—Adverse Childhood Experiences—are literally off the charts. You can't seriously be suggesting we leave safety, our crops, and our winter stockpiles to go wandering through the forest? A forest, as you say, that is infested with Chosen slavers. I'm sorry, but there's got to be another way."

Many were nodding or voicing agreement, especially the adoptive parents.

Sadness etched Elena's face as well. "I understand your frustration, Ms. McIntyre. But it's not my Sentinels I'm thinking of in making this recommendation. It's the children." Expression still grave, she called on the next raised hand. "Pastor George?"

A barrel of a man rose slowly to his feet; Mukwa had often seen him working with the livestock. The pastor's voice carried clearly as he said, "Thank you, Elena, for your honesty. We know you have our best interests at heart. I also thank your Sentinels for their vigilance. If harder times are indeed on the way, no doubt you warriors will bear the brunt of it."

George paused for a moment, then continued, "Before Covee, before Stinger, I was a Lutheran minister. I tended my human flock, and also raised horses. I had been blessed with children, even grandchildren. All that is gone. I am still a man of faith, but don't know where to put it. In God? Nature? In each other?"

Mukwa liked this burly dude; he hadn't met many church types he couldn't out-wrestle.

"When in doubt, I fall back on the familiar. This is from Exodus," George said, then recited from memory:

"Pharaoh called for Moses and Aaron at night. He said, 'Get up and go away from my people, both you and the people of Israel. Go and worship the Lord. Take your flocks and your cattle, and go.'"

George translated, sermonic: "Moses led his people out of slavery, away from Pharaoh and his chariots, to a land of milk and honey. I know that all of us," here he nodded toward McIntyre, then Rodriguez and farmer White, "hoped that here, under benevolent trees, we had reached our promised land. I am not Moses; none of us are. But I have heard enough to know we are not safe here. This has become a land of Pharaoh, a land of slavery, plague, and war. If this council wills it, then I will go. We have horses, donkeys, even llamas to help us transport what is necessary."

He resumed his spot on the ground. Naturals nodded approval, patting his shoulder, his knee, his hand. Their pastor had spoken well.

Mukwa, from the outskirts, saw Miin leave her place and go to George, surprising the Lutheran with a hug. Barefoot and brown-eyed, she looked towards Brian, then Grace. Both mentors maintained their neutrality. This was her call.

"My name is Miinan. It means blueberry, but most call me Miin."

She looked around at the gathered Naturals, smiling. The people smiled back; how was she not terrified? Muck would rather face a hundred shrieking Raiders.

"*Miigwech*, thank you for taking us in. You've been like family to me and my friends."

She smiled at Uncle Crow, then winked at Mukwa, though her face became solemn as she turned back towards the tent.

"We brought trouble with us, and death. Duck and Sarah—I mean Squirrel—would be alive if we'd left you alone."

The crowd protested.

"My hope is that some good can come from this harm."

She bowed her head and submerged briefly, tapping into something. Was she reaching out? Mukwa guessed it was to the trees.

Miin resurfaced, ready now to share. "I experienced something today with Brian."

She looked at the ELF shaman. He stood up from behind his drum and said, "Nature has opened her doors. Most of you know about my connection to birds, to fliers?"

A raptor, winging across the moon, pierced the night with its cry.

The crowd stirred, Mukwa too. Nighthawk squeezed his padded paw.

Brian continued, "Miin's connection is similar, but with trees. Earlier today, we used our green abilities to gather information about those who threaten us. What the trees told her, I confirmed soon after with a flyover." He frowned and ran a hand through his curly beard, adding, "I wish we had better news."

Miin resumed her thread, saying, "With Grace and Brian's help, I've found a way, crazy as it sounds," she acknowledged Daniel Chow with a nod, "to access the root network and tap into the wood-wide-web."

To Mukwa, the crowd's reaction seemed mixed. Fliers were one thing, talking trees quite another. Whispers spread like sparks through the dusk.

"This morning I connected with a beech tree. I was searching for Chosen, for threats to ELF Country; eventually the old one understood, and away we went. It's difficult to explain, but I'm sure it could be taught."

Ms. McIntyre frowned at Miin's curricular suggestion as the camp's youngsters grinned, picturing their severe principal with the too-tight bun leading a lesson in tree speech.

"This beech—nerve center of the web, fiber-connected to hundreds—showed me a place where the Chosen signature was strong. Sounds, smells, and vibrations flooded me through the filaments of the forest. My impression, through the trees, was of a *violent force* assembling. The exact location was tricky to pinpoint, as you can imagine, trees don't do highways, street names, or townships. Instead I was shown coastlines, hills, and valleys. It was one of the most powerful experiences of my life."

Miin stopped speaking for a moment, sinking into a treeish stupor. The council waited, a bit confused; again came the circling of whispers.

"When I emerged, I spoke with Brian. Together, we decoded the location, narrowing it down so he could do a flyby."

Brian gave her a kind look. "Thank you, Miin. None of this was easy, as we are both novices. I hope someday to meet others with more skill." He sighed then, leaning wearily upon his drum. "I found a strong flier, a vulture, *Cathartes aura*, that I'd used to assist Diving-Duck—but, that's a story for another time."

Elena, Diana, and even Keith looked sharply up at him. Brian helping with Duck's mission was news to them.

Brian continued, narrating from his bird's-eye view. "Using the trees' topography, we flew south, to the edge of the vulture's range. Just before exhaustion, we scented belching fumes—Miin's clanking column. It was just leaving Grand Rapids, northbound; I counted 20 vehicles, including a semi and a tanker truck. Getting a head count was harder, but I'd estimate around 100 Chosen. The lead truck was painted a fiery red."

Elena's face and tone grew hard as she said, "I need to know more about you and Diving-Duck. We will debrief that later." Brian nodded, then sat down to rest—he still looked exhausted from his flight. Elena absorbed their intelligence. "Thank you both for your work this morning," she said at last, in a gentler voice. "I don't doubt it was difficult. Trees and birds? Incredible, almost impossible to believe. Gaia's new world can feel like a dream." She shook her head, clearing away any cobwebs of doubt. "How soon could this column arrive? Is it headed to Charlevoix? A response, maybe, to our recent resistance?"

Brian answered, "The roads are shit, and old gas is even shittier. I'll fly again at first light, but based on what we saw these Chosen could make Charlevoix either late tomorrow or the day after, depending on whether they raid along the way."

Elena calculated.

Pastor George powered up his pulpit voice. "Pharaoh is coming," he declared, "with all his chariots too! They want to chain us, enslave us. In the Old Testament, Yahweh spoke to Moses through a bush. Perhaps now it's trees and birds? The time has come for us to decide."

Rodriguez checked with his partner, then spoke for all the farmers. "If we abandon our fields and risk our flocks, where will we go? What is the destination?"

McIntyre was skeptical. "How do we keep the children safe? What good are bows and arrows," she challenged sharp-eared Elena, "against trucks and machine guns?"

Diana bristled on her partner's behalf, rising in the firelight. "Sentinels can't defend this place, not against a hundred. They would break through and destroy us all. We must make an organized flight. Our squads will guard the approaches. If they come, we'll fend them off, buy time to pack up."

Many voices crowded the council tent.

"Where to?"

"What do we bring?"

"What about toddlers, seniors, pregnant women?"

The doctor raised his hand for quiet.

When he had it, Chow spoke. "You know me, my profession. I'm a man of science, of logic, of proof and repetition. And yet, if I'm honest, if I turn my calculating eye to the moment, then this is what I observe." Daniel Chow surveyed them, leaning on his years at the lectern. "Nature is speaking. Perhaps, like Moses of old," a nod to George, "it wishes to bring us to safety. With unbiased eyes, we can see that even the birds and trees are with us."

The doctor winked at Miin. "Perhaps nature has sent us blueberries, too?"

Smiles bloomed in the crowd, alongside a willingness to hear more.

"It is my vote that we leave. We should begin immediately. The way I see it, there is only one place to go."

Chow looked directly at Keith, who sat stone-stubborn and silent.

"The scouts are here for a reason. It's an invitation; we must head for their island. It's the logical choice. One question though, will they have us? Will they make room? Will they trust our immunity? It is a great deal to ask. Our future depends on it, and their future as well. Keith Two-Crow, the time for silence is past. Will you have us? Will they? Who will plead our case? Our lives are in your hands. Keith, Miin, and Mukwa, we beg you, please don't drop us."

The Departed (Pastor George)

Carol Halverson, 70 years old, daughters and grandkids, August of Year 1

When their northern county shut down, Carol gathered her brood at "The Ranch." The fenced acreage included outbuildings and ponies; she and George, recently retired, were living happily ever after.

It was wonderful to have her daughters, their husbands, and all the kids under one roof. With eggs to gather, animals to feed, and hay to mow, the pandemic months were the best of their lives. Grandkids grew ruddy and spent their summer barefoot, her daughters played music in the evenings; the piano, long-neglected, never sounded so good.

Her sons-in-law were handy and kept the John Deere running—all its implements too. The only missing piece was her George. Supposedly retired from pastoral work, the man answered every call and said yes to every parishioner.

He held a hundred hands that summer as the variant stung his flock. Virus-vigilant, George moved into a horse trailer behind the barn. His hospice work put them all at risk, and he insisted on safety. The grandkids took his meals out to the barn, also clearing away his empty dishes. They could only talk to papa through walkie-talkies. George watched them ride ponies through binoculars, lenses misting with grandfatherly tears.

But Stinger's virions had gained function and could live for days upon surfaces, a contaminated cup proving to be the ranch's undoing. A single strand of RNA spread from a parishioner to George, to a grandkid, then to the family. True to form, George held every dying hand and dug each grave afterwards, blistered hands burning as he shoveled through sorrow.

By August of Y1, five months into Stinger's contagion, the grid had gone dark, along with the regional hospital. The last hand he held was Carol's, by candlelight. Their dream, brightest at the end, snuffed out when she died.

Annie's Friend

"WHEN WILL YOU BE HOME TONIGHT, TOM? I could make us something special."

Doyle, rising early, grunted in the dark. "Got a late night, Annie. Don't wait up."

Her husband dressed himself with thick fingers, then chastely kissed her cheek. She watched him shoulder his duffel and stump past her heat-wilted garden, going out through the gate, bound for the docks. Her man never looked back.

Annie, frayed like her robe, observed the rising sun with a sinking heart. Four damn decades of early alarms, brewing coffee, packing sandwiches, seeing him off, and he can't even look back? If she didn't know better, she'd suspect another woman. Well, maybe he'd got one? Maybe this is what affairs felt like?

A few days ago, at the ferry dock, he'd left the same way. He'd asked for extra sandwiches, just like this morning. He'd mumbled about a late night, then steamed away—supposedly to check the Watchers—but Tom never came home.

Annie hadn't slept a wink that night, picturing the worst, left all alone with her fears. Agitated, she'd gone down, filled a jar with Sam's wine and sat on the porch, getting tipsy as the first quarter moon sailed sadly through the sky.

Returning at last, Tom found her the next morning, passed out with her indiscreet jug in her lap. They'd fought, then he'd stumbled up to bed, exhausted and guilty. They'd yet to make up. In their younger years that had been the best part. Tom Doyle was fiery, hot-tempered, and difficult to get along with, but they'd always patched things up with passion.

Annie, sober this time, mourned the sunrise with a sigh. Tom's passion, at least towards her, was something she hadn't felt in quite a while. She really couldn't handle another day of moping. A long walk never hurt. She'd visit some friends, force her mind from Tom. Lord knows he wasn't minding her.

An hour later, and St. James and its harbor were behind her. The June morning was muggy with heat, sweat beading her brow and dampening her pits. She sojourned south on King's Highway, waving at women in the fields, at menfolk hanging laundry. The wildflowers nodded waist-high along the right-of-way.

She passed the weedy airstrip, its runway rusty with Y1 barricades and busted Cessnas, some windshields still spattered with dried blood.

After five miles she felt thirsty and overheated. Stopping by the schoolhouse on McCauley Road, Annie primed its old pump, wrestling the handle till cold water gushed. She filled up a dented dipper and parked herself in some shade.

Summer clouds billowed white above a marsh, the woods and fields shimmering green. Indian paintbrushes stippled red on a grassy canvas. Lake Michigan, huge and blue, delighted in its necklace of sparkling diamonds. Annie sat there for a long spell. There were no cars, no tourists, no swarms of Spandex-wearing cyclists. She looked up, seeing a sky clear of airplane exhaust.

Annie closed her eyes, allowing her many knots to unkink. She opened herself to the breeze, its leafy lullaby absolving her, briefly, from consciousness.

She returned to herself refreshed, replaced the dipper and resumed the road. Her feet knew what her head did not: their destination.

She passed friends, fishwives she'd known for years, but never halted. Asphalt gave way to gravel. Entering the state forest, the gravel devolved into dirt. Finally, Annie admitted she was visiting Samantha. Cranberry Bog must be close; the path had roughened, trending downhill. She'd never been to Sam's shack. Weary, she was ready to arrive. Her heartache had been blunted by blisters and an empty belly. A humid noon hung heavy on Beaver Island.

Finally, the path dropped her at a clearing. Annie saw a sun-warped shack, a well-tended garden, and a springhouse—she'd found Samantha's place!

Flushed and thirsty again, Annie knocked, but her friend wasn't home. Water burbled behind the shack. Seeking shade, she entered Sam's springhouse and ladled out a drink. Nothing had ever tasted so good. Dead on her feet, she forced herself outside and sat on a shadowed bench. The garden observed her with a million eyes, butterflies fluttering while fussy bees droned on about trespass. Perhaps she nodded off.

Awake again, she blinked several times to clear away the webs. A silver-haired woman stood before her, barefooted, carrying a basket of greens. Her smiling face was crinkled with laugh-lines. "Annabelle Doyle, you shouldn't have!"

Half an hour later, Annie, tuned up, felt right as rain.

Sam ushered her inside, the two sharing a spring-chilled jug of wine made from fruit picked by Miin. Now both wore smiles, talking towards some truth.

"I just don't know about my Tom. He's always been distant, but now we're miles apart, in more ways than one."

Sam saw the little girl inside Annie: her heart, her loyalty, her need to get swept off her feet. "And where do you think he's off to, when he spends nights away?"

Annie shook her head. "Maybe an affair? Plenty of that going on these days. But I swear, Samantha, I don't think it's in him."

Samantha, recognizing Annie's marriage neared the rocks, navigated carefully. "What would you say if I told you Tom's been running missions to the mainland, helping out some friends of mine?"

For a second, Annie looked shocked. Then less so.

"The mainland, and not a mistress? Sounds more like Tom Doyle for sure."

Sam refilled Annie's cup, reflecting on fate. "You say he's off again? Won't be back till tomorrow?"

"I expect so. He wanted extra food, and packed his sea bag too." Annie yawned and stretched, feeling suddenly tired. "I haven't seen your Miin around lately," she said, eyeing the girl's empty cot. She yawned again.

"Tell you what, friend Annie, why don't you rest here a bit? You're in no shape to walk home, and I've got things that need doing. You just make yourself comfortable."

Too tired to protest, Annie let Sam lead her to the cot. Mrs. Doyle laid down, closed her eyes, and was soon asleep. The smile, one of marital relief, never left her face.

Sam slipped into moccasins, provisioned her pockets, and hiked towards the nearest road, hoping to hitch a wagon ride to the harbor.

Midnight Rendezvous

TRUE TO HIS WORD, half-surprising himself, Doyle positioned *Mary* just off-shore, awaiting Two-Crow's pre-arranged arrival. It had been four nights since their last comms. The big lake was a mirror, both the moon and its mirage waxing towards full. Doyle killed the motor, doused his lights, and bobbed at the rendezvous point.

He'd had to lie again: to Annie this morning, to Keller in the lighthouse, and to himself about what the fuck he was doing. Beaver Island's diesel reserve was dangerously low. The council needed gas for winter, for its clinic, to keep folks from freezing. Doyle's confidence, like the harbor gauge, was plummeting.

Was Keith still alive? The old man signed off last time in the middle of a damn gunfight. What if he'd been killed, or worse, captured? If Crow had cracked, tonight could be an ambush.

Mary's captain ducked into the forward cabin, opened the gun locker, and hefted out his well-oiled rifle. He thumbed it full of brass cartridges, locked in a round, and stepped out on his fish deck. Doyle squinted at the grinning gibbous moon. Four nights till full; it cast a ghoulish glow on the highlands of Little Traverse Bay. The lack of light from Harbor Springs and Petoskey still weirded him out. No winking towers, no beaming trucks, every billboard gone black—the electrified world was extinct. Would it ever come back? Tom didn't think so.

Blink, blink, blink, went the signal in the night, across the open water.
Here we go!

Doyle sharpened his senses: no time for fuckups. He got into a firing position, shielding his bulk behind steel rails. He eased open the action, double-checked the chamber, and then reached for his spotlight.

Blink, blink, blink, Doyle flashed back.

His night-sharp eyes limned the shape of a canoe, its two occupants paddling towards *Mary*. Ready for a trap, Doyle scanned the silver horizon, but the canoe was alone.

Keith, hooded, sat in the stern, looking like a pilgrim from another age. Two-Crow cradled a lantern in his hands. *Blink, blink, blink*—his fingers flashed with fire.

Doyle signed again, careful with his weapon as the canoe drew closer. When it reached hailing distance a voice rose above the lapping waves between them.

"Doyle, it's Two-Crow. Kindly lower your rifle."

Reluctant, Doyle complied. Squinting, he could just make out Keith, a shadowed stranger sat in the bow, in front of the old man.

"Who's that with you?"

Keith answered, as quiet as he could, "This is Doctor Chow, a friend. May we approach? We have much to discuss."

"Is he infected? Contagious?"

A pause before Chow answered from the bow. "Captain, I am not. I have immunity. That's why we're here."

Ten minutes later their canoe was aboard, the weapons safely stowed. Doyle stood at the helm, furthering them from shore, while Keith and the doctor sat at the galley table awaiting *Mary's* captain. Chow had brought a file—facts about infection, the foundation of his hypothesis. Keith shook his head—the time wasn't right, keep it secret, and safely out of sight. Stale coffee percolated through recycled grounds; aromatic, the welcome smell helped prep them for conversation. Keith was rolling cigs, one for him, one for Doyle. The good doctor didn't smoke.

Soon *Mary's* pistons paused, the steel boat drifting, becalmed upon the deep. Time to parlay. Doyle abdicated his wheelhouse throne. Eyeballing the guests, he filled three mugs. Lacking cream since collapse, utterly un-sweet, the captain's coffee was black and bitter. A moment of silence as they sipped the hot brew. Keith slid a rollie and his Zippo, *Semper Fi*, toward the captain. Doyle thumbed the wheel, sparking steel against flint, no ritual more ancient. The herbs ignited, Tom lit up, took a deep drag, and Keith did the same. The galley fugged up with smoke. The only light, a red bulb for night vision, dimmed on its mount. Doyle adjusted the galley's blackout curtains. The three men— Cro-Magnons in a cave—regarded each other in the gloom.

Keith cracked the ice. "Thank you, Captain Doyle, for making the trip. This is something you didn't have to do. It's risky, and it's appreciated."

He blew a thin stream of smoke towards the overhead, and was quiet.

Doyle took a drag, tapped ash, and squinted suspiciously at the stranger, Dr. Chow.

"What exactly do you mean you're *immune*?"

And away they went.

After two cigs and a second pot of coffee, tensions had eased, though not Doyle's doubts. Keith's pilfered map lay spread across the table. They'd scrutinized its details. Doyle, quick with charts, soon learned the lay of the land. Nervous system humming with leaf and bean, he tapped a heavy finger over Bear River, the aquatic artery of ELF Country.

"You're tellin' me there's 200 of you, all immune, caught between the hammer," he pointed to Charlevoix, "and the anvil?" He then stabbed a finger at the XCon notation near Clare.

Daniel Chow nodded in confirmation. "That's right. And we've got intel that more Spreaders are coming." The doctor's delicate finger traced the route north on 131, from Grand Rapids to Charlevoix. "The Chosen compound in Charlevoix might be reinforced already."

Doyle took it all in. "And none of you *Naturals*," he sneered a bit at the unfamiliar concept, "will handle a firearm, even to protect your own kids?"

A clinical nod from Chow, no apology in it.

Keith cleared the air. "They're not hippies, Doyle. I've fought with them twice. Their kill ratio so far is 16-2. They're guerrilla fighters, motivated and tough on their own turf."

Doyle still doubted. "So what's the problem?"

"Their turf is shrinking. They've got children. They're outnumbered, or will be soon."

A gentle swell lifted the boat, freshwater fathoms yawning below. The doctor coughed, the secondhand smoke irritating his throat. Doyle, taking the cue, stubbed out his cig and opened a porthole. The night gushed in.

"What's this got to do with me, with the island? You want a rescue? Impossible."

Keith fixed the captain with a rifleman's steady gaze. "They want more than that."

Anger flashed from Doyle.

Before he could speak, Keith rumbled in response, "They want sanctuary. For us to take them in. Your fleet can meet them, full moon at the latest. We'll evacuate everyone and their livestock to the island."

In the red light, Doyle's face twisted. He banged both fists on the table, making the mugs jump. "God damn it, Keith! Are you out of your fucking mind?"

The captain stood abruptly and adjourned to his wheelhouse, leaving a trail of profanity in his wake. The doctor, alarmed, looked askance at Keith. The weary veteran shook his head. Unwelcome, the guests ducked through a hatch and onto the fish deck.

A flick of movement by the canoe, a furtive *something* snagged Keith's eye. He put a hand to his knife's hilt and moved cautiously, signing to Chow: *Stay back!*

A woman's wizened figure unfolded, her white hair garlanded by moonlight. She smiled and raised a hushing finger to her lips. "That went rather well, don't you think?"

Keith couldn't help himself. He opened his arms wide, grinning.

Samantha, a stowaway, stepped into his embrace.

Doyle's Return

THE HORIZON HID THE MOON, the Milky Way mirroring *Mary's* transit as Captain Doyle helmed her homeward. His two guests had departed. He'd helped launch their canoe, even lifted a hand in farewell.

But had he lied to them? To Keith and that damn doctor?

Grudgingly, Doyle promised he would confer with his captains. As a group they'd discuss an evac of the Naturals, and their fucking animals too. *If* the captains agreed, then four nights from now, the full moon would aid them.

Even as a greenhorn working his father's boat, Doyle had done his best thinking while steering a course. He minded the compass and heading, then examined his own, trying to remember everything they'd discussed.

When the shock of Keith's request had subsided, Doyle left his wheelhouse and its cloud of curses. He'd gone out on deck to find his two guests lingering by the rail. Doyle, rage spent, had asked questions and listened. These men weren't fools. He'd hear them out; Doyle owed it to his Annie, to Maggie. Whatever was best for Beaver Island, that was the course he would steer.

So he'd sparked another rollie gifted by Two-Crow, inhaled, and asked his first question: "Why the big hurry?"

Keith admitted it was a huge ask, but Charlevoix's Chosen were being reinforced, the XCons a complete unknown. If the Naturals waited even one day too long they'd be pinned down in their forest, out-gunned and enslaved.

"Think now, Doyle. Does that make our island any safer?"

Doyle, clearer-headed about his course, admitted Keith's point.

Next, Tom had queried the doctor, asking, "What about infection? Islanders have been killed repelling mainlanders like you. Explain again about your *immunity?*"

Dr. Chow did his best, relating how Naturals produced antibodies which targeted the variant. Was it their lifestyle? Their affinity with nature? A mutation unique to their immune systems? Something shielded them from Stinger; but so far, the exact mechanism was unknown.

Doyle had scowled at this. *Definitely some hippie crap.*

But Chow insisted he had proof, hard data to back up his claims. He'd begged Doyle to alert the island doctor to these findings.

Doyle pictured telling Doc Newsome. Shit! He'd be called crazy, shooed from the man's clinic.

What else had Chow said? Immunity might be something the islanders could *learn?* Something they could *acquire?* Tom should have attended better. That last part was important. If true, it sweetened a pretty sour deal.

At the end, Doyle had looked hard at the diplomats. He was gambling everything, and wanted them to know it. He respected them both, Keith for his service, Chow for his expertise.

"It's clear what *you* get from this deal, but what about the island? Its people? What's in it for them?" Shit, this was life and death; 300 lives actually, the island's post-collapse census.

Keith had answered this one, locking eyes with Doyle. "Beaver Island, *my* island, gets a lot. First, it gets fighters, 100 of them, best commandos I've ever seen. Second, these people are industrious. They farm, they hunt, they fish, and they've got livestock. Doyle, they eat well. How many islanders have died hungry? Third, there's a chance for immunity. You know we won't stay isolated forever."

Two-Crow halted there, giving Doyle a chance to digest it all.

After brooding for a long moment, the captain had offered his calloused hand, first to Keith the hunter, who shook it, then to delicate Chow, who—flinchingly—did the same.

"Well, shipmates," he'd said, assessing the moon's phase, "looks like we've got lots of work to do and only a short time to do it."

Then the host had gestured them inside. Seated in the galley again, they'd elbowed around Keith's outspread map.

"Now, about this possible evacuation," Doyle began. "There's a threat, a ferry in Charlevoix's inner harbor that needs taking care of."

The three men had gotten granular.

"Surely some revelation is at hand"–Yeats

GIVEN THE CATACLYSMIC NATURE of our global pandemic, I was not surprised to see a rise in radical religion once our variant went viral. This resultant surge in cultism and firebrand demagoguery is not at all unique to our era. History's plagues have spawned similar sects.

In Exodus, a pestilent Egypt, infected by a strain of morbillivirus—a member of the paramyxoviridae family—strengthened the faith of Moses and his followers. Jews took advantage of the epidemic and escaped the whips of a preoccupied Pharaoh.

Speaking of whips, two millennia later Europe's Black Death gave rise to the Flagellant movement in the medieval church. Zealots roamed the countryside whipping themselves raw for the sins of humanity, falling to the ground in penitential frenzy, hoping to assuage an angry God with their suffering. When this didn't work, they'd slaughter Jews and Gypsies, scapegoating them for the insidious work of bacterium Yersinia pestis.

Even our knave of a president enjoyed a surge in his personality cult. Riffing on xenophobia, evangelism, and chaos, he sued for a second term, supremely shielded by his court and a contingent of alternate electors. The subsequent crowing of the man and his lickspittles grew insufferable till my Aghori put an end to it, and a pointy end at that.

As far as I know, no denomination on the planet has placated Stinger. No smear of lamb's blood has persuaded my virulent angel to pass over. Could there be such a religion, a belief capable of holding contagion at bay?

I suppose it's feasible.

A founder-effect scenario could be possible, where a society—perhaps isolated for millennia like Zoroastrians, or centuries like Mormons—might fare better against my variant due to a quirk in their immune response. Also, groups practicing endogamy, where marriage is strictly intracommunal, could hit the genetic jackpot and find themselves less susceptible. The Amish are an example here, as are Assyrians, Druze, and Yazidis.

Could a person's faith alone shield them from my creation's cytokine sting?

Not that I know of.

Churches and mosques served wonderfully as temples of transmission; the singing, praying, and exhorting that occurred at such gathering places helped super-spread my contagion. The spiritual desperation of congregants fanned the flames of infection. The transition from fervor to fever was a quick one. In the end, the religious fared no better than the rest.

Here Comes the Cavalry!

IN THE WHEELHOUSE of the *Emerald Island* ferry, Cowboy drained the dregs from his mug. He wiped at his mouth, blew out a big breath, and picked up his walkie-talkie, calling his fixer in the engine room. "Ready down there, Mikey?"

The moment of truth. They'd been overhauling the big boat for the last 48 hours, per the orders of Dr. Liz.

"Ready boss! Should I start her up?"

Cowboy had gotten dirty too, helping Mikey go over every component in the engine room: fuel lines, filters, generators, hydraulics, pumps, gauges, batteries, electrical, the works. It had been over a year since anyone went down there, since its engines were started. Anything could happen. Mikey insisted on being thorough, taking their time, doing it right. If they started her up too soon, all kinds of shit could go wrong, then where'd they be?

Cowboy crossed his fingers and keyed the mic. "OK, Mikey, let her rip!"

A few seconds of silence, then whirring as Main Engine Number One turned over.

"Come on, baby!"

Cowboy prayed aloud as the engine sputtered and struggled. Finally it caught, and the big fucker roared to life with a gassy growl.

"We did it!"

Cowboy walked out onto the bridge wing. A dirty plume of exhaust spewed from the stack; he could feel the engine bucking beneath his boots, 1000 horsepower at his command.

Mikey came on the radio. "Should I try number two?"

"Start her ass up!"

The process repeated, the second engine turning over right away.

Yeah baby! Another thousand ponies!

Bob felt aroused; his very bones were vibrating. Fiery Liz would love it too.

"Oil pressure looks good. Seals are holding. Boss, I think we did it!"

Mikey's happiness rippled through the radio. As for Cowboy, his blood was up. Hell, he felt downright giddy. Why hadn't he thought of this before? Fucking Liz. He owed a lot to that fire-baller. Bob promised himself to do right by her, come hell or high water.

Mikey monitored the engine room while Cowboy made his rounds. Half a dozen Chosen had been tasked with various ferry projects. He'd motivated them with the promise of booze. Best move he'd ever made, putting a padlock on the alcohol. If his men wanted a drink, it was on his terms, his schedule. Some were still acting mutinous, derelict in their duties. He'd deal with them later.

He toured the ferry, slapping backs, slapping fives.

"Hey! Boss is in a good mood."

"Might be a party tonight!"

Everywhere Bob looked, shit was getting done. Sparks flew from grinding tools, arc-lights flashed from welders. Guys were mounting machine guns and stocking cans of ammo.

The USS *Chosen* girded for battle.

He and Mikey drew up big plans for weaponry, the one thing they had plenty of: a whole shipping container of armory-looted firepower. Two .50 caliber Brownings were mounted on the bow, another sticking out from the stern. His mechanic placed two .30 caliber SAWs, one on the port side, one starboard. Cowboy had the idea to stock grenades, ammo, and small arms in one of the lockable cabins. They'd topped off the ferry's fuel tanks with the last of their diesel.

When Liz arrived, she'd be fucking blown away. Bob grinned. *Bet I get blown too.*

He left his fixer to it and disembarked to continue his tour of the compound. The drawbridge was up, the first thing he'd done.

"Reinforce your castle," Liz had prescribed.

No patrols had gone out, and no primitives had attacked. With the bridge up, he and his men were sealed off from the north, from "elf" territory. That bloody tree still graffitied Bob's brain; sealed off was just fine by him.

Liz's convoy was in-bound from the south. He checked his watch; they'd arrive any minute now. Boat ready, bridge up, booze rationed, Bob was feeling good. Good and horny. It had been a long week since she'd straddled him on his office chair.

Newly responsible, Bob thought of his men. Liz had removed all the Candidate females; his garrison, some sodomy aside, needed uncorking.

Cowboy pictured Beaver Island. The name alone sounded promising—he'd have to share that joke with his men. Bob didn't know Liz's plan, but he guessed they'd hit the island first. Stock up on supplies, do their rape-and-pillage thing, then return and deal with these fucking elves properly.

He'd eulogized Heavy, Hernandez, Barnes, and all the others. With 16 dead so far, the Raiders' revenge might get heated. It would be impossible to rein them in once the murderers were captured. He'd give his boys plenty of slack. If it got nasty, oh well. Got to send a message: you whack a Chosen, you pay a price.

At the motor pool, he was down to six vehicles; they were fueled up, but too few. Next stop was the mess hall. He visited his man there, reminding him to serve their best to Liz and her crew.

"Best? Boss, we got nothin' but old MREs, meals-rarely-fucking-edible."

Well, all that was about to change. Bob drooled over the food cache they'd find on Beaver: pork, beef, fresh eggs, bread. It'd be like before—pre-collapse—only better, because they wouldn't have to pay. Outside his office, he inspected the generators, all running at capacity. He was splurging on full electrification for his Lizzy.

Cowboy's last stop was home-sweet-home, his hooch. Here he'd outdone himself, had bent his own rule. The rooms were air conditioned! It was a hot fucking day, and tonight would be hotter. His stereo was ready, greatest hits all queued up. He'd stocked some whiskey, had even splurged and made ice. The bed was made; he'd horned up while tucking it in. Wildflowers stood erect on the table.

All in all, he felt fantastic. *Can't keep a good man down.* It seemed like forever since the massacre. Five nights ago? Why mope about the past when the future was so bright?

Bob's walkie buzzed, and he turned up the volume. It was one of his best Raiders, manning the barricade south of town. Dude sounded excited.

"Boss, you there? Dust cloud comin' toward us. I hear vehicles."

Cowboy heard them too. Long blasts sounded from a semi-truck, followed by throbbing music. The tune was an inside joke, and he was tickled Liz remembered—RIP Willie Nelson.

My heroes have always been cowboys, and they still are, it seems.

Another long blast.

Cowboy spurred himself towards the checkpoint, *giddy-up!*

The sentry radioed his excitement. "Boss! They're here! Here comes the cavalry!"

Back in Black

COWBOY RADIOED TO HIS MAN. "Roll back the barricade!"

When he arrived the dozer had already been moved, Liz's convoy snaking its way into the compound.

Holy shit! She'd brought an army. Cowboy, strutting towards her truck, counted 20 vehicles packed with Raiders, a piratical-looking bunch. Co-ed too; he saw some badass mamas in the mix—good for them! Equal pay for equal work. His men were excited, making jokes, even Mikey. His fixer stood wheezing in the parking lot where Liz had halted.

Cowboy ogled her fuel tanker and semi-truck. A few vehicles had been rigged with kennels, oversized dogs pacing in their cages, ferocious at confinement. Collapse had been tough on man's best friend; the less fit breeds were cannibalized quickly, survivors coming together in wolf-like packs.

Campbell looked closer: where the fuck had Liz found pit bulls? That girl had spunk for sure.

Bob fist-bumped a nervous-looking Mikey as Liz dismounted from the cab. She stretched like a cat, her ample curves sheathed in black leather, then Liz gave a signal, cutting Willie off in mid-verse.

Knowin' well your best days are gone—

Sexy, Liz grinned and gave her ass a shake. Cowboy feared for his horny heart. The gathered Chosen, his and hers, exploded into hoots and cat-calls.

Oh man! You gotta love the lifestyle!

She sashayed towards him, with everyone watching. Bob's jeans bulged as she came close enough to kiss. Looking down, Liz sized up his package with a wanton wink. "That a pistol in your pocket, Cowboy?"

Their old joke! He loved it, loved her. They'd stay together this time.

Face-to-face, she flicked out a lizard tongue. Bob's pulse was a jackhammer. *God damn!*

Leaning close, she whispered something he couldn't quite catch. *Forgive?* What did she say? Even as he wondered Liz stepped back into the sudden silence, her grim-faced Chosen waiting on her words.

She addressed them, a judge to the jury. "Ladies and gents, you all know this man. Cowboy Bob made a name for himself back in the day," here she shook her head, "but sadly, his day has passed."

She nodded to Mikey. The mechanic approached, sweating bullets, sparking a taser.

What in the fuck?

"Boss Cowboy here has led you poorly. He's fucked things up, and gotten good men killed. In the ranks of Chosen there's no room for deadbeats."

Two of her men stepped up, roughly pinning Cowboy's arms.

Bob didn't struggle. What was happening? *Lizzy?*

She looked right through him, pure calculus.

"Bob Campbell, you are relieved of command. You are my prisoner until a trial can be held. Do you have anything to say for yourself?"

"But—I picked you flowers."

A hundred grizzled Raiders laughed their asses off.

Liz shot him a pitying look, then nodded permission to her snitch.

Mikey moved to comply. "Yes boss," he said, then raised his taser and blasted Cowboy in the chest. "Sorry boss," he said just before Bob's world went blank.

Fifty-thousand volts blew through his mind. Bob's body spasmed, then slumped. The two thugs dropped him to the ground, his battered hat lying in the road. Plastic cuffs zipped tight—ankles and wrists—ol' Cowboy had been trussed.

Liz addressed her leering audience: "Let this be a lesson! There's no place for slackers, no tolerance for fuck-ups!"

She picked up his hat, slapped it on her thigh, and crowned herself. The cowboy-queen planted a boot on Bob's back. "To be Chosen is to be ELITE!"

She drew a pistol from her waistband and fired at the sky. Her crew cheered, Cowboy's men too; there was a great honking of horns and long blasts from the semi. She nodded to her DJ, and he flicked on the amps, blaring AC/DC. Liz's theme song bounced off the buildings, an electrified warning to the whole northern world.

Back in black, I hit the sack
I've been too long, I'm glad to be back

Music shrieking, her Raiders got to work, parking their vehicles in an orderly fashion. Semi doors were opened and supplies unloaded. An SUV towed a barbecue rig, Lizzy's chef already lighting the coals. Soon the compound smelled of charcoal and the sweet scent of lighter fluid.

Yes, I'm let loose, from the noose
That's kept me hanging about

Handlers opened their cages, leashing the red-eyed dogs for exercise. Her lieutenants shook hands with Bob's remnant garrison and were shown around the compound.

I've been looking at the sky, 'cause it's gettin' me high
Forget the hearse 'cause I never die

M-31's bulldozer barricade was reinforced, Liz's gunners selecting fields-of-fire for their weapons as Charlevoix crackled with energy. Liz looked at Bob, still face-planted on the asphalt, and shook her head.

She nodded to the ferry. "Put him aboard and lock him in a cabin. Fill a dog bowl with some water—and leave those fucking cuffs on!"

Two men dragged Bob's boneless body towards the pier.

Mikey attended, hovering close. Liz looked him over. "Conscience nagging you, big man?"

"No problems here, boss."

She nodded. "How's my checklist?"

He grinned. "Done, done and done. We're ready for anything."

"The ferry?"

He nodded.

"Radio scanner?"

Another nod.

"Drawbridge?"

"I've got it lifted now, boss, but it's working. You can roll north anytime."

Liz looked satisfied. "I want someone monitoring that scanner 24-7. If we can force them to broadcast again, we'll nail their asses. And this time we'll bring the fucking heat. Have there been any transmissions? Any recent contact?"

Mikey wobbled his chin. "Not since the massacre."

She winced at the word. "That was some fucked up shit, Mikey. Not your best night. Better not let me down like that. Not ever, you got me?"

The man nodded, gulping as Bob was dragged away. "Loud and clear, boss."

She dismissed him.

Liz stood a moment, hands on hips, his hat on her head. It was a start anyway. She looked over the ferry, the stack exhaust, the heavy weapons. Big fucking boat. A game changer. *Sky's the limit with a rig like that.*

First things first, she'd mop up local resistance: these *elves*, these fairy-fuckers, they had a good run. She'd hunt 'em down, smoke 'em out, track 'em with dogs, whatever it took. Liz needed a win that would prove herself to Cowboy's crew, make her mark up north, and set an example.

Do NOT fucking cross Red Liz!

She'd make it public, execute their leaders, hang 'em high, pull their fucking guts out. Sure, she'd lose them as Candidates, but there was more to reputation than stats alone; there had to be fear.

She'd keep any kids, though. Little tykes were golden.

The dirty secret of the Chosen?

They were all fucking sterile. Birth control by virus! The laugh was on them, but who'd laugh last? Ol' Liz had a plan.

She climbed to Cowboy's office. No glass ceiling; the place was all hers—maps, radios, windows, and the big blue beyond. It would do—for now, anyways. She thumped her pistol on the desk, invaded his drawer and liberated a drink.

From her motorcycle jacket she unfolded a list of frequencies and phone numbers, smoothing it out on the desktop. Her ass was grass if anyone deciphered it. Liz took off Bob's hat, ran fingers through her frizz, and slugged some whiskey. She locked the door, then switched on her satellite phone. It still had some juice.

She punched in the numbers next to the name *Mustafa*.

Red Liz pressed "send" and made her next move.

Strawberry Diplomacy

SAMANTHA—THE STOWAWAY—RETURNED as a golden sunrise painted her shack. Intimations had gone ahead, tree-to-tree, trilled by birds who'd spied her wending home. Fruits and veggies plumped in welcome; mycelia rooted her on, vibing with her signature gait. All was well in this place. Samantha wished it were so everywhere.

She nodded her hellos to the garden, then stumbled inside to lay herself down. Sam was exhausted, her mission a success. She'd heard what she needed to, received Dr. Chow's file and strategized with Keith. Captain Tom Doyle, duped, was none the wiser.

Had her friend Annie made it back home in time?

Samantha smiled, thinking of Doyle's explosion if she hadn't. Would serve the man right, give him a taste of his neglected wife's trauma. Then he might understand the treasure he'd been taking for granted all these years.

Sam's thoughts blurred, deprived of sleep's focus. She shuttered the peeping sun and slept till Miin called her. It started as a dream, subconscious, a connection to her foster daughter. Then Samantha's slumber was interrupted by Miin's urgent messaging:

A peaceful forest, above ground and below.

Trees, slow-growing, symbionts with simians, cradling hammocks with burly boughs.

Peace and green, the world as it should be. As it was. As it could be again.

Miin's sending was lovely, and Samantha felt strengthened. But then:

A mechanized gnashing chewing through the trees: pulping life, sap running, splashing blood. Screams, terror, fear. Saplings and children splintered and split. Miin's sylvan society forced from their forest into an exodus of exposure, refugees desperately seeking sanctuary.

Samantha startled awake. The maple trees surrounding her shack were trembling, their leafy limbs shaking with worry. There was much to be done.

Twenty minutes later she secured the last bottle in her handcart, contents cool from the springhouse, its fruity elixir still potent. Sam covered the load with a blanket and heaved on its handles, finding it too heavy. She pinched a joint from her smoking pouch, straightened its kinks, applied flame to one end and dragged upon the other.

Eyes closed, she pulled spirit inside her, embracing its green magic and exhaling gratitude towards the trees. Her vaporous cloud ascended through the leaves, stomata sniffing the skunky herb as it climbed. Flower-fortified, she regripped the handles, the load was less heavy. Off she went, her clinking cart trundling behind.

It took an hour to exit the bog, its easterly path smoothing itself to help her along. By late morning she hit the beach road. The first farm on her route was the Greene's, outbuildings surrounded by a scattering of chickens—too scrawny and too few. By the time she set down her load the family and its two collies had gathered in greeting.

Amanda, mother of four, held a baby swaddled tight against her chest. Shawn, bearded and gaunt, brought the eldest some water. He turned the bucket so she could reach its ladle. Sam imbibed the mineral brew, ice-cold, from the farm's 40-foot well.

"*Miigwech.*" She nodded at the children, and all the Greenes smiled back. Samantha and her lessons were always welcome.

Their oldest child Josie, a young teen, replied, "*Chi-Miigwech,*" without stumbling.

Sam's face wrinkled as she smiled at her student, gifting strawberries from the cart.

"And these, Josephine?"

The girl foraged through her memories. "*Ode'iminan,*" she said at last, in triumph.

Her siblings echoed the Anishinaabe as Josie shared the red fruits.

"What can we do for you, Samantha?" Amanda, tired, tried to smile. "We're breaking soon for lunch, won't you stay?"

Sam reached for another gift, dusting off a bottle for Shawn. "I can't stay that long. A quick word perhaps, with you and your man?"

The buzzing kids were shooed away, and Amanda led the adults to shade. They sat themselves on a bench beneath cottonwoods in bloom. A moment of quiet; then the breeze blew, and a million white-sailed schooners cast off from the canopy, carrying their cargo of seeds towards Lake Michigan and beyond.

"I've got news," Samantha began, brandishing a file folder, "from the mainland. And I need your help spreading it."

Her baby hungry, Amanda adjusted to nurse. Shawn pulled the cork and passed the fruity wine. They sipped the sun of last summer, feeling refreshed as Samantha told her tale.

An hour later, Shawn had hitched his horse to a wagon he'd jury-rigged from a pickup. Their bay mare Montana, aged 20, was an old gal for sure, but dependable; Samantha's fermented cargo nestled safely in straw. She rode on the bench next to Shawn Greene, who handled the reins. Recreational no longer, the island's equines had been shanghaied into service. Samantha, riding high next to Greene, left her empty cart behind.

The Martins were next. Sarah and William, parents of three skinny children, asked hard questions before finally coming around. Another bottle was gifted, another family acquired. Just like the Greenes, the deciding factor was the chance for immunity based on Dr. Chow's hypothesis, backed up by his file. Samantha made no promises, just repeated the facts. A *chance* was all she offered, but for worried parents, this chance was enough.

Then came the Fernys, another old family, rooted deep in the island's sandy soil. Bill was ornery like his father, and his father before. One of Doyle's captains, he didn't like what he heard; the whole "stowaway business" Captain Ferny just couldn't forgive. Sam's wine went unopened, her generosity unthanked. His wife Ashley, pregnant and defeated, extended no invitation.

Greene, driving on, shook his head. "Always thorny branches on that family tree. My dad used to say there are all types on this island: hayseeds and fish-chokers, you take the good with the bad."

The noon hour came and went. The diplomats devoured the food Sam had packed in the basket. Montana clip-clopped steadily towards the harbor, making stops along the way: Kellers, Hannigans, O'Donnells, and Reddings, each household offered welcome.

Weary fieldwork made breaking for guests a pleasant respite. Most of the family men were boat captains, stranded ashore by diesel's slow ebb. Farming was new to them: frustration over wilting crops and poor yields colored their talk. Samantha's wine, fermented from berries picked and pulped by Miin last summer, was sipped with savor.

At each farmhouse, cottage, and cabin, Samantha's story stayed the same. No promises, just facts, as plain as she could make them. Shawn's presence helped: bright-eyed and grim, he was a man in his prime, respected both pre-collapse and post.

Islander softness had melted away. Folks were worried about the dark months ahead. Last year's cold had been cruel, and the coming cull from Y2's winter would be worse. Their cellar calculations all came up short; there were too many months between harvest and spring. Ancient arithmetic was relearned, the additions too few, the subtractions too many. Most ears were open to Samantha's tall tale.

"*Naturals*, eh? You say they're good farmers?"

"They've got green thumbs, Samantha? Know their way around a field?"

"Livestock too? How many? What kinds? We could sure use some stock to build up our herds."

"They had how many die last winter? None, you say?"

"Handy with tools, resourceful in a pinch?"

"Two hundred or so? Well, we've got the whole state forest sittin' there unused."

"Our island used to feed thousands."

"What about the variant? *None* killed by Covee? How can that be? Who's this Doctor Chow? What's Doc Newsome say about this? That's what I'd like to know."

"Hunters? Fishermen? With their own weapons and tools?"

"The bad guys, these Virals, you say they're called 'Chosen?' Sounds like our worst fears coming true."

"Chosen are infected? Armed? Raiding and killing as they go?"

"They'll find us sooner or later. Can't hide forever, we know that for sure."

The sun arced to its zenith, then fell slowly westward, the longest day of the year hazing the islanders with heat. The mare had been watered at Hannigan's; Montana pulled Shawn and Samantha through town. St. James had few streets, all of them tidy. Back in Y1, cars and trucks had been repurposed as Cessna barricades, their fuel siphoned off. Most of the storefronts were now shuttered, though Shamrock's, of course, was still open.

Branded booze had been eighty-sixed months ago. However, the tavern kept itself well-stocked with homebrew and shine. Sam and Shawn ducked inside the shaded public house, gifting a jug to the barkeeper, Alice. They sat at the bar, repeating their story and fielding questions from the patrons as Alice portioned out Samantha's wine.

Their final stop was the clinic. Doc Newsome had already heard of their mission, and met them in the parking lot. No, he didn't need any wine, but would they please tell him what the hell was going on?

The health center ran on a diesel generator, a rare drain on Doyle's reserves; during summer it mostly sat silent. He was a tall man, near 70, clean-shaven and staying fit. For decades he'd delivered the island's babies, and later set their broken bones. He'd saved lives during the collapse, and lost some too, the diabetics breaking him in particular. He'd been making amends, or trying to, ever since.

Newsome was skeptical of their story, and detailed his doubts. Shawn Greene did the talking as Doc tried to take it all in: Gaia theory, antibodies of Naturals, super-spreading Chosen, and data sets collected by some bush doctor character. Greene handed over Chow's file.

Newsome, like his islanders, was searching for solace. He scrutinized the folder: the title, its author. Of course he'd heard of Dr. Chow, the pre-collapse president of the northern health system; the man, a fellow Wolverine, had a fine reputation, or at least he used to. Newsome said he needed time to do some reading and to think.

Samantha, as a stowaway, had been tasked by Chow, so she asked her last question. "Doc, do you have what you need to run tests of your own? How soon could you get results screening for infection?"

"You're talking about RDT, a rapid-detection-test. I'd need a blood sample, just a finger prick would do. I've got a fluorescence microscope and a generator for juice. I'd sample for antigens, which are proof of infection, and antibodies, indicators for immunity."

Newsome stroked Montana's flank as he spoke.

"I'd need a reagent, though maybe Doctor Chow could help? It sounds like he's already got one."

Greene readied the reins.

"Neither test is perfect, but they're quick. Thirty minutes or less for results."

Montana and her wagon were ready, waiting on Sam. She thanked the medical man for his troubles. Newsome asked a final question as Shawn clucked his mare into motion.

"Do you have something up your sleeve, Samantha? Anything I should know about?"

She grinned back at him as they exited his lot.

"You're a good man, and a good doctor. This island has been lucky to have you. Are you sure about that wine now?"

Newsome shook his head. Sober, he watched them disappear down the road.

Mustafa

HIS NAME MEANT *Appointed One* and sounded foreign, maybe African, though he himself was as white as his collar. He'd been a hotshot EV engineer, a disrupter; as techno-king, he'd dethroned Detroit's Big Three. He'd founded several start-ups, fathering kids along the way, until that whole industry—like the dinosaurs—ran out of gas.

He'd picked the name himself, pre-collapse. He'd been serving 10-to-20 for a passion killing, it didn't matter who, all that shit was in the past. After a 40-day stint in solitary, he'd emerged messianic, claiming he'd been appointed by God, Allah, the big man upstairs, whatever. Appointed for what, he couldn't say. It didn't mean much to him, but his followers seemed to dig it, so Mustafa he became.

ICF is where he'd been rotting, Ionia Correctional Facility its fancy name. He remembered how that bitch judge had pronounced it, all hoity-toity and polite; she made it sound like a damn hospital, clean and helpful. It was known as I-Max to those they'd penned inside, a jungle of rape, pervy guards, and beatings.

The judge had got hers, though. He made sure of that. When Stinger sprang them she'd topped his to-do list. He'd had plenty of time to work out all the details.

I-Max was level 5, one of four supermax prisons in Michigan, probably the worst. Administrative segregation is what he'd been assigned, another fancy phrase for hard time. He'd spent his days in solitary, and all his lonely nights too. Even during rec time, his few minutes in the yard, he'd been caged like a chimp. The "single occupancy security exercise module" was another white lie, peddled to politicians to line prison industry pockets.

ICF was no joke: razor wire, stun fencing, and towers manned by COs with rifles. There were plenty of fights, crazy riots; he'd been tased, gassed, and shot in the arm. The chickenshit guard had missed—dude had been aiming to kill.

Mustafa, charismatic, had CEO skills, and led his people well. He'd brokered deals with other factions; something told him the shit-show couldn't last. Change was coming, the whole world was rotten. Life is too short for long term grudges. So he'd consolidated, patched things up with rivals AB and *La Eme*; he merged his corporation with the Aryans and Cartels. The coming collapse was bigger than I-Max, so he networked, prison-to-prison, connecting dots, prepping for change. It wasn't quick, but Mustafa had time.

When the variant started stinging, his people were ready. They embraced what united them, hatred for the Man and his system. Ionia's warden tried banning newspapers, even the internet, but that didn't matter once corrections officers started dropping like flies, leaving gaps in their ranks. ICF's general population spent whole weeks in lockdown. All food had been stopped, and their health care was a joke.

Covee cut them to the quick, and there was nowhere to hide. Race and class didn't matter; one day they were fine, then they'd go all twitchy and die. No one collected the bodies. Locked down, the prisoners bunked with corpses, had to smell the stink, watch them bloat till they burst.

Stinger left alone the baddest: skinheads, *La Raza*, Crips and Bloods—they all had survivors, more than they should. Sometimes it was exactly who you'd think, sometimes a surprise. Little guys that bothered nobody turned out immune, while big muscle heads would flame out and die. Mustafa helped the survivors incorporate, re-brand, and emerge as XCons.

And it wasn't just the prisons. There were other kinds of cell blocks—Mustafa knew them well—office-hives where the venom ran deep. These corporate drones, Covee's stingers, wore blue suits instead of orange, and after some restructuring, these infected became the new bosses.

Being a higher-up, he had access to guards and knew how bad it was, real biblical shit. With a name like his he should be read up on Revelations and all that. He faked it mostly—who could call his bluff? It was a straight-up Apocalypse, four horsemen and all; the COs panicked, their whole privileged world coming apart. At the end, he worked with a guard he knew and the fool let him out. Mustafa, Prince of Ponzi, had promised cash, promised stock, then hit the guard with a shank, took his keys and his radio. After that it was easy.

Mustafa, right? The Appointed One. Once his reputation took off, went viral, his followers grabbed shotguns and rifles, settled scores, and I-Max was theirs. Old Law formed up quickly, some guards resisting and putting up a fight, hero types who'd watched too many movies. Mustafa could only wonder at their persistence: the fucking world collapses, and they had nothing better to do than form a posse and play sheriff? Old Law wasn't immune, though—and a good thing too. They'd trade their lives to stop Spreaders, and many did.

Red Liz had just called him on the sat-phone, the Chosen Raider with flaming red hair. She'd been wanting to make a move, break the glass ceiling, climb on some Cons to boost her career. Mustafa didn't mind; he'd done this before, and it helped that she was hot. Mustafa always came out on top, though, something little Lizzy would learn the hard way. The XCons weren't going back. They held the whip now, and weren't letting go.

He'd met Liz once, trading dogs for her guns. The Chosen were strapped; they'd taken the armories first, another mistake he'd made. His Cons had gotten carried away, spent too much time on revenge. The dogs had been a lucky break. The variant killed most pooches pretty quickly, being too close to people. Domesticated breeds went soft and sickened with their masters, stung the same way. But his pit bulls were different. Experimental, they'd come from a kennel and escaped like the Cons. Man's best friend? Yeah right.

Mustafa placed his call, part of Liz's deal. Some sat-phones still worked, holding their charge, but electricity was going, gasoline almost gone. There was no one left to run the grid. That meant old school or no school, at least for now.

There was a forest up north Liz wanted wiped; one of his best would run the raid. His man managing the region called himself LeBron, and the dude ran a tight show.

He heard LeBron pick up. "Mustafa, is that you? What's the word?"

"You're moving tonight, LeBron. I want you rolling in heavy. Do you have it scouted? Do you have a plan figured out?"

He trusted this guy; they'd been at I-Max together.

"Mustafa, we're set. Going in with dogs and 20 guns. Roads are shit though, and they're hiding in the woods. We'll roll up close, nice and quiet, then follow the pits to their camp. How do you want this to go down? Are we nabbing prisoners, or just killing?"

Red Liz made it clear this hippie bunch had done her some harm. Slaves had value for sure, call them Candidates or what you will. But sometimes you needed to send a message, propaganda over profit. A brand—and his came with an X—is just perception, and perception shapes reality over time.

"LeBron, this one is strictly search-and-destroy, you got me?"

"Got you, Mustafa. Pits are hungry. When we're done tonight, there won't be anything left."

He hung up on LeBron, put on headphones, and turned up the EDM. Neurally linked, and artificially intelligent, Mustafa canceled out noise, canceled doubts. Don't doubt your vibe. Nothing better than getting lost in a beat.

Stretched Thin

MUKWA WENT THROUGH THE CHOW LINE with his squad. Matador's team had duty tonight, which meant first dibs on dinner. The feed was good: roasted meat, early greens, fry bread and the like. The Sentinels packed it in. Night watch was hungry duty, and breakfast a long shift away.

Things had gotten hectic since the big council three nights ago. The whole ELF world had been rocked, and shit was in motion. Leadership argued for re-settlement; Elena, Chow, Pastor George, Brian, and eventually even Ms. McIntyre advocated for the move, "Whatever's best for the children," always her flustered line.

The rest of the Front was coming around. As a foster, Mukwa sympathized. It sucked to leave, to pack up, to abandon the safety of the trees. And for what? Beaver Island? A tourist trap? America's Emerald Isle?

A few Naturals had been there pre-collapse, reporting sandy soils and depleted fisheries. Some even knew about the 19th century Mormon leader, "King" Strang, who tried to establish a makeshift monarchy, crowning himself as divine ruler. All in all, the island seemed an unusual sanctuary. Should they put their faith in it? Trust their lives to its insular people?

It was a lot to ask. Mukwa understood the grumbling.

But if they'd seen what he had—Chosen executioners, machine gunners, rapists and slavers—they'd be hustling to leave. Anyway, few elves complained, and none of the Sentinels. The warriors understood the threat. Mukwa just hoped they still had time.

He and Nighthawk had grown closer over the past several days. They'd found some quiet moments, though when alone she'd been anything but; Hawk had passion, and he the bruises to prove it. Mukwa just hoped no one overheard them.

Now, shoveling chow, the Sentinel sharpshooter was all business. His girl wore braids and was ready for battle. Little Sparrow was there, and Diana too. Matador's squad wore their headbands; they had parkas on, and also issued one to Mukwa. Looted from a Pentagon supplier, supposedly the garments could blend with any background, even cloaking heat signatures?

Sentinel training had intensified since Duck and Squirrel were killed. Elena pushed them hard, and Mukwa had never felt stronger. He could run, could climb, and could fight from the trees. He wasn't bow-ready, though. Not by a long shot.

Matador had laughed right in his face. "Not yet, oso. Spear and knife-work for you, *güey*. Less chance of you sticking one of us."

True enough. Anyway, what he really wanted was a rifle like Keith's, something badass and tactical. But it wasn't their way. He'd asked Hawk about it, sitting in a tree together, watching over their leafy realm.

"It's not about the odds," she said, "or effectiveness, or range."

He brought up Duck's .50 cal. Hadn't the taboo heavy gun saved their asses on River Road?

Hawk disputed him. "We're in Gaia's hands. It's who we are, it's inside us. It's why *we* were spared when the whole world wasn't. Keeping their weapons, driving their trucks, would be selling our souls. You get that, don't you?"

He guessed he did. He was crazy about her, and admitted these elves had some mojo. *Strong medicine,* the elders would say back on Beaver Island. Take Brian with his birds, or Miin with her trees, or the way Sentinels shimmered in moonlight. Parkas or no, these elves had some magic.

Downright creepy. Mutant shit, he'd said it before. Hard to argue against that, especially with one as attractive as Hawk. She liked him too, and Mukwa thanked his lucky stars. The whole world was dead, yet he'd never felt more alive. Strong medicine indeed.

Hawk told him to stop thinking so much.

"Just go with it, man. Aren't you happy? Don't you feel good? Aren't you satisfied?"

She slipped off her top as she said this, showing her perfect self just to him. She was always doing stuff like this, and it blew his mind every time. Damn right he felt good.

Unfettered, she descended; clumsy, he followed. Hawk let him catch her. They rolled on the moss, flashing the stars and the flushing fireflies. Gaia is good! Muck was converted for sure.

Naturals were busy packing up camp; their herds were coming in, shepherds summoned from summer pastures. A final haul of fish had been smoked and stacked for travel. Fruits and vegetables were harvested early. Shelters were coming down, canvas loads cinched tight. The whole place was astir, elves were on the move, a great migration.

Elena briefed the squad leaders, and word trickled down to the encampment. Keith and Dr. Chow had worked a plan out with an island captain, a cranky Mr. Doyle. The evacuation was on, two nights from now in Charlevoix, when the full moon could light their way. More details would follow, but tonight their mission was simple: guarding the western border. Padgett Road, potholed and ungraded, was the nearest approach to ELF Country.

Mukwa, days ago, had been told the name of the river, of the whole watershed really: *Mukwa Ziibing*. His squad thought it a good sign.

"El oso is home now," became their running joke. They'd ask him for directions, or advice about living in "his" forest. There were endless grins to be had when he got lost or tripped by a tree root. The squad would gather around him as he lay sprawled in the mud, smiling even as they shook their heads.

"What's wrong with our bear? Is he sick? Why doesn't he remember? Maybe *el oso es de mente débil?*"

They'd leave him behind and sprint off in the correct direction. He'd follow, limping, right into some prank they'd concocted. More laughter, more cheering. Nighthawk was as bad as the rest. Oh well, at least she made it up to him. Muck had no complaints about that.

Hawk had been training him, or trying to, in more ways than one.

"Each Natural has a *connection*," she'd explained almost tenderly.

Mukwa, high on hormones, had felt floaty. He'd tried to focus on her words.

"It's what's kept us shielded from Stinger, it's why we're alive."

He understood this, he really did.

"Listen, dumbass!" she'd chided, swatting aside his exploratory paw. "I'm not asking you merely to believe. You must develop your own senses. A green *connection* could keep you alive, could keep *us* alive."

The archer explained how her ability to bullseye each shot was directly related to nature, specifically to hawks.

"When I'm in the flow-state, the zone, *connected*, I swear I can see like raptors do. The target moves in slow motion, every detail sharply etched. I control my bioelectricity, the forcefield between bow, string, and arrow. I'm a hawk-in-flight. Poor rabbit doesn't stand a chance. Foolish Chow credits these headbands, and maybe they help, but in my heart I know it's Gaia, and what Gaia does is *good*. Mukwa, do you get it?"

He got it. And he wasn't just saying that. The harder part, though, was cultivating his own connection. For sure, his affinity was with bears. He'd known this for years; the whole island had. But knowing and being were two different things.

The dirt road they watched was in rough shape after a year and a half of county neglect. Elves had rigged roadblocks at ambush points, manned at all times; every approach road was the same. Watches had been doubled while the Naturals packed up. The Sentinel squads were run down from the extra shifts, but no one complained. They knew the looming danger: Chosen from one side, probably north, and XCons from the west, or maybe south. This is what they'd trained for.

Meal over, Matador's squad collected weapons, said farewell to their friends at camp, and filed onto the trail heading west. Mukwa smiled to see Miin waiting beside the path, but his foster sister looked worried. Diana circled the squad around the girl, and they all took a knee. Miin gave her brother a smile, then frowned, more serious.

"The trees are uneasy," she began. "Something strange is approaching. Not Chosen; this strangeness is different. They don't like it, they're afraid. I'm sorry, but that's all I know."

Diana probed for more. "Anything from Brian? Can he confirm?"

Miin shook her head. "I haven't seen him. He's west of us, watching the Chosen, and Charlevoix has been busy lately."

The elves were stretched thin. No one felt good about the situation.

"Be careful tonight," Miin begged. "Expect something strange."

Diana, grim-faced, straightened and thanked Miin with a hug. The tall woman then turned and jogged off, the squad following at her heels. Mukwa, last in line, looked back at Blueberry. His little sister—*nishiime*, Sam would correct him—was close to tears. He mugged a face at her, trying for a smile, but nothing doing. Mukwa waved goodbye and sprinted to catch up, his two spears tripping his feet. Cursing, Muck clattered on his way.

An hour later and they were in position, the squad they'd relieved wanting to stay and double their numbers. Their leader was a college wrestler, known by the war-name Thorn; dude sported a full torso tattoo of a rosebush in bloom. He claimed his squad was good to go and, Gaia willing, could pull an all-nighter, no problem.

Diana sent them back to camp. Thorn's squad had been on duty since daybreak, with another shift coming soon. Departing, Thorn and company wished their fellow Sentinels well, gifting snacks before disappearing down the path. The sun departed as well, darkness descending earlier each day. Solstice over, the northern hemisphere tipped slowly towards winter.

The Departed (Matador and Tigre)
Jesus and Andrea Garcia, in their 40s, September of Year 1, parents

Their two boys—ever boisterous—had always been a handful. Close in age, they were even in the same grade; natural pranksters, they spent much of high school in detention. Athletic like Dad, their soccer prowess balanced out their demerits. When Miguel got a scholarship to Central Michigan, he wouldn't commit till his brother got a tryout.

After the coaches saw his combine, Tomas, the younger brother, was offered one too. Mom and Dad couldn't be prouder. They'd migrated to Michigan as H2A workers, but had escaped the orchards due to Andrea's cooking. The taqueria they'd opened, offering authentic Mexican food in bland northern Michigan, quickly became a local favorite. The restaurant kept the family busy till Covee closed its doors for good.

Jesus and Andrea never saw their sons play. The NCAA imploded before their first match. The brothers' dorm went dormant; Mt. Pleasant was anything but. Campus became a ghost town. Even online, attendance was skeletal.

Their parents called every day, and all four were comforted. The last talk they held, Jesus covered for his wife. *Mamá* wasn't feeling well, he said, but she'd be on her feet soon.

After hanging up, the brothers, unconvinced, drove home. By the time they arrived both their parents had passed, just like billions all over the globe.

Ellen, duty nurse at the regional hospital, gave the asymptomatic athletes a long look. Could they spare a minute? She knew a doctor that would want a word. Through tears, both brothers nodded.

They met the physician, tag identifying him as "Dr. Chow."

Tomas and Miguel, weepy-eyed, aced Chow's final exam, a blood test.

Both brothers were congratulated. Gaia willing, they'd soon have new names.

They didn't know it, but Matador and Tigre had just made varsity for the ELF.

Buenas Noches Hermanos

AN HOUR PAST MIDNIGHT, and the moon, almost full, silvered the squad dug in along the rutted road. They'd felled a huge pine across the track, forcing any approaching vehicles to stop. Another tree had been notched so that, if needed, it could be toppled behind the threat, trapping vehicles and invaders in a kill zone. The squad faced west, arrows nocked, spears ready, sharp ears open to nature's nocturne.

Their line of battle consisted of Diana, Bull, Nighthawk, Matador, Mukwa, Sparrow, and Tigre. Each Sentinel could be hailed by the next in line. Diana was closest to the roadblock, while Tigre, at the south end, held an ax and could fell the notched tree if necessary. Sparrow, wing-footed, was their messenger. If they were overrun or outnumbered, she would fly back for help. The rest were to scatter, fight rearguard from the trees, stall for time and rendezvous with reinforcements. The protocol was strict; Diana had made them repeat it.

Mukwa felt tense. He was disturbed by Miin's warning, and even more by her worry. It reminded him of hanging-town, his sister having a premonition that night as well.

Too late, he turned and asked Hawk, "You guys never wear masks? PPE? Won't invaders be infected?"

The Sentinel shrugged, an extremist. "We're either shielded or we're not, Gaia is good."

"Gaia is good," the other elves intoned, relaying her prayer down the line.

Mukwa shivered and felt nauseous. Something shitty was happening; the squad sensed it too. Centering himself, he channeled ions, breathing from his belly. Recalling Hawk's instructions, he pictured a bear, then tried merging the bruin's brain with his own. Olfactory-focused, he scented the night, its piney pungency, mulling over its molecules. Mukwa felt a micro-current, a mini-merge, and tried for more, electrified by the thrill of transformation. Was this how Miin and Nighthawk felt?

Bears were HERE!

He could feel them clearly. They'd never left this forest, never had to. Their signature was strong. Mind wide open, he observed the road through half-closed eyes. Other Sentinels did the same, each in their own way; the squad of mutants had its feelers out, all antennae returning the same vibration. Something was definitely happening, something strange.

Tigre, closest to the approach, signaled first, his owl cry heralding an intrusion. The squad attended: no engines, no lights, no sign of disturbance. A false alarm from Tigre? Doubtful.

Seconds of silence as Mukwa furthered his merge. Opening apertures, he was ready to receive. All at once, an *odor* lit up his olfactory lobe.

Who'd sent it? Bears?

There it was again: Foulness! Danger! Foes!

Dogs! That was the sending from the watershed, from the resident black bears of *Mukwa Ziibing*. Some red-eyed breed of pit bull raced up the road, nostrils flaring, seeking their scent. The dogs were coming! Coming fast!

Mukwa returned to himself in an instant, his body amped with adrenaline, mind alert and cleared for battle.

Tigre hooted again, his barred owl sounding scared. Silence resumed.

What the fuck?

Mukwa was sweating, and he wiped his hands before re-gripping his spear. The road remained empty. Then, all of a sudden, it wasn't. Hell hounds coursed into view: one pair, two, then many more, until the entire road seemed to slither with snapping, slavering forms. He heard a bowstring's *twang*, then another, then another.

Three shadows tumbled, shot down by Sentinel archers.

He couldn't see for shit!

Moonlight bathed the road in silver. If the dogs got behind them, the squad, the entire ELF, were fucked.

The canines cast about for scent, their muscular bodies magnified weirdly by moon-glow. What the hell were they? Devil dogs? Muck felt fear; his hands, two strangers, were shaking.

A lone Sentinel left the treeline and charged the red-eyed pack. Shimmering, the elf wielded a spear. It was El Matador, team captain, voice rising in command as he raced toward the melee: "Sparrow, fly! Archers, use the moonlight! Now shoot!"

The beasts fell upon him. Arrows zipped into the fray, shattering ribs, feathering throats. Matador, goal-keeper, played defense, parrying with his spear. Blocking their jaws and shielding his throat, he kept the dogs fixed in the light, marking them for Gaia's sharpshooters. Moonlight glinted on stainless steel as broadheads flashed from shadow.

The bodies piled up, a heaving heap, but Matador couldn't hold. The dogs coursed behind him, gripping his spear in their jaws; then he was down, teeth tearing into his flesh. Tigre sprinted towards his brother, a wordless scream his battle cry. The nearest devils turned and bounded his way, but a scythe of arrows mowed them down.

Another sound, amplified bass notes, began thumping from unseen speakers. Headlights bounced in the black as probing vehicles prowled up the road.

Diana took note and shouted orders. "Sentinels, scatter! Fall back! Fight from the trees!"

Mukwa ignored her and ran toward Matador. The man still struggled as infected jaws tore at his flesh; Tigre was nearly there, fighting to reach his brother. Blocked by hounds, Tigre's spear was a bloody blur.

An oversize pit bull knocked Mukwa to the ground. He couldn't breathe, like he'd been tackled by a truck. Muck curled up prone, hot slobber on his neck, jaws snapping as the beast sought his throat.

An arrow thumped into its body. Mukwa smelled blood, but not his own. He rolled free, gasping, alive, clumsily fumbling with his spear. Then Nighthawk swooped in, nocking again and again; her avian eyes darted everywhere.

Floodlights from the invaders seared the scene.

The biggest dog jumped atop Miguel, a matador no longer, burrowing for his throat. Tigre couldn't get there in time. Goaded by the scent of wounded prey, the pits leapt in triumph towards their kill. Miguel, jugular shredded, bled out in the road, lifeblood pooling in a pothole as he died.

His brother Tigre screamed, and a heavy gun barked back above the headlights: *Brap! Brap! Brap! Brap!*

Every bullet bit, killing the tiger, Tomas torn apart by large-caliber lead. Gnashing canines reduced him to chunks as harsh laughter rose from the vehicles, mingling with the thump of bass notes. The feasting dogs made no sound beyond rending flesh and crunching bone.

Nighthawk took hold of Muck's parka, pulling his dumb ass off the road. Spotlights searched for targets. Sparrow had flown, Bull and Diana too. They'd followed protocol, what else could they do?

"We've got to fell that tree," hissed Hawk, "trap them here. Can't let any escape!"

Mukwa nodded, numb, then followed Hawk from trunk to trunk.

X-branded gunmen exited from vehicles; the pits were leashed and kicked from their feed. Mukwa looked back, then wished he hadn't. Sentinels no longer, Tomas and Miguel had been mangled; their bones, stripped of meat, gleamed white, ghastly in the moonlight. Dead dogs littered the road, stuck like pincushions with carbon shafted arrows.

Hawk halted him; so far, so good, they'd reached the notched tree undetected. Mukwa set down his spear and hefted the ax, eyeing the cut he had to finish. Nighthawk counted vehicles, counted men, counted dogs, tallying the invaders under her breath. There were way too many.

They stood in darkness, not far from the headlights. Mukwa hoped the others had gotten clear. Hawk nodded, an arrow held nocked and at the ready. She'd give her life, and his too, helping the Front survive.

Shit, this is IT!

The vehicles would be trapped, blocked in by fallen giants, which was the whole damn point. Mukwa swung the ax, its filed edge biting deep. He recovered and swung again, the thumping bass notes covering his chopping. He cut into the pine's heartwood, alternating flat and downward strokes; resinous chips flying in chunks. Finally, the great tree groaned and began its slow fall. *Timber motherfuckers!*

Both he and Hawk were running. The earth shook as the green Goliath collapsed; three centuries to grow, three seconds to fall. They sped through the trees towards the rally-point Diana had named. He hoped more squads were on the way—they'd need every Sentinel.

"Five vehicles," she panted, "maybe 20 men, 20 dogs? Half the beasts are still alive."

Muck tried to fly, but his chest was hollow. He gasped for breath, choking on tears. The Garcia brothers, Miguel and Tomas, were dead.

Exodus

A THIN RAIN HAD BEEN FALLING all morning, the sunrise smothered by woolly clouds from the west. Pastor George was weary—they all were. It had been a night of alarms, of panic, of crying babies and displacement. Pharaoh had come; he'd rolled up with his chariots and loosed the dogs of war. Sentinels had been killed, though how many they still weren't sure.

Sparrow flew in after midnight, rousing the camp; Elena had rallied all the remaining Sentinels. They'd sped away to hold off the invaders, buying time for Naturals to finish their packing and depart. George and the ELF leadership had prevented a rout.

And Moses said, We will go with our young and with our old, with our sons and with our daughters, with our flocks and with our herds will we go...

The rain increased its tempo, driving slantwise, stinging George's eyes. His people were spread out on the road; strange to see everyone in the open after a year under trees. They numbered 200 souls, and their livestock about the same; the sheep were moving quickly, as were the pigs. Their shepherds, mostly teens, drove them well. The cows, milk and beef, were more balky, and some had dropped behind. George doubted they'd make it. Overland, it was a long trek to Charlevoix.

Its harbor was their destination: on the surface, a strange one. Straight at the Chosen, hopefully the last thing they'd expect? The ELF's emergency council, mere hours ago, had been brief; it was not the time for long questions.

Elena had been girding for battle, ordering the squads.

Chow's thoughts were on his lab and what could be salvaged.

Grace had consoled the newcomer Miin, weepy with worry.

Rodriguez and White, rooted to the earth, were calmer; their farmer folk stood ready.

Shaman Brian would be busy; he'd fly at first light.

Ms. McIntyre had surprised them all, her quick response to the active shooters—last night was no drill—had been highly qualified. The camp's children were lucky to have her.

Keith, the storm crow, had exchanged some whispered words with Elena. He then nodded good luck to the Front's leaders before slipping away into shadow. The old man's departure seemed strangely final, George wondering if they'd ever see Keith Two-Crow again.

The people trudged westward along the road. Walloon Lake, gray with rain, glinted to the north. They were taking back roads to the small village of Horton Bay; from there they would pivot northwest to Charlevoix and its harbor. The plan, as George understood it, was to rendezvous there with rescue boats from Beaver Island. Tomorrow night the moon would be full. They'd evacuate the mainland and seek refuge with strangers.

But for now, it was one squelching step at a time. George conducted the train of horses; the equines, heavily laden, were hardy. They ignored the rain, content with an open sky, even a wet one. Walloon Lake fogged on their right, Lake Charlevoix glum on their left. George looked over the soggy line of marchers, feeling humbled by their resolve. Bowing his head, he resumed tending the animals—and himself—by reciting bits of scripture.

But the children of Israel walked upon dry land in the midst of the sea; and the waters were a wall unto them on their right hand, and on their left.

During collapse, the village of Walloon had burned down, including its old hotel. Hemingway's statue had melted, forever fusing the old man with his cat. Blended groups trudged together, mixed by the melting pot of plague; no family survived intact, unstung. His own family tree, from wife to grandkids, had splintered, every branch ruthlessly pruned by the variant.

The whole world was the same. A population of Jobs remained, Lord-tested, and for what?

Was Jehovah made jealous by the entertainments of Man?

Was Stinger the punishment for idolizing screens?

Or were the Naturals—Brian, Grace, and Elena—right?

Was Mother Nature resurgent, reclaiming her Earth?

Or was Dr. Chow closer to the mark, with his proteins, aminos, and RNA strands?

Was apocalypse mere mutation, a zoonotic zest for new life?

George gave thanks for the rain, no matter its sender. He felt concealed in the mist, cooled by its damp. If it was 90 and humid they'd all be in trouble. His horses bore their loads bravely, precious cargo for a new life ahead. The people were the same, none marching unburdened; adults and kids, they all carried packs. There were no weapons in sight, most Sentinels elsewhere engaged, though a small screening force went ahead, scouting the path. The reserves had followed Elena to the rally-point, bartering their blood for more time to get away.

Would any warriors survive? Had they been overrun? Were they pursued even now? George looked behind, the road veiled in a curtain of rain. He stroked the ears of his lead packhorse, soothing them both with words long-familiar.

And the waters returned, and covered the chariots, and the horsemen, and all the host of Pharaoh that came into the sea after them; there remained not so much as one of them.

Thunder pealed as the clouds opened further. The refugees looked up, eyes streaming in supplication.

Doyle Calls His Captains

"SHIT, DOYLE! The full moon is tomorrow night!"

Big Hannigan fumed in the lantern-light of Doyle's dimly lit workshop.

"Not a lot of heads-up you've given us, is it?"

"What really chaps my ass," carped Susan Keller, a charter skipper who delighted clients with both her catches and curses, "is that you've run your boat *twice* now to the fuckin' mainland without breathing a word to us. It's like gettin' reamed, without a courtesy reach-around!"

Coarse laughter rose from the captains as Captain Sue mimed the maneuver. Doyle kept his cool—he had to.

"How many did you say?" asked seven-fingered Redding, digits lost years ago to a hungry winch. "Damn near 200? Maybe more? Animals too? Pissin' and shittin' all over our decks? Come on man, what were you thinking? No fucking way we'll be pulling that off! Not by tomorrow night, it just ain't gonna happen."

"Plus, there's opposition!" Miller spoke next, Navy man, gunner's mate. "Let's not forget that little fact."

Doyle had laid it all out for his captains, holding nothing back.

"Heavy weapons, .50 cals? Shit, these pox-riddled 'Chosen' might have bazookas for all we know. Blow our little boats right to hell! Is that what you wanna see?"

Doyle's garage, even with the doors open, was thick with fumes. Kerosene smoked from the lamps, stale tobacco stank from pipes and hoarded cigs. The rasp of alcohol sharpened their tongues; the stills on Beaver Island—as always—produced a mean shine.

It had rained all day, a real soaker, and good for the crops, though on most island farms the weeds were winning. By nightfall the rain had ceased, lightning from storm cells flashing over a dark horizon.

For a minute there was a lull in the garage's shit-squall, till Bill Ferny started gusting. "What bothers me most, *Cap'n* Doyle," Ferny sneered at the title, "is how you let that old biddy, Samantha, hitch a ride on your boat. Now that wrinkled crone is making her rounds, preachin' how these so-called 'Naturals' are the answer to our prayers."

Stunned silence at the insult. Some nodded, though most kept their peace.

Ferny raised his voice, a blowhard. "Now I don't know about the rest of you," he eyed the smoky dozen, "but me and my Ashley, we threw Samantha and her witch's brew right off our land. Last thing this island needs is more mouths to feed. And what if they're infected? Are you willing to take that risk? Honestly, Doyle, yer gettin' right soft. Might be time for a leadership change around here."

Bill spat his words, itching for a fight.

Total silence, no nods this time. The captains weighed the wishes of their wives, Samantha's welcome-wine, and the advice of the farmer, Shawn Greene. They'd had time to talk it out, to converse with their neighbors. The tide seemed to be turning against Ferny and his bile.

Doyle glared at his guest. "Bill Ferny, now you and I go back a ways, and our fathers before us. For their sake, I'll not knock yer fuckin' head off."

Tom took two quick steps and faced the wilting Ferny. "Now if you're quite done, I've got a few things to say."

Cow-eyed, the crooked man chewed his tongue and kept quiet.

"First, Samantha stowed away on her own." Doyle canvassed those assembled in the garage with a keen eye, making sure this was understood. "Second, as you all know, I've got little love for those Indians. But Keith Two-Crow is out there risking his life for this island, which is more than I can say for the lot of us."

Doyle surveyed his skippers. "You all raise some good points. Believe me, they've kept me awake too. And to be honest, my mind ain't made up. No matter how I think everything over, doubts creep in; that's just the way of it. Ain't nothin' been clear since collapse, and don't we all know it?"

Nods from around the room. Pipes and bottles stood neglected; they'd reached the tipping point.

Doyle pressed on. "We're gonna vote, right here, tonight. That's the way we do things, ain't no virus gonna change it. But there's one more thing we need to consider. It's that fucking ferry, *Emerald Isle*. You all know this boat; we've talked of her plenty. She's a real threat to us, ain't no way we can stop her. She's tied up in Charlevoix, surrounded by these Chosen. Sooner or later they're gonna rig her up and come right fuckin' at us."

He paused, inviting them to his nightmare.

"Now, what Keith is offering is help. These Naturals have some fighters, handy with weapons from what he's told me. The reason he and I picked Charlevoix is so we could join forces there and scuttle that fucking ferry. Open her valves, flood her engine room, put that big bitch on the bottom where she belongs."

Hannigan spoke next—amateur historian, the biggest man in the fleet. "I'm not afraid of a fight. Me and my Nick, we'll do our part. But what about these Chosen now? How exactly do we get inside the harbor? What if they've got the damn drawbridge down? Caught in that channel, no room to turn around, we'll be fish in a barrel. Beaver boats have been beaten there before. Battle of Pine River, 1853—"

"Ancient fuckin' history, Hanny." Doyle cut him off; otherwise the big man would be citing sources all night. "But you all make good points. Of course I raised 'em, every one, with Two-Crow. Man has a plan. Keith's got a way to empty the town, even the odds, give us a fighting chance."

Hannigan still doubted. "And that bridge, Tom? None of our boats can clear it if that clanker is down."

A headshake from Doyle. "Crow says it'll be up, it damn well better be."

McCann spoke up, battle buddies with Keith since their tours in Vietnam. "Let's fucking vote and get on with it. We're wasting time."

Rumbles of agreement, the gathered captains more thunder than flash.

"I say we go," McCann continued. "I've known Keith near forever, and his word's good enough for me. My boat and my crew will do what we can."

Knuckles rapped on tables while others shook their heads. Voices were raised, and the fetid air thickened.

"*Go?* Damn fool! It's a death sentence!"

"Do we even have the fuel? What's council say about this?"

"Death sentence? We've got that already. We'll not last the winter, and you know it!"

"We can't stand the man up. Keith's life is in our hands!"

"His fuckin' problem, no one asked him to go!"

"Screw the damn council, *we* make the call!"

"We've got no proof, just the word of a kooky old man!"

"If our fleet is sunk, then the island's left undefended. That's 300 lives we're risking!"

"What's the damn rush anyway? I vote we wait, send a scout of our own!"

"Rush? You heard Doyle, those people will be slaughtered!"

"Better them than us! Who even knows if it's true?"

"Good men have died protecting this island! Did you forget their widows? Their kids? They'd be rollin' in their graves if we risked it all for strangers!"

"Might be a whole new crop a' widows, we go steaming off like fools!"

"Enough!" roared Doyle, clanging a pipe wrench, alarming Annie in her bed.

The room hushed, all eyes on their angry host.

"I said we'd vote, and vote we damn will. But proper, not clucking like a bunch of hens!"

Doyle took a breath, and the skippers did the same.

"Now, here's a scrap and stub for each. You print *Go* or *Stay*. There's no in-between."

The mariners shot each other looks and made ready.

"Now, whatever we decide, we all stick together. If you don't like it," he flipped a finger at Ferny, "then get the fuck out. We'll not be divided."

He paused, but none left. Doyle nodded, dumping rusty bolts from a container. Tom made his mark, folded up his future, and dropped it in the emptied jar.

Merch Biotech HQ: New Jersey

ARE YOU READY to meet my Gories? I've hinted at their creation, laying track for their arrival. Earlier in this memoir-of-sorts, I dictated "hedging my bets," "side projects," and "putting my house in order."

I'm warning you, future jurists: the more you learn, the more fantastical they will appear. Just keep in mind that at the time of their formation, just before the US was stung, my access to equipment, expertise, and funding was unparalleled, perhaps in the history of scientific endeavor. The budget for NASA's moon landings, or the Manhattan Project, was a mere fraction of what the American taxpayer paid me to save them from extinction.

Even for an audience desensitized by Asia's apocalypse, the brazen daylight raid on Merch Biotech's campus caused quite a stir. The security footage, salvaged from conflagration, would be analyzed later. The first videos were from panicked employees live-streaming as they fled from death, slip-sliding in the blood of slain security personnel.

Screams could be heard, and the *Brap-Brap-Brap* of automatic weapons. Crowds of people were seen running. The headquarters housed 10,000: doctors, lab techs, daycare staff, and the world's top specialists in pharmacology and epidemiology. Their corporate hive was under assault from my determined drones, the cubicle-combed structure soon to burn.

It didn't take long for content creators to sift through the footage and reveal my assassins. These highlight posts garnered many millions of views, and were shared around the world, their comment sections quickly cluttered by the *Sturm und Drang* of internet discourse, ALL-CAPS BRAVADO!! And misspelld emoshion.

Zoomed and enhanced by A.I., terrifying *totenkopfs* emerged. They moved like trained infantry, cleared rooms like special operators, and were as remorseless in execution as cartel *sicarios*. All this was mere background, as their physical appearance is what gave the world chills; entirely hairless, individuals were impossible to ID. Over every face a grinning skull had been tattooed. Their idea, dear reader, not mine, I assure you!

Their torsos were bare. Well-muscled, my warriors disdained Kevlar, inked-on skeletons covering every inch of exposed flesh: a terrifying *Danse Macabre,* medieval scythes upgraded to Mk18 carbines.

My "side-projects" sacrificed the tactical surprise of a nighttime op and hit the pharma headquarters on a workday afternoon. It's not like they needed an advantage, plus I selfishly wanted to make a splash with their reveal.

Two ODA teams of 12 were deployed for the mission. Alpha, to secure the perimeter and ward off any SWAT response; Bravo, to penetrate the building, assassinate the hit list, and set the pyrotechnic charges that would burn the place to the ground.

Merch's modernist architect had constructed a "corporate cottage in the woods." The 400 acre campus was revered for its old-growth trees, renewable energy, underground parking, and child care. I wanted the whole place erased, specifically its data servers, labs, head researchers, and stocks of vaccines and antivirals. It was all too easy, quite literally a walk in the park.

The variant at this time was swarming Asia, early cases of Stinger also appearing in Europe; Merch Biotech was leading big pharma in the development of countermeasures. I don't take kindly to competition, never have. My teams trained for a month on mock-ups, refined their plan, selected weaponry, and loaded themselves into—you guessed it—unmarked vans.

Ten thousand squealing bystanders meant plenty of video captured the attack. Security footage was later salvaged, and for weeks afterwards my bizarre-looking unit was must-see-TV. Cable news and the networks showed censored versions of course, but the full bloody Monty was just a few clicks away. Merch LLC had decent security; firefights with guards had a Hollywood look that didn't raise too many eyebrows. Even Alpha's use of LAW rockets to incinerate SWAT vehicles didn't move the needle much. It was the cold-blooded executions that gave viewers pause.

Scientists kneeled, men and women begging for mercy, not for themselves but for their children in the daycare. My assassins methodically checked IDs and sorted employees, stylized skulls leering from every fanatical face.

Once sorted, sobbing ignored, my creations opened fire. Muzzles barked and bullets bit, reducing researchers to shreds. Spliced footage of these blood-spattered killings went viral on social media, infecting viewers by the millions. Law enforcement and ink enthusiasts analyzed the Sanskrit on their necks: "Aghora."

In minutes, the world's algorithms—artificially intelligent—started auto-filling "Aghora" after all queries beginning with "What does..."

For a day or two, the babbling billions debated terms. Aghori, Skulls, Ghoris...

By the time we hit the CDC, consensus had been reached. The headlines blared:

"Gories Attack Again! CDC Headquarters Engulfed in Flames!"

Eating Crow

LAST NIGHT'S GARAGE VOTE had been close, but no cigar. The Beaver boats weren't going.

Doyle's captains, a few with shame-flushed faces, had exited his workshop. Some, like that rat fink Ferny, wore smug expressions of satisfaction. Doyle, Keith's betrayer, had slunk upstairs to bed but hadn't slept a wink. He'd kept Annie awake with his muttering till she elbowed him out; then he'd gone below, darkening her galley with his doubts.

Should he make the trip alone? Round up those who'd voted to go, men like Hannigan and McCann, divide the fleet?

Tom was a mouse caught in a trap he'd set up for others. Exhausted from the garage caucus, he left home near midnight to walk around the harbor. Down Michigan Avenue, then Main Street; Doyle grumbled and schemed to himself, determined to do what he could. But it wasn't much.

He turned his back on the old black and white tower. Broadcasting to the stranded scouts wouldn't work. First, the range was too far, even from Whiskey Light's elevated antenna. Second, Keith wasn't listening. Third, any radio signal must be sent in the open, where any asshole could hear it. For a year and a half now this sort of risk had been strictly forbidden, usually by Doyle, backed up by both fists.

Tom, doubt-filled and penitent, approached town, a midnight moth drawn to the lantern-light of Shamrock's bar. At the ferry dock, *Bloody Mary* was tied up tight, probably spied on by Ferny or his ilk. After Doyle's "we all stick together" stump speech, taking *Mary* to the main was impossible.

Standing outside the still-open 'Rock, Doyle pushed through the tavern door, its little bell warning the patrons: *Ding-ling!*

Five heads turned to regard him, but one, silver-haired, did not, exclaiming instead, "Captain Tom Doyle! Up past your bedtime, aren't you?"

Samantha, island's eldest, stood from the bar, beckoning Tom to a booth. Laugh lines etched her face, but the woman was worried. "Have a seat in my office, Cap'n Doyle. And Alice, how about a couple glasses of my wine?"

Tom sat in silence as barkeep Alice delivered a dusty jug and two Mason jars. Samantha eyed him for a long moment, then said, "Everything OK with the Watchers, Tom? And how's our Annie doing?"

A bare nod was all he could muster. When Alice retreated, Tom turned the booth into a confessional. "I've let Keith down," he admitted, his own eyes downcast. "The fleet won't go. He and your two foster kids are stranded on the main."

Sam, wordless, forgave without penance.

Doyle smoldered. "And I *know* you stowed aboard the other night! Made me look like a damn fool! You need to see your Two-Crow so bad, why not just ask me?"

Samantha kept quiet.

Doyle blew off more steam. "Didn't you hear me, Sammy? There's no evacuation! You'll never see Keith and those kids again! And there's more, hundreds more, refugees, innocents, all uninfected. Those families will be slaughtered, or worse!"

Heads turned their way. Alice gave last call and lowered the lantern wicks.

"Things could be better for sure," Samantha said from the shadows, "but, Thomas, they could also be worse."

"Worse? Aren't you listening, old woman? I've *betrayed* them. I made a promise to Keith. Now I can't keep it, and there's no way to warn him!"

The oracle filled both glasses and raised hers, but Tom didn't clink.

Samantha took a sip, still serene. "Where there's will, there's a way. I'll see what I can do. As for Keith, that graybeard has been through worse. Miin and Mukwa are still in good hands."

"And the refugees? These Naturals?" Doyle's eyes were bleary.

Samantha sighed. "That, I can't say. There are many possible futures, and only one will come to pass."

"So what do you advise me to do?"

"I give no advice, Tom Doyle. I am not your counselor. You have courage, you have wisdom. Do what you can, and I shall do the same."

"Can *you* call them, Samantha? Will you please try?" Doyle, once doubtful, was now begging. "I know you have your methods, witchcraft or mumbo jumbo, but if you can reach the girl, then do it. They expect our boats tomorrow night."

The Shamrock had emptied, its little bell ceasing to toll. Barkeep Alice addressed her oldest patron, gesturing to the storeroom. "Lady Samantha, your guest cot is ready when you are," she said.

Sam nodded her thanks and stood, forcing Tom to do the same.

"I'll try," she promised him. "Do what you can as well."

Disbelieving, Doyle watched his hand as it slowly extended. Samantha shook it, more strength in her claw than he would credit. He returned a tight grip of his own.

Reluctant, flexing his fingers, Doyle went out the door, the last *Ding-ling!* of the night.

Indeed, Tom Doyle would do what he could.

✦✦✦

And he had, all that night and the long day that followed. Doyle added juice to their signal strength, broadcasting loud and proud for every scumbag to hear: "Crow, this is *Mary* in the tower. Evacuation NOT possible. How do you read? Evacuation NOT possible. Over."

On the second night, the night they weren't coming, Doyle circled the tower's catwalk. The sun had set, a full moon rising in the east, over the main. Doyle visualized Earth as a marble, a tiny blue-and-green planet rolling darkly through space.

Tom's thoughts were bitter, bile harsh in his throat; he'd overestimated his captains' courage, underestimated their insular fears. He'd rushed them, gone too far—and far too fast. Two-Crow and his quiet heroism had opened Tom to something that others couldn't see, not yet anyway.

A radio squelched from the lantern room. Doyle ducked inside, adjusting volume and gain. Tom heard static; then, a voice came whispering through the ether. *Keith Two-Crow? Is that you?*

A minute of silence. Then, the spirit breathed again. But the range was too far, the atmospherics not conducive. Doyle set the mic down. If this ghost *was* Two-Crow, then what could Tom say?

He checked the tower clock against his wrist: almost time for another round of reports. Doyle was readying the log when something strange happened. From the corner of his eye, he saw a bright FLASH strobe to the southeast. *Heat lightning?*

Another FLASH followed, then ANOTHER!

From the mainland, a sine wave of SOUND flooded the island. Too sharp for thunder, Doyle heard explosions going off in deadly succession, a Morse code of murder.

BOOM!

BOOM!

BOOM!

BOOM!

BOOM!

His radio beeped, the Watcher calling from Kilty Point. "Whiskey Light, this is McCann. You seeing this, Tom? Over."

Doyle's hands clutched at his head, the radio going unanswered. He pictured Keith, Dr. Chow, those two kids, the slaughter of innocents—and he, their Judas, sitting safe in a tower.

One Step at a Time

LIZ, NAKED BENEATH HER BLACK SABBATH SHIRT, took a break to light a cig and watch the sun go down upon the lapping waves. Her bedroom, once Cowboy's, overlooked the harbor. The drawbridge stood erect, the channel that connected Lake Charlevoix to Lake Michigan flaming with brilliant light. Up north, the summer days were long; she'd forgotten how outpost duty could drag. Still, in the two days since she'd taken charge, shit had gotten done.

Cowboy's sorry ass had been locked in the ferry. Liz hadn't visited yet, still disgusted by Bob's slipshod leadership. She couldn't believe he'd been feeding his men MREs for over a month! *Come on Campbell!* That goop got old, even the best of it. Also, the compound had been coasting on fucking fumes till her tanker truck showed up. Survival 101: gasoline was gold, for as long as it lasted anyway. After that, shit got ugly.

She took a deep draw, nicotine tickling her cortex; those hoarded cartons wouldn't last either. Talk about shit getting ugly.

The dusky sky purpled, the big lake looking bruised. Liz reviewed the checklist in her head. A good leader was always prepared, and she had a hundred Chosen to look after.

Were they healthy, were they fed?

Check and check.

Was her compound safe from attack?

She considered. From the north, the drawbridge was up, and she'd parked trucks on the approach road just in case. From the south, she'd improved the barricade, positioned heavy guns, and even deployed a scout truck with a radio down the road a few miles to pick up anything on the move.

So, for the moment, was Charlevoix safe?

Check.

Finally, did she have a plan? Was she actively leading her crew towards an achievable objective? That had been Bob's biggest problem. Burned out, the man had grown stale.

Damn right she had a plan. A bold one, a real game changer. She'd start by wiping out the local resistance.

Red Liz inhaled again, stimulated by what the future held. Her planned rebellion against the Big Boss downstate, her risky alliance with X-branded Cons, her scheme to topple the whole rotten structure of post-collapse Michigan—damn, she got tingly just thinking about it.

Tapping ash, Liz focused on the present. Bob's fixer, Mikey, was monitoring his radio scanners. Tonight's moon would be full, meaning plenty of light for some solid action. Earlier, they'd gone over the maps together, pre-positioning a dozen vehicles. Her own column was gassed up and ready to deploy; *her* Fox-Hunt would be a whole different show.

First, she'd hit these resistors with 10 times the force as blundering Bob.

Second, she had fucking hell hounds, and those pits were terrifying.

Most importantly, instead of the resistors flushing *her,* she'd be the one flushing *them.* Here's where Mustafa came in. His crew was in position and would be attacking soon, if they hadn't started already. She figured that between canines and Cons, any local "elves" would panic, break radio silence, and give away their position. Then she'd rush in and annihilate them with overwhelming force.

She stubbed out her smoke and scissored her thighs. Tingle nothing, she was straight up aroused. Well, Liz had a plan for that too. Keeping her back towards the bed, she poured herself a drink from Bob's bottle, horny heart pounding.

A deep voice grunted huskily from the bed. "How 'bout a taste for the help, huh boss?"

Another voice, female and frisky, rose in agreement. "Come on Liz! This is thirsty work, and you know it."

"Shut the fuck up, both of you!"

Her exclamation was a whip crack. Turning, she faced her impatient captives. Her two best lieutenants lay naked in Bob's bed, their feet and hands strapped down by leather thongs; the pair were trussed side-by-side, awaiting her pleasure.

She came first to Lacy, whose well-toned arms were sleeved in tattoos. The Raider grinned up at her boss. Liz took a sip of whiskey and held it in her mouth, squatting beside the bed. Leaning in close, she kissed the woman, letting whiskey trickle out for her lieutenant to taste. Lacy gagged, swallowed, then smiled.

"Better?" Liz asked.

"It's a start," Lacy answered, licking her lips.

"Boss, don't forget me," moaned the man bound at Lacy's side.

He'd been hog-tied, bindings stretched tight so the two couldn't touch. Only Liz could unite them: how she loved that control. Collapse had been wild downstate, the dude's muscled torso puckered with scars. Some Liz had inflicted herself.

"What's that, Hammer?" Liz climbed atop the big man, bringing her bottle with her. She took a swig as she straddled his chest. "You weren't complaining now, were you?" Liz gave one of his nipples a twist.

"Fuck no!" Hammer yelped.

Liz looked him over: her tool, her handle. "Always liked how you rise to a challenge."

She brought the bottle to his lips and poured for her pet. He gulped it down, eager for more. Liz set the whiskey on Bob's nightstand, was beginning to lift off her shirt when the walkie-talkie buzzed, coitus interruptus.

Mikey's voice squawked triumphantly, "We've got something, boss! It's that old man again, the crow, same as before, sounds terrified too! Liz, you there? Over."

Liz grabbed up the handset. "Mikey, call the trucks and meet me at my rig. I'll be there in a minute!"

Her lieutenants flushed with excitement. Liz cut them loose and they sat up, rubbing at their wrists. All three were grinning.

"To be continued, eh boss?"

"Damn right, Hammer."

Lacy squirmed into her leather pants. "Might have some fresh faces next time, right Liz?"

Liz swatted her ass. "One step at a time, you minx. One step at a time."

They buckled on gun belts, sprinting for the column. Mikey had roused the whole compound. Her Raiders were laughing as they raced to their vehicles. Engines revved as weapons were loaded, both halves of the drawbridge coming down and clanking loudly.

A full moon, fireball red, rose just above the harbor.

Night Swim

ELENA AND HER SENTINELS were at their marks, set on action, ready to go. Two nights prior, ELF Country had been overrun by XCons. Evacuating, Keith had coordinated with Elena before departing. "Wait for the full moon to rise," had been the veteran's last instruction. "Don't count on the Beaver boats. If you have to, take the ferry. I'll lure them out."

There'd been no communication with Two-Crow since then.

Elena flinched at the risk they were taking. Surprise, surprise, the rescue fleet hadn't shown. Brian, flying over the lake, confirmed it never would. The ELF were on their own.

Diana crouched beside her partner in the dusk. The tall mariner had stripped down to a sports bra and leggings for their night swim across the harbor, the whole commando team likewise getting undressed. Two rafts had been hastily constructed, each floating enough gear and weapons for a dozen fighters; bowstrings and fletchings needed to be kept dry. Their mission stood no chance otherwise.

Elena's elves, half-naked, looked athletic in the low light. She'd picked only the strongest swimmers, though many more had volunteered. Looking closer though, her fighters were haggard. Most hadn't slept in days, the shock of trauma hitting hard; comforted by comrades, some were shaking, stifling sobs. Mukwa was there, slab-muscled, impossible to mistake. He sat on the dock, bared to the waist, side by side with Nighthawk. The pair of warriors waited in silence.

The surprise attack, Cons and canines, exacted a bloody toll; many elves were missing. Some had been killed, gunned down, shredded by dogs, but the fate of others was less certain. Sentinel Thorn and his squad had fought rearguard, screening the retreat by drawing XCons away. Thorn told Elena his team would make for the river, skirmishing as needed, then flee in canoes once the Naturals were clear. He hadn't resurfaced, and probably never would.

When it was clear the Beaver boats had bailed, leaving them stranded, Elena assembled her most able-bodied Sentinels, briefing them on the new objective: escape. Diana's team would board the big ferry, overpower any guards, and commandeer its engine room and wheelhouse. Elena's team would assault the compound, neutralize any Chosen, cut off reinforcements and ensure the drawbridge was raised.

The big ferry, *Emerald Isle,* was their one remaining chance; everything depended on it. Diana assured them she could handle its controls. Once stolen, she'd steer the boat across the harbor, embark the Naturals and their livestock, maneuver under the open bridge, out the channel, and steam towards sanctuary on the island. Elena and her security force would counter any attack from the town. Both teams would be amphibious, taking advantage of surprise.

Elena, awaiting Keith's moonrise-signal, visualized mission failure: her frog-team discovered, pinned to the surface by spotlights, dissected by direct fire.

Or another: the elves captured the ferry, but it was non-functional. Evacuation impossible, the 200 refugees would be taken.

Elena filled her lungs as the full moon floated above the eastern hills.

Come on, Two-Crow! Isn't that your sign?

They'd have to strike soon, or the waxing light would betray her swimmers. The two commando teams, keyed up, encouraged each other.

An intuition turned Elena's head. *Something's happening!*

Three hundred yards away, across the harbor, engines roared to life as rock anthems blared from truck bed amps. Rough voices shouted as the drawbridge clanked down, allowing a column of vehicles to sortie across. In a minute Castle Charlevoix had emptied, and the rusty bridge was drawn up again.

Elena kissed Diana for luck—*Gaia protect us!* The two teams then slipped into warm water. Loading their weapons onto the rafts, Diana's squad stroked towards the ferry, Elena's towards town. The moon beamed brightly, a lunar guide not just for the ELF but for all of Earth's Amphibia.

PART 4:
Animikii

Stranded

MIIN SAT ALONE, sundered from the others, as the sinking sun quenched itself in Lake Michigan. Behind her, the crowd of Naturals waited for a sign, wondering in nervous whispers whether Doyle's fleet would come. A hungry infant was quickly nursed, braying herds harder to silence; Earth's Liberation Front endured, plagued by a great unease.

Where were the rescue boats?

Had Beaver Island abandoned them?

The refugees, footsore, had reached Charlevoix's inner harbor by late afternoon. People hid themselves and their animals along the wharf, their lookouts reporting good news: the bridge was up. Less good, no evacuation boats could yet be seen.

Elder Grace approached Miin's sitting spot. "Won't you eat?" she implored the girl. "It might be hours yet, and I know you're famished, you always are."

The girl waved her well-wisher away. The past few days had stretched her, stretched them all. The Strawberry Moon, *Ode'imini-giizis*, would rise any minute, Elena designating that as the signal. Plan A, though fraught with danger, was their best chance: evacuation via the Beaver fleet. Plan B, if the boats didn't show, was still a mystery, though many had witnessed Two-Crow's hasty plotting with Elena. Since then, the old man—her beloved uncle—hadn't been seen.

❖❖❖

One night prior, the rearguard Sentinels had caught up as the small host camped near Horton Bay. The timeless village had been spared by collapse, the Red Fox Inn and its cluster of cottages providing shelter for a night.

Grace had tried to cheer her up. "Look Miin, it's a mini Shangri-La. There's clean water, dry cabins, and fish in the creek."

Miin remained morose. She couldn't shake the feeling this was the end of something. Grace had left her to it and walked downhill to the old dock, where some refugees were bathing in the bay.

Leadership visited Miin's tent, staked away from others beside a minty spring and an old tin cup. Elena and Diana thanked the island girl, each in their own way, awed by what they'd witnessed last night in the woods. Along the stony fords of the river, the trees themselves had seemed to fight. Miin brushed aside their thanks, dodging questions. She'd done her part, nothing more. Her foster brother lingered longest, looking hollow-eyed and run-down; Muck's jesting days were over. He'd seen friends killed by demon dogs and their X-branded handlers. Others died, kids too, in the assault on ELF Country that had followed.

"Miin, it was terrible."

The siblings sat outside her tent. Lightning, thunderless, harried the horizon. Miin's tent-mate, the art teacher Grace, had made herself scarce.

"I'll spare you the details, because little sis, you were there too somehow. Weren't you?"

He thrust his theory at her, and Miin, exhausted, neglected to parry.

"Strangest thing," Muck said, and looked away. "Time after time, despite the darkness, I knew just where they'd be. Was I scenting them somehow? We'd get there and find the dogs either trapped by trees or tangled up in vines."

Post-traumatic, he shook his head. "Elves believe this was your doing. Tree-talking, green witchery, and all the rest."

Miin shielded herself with silence.

"Sometimes it was thorns. Next it would be roots, or a ditch they couldn't climb," brother bear flashed back, "but killing them wasn't easy. Even trapped, those beasts were terrifying."

Lightning, far away, danced in pantomime, muted by mileage.

Mukwa described the mop-up. "Without their dogs, the Cons mostly panicked. They were no match for us in the woods."

Fostered by Samantha, they said the rest with silence, accompanied by the camp's twilight concerto: cookware, lullabies, and the lowing of livestock. Mukwa shambled off soon after. Miin hoped that Nighthawk and her brother could help heal each other.

◆◆◆

Now, one night later, Blueberry sat depressed in the dark as generator-powered lights glittered from the 'Voix. Strange to see electricity after months of no grid. A stir rippled through camp; Grace returned, patted Miin's shoulder and nodded east. There, a ruby moon ballooned above the hills.

The people gathered, pointing, anticipating action. Brian, wingless, staggered her way, leaning hard on Dr. Chow. Both men were grim with bad news.

"I'll tell you what I just told Elena. I've flown it. The whole thing, there and back from Beaver Island."

Brian's voice cracked, Blueberry's eyes brimming with unshed tears.

"Miin, there's nothing, not a single boat. The rescue's not coming."

Blueberry wasn't surprised. Since last night, the vibrations from the island had been bleak and filled with fear. *Samantha, is that you?*

Miin had no faith in the fleet. Gutted by grief, the trio observed the climbing moon in silence.

Thunder Spirits

EXHAUSTED AND ALMOST OUT OF TIME, the old man wired up his ambush. Earlier, Keith had wrenched his back on a portage; the gear, plus canoe, were too damn heavy. He wished Muck was here—Mukwa, he self-corrected. But the young man's place was with his squad, with his woman. Who knew if any Sentinels were even alive?

During the XCon attack, Keith made a hurried plan with Elena. "Don't count on the Beaver boats. If you have to, take the ferry yourself," the old man said. "I'll lure them out." He'd slipped away to do so while the tall elf rallied the Front's defenders.

As Two-Crow hunched over his work, he kept a corner of his mind open for Miinan. He needed her too; the girl's green strength was growing fast, just as his was ebbing.

The moon was rising now, full-blooded, above the eastern hills—Indian Hills, the locals called them. Keith's aching wrists struggled with the task. Doing his duty by Elena, he'd initiated a series of transmissions, placing the radio and its back-breaking battery—stolen from that first truck—a quarter mile further up the road. Locked in broadcast mode, its repeated signals were the bait for Keith's electronic trap.

M-31 hugged Lake Michigan's rocky coast; he'd stashed his dented canoe nearby. Susan Creek rushed through its culvert, while boulders and trees crowded the road, creating a perfect pinch-point. The driving time from Charlevoix was short, though. If his plan worked its garrison would arrive any minute.

The day's last light was fading fast. Keith's battered rifle was propped nearby. He'd emptied the duffel and was rigging the final charge, last link in a daisy chain of destruction. Squinting at the mine case, FRONT TOWARD ENEMY, his arthritic fingers fumbled with the fuse well and firing wire.

Engine noise growled up from the south, coming from Charlevoix; the old Marine—Private First Class Two-Crow—had run out of time. The trigger assembly was lying just over the ridge. With only seconds to spare, his fingers remembered and clicked the cap home. A pack of vehicles, beaming brightly in the dark, raced towards his radio-trap.

Would he make it?

Just ahead of the headlights, Keith grabbed his rifle and rolled over the rise. Where was that detonation trigger?

The lead truck, blaring music, had almost drawn even. Two-Crow had no way to stop them; they'd be in and out of his kill zone in seconds. Too dark to see, frantic, he felt the ground for his wire. Suddenly, a corner of his mind was flooded: Blueberry! He even caught a whiff of Cranberry Bog!

A slow motion *Craaaa-ACK!* assaulted his eardrums.

Brakes squealed and rubber burned as the old timer peered over the embankment. A massive maple, rotten with age, lay sprawled across the road. The lead truck fishtailed to a halt, the column behind it screeching and swerving, every vehicle askew and spouting profanity.

At last, guided by Animikii, Keith found the assembly and pulled the trigger. Then, the thunder gods exploded.

BOOM!

BOOM!

BOOM!

BOOM!

BOOM!

Park Island

THE FRONT, hidden along the harbor, stirred, fingers pointing west towards the town. Headlights brightened, engines coughed carbon, and the drawbridge clanked down. Raider trucks were tallied as Charlevoix emptied out; it took only seconds. A column of vehicles sortied across the Pine River channel. When the last crossed over, the bridge was re-raised, once again sealing off their compound by moat.

Miin felt a familiar green twitch; the tree-talker knew she had to get clear. The girl excused herself from company, shaking off their concern. Blueberry knew exactly what was needed.

Park Island, it was called: a leafy peninsula near the harbor's Coast Guard station. She footed across its bridge and embraced the tree-loud dark. Miin opened every pore, to the good, green smells around her.

Miin found the tree that wanted to be found: a talkative old *pinus*, centuried and wise. She trailed twig-like fingers down the pine's gnarled bark, breathing deep and even, a druidess of dendrons. Bioelectric, their minds merged, cranium to cambium, brain-stem to tree-stem: two became one.

Her mind quickly flooded with information, Miin sifting through the mycorrhizal missives.

There! An elder maple, a few miles north, was frantically messaging.

A package of scent particles was forwarded by fungi, priority-urgent: Two-Crow's signature, vehicle exhaust, and the stink of human fear.

Miinan mentally composed her response and hit send. A bolt of GREEN flashed underground, root-to-root, speeding to her uncle in his moment of need. Seconds later, to the north, lightning forked and the ground shook, a daisy-chain of detonations unleashing their own heavy thunder.

BOOM!
BOOM!
BOOM!
BOOM!
BOOM!

Fireball

LIZ SHIFTED THROUGH THE GEARS of her blood-red truck, its vibrating motor tickling her fancy. Mikey, lap full of gadgetry, grinned as he gave his new boss a grimy thumbs up: they were closing in fast on the old man's frequency. Hammer drove hard behind her, riding her ass. Lacy, her next-best lieutenant, came third. Charlevoix's column of Raiders converged on the geezer's distress signal.

We've got those fuckers now!

Liz cranked the volume, Steppenwolf growling from her speakers.

The old crow had broadcast, in the open, several times. Liz's fixer had him dialed in; their plan was working. Flushed from the forest by XCons, the resistors indeed had panicked: "Dogs...surprise attack...surrounded...trapped!"

Liz pressed down on the gas pedal; her crew had to beat those fucking Cons to the prize. She knew the juiciest Candies would be snatched up quick.

Damn, she felt hot though!

Liz balled a fist between her thighs. She stroked the gear shaft, then downshifted as M-31 narrowed between embankments. Something scurried up the slope.

What the—? An animal? No! There again—a MAN!

Just beyond her beams, a massy *SOMETHING* crashed down in the dark. Liz slammed her boot on the brake, truck skidding to a halt, her whole column the same. A thick trunk of hardwood now blocked the highway.

What the flying fuck?

Drivers radioed their confusion; Mikey, dazed, flapped his gums. Liz examined the fallen tree-corpse, an autopsy by headlights. She blinked. Did the bark blink back?

What the hell?

Eyes of burl were watching, every leaf peeping.

Her wolf pack, penned in, howled its frustration as Liz's stereo screamed:

Fire all of your guns at once, and explode into space!

From behind, a bright *FLASH* was capped instantly by thunder, *BOOM!*

Compressed air spattered her nosebleed across the windshield. In her rear-view the column erupted, trucks and SUVs tossed about like toys. Explosion after explosion ripped through their ranks; ear drums ruptured, Red Liz couldn't hear. She felt pukey, could smell piss and shit. *Fucking Mikey!*

She revved the engine, but there was nowhere to go.

BOOM!

Limbs—dog and human—cartwheeled across the roadway.

BOOM!

Lacy's truck flipped next, long legs torn from her torso.

BOOM!

Then her big man was hammered, tenderized by his own Toyota.

BOOM!

Red Liz faced the fireball and screamed her defiance.

Climb so high, I never wanna die!

Ninth Hour

GEORGE WORRIED OVER HIS FLOCK, having no time for moonrise. He'd not seen the town empty out, nor felt the stir move through his people. The pastor's heart was heavy with rumor; some said the boats weren't coming, that the Naturals had been abandoned by Beaver Island, stranded ashore.

Eloi Eloi lama sabachthani?
"My God, my God, why hast thou forsaken me?"

George put the question to his wisest horse, an uncomplaining gelding who'd hauled a double load. Per usual, the equine offered comfort but no answers. George was weary from the road, from collapse, from his faltering faith. He looked north to the horizon, towards salvation, and there beheld a great *FLASH* of light.

A rumble followed seconds later—*BOOM!*—like no thunder he'd ever heard.

The people rushed to bear witness, shaking their heads in wonder.

Another *FLASH*, and then *ANOTHER*. The ground itself seemed to shake.

The gelding observed his master.

George's eyes were shining.

And the Lord went before them by night in a pillar of fire, to give them light.

PART 5:
A New Dawn

Vision Quest, by Susan Seddon-Boulet

Waagoshii-Mindimooye

BEAVER ISLAND'S ELDEST GAZED SOUTHEAST from a bluff overlooking Lake Michigan. She watched as the full moon furled its silver sails, the eastern sky turning pink.

Above Samantha's head, birch leaves were stirred from their sunless slumber. Freshened by daybreak, the onshore breeze gossiped with the grove. Once awake, the chatty leaves were all aflutter; Samantha, vigilant for hours, opened herself to their news from the main.

But trees won't be rushed, even birches. Salutations and small talk were expected, photonic prospects debated and rainfall rates exchanged. At last the eldest heard their tall tale. Astonished, she queried further, receiving confirmation.

Samantha brushed her hands through the leaves, grateful for their green reporting. There was suddenly much to do. The old woman turned quickly and, foxlike, disappeared towards the interior.

Incoming!

"UNCLE TOM, WHAT'S WRONG?"

Maggie Doyle had arrived early, pre-sunrise, for her tower shift. Her uncle looked terrible, skin pale and expression grim. Had Tom been wrestling with ghosts all night?

"Gonna be a beautiful day," she stalled, letting the old guy recover. "And did you *see* that moon last night? Amazing! I went swimming with friends. Donegal Bay was as bright as day."

Maggie was worried. Her shaky uncle couldn't even unscrew his thermos.

"Let me," she said, and filled his chipped mug.

Uncle grunted. Niece took it as thanks. She would *not* be sharing how she swam with Nick Hannigan. Going topless, she'd kissed him in the warm water beneath the moon's ruby glow.

Maggie carried their best binoculars onto the catwalk. Uncle was in a mood. Leaning against the handrail, she took a deep breath of sand-scented air. Overhead, gulls hovered hungrily on the morning breeze, hunting for their breakfast. A few puffy clouds reflected gold in a blue-washed sky; the sun would roll up any minute now.

She put the cups to her eyes, found her focus, and slowly scanned the morning's horizon till a sudden *something* filled her visual field. Her throat caught in surprise; backing up, Maggie found the object again and refocused. *What on God's green earth...?*

She spun the dial, sharpening its shape. *Oh my Lord!*

"Uncle!"

In three strides Doyle was there. He had binos of his own, and followed her point. The tower radio began beeping: Watchers were calling, broadcasting panic.

"Pan-pan, pan-pan, pan-pan. Whiskey Light, this is Point LaPar. I've got an incoming vessel at zero-four-five, looks like a big one, over?"

"This is Kilty Point. Vessel inbound, headed your way, pushing quite a bow wave. Doyle, you seeing this, over?"

"Uncle Tom? What is it? Are we in trouble?"

Her uncle looked ashen. "It's that damn ferry."

Doyle's nightmare had come true. "Sound the alarm, Maggie! SOUND—THE—ALARM!"

A Motley Crew

CAPTAIN DIANA, ACADEMY-TRAINED, helmed their stolen vessel. Her gauges looked good; the ferry's two big engines—for now—were behaving. The full moon was setting off the port bow, its final blush reddening the waters. She'd been steering three-three-zero since midnight, when they'd passed, unmolested, beneath the open drawbridge, leaving Charlevoix and its Virals in their wake.

The big boat felt sluggish though, and no wonder: they were grossly overloaded. Just before departure it was decided to drive the compound's tanker truck aboard. As the only licensed mariner, she'd been against it, but Dr. Chow had insisted. The rig was full of Chosen-hoarded fuel, and Chow argued that gifting gas to Beaver Island might sweeten the deal.

Diana had found the specs for the ferry. *Emerald Isle* was rated for 294 passengers; no mention was made of horses, sheep, or pigs, let alone large fuel-laden trucks. However, they'd almost made it. Beaver Island loomed, dead ahead, in the predawn.

She called for a runner, and a teenaged boy stepped into the wheelhouse, wide-eyed from the dewy bridge wing. Captain Diana sent the young shepherd to fetch leadership: Elena, Chow, Brian, and Keith. She still couldn't believe that old man. What he'd done for the refugees, and how he'd survived....!

Last night, after *Emerald* cleared the raised drawbridge—Gaia is good!—her starboard lookout had spotted Two-Crow alone in his canoe. The old wizard, reborn, floated ethereal in the moonlight, glowing white. The fires from Keith's ambush still burned along the coast road, and there he bobbed, just outside the channel marker, waiting patiently, as if he had all the time in the world. Fucking badass is what he was. Diana hoped to be the same at 80.

After bringing Keith and his battered canoe aboard, they'd spent precious time searching for Sentinel Thorn and his rearguard canoes. Finding no trace, they reluctantly set a course for Beaver Island, assuming the worst. This bad news hit the ELF hard, more names added to the lengthy list of MIAs.

Diana's assault team, as planned, took the ferry; it hadn't been easy. There were guards everywhere, infected on the gangway, in the engineering spaces and wheelhouse.

The first few kills went quietly. Caught by surprise, they'd choked on arrows or knives to the throat. Eventually though, some asshole had pulled a trigger, gunfire alerting the garrison. Then things got ugly. Two of her Sentinels had been killed, their parka-shrouded bodies now stowed in the ferry's lazarette awaiting burial, hopefully on the island.

Much blood had been spilled, mostly Chosen. Diana deployed the ferry's deck hoses before taking on passengers; traumatized already, she tried to shield her Naturals from further gore.

Elena's team had secured the compound. They'd fought two skirmishes, one at the drawbridge and one at the southern barricade. Mukwa and Nighthawk did most of the killing; Elena reported they'd been something to see. Hawk, swift-flying, fired arrows inches from Mukwa as the big man closed in, freakishly fast, to fight hand-to-hand. Once a few defenders were feathered or ripped open by Mukwa, the remaining Chosen fled. Few shots had been fired—none of Elena's commandos were killed in the fray.

The loading process, however, had taken forever, their livestock balking at engine noise and fumes. Thank goodness for Pastor George; the brawny Lutheran had a gift. Who knew animals could be soothed by scripture?

Pairs of creatures came to Noah and entered the ark—

Diana shook her head, remembering. Never a dull day in the ELF.

The runner she'd dispatched returned with the leadership team. Sleep-deprived, the bleary adults now cluttered up her wheelhouse. Ahead, the island loomed larger. Diana reduced her RPMs, delaying their arrival, allowing time to talk things through.

Speaking with authority, the captain began, "Brian, can you fly? Take a peek and see what's waiting for us?"

The bearded man shrugged; his blue eyes had lost their sparkle. "I'll see what I can do. Never had much luck with gulls, though."

Diana, depressed, kept her chin up. "Very well."

Seamanlike, she moved to the next. "Doctor Chow, the islanders will be nervous, and it's not hard to see why. Is there anything we can do to reassure them?"

The medical man considered. "When Keith and I met with Doyle, we discussed administering antibody tests in conjunction with the island's clinician, Doctor Newsome. We believe he has my file on infections? With your permission, I'll set up a health station to screen our people before they disembark."

"Make it so," Diana delegated.

Relieved by daybreak, the lusterless moon had gone below the horizon, the loftiest birds basking in gold from the almost-risen sun. Diana turned next to Elena and Keith.

"The Chosen have armed this vessel to the teeth. Gaia forgive, it's bristling with forbidden weaponry."

Elena nodded her agreement, while Keith just stared.

Was there something wrong with his hearing? The old man had never been a talker, but now he seemed deaf.

Elena spoke up. "We should disarm ASAP," the elf said, grimacing at the twin machine guns mounted on the bow. "No scenario has us fighting our way ashore. We're not here as invaders; this resettlement only works if we're invited."

Diana looked to Keith, the Native islander. Numb, the old man indicated nothing.

Dr. Chow cleared his throat. "I agree with Elena about the guns, but Captain Doyle is a practical man. Maybe we should take the fuel tanker approach, gift him the weapons as carrots?"

Diana considered. She looked to Brian, to Keith; the two longbeards kept quiet.

"Very well. Disarm immediately, before the islanders notice. But find a compartment where the weapons can be stowed, and do it *safely*. The last thing we need is an accidental discharge."

She looked them over. "Anything else?"

The leaders propped themselves up, dead on their feet, a motley crew for sure. Diana had driven dozens of freighters up and down the Great Lakes; she could not imagine a weirder wardroom. And yet, she wouldn't trade a single one of them.

Dr. Daniel Chow, reluctant, had the last word. "Pastor George has an idea we might want to consider."

Holding the Line

DOYLE'S CAPTAINS, all early risers, responded quickly to Maggie's alarm bell. Beaver's fleet, twelve boats—gill-netters and tugs sporting homemade armor—had cast off from the municipal marina. They formed a rusty line of battle, forbidding access to the harbor and the town of St. James.

The boat crews were all experienced at fighting off invaders. Rifles and shotguns had been loaded, toted by men and women who knew how to use them.

Might as well be peashooters, Doyle thought, *when it comes to stopping that ferry.*

His *Bloody Mary* was the flagship of the squadron. Niece Maggie, excited by danger and the clanging alarm, had begged to join his crew. He'd squashed that idea as his deckhand, O'Donnell, tumbled aboard, a silent man with an island name and long experience offshore.

Doyle keyed his mic, broadcasting to the blockade. "Easy now, here she comes. Let's not do anything stupid. Hold your positions."

Deckhand O'Donnell, with binoculars and a rifle, nodded at the streets and rooftops near the harbor. Doyle looked: word must have spread, many islanders were gathering. He could make out at least a hundred already, and more were coming in—by foot, by bicycle, singly and in groups.

"Fucking great. Just what we need, a goddamn audience."

O'Donnell swore in sympathy.

Doyle's initial panicked fear of Chosen marauders had been quickly erased. Studying the ferry through binoculars, he could see clearly that these were Keith's Naturals.

The big boat was packed with people and animals. Survivors from last night's explosions? Had they somehow stolen *Emerald Isle* from the Chosen? The trip across would mean dead-reckoning 30 miles of open water at night.

Doyle, grudgingly, was impressed. His conscience was glad they hadn't been slaughtered, but that didn't change his response: there was no fucking way they were coming ashore. The garage vote was still valid. He and his captains would hold the damn line—what else could they do? Island safety depended on his fleet. The lives of innocents, gathering near the harbor, were in his hands.

Standing at the helm, he braced his binos for another long look.

Mary's marine radio beeped.

It was Redding, acting as Watcher in the tower. "Doyle, I just caught a glimpse inside the ferry. There might be a tanker truck aboard, maybe diesel, you copy?"

Diesel? What the hell!

Doyle's heart revved towards its red line, his chest constricting as he pictured a fireball.

Tom keyed his mic and barked an order to the fleet. "No shooting! I repeat, no shooting! Hold your fire, there's flammables on board!"

Old Fox-Woman

SAMANTHA OBSERVED THE HARBOR. The people had come, answering her summons.

After breakfasting with the birches and hearing their news, she'd called upon the nearest families, sending runners to others. The Greenes had gathered, Kellers, Millers and O'Donnells too; they carried the bundles she'd been hoping to see. The roads and terraces around town were packed with nervous islanders, and more were streaming in. All eyes were on the harbor mouth and the home fleet's blockade.

Twelve boats were crewed by men and women with rifles. Their battle line formed a crescent denying entrance to the approaching ferry, which rode low in the water, crowded with refugees and livestock. Samantha's intuition had manifested, her vision clear; the big boat slowed to a stop 100 yards from the fleet. Its idling engines could be heard, and occasionally the bleating of animals or clamor of people.

The island's eldest, alone above it all, closed her eyes and filled with light. Breathing slowly, she thrummed with tension: the gathering islanders were of many minds. They swayed back and forth with indecision. The fleet below was also divided, the discord in their ranks easily felt.

Samantha sensed the signatures of her returning scouts:

Miinan, even stronger, empowered by green.

Two-Crow, storm-damaged, resurrected, and still alive.

Mukwa, larger-hearted and wiser than before.

She felt the watchfulness of trees, terns, high-flying gulls, fish in the water and families ashore. The sun also was about to rise, radiating warmth and light. It, too, would watch these events unfold.

The balance was exquisite, unbearable; something had to give. A premonition hit her. She heard the song before it was sung, saw the banners before they unfurled. Samantha smiled as the first ray of a new dawn illuminated her joy.

Her sacred mission—*allies to be found, survivors on the main*—was almost fulfilled.

The Redeemer

CAPTAIN FERNY TRAINED HIS BINOCULARS on the big boat. It appeared unarmed, but he didn't like what he saw: a dirty crowd of beggars, desperate with disease, and filthy animals too, their coats all matted with shit. And were those *gun mounts* on the bow? And *welded fucking armor?*

He wouldn't put it past 'em. For now the gun mounts were empty, no weapons could be seen, but that ferry could deploy its firepower in seconds. Then where'd they be?

Tommy Doyle whined on the radio. "No shooting! Hold your fire—"

Ferny turned the thing off. *Damn coward!*

Stinger, Covee's variant, was aboard that vessel: he could feel it. The fucking plague ship had to be stopped! Ferny studied the boat yards, the rooftops. He saw the faces of worried islanders, heard their distant voices pleading for help, for someone to check this madness. *It's all up to me,* he thought, and stepped out on deck, toting his rifle.

"Cap'n, you see this?" His deckhand pointed to the ferry. Ferny saw it, all right: the veteran Two-Crow, supposed war hero, limping towards the ferry's bow. He carried something, a weapon? Was he armed? Passengers surged towards the rails, their hands full as well. An attack?

Above the engine noise, a harmony reached his ears; *Emerald's* passengers were singing, well-conducted by a pastor in a collar. Ferny recognized the tune, an old Shaker hymn carrying clear across the water. *Probably just buying time to arm themselves.*

> *I will bow and be simple, I will bow and be free,*
> *I will bow and be humble, just like the willow tree.*

Ferny grimaced. They were being DUPED!

He eyed the line of Beaver boats. IDIOTS!

No one made a move, not a single island weapon raising in defense.

Keith and his bundle were almost to the bow. NO!

Then he saw Samantha manipulating the crowd, arms raised in triumph, her wicked smile, her scheming face: a goddamn AMBUSH!

The ferry's guns would be ready in seconds, Beaver's boats shot to shit. He put his scope on Two-Crow. That Indian bastard was smiling too!

Ferny, a draft-dodger decades ago, aimed at the veteran, the helicopter Marine. "Fly *now*, you old fool!"

Whip-crack! went the rifle shot.

Ferny's firing pin struck the primer, detonating its charge; the weapon recoiled against his bony shoulder. His bullet blasted Keith square in the chest, blowing Two-Crow right off the bow. Hooded, his broken body splashed into the bay. The package unfurled as he fell: a white banner, brightly spattered by arterial blood.

From the ferry rails, a dozen flags were now flying; tablecloths and towels blazed, argent against the blue. *Emerald's* passengers froze, the gathered islanders too, as a thousand eyes blinked in disbelief.

"Noooo!" A broken-hearted cry was heard as a man, bear-sized, dove from the ferry.

Captain Doyle stood stunned. Keith? Shot? Who the fuck pulled the trigger?

Big Hannigan roared to life, ramming Ferny's boat; his son Nick jumped aboard, followed by a woman. What the hell? Niece Maggie?

Nick tackled the deckhand that tried to block them. Ferny still fingered his smoking rifle. Maggie narrowed the range, aimed her punch, and crumpled the shooter.

A lament rose from the islanders, from the ferry, from the whole watching world. Banners were blooming from roads and rooftops: one, two, a dozen, then more. The Greenes waved white sheets from a horse-drawn wagon, O'Donnells flapped linens, Alice and her staff twirled Shamrock's bar towels. Then the islanders picked up the song that the ferry had dropped. The tune had first been sung, long ago, in an un-Civil War.

I will bow as a token, I will wear the easy yoke,
I will bow and be broken, yea I'll fall upon the rocks.

Doyle shoveled the lump from his throat and radioed, "Weapons down! Weapons down!"

He looked across his line. Hanny's boat was still tangled with Ferny's, Maggie rubbing her knuckles as Nick and his cousins disarmed Ferny's crew.

"Captain Hannigan, secure that damn boat! And get my niece the hell out of there!"

Muck sobbed in the reddening bay as he wrestled with Keith's corpse, Two-Crow's life-blood diluted by a quadrillion gallons of fresh water.

"God damn it McCann, you're closest! Throw a line and get them both aboard!"

A new day dawned, white sheets stained by a red-risen sun; a great grief fogged the harbor. Doyle choked up, rasping his orders by radio. "All boats! All boats! Let them through! Captain Miller, escort *Emerald* to the ferry dock. Crews, stow your weapons!"

The blockade parted as the ferry revved its engines, smoke curling in plumes from twin stacks. *Emerald Isle,* after two years of quarantine, bumped back to its familiar berth, the townsfolk looking on.

The sun wheeled through its morning colors—red, amber, and orange— sheets and linens shining white once more. Break over, back to work, the watchful trees resumed their solar shift, hoary alchemists transmuting gold into green.

Sanctuary

THE FERRY HAD DOCKED; old sheets and towels—the morning's truce flags—had been folded away. The blockade boats returned to their berths, crews topping them off from the island's dwindling stock of diesel. Mukwa, plucked from the bay as he grappled Keith's corpse, had been dropped at the ferry terminal by a tearful McCann.

The big boat and its refugees were quarantined—no one on, no one off—*Emerald Isle* was shunned. Looking medieval in full PPE, Doc Newsome and his two island nurses approached the plague ship and its mysterious passengers. Standing at the rail, Dr. Chow—masked and distanced for courtesy—welcomed the alien-looking ambassadors aboard. Newsome nodded, handed back Chow's file, and together they planned out the protocol. Chow volunteered to be the first one screened.

Doc Newsome took a blood sample, testing Chow's serum with two different kits: the first for antigens, indicating the variant, the second for antibodies, evidencing exposure. This point-of-care test was fast but imperfect, both doctors, island and main, hoping for unanimous results. After the proper interval, Newsome examined both test wells, showed them to Chow, and then dictated to Nurse Mathew, who scribed in his notebook:

"Patient Daniel Chow, number 001: viral antigen results negative, antibody results positive. Patient Chow does not carry the virus, and instead has antibodies against it. Doctor Chow is cleared to exit quarantine."

The two doctors—Michigan grads, though decades apart—fist-bumped through multiple layers of latex. "Hail, Doctor Chow. Hail to the victors!"

Thus it began. All day, passengers lined up two by two to be tested, cleared, and given permission to go ashore. After that, each animal was also sampled. *Emerald Isle*, their improvised ark, slowly emptied; Diana's two dead Sentinels were raised from the lazarette and, post-mortem, tested as well.

Miinan and Mukwa had deferred—the native islanders were among the last to be tested. Doc Newsome shook his head at their results. "Muck, Miin, I don't know how you kids did it. There and back again without a scratch, without infection. What's more, you both have high levels of variant antibodies. And here comes Samantha to welcome you home!"

Their foster-gran strode up the dock, townsfolk and well-wishers clearing a path. Samantha's eyes were shining as she opened her arms. Blueberry skipped ahead and into her embrace. Mukwa hung back, hung his big head; Keith's body, possibly infectious, was tagged and bagged by Deputy Williams. Muck couldn't look away.

His foster-gran took one paw; little sis held the other. Together they pulled him off the dock and through the crowd, toward Shawn Greene's waiting wagon. All eyes were fixed upon them. Muck's old principal was talking with his coach; both men beamed at Mukwa. They began clapping, and soon the whole wharf joined in the applause.

The familiar mockery of, "Muck! Muck! Muck!" began to morph as more fans joined in. "Mu-KWA! Mu-KWA! Mu-KWA!" they chanted with new-found respect, voices overwhelming in spontaneous praise.

Shawn Greene settled Samantha's adopted family on a wagon bench and clucked at his old mare, Montana. They clip-clopped away from town, south on King's Highway towards the state forest, Sam's shack, Miin's maples and Cranberry Bog.

◆◆◆

"Nookomis, what about our friends the Naturals? The ELF needs a home."

Apprentice Miin busied herself with small chores around the shack. Mukwa hulked in a corner, shadowed by trauma, taking too many sips of strawberry wine. He pawed his tiny pencil as he sketched foster-gran and sis, depicting them as two plants growing right through the floor, roots intermingled, entwined with their chairs. Passing between them were complex molecules, Mukwa shading these green.

"I've been making my rounds, gifting our brew," the eldest said. She grinned at Miin's sweeping, happy to have her back; despite nature's omnipresence, she'd still felt lonesome living alone. "Your friends will find sanctuary across the Jordan in the old state forest. Plenty of room for them and their livestock, and most islanders agree."

"Most?" There was little dust in Miin's pan. She dumped it out anyway, then turned to the kindling.

"Oh, Ferny and his cronies, no surprise there. But Beavers are sensible; they fear the long winter. Island cellars are empty, and the crops don't look good. Whatever aid we give now will be repaid tenfold if famine can be avoided."

"You planned this all along?" Miin's hatchet never stopped, the split wood soon overflowing its box. Sam knew the girl had traumas of her own.

"Planned? No, Miinan, this is too big for me. I felt it coming, kept myself open and reacted, same as you and Mukwa. And Keith too, of course."

At Two-Crow's mention, the big man stifled a moan and shambled out to the garden with his grief.

Samantha sighed. "It will take time, and even then some wounds won't heal. Our Mukwa will be scarred, as you will, for life. Keith bore his own scars well, and should inspire you both."

No words for this. Samantha halted Miin's hatchet as the girl brimmed over with tears.

After a time, Sam pulled her foster child, her granddaughter, upright, and they embraced again. "Will you help me, Miinan, to get the sweat lodge going?"

The tree-talker dried her eyes. "Of course. But Grandmother, let me go to the grove first. The maples and I have some catching up to do."

Samantha smiled at her Blueberry, glad wrinkles creasing her face. "They'll be thrilled, I'm sure. Take all the time you need. Trees won't be rushed, as well you know."

Miin flashed a smile of her own, remembering Charlevoix's harbor, Keith's need, the talkative pine and the bolt of GREEN that had forked from its roots.

EPILOGUE

THREE FIGURES SLOWLY CLIMBED Kilty's Hill at twilight. It was September, nearly three months having passed since the ferry's arrival. The moon phase was waxing crescent, little warmth in its smile. Campfires winked from the settlement of Naturals below, ELF Country II now established in the Jordan State Forest.

Sleepy squirrels watched the supplicants genuflect in their grove. An old mama and her fawns—a spike and a doe—scent-checked the visitors before resuming their acorn repast: the three signatures were known, and none posed a threat.

The warm day was easing into dusk, eager stars beginning to shine as the hemisphere tilted towards darkness. Daylight's long summer reign was dimming.

Atop the hill, a sapling had been planted over freshly turned earth. Keith's other grave marker was his .22 rifle, standing upright, rusted from three months of rain. The trio sat themselves down, bowed heads and joined hands in a circle of power. Unseen, a squirrel family eavesdropped from above: words were spoken, and a pipe was passed. Fragrant smoke soon tickled the leaves. More words were said, then a starry silence resumed.

The eldest, white-haired, lifted her lids and greeted the watchers. A squirrel kit chittered back and was hushed by its parents. Beneath their tree, the big man kept his eyes on the ground. A heaviness was in him, a weight that the whole grove could feel: thunder before a storm. The youngest was a girl, and her sadness burned bright. She gathered sticks as she sat, deftly weaving a nest.

The scolded squirrel was shocked, and looked to its parents. What was happening? The big oak they lived in was bending down its branches. As above, so below: the oak's twiggy fingers repeated the girl's pattern. Now the whole canopy was chittering, and even the heavy man looked up, briefly baring a grin.

Vega, the first star, peeped brightly through the leaves, followed by a second, then a third; Altair and Deneb swanned through the sky.

A bell began to clang, and all ears bent towards its clamor.

The three humans stood and quickly descended. Nearby, an osprey stirred himself to flight. Several powerful wingbeats, and the sandy island fell far behind. A few more, and the flier spied the reason for the ringing alarm: a trio of oversize canoes approached Beaver Island from the darkening east. Paddles flashed in synchrony. Singing was heard from many strong voices.

Clang! Clang! Clang! the warning bell insisted.

Stroke! Stroke! Stroke! the newcomers replied.

This Ends Book One of *Sudden Quiet*

ACKNOWLEDGMENTS

JRR TOLKIEN ONCE WROTE, "I wisely started with a map, and made the story fit."

Though certainly less wise, my own story began the same way and I want to thank the two map-makers that helped inspire this book: Irene Harsha Young of Charlevoix, and Ed Wojan of Beaver Island. I also wish to acknowledge the lands and waters of northern Michigan and their caretakers—the Indigenous communities of the upper Great Lakes. This book would not exist without them, Miigwech! As a reader, I never understood why editors featured so prominently in acknowledgements. Now I know. I am incredibly grateful to Scott Couturier and the entire team at Mission Point Press. Next, a huge thank you to everyone who supported this project, financially, emotionally, and otherwise. A special thanks goes to my mom, mom-in-law, brother, cousins, my two sons, and the greatest thing to ever happen to me, my wife Katie.

ABOUT the AUTHOR

Joshua Veith is an educator, adventurer, and outdoor enthusiast. He has traveled to more than 30 countries—including China, Nepal, Syria, and Turkey—and once made a 19-day Pacific Ocean crossing on a cargo freighter from Seattle to Hong Kong. For three years Josh worked as a deckhand on commercial fishing trawlers out of Newport, RI and Cape May, NJ. He is a graduate from the same high school—Oak Park, IL—as Ernest Hemingway and spent a year studying at the Albert-Ludwigs-Universität in Freiburg, Germany. He played club lacrosse and graduated from the University of Michigan, later earning an MA in Literature from Eastern Michigan University. Today Joshua lives with his wife and two sons in northern Michigan, fishes and hikes in the same spots that Hemingway enjoyed as a young man, and teaches a literature class on JRR Tolkien. As a public school teacher and writer, Josh strives to be an Indigenous ally, recognizing that traditional relationships with the environment offer the most sustainable pathways for humankind's interaction with the planet.

60187706R00205